BITTER NOTES

ALY BECK

- ➢ Cover Design: Pretty In Ink
- ➢ Editing and Proofreading by Jenni Gaunt
- ➢ Developmental Editing provided by RawlsReads

"Music is the balm that soothes my broken soul and Whispered Words took me to another plain entirely, healing me with their music."

RIVER

When the first note fills the tension-filled room, every woman's panties in a five-hundred-foot radius disintegrate into thin air, and the crowd goes wild. Poof! Panties be gone! Mine included.

A sigh of admiration rocks through every patron present when the six-foot God towering over the crowd on stage opens his fucking mouth, belting out the first note of the night. Heaven shines down. God himself shows up and blesses us individually. Miracles happen simultaneously. The lead singer's smooth, gravelly voice echoes through the bar, and we all die a happy collective death.

What an excellent way to go.

My mouth falls open. Watching the stage from my chair at the front door, I sit on the edge of my seat in anticipation, letting their sound envelop me entirely like a hug. With my arm resting against the small podium raised in front of me, my admission stamp hovers mid-air over the back of some poor patron's hand, waiting for their approval into the bar.

Four of the hottest guys I've ever seen demand attention on stage, drawing every eye to their performance. Proving to me they aren't the same four guys I knew in high school. And hell, it's not even their performance that draws everyone's attention to them. It's the way they command the stage, like kings ruling over their subjects.

Kieran, the lead singer's mismatched eyes squeeze shut, and his body bows back when a particular high note slips out of his mouth, drawing us in more. His beefy body bulges, and veins protrude as his fingers wrap tighter around the microphone. His jet black hair plasters to his head from the sweat glistening across his tanned skin. He kicks a leg out and then works the stage like a pro, making love to everyone in the room. My ears rejoice in his melodies, and when I shut my eyes, I see the ghost of my past peeking through.

Kieran waltzes toward Asher, the grumpy, dirty-blonde guitarist, and leans in. Asher's bushy brows raise into his forehead until a smirk pulls at his lips. His hazel eyes watch Kieran's every move until they sing a line together, leaning into the same microphone. Asher bobs his head, belting out every note on key and in perfect harmony. Eventually, Kieran's growl echoes through speakers, curling my damn toes.

Moisture pools in my panties when he struts to the nearly naked drummer, Rad, and ruffles his mullet as he pounds his sticks into the drums. Yeah, his curly, 1980s-era mullet, drenched in sweat. His lean body constantly moves with every pound of the drum, and his dark eyes sparkle with life, something mischievous hiding in their depths when he looks out at the crowd. A dark tattoo crawls up his chest and neck, displaying a design I can't distinguish from here. But it's something I've studied before on the worst day of my life.

"It'll be okay, I promise. I'll get help," Rad's dark, faint voice echoes in my memories. I can still feel him pulling a coat over my body.

My body shudders, blinking up at the music notes and splotches of black ink dotting his neck and chest. How the fuck? Panic crawls up my throat, and bile burns on its way up.

"I'll take care of you, okay? Do you need a hospital?" he croaks, holding my hair back as I puke on the lawn of someone's home in the middle of the night as music blares in the background.

I shake myself from the awful reminder before it plays back in vivid detail, running my fingers over the knife nestled deep in my pocket. I've shoved that memory into a solid black box in the back of my brain since the night it happened when I was fifteen—four years ago. No reason to think of it now. Except him—Ashton "Rad" Radcliffe. I must have been nutty to think emailing them and inviting them to perform at the bar I currently manage was a good idea. They're nothing more than a stark reminder of two different points in my life. Taking a deep breath, I focus on the men on stage.

A grin splits Rad's lips, and he doubles over laughing, managing to keep his rhythm when Kieran makes his way to Callum, the last person in the four-member band, strumming his bass with such concentration his tongue pokes out.

Kieran whacks Callum on the ass, jolting him from his concentration pose. His shaggy blonde hair flies with his movement, falling into his pure gray eyes. Like the badass he is, he doesn't miss a note and scowls as the song comes to an end, and the crowd formed in front of the small stage at the front of the bar erupts in whistles and cheers.

I smile at their carefree escapes and clap when they go into another song without addressing the drooling crowd. The atmosphere tonight flares when everyone jumps on their toes, throwing their hands in the air, and rocks out to the beautiful sounds of Whispered Words—my newest discovery—and possibly my worst nightmare.

My heart rate picks up, and sweat prickles at the base of my neck. I can't take my eyes off their cocky grins and swaggering steps. Girls swoon. Guys swoon. Everyone in the fucking bar swoons over them.

I've known most of these guys since high school. Well, I didn't know, know them. I knew of them–ego and all. Two years ago, we roamed the halls of Central City High School together, and then they graduated when I was a sophomore. Watching them command the stage for the second time, I can tell they haven't changed much. They've always been the same demanding pricks, making their presence known. They're larger than life. And yet, they have no idea I exist. Hell, they probably don't even know my name—not anymore, at least.

I was just the poor Central City girl showing up to school with ripped, out-of-date jeans and messy hair, not caring what they thought about me. Or anyone, for that matter. They live the good life in Lakeview, on the good side of town, with two-hundred-dollar shoes and expensive clothes, living off their mommy and daddy's money. At least, that was then. And now? I have no idea what their lives are like. But judging by the name-brand shirts and shoes, I'd say they're still doing pretty well for themselves. Even Kieran....

Kieran and I grew up together in the trenches of Central City. Once neighbors, now—he stares at me like we weren't friends hiding under the stars, talking about our tiny lives. We had experienced so much in such a short time and related to one another on many levels. Even when I was seven and he was nine, I thought Kieran was my knight in shining armor. The hero who saved me over and over again from danger.

My heart aches at our shared memories, and I shake my head. I always wondered what had happened to my best friend, who vanished and was nowhere to be found. Every day I looked for him.

In the halls of our elementary school, on the streets walking, or on the shared bus we took home. But he was gone.

It wasn't until I got to our only high school, where every student in town attended, that I learned the cold hard truth—he moved on to bigger and better things on the other side of the city, seemingly forgetting I existed. His new reality was the rich side of town, lined with mansions and money, leaving me in the poverty-stricken apartment complex with nothing but his memory.

"Ahem, bitch!" A whiney voice breaks me out of my little pity party, bringing me back to the present.

Right. I'm at work—time to return to reality.

I jerk back, narrowing my eyes on the pearl-wearing, plaid skirt-toting woman standing with an unattractive sneer on her lips. Great. It's her. Tessa. My snobby bully from high school who has never decided to grow up. Ugh. Gross. She taps her fancy-ass heels on the sticky floor and scoffs at me like I'm an idiot.

"You stupid Central girl, stamp my damn hand so I can watch my man perform." A warm smile glides across her face when her crystal-blue eyes land on the boys on stage with hearts floating above her head.

More specifically, she stares at the delicious morsel singing like someone punched his puppy, and he's been crying for hours. Deep anguish lives in the depths of his voice, and I want to fucking hold it in the palm of my hands and bathe in it and keep it for myself. There's something so right about Kieran's deep voice that calls to me. Or maybe it's the nostalgia of a former friend who is now the ghost of who he was. The only thing that never changed was his love of music.

"Let me play this for you, River Blue. Mom's new boyfriend got me this," Kieran's small raspy voice utters, sitting beside me in the grass, overlooking the parking lot of our dismal existence. Setting a small, janky-looking guitar on his lap, he strums the strings, tuning them by ear, and he hums, playing me our favorite country song by Garth Brooks, as my head rests on his shoulder. Laying his head on top of mine, he plays into the night, drowning out the sounds from his apartment that I was way too young to understand.

"Right, that'll be a ten-dollar cover charge," I say, returning to reality and extending my hand while wiggling my fingers expectantly.

Glaring in my direction, her face heats. Did she expect to get into this bar for free when a popular local band was playing? Probably. She's entitled like that. But not today, Tessy-boo. Pay up or leave before I sic my bouncers on you.

"The audacity," she murmurs through clenched teeth, acting like I'm putting her out by asking for money.

Hello, it says cover charge right behind my head, bish. Can't you read? But I remain as professional as I can when she continues her tirade on the ethics of our bar. The audacity is correct. Fuck.

I want to bang my head against the wall and crack my skull open when she murmurs more angry words under her breath, digging into her tiny purse. Her nose crinkles when she takes out a few hundred dollar bills, looks through them, and finally finds a ten in the stack. And she was complaining? Jesus. She has enough money in her purse to feed Ma and me for six months and pay all our bills. She thrusts it in my hands with a sneer and holds out her hand for me to stamp.

I raise a brow, stamping her hand. "And your ID?" I ask again, earning another huff.

"I'm twenty-one," she says, digging in her purse again. "You should know that," she hisses again, finally acknowledging we also knew each other from high school.

Sure, high school was big, but when you're a punching bag for half the school, everyone knows who you are. And she's no different, seeing as she was the ringleader of it all.

"Yeah, well...this is a bar, and there's the sign to enter for the show," I say in a bored tone, pointing to the sign behind me. "You either show your ID or get an underage stamp, so they know not to serve you any booze." I shrug when she scoffs again, throwing her pretty blonde hair over her shoulder.

"Here," she grumbles again, flashing me her ID, and confirming the bitch is twenty-one.

"Thanks a bunch," I say sarcastically with a sugary, sweet grin.

Stay professional. Stay fucking professional.

This earns me a mean scowl when I throw her ID back at her, and it falls to the floor. Her blue eyes connect with mine with disdain; it would kill me if it could—cue eye roll.

Was it a classy move? Hell no. But I'm tired of these grown adults insulting me and giving me attitude because of where I live and work. Grow up, already. This isn't high school anymore.

Besides, it's not my fault my father decided to kick us out and leave us destitute when he found a new woman to put his wandering schlong in. Gross—shudders—I shouldn't think about my father's dick. Like ever. Also, fuck him for leaving us poorer than shit, forcing us to return to my mom's hometown without a penny to our name. What we've made here is all our own. We didn't need his help, and we never will.

I wave her along, getting the same reaction from her friends behind her. And the people behind them. And so on and so forth. Where's the common decency these days, people? The compassion? The respect for humankind?

Nowhere, that's where. Why would there be any here in Central City, Illinois? We're the poor people, the people breaking their backs to earn our money. At the same time, they live in huge mansions and turn their pointy noses down at us from the outskirts of the same damn town just because of our financial differences.

My wandering gaze lands on Kieran again, singing his life away into the microphone. A dreamy sigh slips between my parted lips. Sometimes I miss the boy who told me everything would be okay.

I wonder if I ever crossed his mind. Probably not. Now he lives the good life with his new stepdad in a mansion overlooking the lake.

What I wouldn't give to have a conversation with him, or you know, a good romp in the backseat of my car. That would suffice, too. Because he may have been my bestie as a kid, but I always harbored an insatiable crush on the tall, dark, and handsome singer.

Ma always said I shouldn't touch poisonous things, but I can't seem to stay away from the bad boys who will bring me nothing but ruin. Getting Kieran Knight in the backseat of my car for a quickie is nothing out of the ordinary for my toxic ass. In fact, it's right on schedule.

It's happened a few times with other bands that passed through. They gave me the best two hours of my life—or, let's be honest, the best night of my life—and then they were on their way out the door with a thank you, ma'am. That's the beauty of it, though. I got mine. They got theirs—multiple times. Threesomes.

Foursomes. Hell, even some fivesomes. It didn't fucking matter. Freedom liberated every inch of me at their hands. Oh, and the orgasms were nice, too. Nothing beats multiple partners at one time. Some call it being a whore, but I call it sexually freeing. Fuck the labels!

Then the sun would come up, stream through my car window, or hotel room that accommodated us for the night, and they'd move on to the next city. We didn't exchange names or numbers. It was just a simple roll in the hay. And the best part? No expectations of a relationship in the future. I have way too much going on to be in any sort of relationship. Besides, I'd never date a fucking musician. Fuck them? You bet your ass. Relationship? No. The last thing I'd want is a relationship with flighty rock stars who are unreliable. Good in the sack, sure. But on the boyfriend, girlfriend end? Nope. Thank God for birth control and condoms, or I'd be tied to them for life.

If there's one thing my ma taught me, it was to stay away from rock stars. They bring you nothing but heartache.

Now, if only my heart would continue to listen to that sage advice instead of falling head over heels.... Thankfully that shit has only happened once. Past best friends don't count.

I smile when my best friend, Odette, comes bouncing into view, wrinkling her button nose at the crowd forming at the front of the small stage. Her beautiful curls bounce with every step she takes, giving her an angelic presence.

Darkness would have taken over my entire existence if I didn't have her in my life. She moved into Kieran's old apartment after he left, and we've been inseparable ever since. Her family is my second family, not by blood, but by our bond. Her mom, Korrine, helped raise me into the woman I am, constantly taking me in when my mom had to work nights. Ode's brother, Leon, is like my brother and treats me as such.

"Girl," she says, as her dark eyes scan the screaming crowd. "What is up with all the...the...." She scrunches her nose, looking back at me with her mouth gaping. "Damn suburban moms and dads in training. Is that girl wearing pearls?" She gapes, pointing to the mean girl from earlier. "By God, it's fucking Tessa, and she's wearing pearls," she murmurs, looking at me with wide eyes.

"You think she clutches them when her boyfriend suggests booty sex?" I snort when she cackles, drawing the attention of the devil herself.

Once again, Tessa's face contorts into a sneer, twisting her gorgeous face into something ugly. Eventually, her eyes drift back to the man candy on stage with a heavy swoon, and dear God, she fucking clutches her pearls as she throws her head back and sings at the top of her lungs, knowing every lyric.

"How's the first day as the head bitch in charge going?" Ode asks, leaning in to talk over the loud music. "HBIC in da house!" she hoots, shoving my shoulder playfully with a proud grin.

A laugh bursts from me, joy filling my being. I've worked long and hard since I was fifteen to get to this point. I've scrubbed toilets, removed trash, washed tables, and cleaned the floors. Slowly, I've worked toward the manager's position over the years, even at a young age. Some consider a nineteen-year-old manager impossible, but I've bled for this place. And Booker, the owner of Dead End, has always had my back like a father. Years before, he dated my mom, and I got to know him that way. Booker was the best boyfriend she ever had. They may have only lasted two years, but he forever cemented himself into my life. By age fifteen, I was begging on his doorstep for a job to start making my own money. Ma did her best, but it was never enough to keep the heat on. So, with reluctance, he started me out small, and here I am today—the manager. And my specialty? Bringing in bands from around the area draws more crowds and money for us.

I pull my loud best friend next to the podium, allowing the rest of the patrons to pile in. I give her a thumbs up, waving more people in line forward.

"Well, I'd say good. This is my doing." I wave a proud hand at the band on stage as more of their fans pile through the door with eager eyes.

It might sound cocky to some, but I've worked my ass off to bring Kieran and his merry band of dickbags here and all the people who follow them from venue to venue. I've stalked them on their barely-there social media, begging them to come here and play. I knew if they performed, all these suburban snobs would turn up, too. Cha-ching, money in my damn pocket. Never mind who he is to me. If it's a chance to make extra cash for my future, I'll take it.

Ode whistles, leaning an arm on my shoulder. "How the hell did you get Whispered Words to come here? They're like the hottest little band in Central Illinois right now."

I snort, waving more people along, stamping their hands, and checking their IDs. "Incentive," I say, biting the inside of my cheek when she throws her head back, laughing.

"Like pussy incentive? Because yeah, Riv, I'd say you'd give them a run for their money. Especially Kieran. I remember him from the school," she murmurs through a whole body shudder, eyeing his thick frame with lustful eyes. "He was so damn dark and mysterious. Who knew he'd end up...up there...." she says, waving a hand in his direction.

"Shut up," I say, elbowing her in the gut, causing her to burst into manic laughter. "I'm not putting out. God, what do you take me for?" I grumble at the last part, earning a few stares from the stragglers handing me their money.

"A Central City whore?" Ode chortles, earning another glare from me.

I frown, pushing my wet stamp right onto her arm. "Way to keep the stereotype going, bitch," I mumble. "Us Central girls have to stick together, especially against them." I nod toward the jumping suburban girls bobbing their heads to the music without a care. They hold their hands in the air, hoping to catch the attention of the four men rocking out on stage.

The boys are too enthralled in their music to notice the bouncing blonde elbowing her way to the front of the stage. Their eyes remain closed and focused on the euphoric sounds spilling from their fingers and vocal cords. I could watch them all day.

"I'm joking, girl," she says through a laugh, tossing her arm over my shoulders. "But in all seriousness, woman. They're like the best band on this side of the Mississippi. How the fuck did you convince the preppy assholes from the burbs to play at a place called Dead End?" She raises a brow in my direction, inspecting my face, and then she smiles. "You bitch, you used your name, didn't you?" My stomach drops at the accusation, and I quickly shake my head.

A lie rests on the tip of my tongue, eager to tell her I didn't. Because if there's one thing I'd never want to admit, it's that I used my name to get me anything in life. I resent the asshole who loaned me my last name for the past nineteen years. If I could give it back and tell him to shove it, I would.

I wave a hand at her, continuing to do my job despite her incessant yapping. "Maybe," I say, side-eyeing her when her mouth drops open in shock and flies swarm out.

Or they would if they were around. Ode's so damn shocked I pulled out the only famous piece of me—my last name. In East Point, California, my last name could get me a limo, a million dollars, and four hunky men willing to do anything for me. But here, in the middle of nowhere Illinois, it got me Whispered Words, and I call that a win in my book.

"River Blue West," she shrieks, hitting my shoulder and nearly knocking me off my stool.

I cringe at the sound of my full name and shake my head, sneaking a peek at Kieran. "Bitch, not so loud."

"I'm just surprised, is all," she says, wrapping an arm around my shoulder. "You hate your name. You hate your father and anything that involves him. Which includes your name, babe."

I scoff, rolling my eyes toward the ceiling. "Hate is a strong word when talking about the West legacy. Besides, I'm not the only loser West daddy dumped. So, I use it when it's to my advantage, like getting bands like this in the door. Besides, they never saw my face. It was only my last name. They probably think I'm a dude, anyway. Plus, I worked it out to get a commission for a good turnout." My grin grows when Ode's eyes turn to the size of saucers. "So, for every person that walks through the door and pays me, I get twenty-five percent."

And the sooner I get the money, the sooner I can get out of town and start my life. Money. College. New life. It's on the horizon for me. Freedom is in my future, far from this shitty stereotype I've had stamped on my forehead since I stepped foot in this town when I was two.

I sigh, thinking about all the shit I'd love to do but can't because I don't have enough money. I've been working here and Dead Records, the only vinyl record shop in town, since I was fifteen, and saving like my life depends on it. I still don't have enough to escape this hell hole I call my hometown. There's nothing here for me in Central City except a shitty stereotype about where I come from and dirty looks. All I'm trying to do is survive and make it from day to day until I can plot my escape. Until then, I'll put up with the Lakeview douchebags from the suburbs, who turn their noses down at us every chance they get.

"Oh my God, you finally got Booker to agree to that? You have that man wrapped around your pinky finger, I swear," she says, shaking her head without judgment.

"What're you doing here, anyway?" I ask, stamping another hand of the elite and watching as they walk to the bar, ordering a drink.

"Leon called. Apparently, the new manager filled the damn house up, so my brother said he needed an extra hand in the kitchen. The man is cooking his life away. But I'm always willing to give, especially since it's cash under the table." She grins at that, rubbing her hands together.

"The best way to keep the government out of our damn pockets," I say in agreement, sighing in relief at the pause from new people coming in.

"Well, tell your brother I said hi, and he's doing good work. I'll be up here until people stop coming in."

"Aye, aye, Miss Manager!" she sings, slapping me on the shoulder, and disappears behind the kitchen door.

We may be a small band venue at night, but Booker runs a bar complete with delicious food and drinks during the day. Ode, my neighbor turned best friend, sometimes comes in to help her brother Leon prepare the food and serve it to our patrons. We've all worked here together for several years—Leon and I, mostly. Ode has been in and out, going to different opportunities, but she always finds her way back. Together, we're a dysfunctional family making ends meet. Even if we still live with our parents on our journey to bigger and better things.

I glance around, taking in the unruly crowd as the music continues taking me out of this world. Building and building, it finally hits the chorus, and the crowd explodes with cheers. Phones light up and lift into the air, swaying back and forth until the chorus falls into the next verse. The beauty behind music never ceases to send goosebumps down my flesh and shivers up my spine. It takes me to another world, letting me leave the one I'm in. Music lives in the soul—hell, it lives in my DNA. Literally.

My pounding heart accelerates through my lungs when my gaze snaps to the one man I've been drooling over since he cockily walked in. His piercing, mismatched blue eyes stare at me from the top of his kingdom on stage, ripping the soul from my body with one devastating look.

But does he recognize me as the girl he used to run to when his mom drank too much and kicked his ass out so she could make a buck?

Deep in the depths of my body, something shifts, leaving me a gasping mess, desperately pulling oxygen into my lungs. It feels like we're two magnetic pieces shifting into place and finding their match—once again. I only experience relief when Kieran's eyes pass over me, running over the crowd of girls shouting his name. The moment he breaks our stare, oxygen floods my body again, and my trembling fingers halt.

Kieran sings the melody of fucking angels, high in the clouds and looming over us. God, he has the voice of a damn siren that makes me want to come in my damn booty shorts before I speak to him face to face. How the fuck can I face him again when the urge to lick him all over becomes overwhelming?

As the song ends and the music dies, he holds up his toned arm, thrusting his fist into the air. Sweat pours from his head, down his chiseled face, and drips off his carved marble jawline. The lights from above shine down, creating a halo around his unsaintly head.

"How's everyone feeling tonight?" His deep, panty-soaking voice breathes through the microphone, and my damn breath leaves my lungs.

"We love you, Kieran!" some girl shouts with desperation, lifting her shirt, and revealing her tits to the world.

Soon more girls join in on the titty show parade, jiggling them as they dance, giggling their lives away. Kieran smirks, holding up a finger as he leans toward the bass player, whispering secrets between them. Callum blushes deeply, staring at their nipples like a deer caught in the headlights. He can't move away until Kieran slaps him on the back with a grin. Callum shudders, averting his eyes to the stage, and avoids the tit show with all his might.

Ah, shit. We can't have titties on display in the bar. Nudity is very frowned upon. Since I'm the damn manager, I have to force the boobs back into hiding, or more will pop out to join the party, and I can't have that.

"Put your tits away!" I shout, cupping my hands around my lips, amplifying my voice through the crowd.

The girls squeal again, shoving their shirts down. Whispering to one another, they collectively throw me dirty looks. Yeah, barbie dolls, I'm the devil for telling you to put your boobs away. Get over it.

Call me the boob police or whatever; keep your damn titties in your shirt, and we'll be peachy. Have to keep this a clean operation, after all.

"What a titkill," the drummer says, leaning into his microphone with a manic grin. He hits his cymbal, tapping out the badum-tss tune.

"Boooooo!" the crowd rings, aiming their displeasure at me with dirty looks and down-turned thumbs.

"You've heard the crowd, Door Girl," Kieran says in a low, warning tone, staring right into my eyes again.

But how much can he see from the brightly lit stage? Can he see who I am? Or am I just another nameless girl to him? My heart plummets into my churning gut with indecision. Do I want him to remember the poor girl from the apartments he left behind? I have no idea. I knew I'd face him eventually, but I'll deal with that when it comes.

"We want the titties!" someone chants, making the rest of the crowd chant right along with them.

I groan, throwing my head back. Jesus Christ. Why do the titties have to come out at a concert? Why's that a thing? Can't we leave the titties out of this and not display nudity? No one bends over and exposes their asscheeks, so why this?

"No fucking titties!" I shout, standing on my chair, raising myself above the rowdy crowd, still chanting. "You get 'em out. Then you're out! No more show! Capiche?" I raise a brow, scanning the group, frowning at me with displeasure.

Frown all you want. I won't change my mind.

"You heard the titkill!" Rad says with a laugh. "Save your pretty titties for later! Now, K, let's fucking do this." The drummer counts them in with the pound of his sticks, and they begin.

Kieran keeps his eyes on me, burning right into my soul. As the music starts, he sways to the beat, watching my every move when I jump down from the chair and stroll into the kitchen. I feel his gaze everywhere, much like a predator eyeing his prey, scurrying back into the field. It's as if he recognized the girl staring back at him with hope in her eyes. The same hope I've held loosely for the past nine years.

"I'll get the front, HBIC!" Ode says, saluting me, heading out of the kitchen with a grin and settling on a stool at the front.

Kieran's heavenly voice blasts through the house speakers again, forming goosebumps across my flesh. Resting my head against the kitchen door, I regain my breath, begging the oxygen to return.

Every time that man pierces me with his stare, I swear my knees wobble and weaken under his scrutiny. Kieran has always had that cocky, dark, and mysterious cloud hovering above him luring me in.

And that's my fucking kryptonite.

RIVER

Walking silently up the steps toward the dark lifted stage, I nibble my bottom lip, careful not to spook the man leaning down. Left behind by his band members, one lone figure packs away his things with measured ease. I huff a breath, eyeing his every move. This is the closest I've been to him since they all graduated high school and started at the university across town.

Thirty minutes ago, the spotlights dimmed, and the music died. The boys took one last sweaty bow, smiling at the crowd, and said their goodbyes, disappearing behind the large black curtain separating the front from the back. Despite the crowd hooting and hollering for an encore, the boys remained backstage, cooling off after a successful show.

Eventually, the crowd gave up begging for an encore by paying their tabs and calling it quits. Everyone except Tessa and the itty-bitty titty brigade who are currently standing by the edge of the stage, looking more like desperate groupies than anything.

Squeals of delight, giggles, and whispers follow me as I head onto the darkened stage. Looking back, I smirk at Bert, our burly security guard, who disdainfully frowns at the girls. Shaking his head, he murmurs a few choice words and pins me with a look, begging for help. I snort, playfully saluting him in response. No can do, buddy. I have one last thing to do before I go home, and then I'm free.

Peering down at the hefty check made out to Whispered Words, I can't help but smile at tonight's success. I knew the raging crowd from before would be my good luck charm but fuck if I didn't make bank. And with our split, the band made bank too. No other band in the history of Dead End has made this amount on their first night here. They're definitely coming back. I could kiss their damn faces for granting me such a payday.

My eyes close on their own accord when the remnants of their songs repeatedly hum through my veins. Echoes of their fans' excited whoops and hollers play in my mind like I'm standing before them again, eagerly hearing their orgasmic sounds. A buzz encases my body, and I sigh. When I open my eyes and look around, reality crashes into me. The show plucked its last string and thumped its last snare thirty minutes ago. All that meets my ears is the whooshing static filling my senses after a long night of loud music and screams.

A heavy sigh rocks me when I take a few more steps, watching Kieran as he packs away his equipment with angry mutters and throws his things around haphazardly—reminding me of his small temper as a kid when things didn't go his way.

His dark, messy, sweat-soaked hair falls into his eyes, and he curses at himself through several frustrated growls. It's one thing when he growls into the microphone. But up close and personal? My core heats to molten levels, heating my cheeks, and my damn toes curl in my shoes.

Kieran throws something into his guitar case with force and curls his fingers into fists. Heavy breaths rock through him, heaving his sculpted chest. My eyes fall down his body, taking in the glory of Kieran Knight. My palms sweat in his proximity, forcing me to wipe them down my jean shorts.

"You guys sounded so good tonight. Good show, Kieran," I say with an enthusiastic smile, stepping up to the massive man with his back to me.

Typically, the musicians happily stay behind for a free drink and a two-a.m. snack before they hit the road again. Usually, we chat about nothing and enjoy each other's company. Some rock my fucking world in the backseat of my car or the back of their small tour vans. And some we just don't mesh well.

And apparently, this guy is the latter.

He grits his teeth, turning toward me with his fists clenched. Those familiar mismatched blue eyes look right through me as if he doesn't know or see me. I frown when he doesn't immediately respond, returning to packing away his stuff, and completely ignoring my existence.

Talk about rude, dickweed. I'm standing right here. I try not to let the hurt infect me and instead try again.

I clear my throat again, hoping to catch his attention without sounding too damn needy. Like, hello, I'm here to pay you, assbag. But it doesn't work. I could dance a jig with tap shoes naked, and this asshole wouldn't look my way. Maybe I should show him my tits like the girls at the show? I peer down at the bottom of my shirt, seriously contemplating showing off the girls for some attention, and shake my head. I have dignity, damn it.

"I said..."

"Yeah, well, I'm not interested. Especially some Central girl," he says in a rumbly voice, perfect for sexy dirty talk.

But this talk isn't the dirty talk I have in mind. I want him to slap my ass, call me a whore, and maybe a good girl. Not a fucking Central Girl. Jeez, this guy, too? You'd think someone formally from this side of town would have more respect for the group of people he was once part of.

My stomach twists at the audacity of his judgmental words. The fucker didn't even look at me to know who I was or where I came from. Instead, he kneels in front of his pedalboard, inspecting them with his fingertips. He shakes his head and ignores me again by busying himself with more packing and grumbling.

A sharp arrow pierces through my chest and embeds in my heart. Old feelings burst to life inside me, and I instantly resent the fucker for ever stepping foot inside my establishment.

"I'm sorry. What the fuck did you say?" I say through clenched teeth, standing rigid.

Fuck pleasantries. Fuck professionalism.

My panties dry in an instant at his attitude, tamping down my attraction. Maybe he has changed so much, and he's no longer like the sweet boy I once knew. And instead, he has turned into the asshole everyone says he is.

A deep heat races up my neck and onto my face, burning my ears with a fury so intense I could take down the fucking devil. Tears well in my eyes, fueled by my anger.

God, be good, Riv. Be fucking good, don't curse out the fucking talent just yet.

Even though he deserves every ounce of my ire coming his way, I bite my damn tongue. I grind my teeth, fisting the damn paper check in my fist, contemplating tearing it up in his face so he sees who he's dealing with. Maybe he'll leave, and I'll take the entire cut. Fuck him.

"You heard me," he grits out, shaking his head. Fiddling with his damn pedals, he tosses them into a case and growls, not paying me an ounce of attention. "I'm not interested. We don't want anything you're giving. You're wasting your breath."

What. The. Fuck. Not only was I friends with this asshole as a kid and went to the same school, but we spoke through email, and I used my name. Hello, River. It's written across my damn boob in tiny writing. I blink a few times, swallowing the angry words in my throat before I say anything else stupid.

His jaw twitches when he stands before me, crossing his arms over his buff chest. I swallow the gasp in my throat, the intensity residing in the depths of his eyes. Two blue eyes stare back at me, but one stands out with a brown stain carving its way through the bottom of his right iris. It's mesmerized me since we were kids, pulling me in again.

"Everything will be okay, Blue," he murmurs, putting an arm over my shoulder after setting his used guitar on the grass. "I'll always be your knight." I always grinned when he said things like that, making a little play at his last name. But it was always true at the time. He was my knight, saving me from the clutches of the bullies at elementary school. Kieran strokes the scratch down my face, given to me by some chick in the fifth grade on the playground who said I stole her kickball.

"But your ma," I say, pointing to his darkened apartment with the curtains drawn and the loud music pouring from it.

"She'll come around," he sighs, shaking his head. "She always does." I lean my head on his shoulder as we fall back into the grass, staring at the stars twinkling down at us.

That was the last time he held me like a precious jewel and our last encounter. After that night, a strange man kept coming around, sneaking around with Gloria—Kieran's mom. After that night, Kieran and Gloria left the apartment without a goodbye. He didn't even have the decency to knock on my door, hug me, and tell me he'd see me later. He simply vanished under the moonlight, and Ode and her family replaced him in a matter of days.

Swallowing my memories, I meet the boy who broke my heart head-on, refusing to back down and break off our stare-off. He's hot now—hotter than before. But his personality could use a little throat punch until he learns how to talk to me appropriately. Or anyone else, for that matter.

"You're still here?" he questions, raising a brow. He may be looking in my direction, but nothing but fury resides in his eyes. It's like he's looking through me and doesn't seem to notice I'm really here. Or human. Looking down, he continues to fiddle with a pick between his fingers, dismissing me. "Jesus," he mumbles, running a hand through his hair. "I thought I told you..."

"Yeah," I scoff, waving a hand. "You told me you don't want anything I have to offer." I hold up the paycheck in front of his face, happily watching the color drain from every inch of him when I tear it in half and then tear it into tiny pieces, throwing it in the air like little pieces of confetti. "I guess you didn't want your paycheck either. You know, the one we bargained for over email? But fuck you and your high and mighty bullshit," I spit through clenched teeth, turning on my heel and storming off the back of the stage without a look back. The heat of his burning gaze stares after me when I march down the stairs, stomping my feet into the old creaky wood.

As I round the stage next to the security guard, he holds his hand in the air. With a smirk, I high-five him, only letting my rage settle for half a second. The girls around him titter and gossip about me, and I laugh internally when Bert finally shoos them away and kicks them out of the bar.

"Way to go, boss," he murmurs with a tiny whoop, barking out a laugh when I nod my head at him. If I speak any more than I have, I'll blow a damn gasket.

My fingernails dig into the palm of my hand, leaving blood-stained crescent moons behind. As I march across the empty bar with my boss's office in mind, a familiar face joins Assface—that's his name now because he doesn't deserve the name Kieran—on stage with a disapproving frown.

Rad looks at me without an ounce of recognition and then at his bandmate, shaking his head. If I had more time and energy, I'd ogle the lean, shirtless man hovering on stage, giving his friend a disapproving look. But I'm all out of fucks to give. They flew the coop the moment that assface dismissed me with a growl and wrist flick.

In high school, Rad sported the most ridiculous-looking mullet, pairing it with his new mustache. He's grown into his style, becoming a man all on his own. But the remnants of who he once was, has my heart squeezing when more unwanted memories pour through my mind at the sight of him, reliving one of the worst days of my life.

"Dude, what the hell did you do?" Rad says to Kieran with outrage, tinting his tone.

Stopping my retreat, I knock away the awful memories pushing at the forefront of my mind and lock them deep inside. They beg to reemerge and haunt me, but I don't let them. Long ago, I forced them down, and I never want to think about that day again. Not even with him, my hero, standing before me.

Leaning against the solid door leading to the long, private hallway, I pause to see what Assface has to say for himself because it had better be good.

My eyes narrow at the shirtless drummer, absentmindedly twirling a drumstick, pinching his face with concern. Dark eyes take me in from the stage above until he growls, focusing all his attention on the rude as fuck singer.

"Come on, man, you can't *not* be an asshole for like all of five seconds?" His shouts echo off the walls. Satisfaction soars through me at his outrage, and I smirk, watching the other guy sputter for words. "Fix it, Kieran!" he shouts, pointing at me before I slip into the long, abandoned hallway, letting the door shut firmly behind me.

Passing the bathrooms and a storage closet, I make my way down the checkered linoleum hallway before I finally make it to the back office and enter the room. The once cluttered space now sits clean and organized.

Becoming a manager didn't happen overnight. Hell, it took four years of hard, greasy work. I've been watching Booker run this place for years, taking the opportunity to learn the ins and outs of everything from staffing to taxes to buying food and alcohol. Last month, Booker took the training wheels off and let me handle it as a test to see if I could hack it. I may be too young to run a bar, but Booker trusts me with his baby. And I've never been more thankful for the opportunities he's granted me. Despite my mother breaking up with him, having him in my life has been a godsend. I don't know where I'd be financially if it weren't for him suggesting this was a possibility

Silence stretches around me when I walk into my shared office and lean against the once-cluttered desk—gripping the edges to collect myself. In ten seconds, I need to slip back out of this office with a new check and present them with their money.

Even though they're dicks. Okay, huge dicks.

This is business, and I need their business to continue to grow. The bigger their band gets, the more money I get, and the faster I can run away from this town to my dream college a few states away. All I have to do is survive community college and work two jobs. Easy peasy.

I swallow my damn pride and lean over to collect the company checkbook and write a new check out to the band.

To the Whispered Words, you sack of shits, here's the money I owe you—one-thousand dollars.

I sigh, rub my tired eyes, and flip to the next check. As much as they deserve the first one, written with all my rage, I make a new check with their correct name and a much friendlier tone.

Whispered Words, $1,000.00.

As I rip the first check out, the office door slams open in a rush, shutting with a heavy thud. An embarrassing squeal leaves my lips as I stare into the same eyes that have left me breathless for many years.

Glazed-over eyes take me in, somehow looking slightly less harsh and judgmental. This time, Kieran doesn't look down at me with disdain or disgust. Nope. It vanished from his expression. His eyes linger down my body, taking in the ripped shorts I stuffed my flat ass into and the tight black shirt clinging to my body. He swallows hard, slowly drifting his gaze up my torso and resting them on the words—River and manager resting on my tit.

"I bet you wish you looked at my tits before you dismissed me, huh?" I growl, crossing my arms over my chest, blocking his view.

Snapping his gaze up to mine, a renewed sense of anger ignites in the back of his eyes.

"If you would have just fucking told me you were the goddamned manager," he scoffs again, throwing his hand in the air like this is all my fault.

What an assface. Seriously? All the oxygen leaves my lungs, renewing my rage.

"Like that would have made a fucking difference?" I growl back, pushing at his hard chest two times. Much to my satisfaction, I knock Kieran back a few steps, catching him off guard. His eyes bulge at me when I curl my fingers in his shirt, holding him upright. "You didn't even give me the time of day. Maybe you should learn some respect, Knight," I hiss his name like a curse, never wanting to speak it again. It feels foreign on my tongue, having not been uttered for so many years.

My Knight—the boy who swooped in and saved my pitiful ass from the bullies around the apartment complex and at school. He saved me more times than I can count and was my closest ally until he disappeared.

Something sparkles in the depths of his eyes. He gives a knowing glance when he looks down at me again and reads my name before meeting my eyes again, searching for the answers. All the color drains from his face, and he shakes his head with confusion.

wallowing hard, he licks his lips with a mist glazing over his eyes. His breaths hiccup until he finally returns to himself, and the realization settles in. Every inch of gruffness he displayed before disappears, and before me is the Kieran I knew when I was a kid.

"It's you," he whispers softly, easing the rugged plains of his face, almost disbelieving. His eyes scan my face like he's trying to memorize every inch. "Fucking Callum. I wished he had told me who he was emailing," he murmurs, shaking his head. Shadows lift from his eyes, and a lightness breaks through, bringing back the carefree knight I once knew.

"Tell me now," he whispers in a softer tone, leaning down so our noses touch and our lips rest a millimeter apart. I'd beg him to close the distance and fuse our lips if I didn't loathe his existence right now. "Tell me now, River Blue," he says the last part so softly I swear I'm getting whiplash.

Anger? Happy? Horny? Who knows? This guy is a friggin enigma I should run far away from. In fact, I should high-tail it out of this office before I do anything stupid. Like, fuck him. Now that would be a huge mistake. I glare into his beautiful, mismatched eyes, drawing me into his dangerous web. Piece by piece, I fall deeper into his gaze.

Holy disintegrating panties. If I don't remove myself from this situation, bad things will happen. Or good things, depending on how you look at it.

Sweat breaks out on my neck, lifting the hairs. His eyes dilate, almost turning black with desire. My fingers tighten on his shirt, torn between throwing him out of the room and having him bend me over. Right here. Right fucking now.

"I am River West, the manager of Dead End," I rasp, licking my lips. His eyes follow the movement, and he steps even closer.

"Here is your damn check. Maybe we can do business again," I say in a breathless voice, loosening my grip on his sweat-soaked shirt and shoving the check into his chest.

Now—this is the moment I should try to back away and fully uncurl my fingers from his shirt instead of standing there eagerly awaiting his next move. I really should go home. Because, you know, he's an asshole, and I shouldn't put up with it. He dismissed me, yet I want to bang him into next week. Just call it scratching an itch and leave it at that.

So, it shouldn't surprise me when he grabs my wrist and clucks his cocky as fuck tongue at me. A smirk lifts the edge of his lip, yanking me forward and pulling my entire front into his. My eyes narrow, dangerously close to stabbing the fucker in the dick for even thinking he can manhandle me. I palm the knife in my pocket, ten seconds away from yanking it out and threatening his manhood. But then he looks at me—really looks at me, taking me in.

My breaths pick up, a strange sensation tingling across my skin. I soften against the rugged plains of his body, soaking in the way he feels against me once again. When he looks down at me, something strange sparks in his eyes, and I can't place the soft expression. His wide eyes drift to where our bodies fuse, where a weird possessiveness vibrates through his chest in the form of a growl, and something stiff pokes into my belly.

My breath shudders and my mind spirals out of control. How can we go from wanting to rip each other's hair out to wanting to tear each other's clothes off? Huh? This whole situation is bat shit crazy, yet my panties cling to my eager pussy, ready to fucking receive him—traitorous hussy.

He bites into his bottom lip and nods approvingly. His meaty grip weaves through my ponytail, ripping my head back with a sharp yank. Embarrassment tints my cheeks when rogue moans leak between my lips, and his rough grip rips my roots out.

Rock stars and their dirty mouths and expert tongues hold me hostage and weaken my damn legs, proving once again to be my fucking kryptonite.

Kieran leisurely holds me by my damn ponytail, gently tugging as he stuffs the check into his jeans pocket. Every inch of my body is apparently attracted to assholes like him. Proving to me I can never get enough. But it's him—Kieran. And that leaves me with conflicting feelings. WHYYYYYY???? Why does it have to feel so damn good and bad and wrong all at the same time?

"Yeah," he groans, getting in my face. "I think we can do business, but not in the future. Right now. We have some fucking business to finish."

The entire world tilts when Assface slams his lips into mine, and fucking seals our fate with his wild tongue diving into my mouth. I loosen my grip on his shirt entirely, dragging my nails through his shaggy black locks. He grunts into my mouth when I scratch his scalp and dig my nails in deeper, loving how his massive body shivers against mine.

His teeth sink into my bottom lip, dragging it out and sucking it. I swear my eyes roll so far into the back of my head I see my damn brain—if I had one, that is. I melt when a metallic taste explodes on my tastebuds, and he thrusts his tongue back into mine, and I moan.

Fuuuckkkk. It's been a hot minute since I've gotten some, and let's just say I'm thirsty, and Kieran is the tall glass of 'What the fuck am I about to do?' I've been craving.

So, I internally make the call. We fuck. We leave. End of fucking story. Just like all the other musicians who have come through. He's a dick. But I'm goddamn horny.

"This doesn't mean anything," I growl out, trying to shove him back to take control, but it does nothing. He's a damn, immovable brick wall keeping me trapped.

Using his grip on my ponytail, he forcefully spins me, pinning me against the edge of my boss's desk. My hips cut painfully into the sharp wood as he jerks my neck to the side, extending it until pain erupts.

I shiver through the delicious sensation exploding through my body when his warm fingers trail up under my shirt, stopping against the ribs near my boob. My heart beats like a damn drum inside my chest, waiting for him to make his next move. Come on, asshole. Do something already.

A small, desperate whimper leaks through my tightly pressed lips when he leans over me, pressing his hard chest into my back. And that's not the only thing that's hard about him. His warm breaths brush against my ear when he chuckles, tightening his grip around my ribs and grinding himself against my ass. His breaths echo in my ear when his wet tongue rolls over my earlobe until he finally latches on and sucks it into his mouth.

"This means everything, River Blue," he murmurs, and my heart cracks in half at the massive emotions soaring through me. It's the name he called me so many years ago.

Sliding his fingers beneath my bra, I gasp when he pinches my nipple between his fingertips and thrusts my ass into his hard dick. "Fuck, River Blue," he grunts, squeezing harder. "Where have you been?" he whispers again, shaking his head. "I can't believe... It didn't even cross my mind that it was you. The girl from my past."

"Where I've always been," I moan when he kneads my entire tit in his hand like dough. "You were the one who left without a word." Hurt leaks into my voice, and he stops, pressing his forehead into my shoulder. "You didn't even say goodbye."

"Let me make it up to you, then," he murmurs against my neck. "Let me show you how much I've missed you."

Kieran doesn't waste a moment when he flicks the button to my shorts and pulls them down my legs to my ankles. He uses his leverage to force me over the desk, and there's not a damn thing I can do about it.

"All soaked for me?" he whispers in my ear, pulling my thong to the side and letting his fingers explore my soaked core. "I want to hear you say it, River Blue." I shiver at the sound of my stupid full name, the one I hate so damn much, falling from his lips.

His fingers go up and down through my slick folds but never plunge in. My back arches in desperation, silently begging him to fuck me before I do it my own damn self.

"Quit playing, Kieran," I moan when his fingers lightly circle my clit in lazy circles. I'm about to bite his damn fingers if he doesn't get me off. "And fuck me like you hate me already!" I cry out in desperation when one finger enters me and swirls around.

"Then admit it," he whispers, nipping at my earlobe. "Admit that you're gushing for me, and only me. Admit it." My pussy clamps around his finger with every word he speaks, begging this asshole to do me in.

"Yeah, I'm wet for you. Now, what the fuck are you going to do about it?" I hiss, jerkily turning my head to the side to stare back at him.

His beautiful eyes dilate, and he looks me square in the eyes. A sly smirk picks up the left side of his lips before he jams his fingers so far inside my pussy that I come on the spot, seeing white stars. I heave a breath, trying to drag oxygen into my sputtering lungs. Sweat trickles down my spine when his fingers continue their delicious assault.

"Good girl. That's what I thought," he murmurs. "You're going to take my cock, River Blue. And you're going to come all over it again and again." Possession takes over his voice, dipping it into a deep growl.

My eyes roll into the back of my head. Like breathing life into me, every inch of my body comes alive for the first time in months under his rough touch. Goosebumps erupt across my flesh, and my toes curl into the worn-out linoleum. This is what I'm talking about. Now, slap my ass and tell me I'm a good fucking girl, and we'll be peachy.

"Whatever you say, Assface." I pant when the sound of a condom wrapper ripping fills the air, and my damn pussy clenches around nothing.

"I have a fucking name, River," he whispers my name into my ear like a fucking prayer he's preparing to chant for eternity. "And I want you to fucking scream it. Say it with me," he grunts, rolling on the condom with one hand, securing my hair, and keeping me still. He kicks my feet apart, forcing my ass to arch into the air even more. "Say it. Say, Kieran. Say my name, the one you used to. I want to hear it fall from your lips," he says through clenched teeth, rubbing the tip of his dick through my folds, sending a thrill of shivers down my spine. "Say it, for the love of all things holy, River! Say my goddamn name so I can fuck you over this desk."

Everything inside me says to walk away, no matter how good this feels. Kieran is a walking, talking disaster. The moment I say his name out loud, it will solidify what we had so long ago.

The memory of my first kiss floats to mind. Kieran and I played in the apartment pool late in the evening alone. One second, he was splashing me; the next, his lips were on mine. Before I could react, he had pulled away with a blush and quickly ran home. Leaving me there to consider what had happened. The next time I saw him, he acted like it didn't happen, and we were just friends like we always had been.

"My Knight," I rasp through shuddering breaths.

Every muscle in my body contracts when he surges forward, growling like a beast and burying himself so deep inside me that I swear my cervix brushes his tip, and I meet God himself behind my eyelids. White static takes over my vision. Stars burst. The fucking angels sing their hallelujahs! I try to keep my moans at bay but fuck it. That won't happen.

"Holy fuck, Kieran," I say through a shuddering moan, my mouth gaping open.

"That's right, scream it for the entire bar to hear," he grunts, slamming his hips against mine repeatedly until the sound of flesh hitting flesh fills the office above my loud moans. "Let them know who's giving you the best fuck of your life."

I grip the edge of the desk with all my might when it scratches against the floor, leaving indents and scrapes.

"Touch yourself," Kieran begs through a rasp. "Come on my cock. Do it!" he demands, grabbing my wrist and forcing my fingers to swirl around my aching clit with heavy pressure. "Good fucking girl," he hisses when my pussy contracts around him, and I gasp for air.

Come," he demands in a single growl, picking up his pace.

With one demand from his gravelly voice, I fucking detonate like a bomb, contracting around him until he stills behind me and moans so loudly with satisfaction that it fills the air. I'm sure everyone and their mom down the block heard precisely what we were up to. Our heavy breaths echo through the room, and his grip on my hair finally loosens.

"Well, Assface," I retort through heavy breaths, returning to the name I initially chose for him. "That was quite satisfactory. I'd give you a six," I say through a lazy grin when his body stiffens behind me in offense.

That's right. You can't waltz back into my life like you're my damn savior again—no way in hell. Maybe I should add the finger guns and a thumbs up to really sell how I'm feeling. My body sags, and every ounce of stress evaporates. This was precisely what I needed to clear my mind.

"A six? I'm worth more than a six," he scoffs into the crease of my neck. His hands wander down my body again, and he pinches my nipples through my bra, sending electricity through my entire body.

"Nah, just a six," I whisper. He kneads my breasts through my bra, drawing more want from my needy body. If I weren't so pissed at him, I'd say fuck it and go another round.

"That performance was way more than a six," a new voice comes from behind us, startling me.

Kieran protectively tightens his grip on me, keeping his body draped over mine and out of view of our newcomers.

"The fuck are you doing in here?" he hisses, and my entire face heats in embarrassment. Great. I just got the best lay of my life in front of an audience.

"Came to find you, K. I had to make sure you didn't kill the poor Central Girl. We see now you didn't. I mean, you beat that pussy up, but God damn," the man rasps, and I recognize him as the asshole who berated Kieran for being a dick to me—Rad.

"Don't ever say beat that pussy up again," someone else mutters through a tired sigh.

"Jesus Christ, you assholes, get out!" I hiss, throwing an arm out, but Kieran holds me tighter. "Get the fuck out!" I screech.

"Aw, how cute," another voice says with a sneer. Instantly, I recognize his preppy ass—Asher Montgomery. The biggest dick that ever walked the halls of Central City High, thinking he was better than everyone else. "We'll be in the car when you decide to think with your damn brain, not your dick. Hope you get yourself tested too."

"Yeah, maybe you guys should learn to lock the door," another voice I recognize now as the bass player, Callum Rose, mumbles, apologizing under his breath.

I blow out my breath when Kieran releases my body and steps back from me so fast that it's like I have a disease. He takes the condom off his flaccid dick and stares at the mess in his hands.

"I can't believe you didn't lock the door, Assface," I say, pulling up my tiny shorts and righting my bra, thong, and shirt. His eyes watch my every damn move with heat resting behind them as he takes every inch of me.

"You could have, too," he says with a shrug, tossing the condom into the trash like a gentleman. Quickly, he redresses himself but doesn't bother to fix his dark strands standing on end. His eyes heat again when he stares me up and down. "So, you're the River West from the emails?" he questions, taking a step forward.

"Um, that's my name," I say sarcastically, tossing my arms in the air with a shrug.

"You're the same River Blue," he chuckles at that, throwing his head back and staring at the ceiling. "Fuck," he murmurs to himself, blinking several times.

"Yeah, that's me too," I huff, crossing my arms. "Are we done here? Or?"

"We are far from fucking done," he hisses, snapping his gaze to me. "None of this is over," he gestures between us. "I'll be seeing you, River Blue West."

And with that, his toxic ass waltzes out the door, looking back at me with a manic, knowing grin.

What the hell did I just do?

KIERAN

"**W**hy the tears, River Blue?" I murmur, rage brewing through my veins at the sight of her shaking shoulders. My fingers curl when her big, moss-green eyes look up at me, glistening with tears. We had just met up on the hill behind the apartment complex—our daily meeting spot.

"Stupid Stacey again," she says, clenching her fists tightly together. One day, I'll show my girl how to use those fists against everyone who decides to put their hands on her.

"You want me to take care of Stacey?" I ask in a low voice as violent images roar through my mind. I'll rip that girl's head off. I don't care if she's in first grade and I'm in third.

"No." Her answer is simple and to the point, like she always is.

I scrub a hand down my face when I waltz out the bar's back door and head down the dark alleyway toward the SUV parked in the back. A faint sense of nostalgia hits me hard as I make my way through the shadows of the night. Being back on this side of town brings so many emotions flooding the surface, even if I fight them off at every turn. For as long as I can remember, I've lived on the greener side of town, never venturing into the dark stain of Central City—where I grew up. It's a vague memory nestled in the back of my mind. One I had forgotten for many years. After losing a piece of myself here when I had to leave her behind, I shoved the memories into my deepest, darkest part and incinerated them for eternity.

After my mother moved us away from the only place I had ever known, that's when my real nightmare began. Each night I sat and cried, longing for the girl under the stars talking to the man on the moon. But I was stuck, beaten down, and verbally harassed by the new man in my mother's life—my stepfather, Nigel Montgomery.

At ten years old, I could only handle so much. There comes a time when the beatings become too much, and you stop longing for the one person you crave. Instead, locking the happy memories away until they fade into nothing more than a vague idea.

Now, the memories pour through my mind like a dam bursting open and flooding my every waking thought. Flashes of River's long brown hair lay past her shoulders and flowed down her back. Those moss-green eyes glared at me when I entered her office, and the pinched look she gave me. Her delicate nose. Those dark eyelashes brushed against her freckled cheeks as her eyes hooded from lust. River Blue, the girl from my old life. The one girl I swore I'd never think about again. Or see again. The girl I forced myself to forget. River Blue was always River Blue to me, never River West. Fuck. I should have read the damn emails Callum wrote to the manager of this place. If I had just seen her name, I could have told them who she was to me—and now, to us.

But now, she's all I can think about as I make the walk of shame toward my friends. Shit. Heat burns my cheeks when I open the driver's door and sit without looking around.

"Oh! There he is! The man of the hour!" Rad whoops from the backseat, obnoxiously pounding his fist into the roof of my Tahoe, making it bounce on its wheels.

I grunt, starting up the SUV, and proceed to the mouth of the alley, waiting for the crowded sidewalks to thin. Leaning back, I stare at the boys and idle the car.

For once, Gloria—the woman who begs me to call her mother—became reasonable when I asked for a larger car. In her eyes, it was a status symbol for the pot of gold at the end of our fucking suburban rainbow.

For me, though? It was a place to store and transport our instruments and the amps we'd bought ourselves over the years. Whatever we got from gigs went straight into our band's bank account so we could afford new instruments, strings, picks, and sticks. We can provide whatever we need without running to someone for a loan. This band will be entirely ours, and I don't want Gloria's money tainting any of it. I've built this with my hands alongside the guys.

"You good?" Callum asks in his usual short words from the backseat, nervously averting his eyes.

Sweat sticks to every inch of the curly blonde hair currently plastered to his forehead. His tired eyes watch out the window, taking in the passing patrons lazily walking down the sidewalks at two a.m.

"I read on Spaceface last night that there have been three attacks in the alleyways in the past three weeks, each getting progressively more violent," Callum mutters to the window, worrying his lip until his worry-filled eyes meet mine.

I raise a brow, turning to look at Callum, and shake my head. I'd hate to have a talent like Callum's, where everything he sees, he stores in his head without effort. Some would kill for a photographic memory, but the cons greatly outweigh the pros. Every event—good or bad, stays with him for the rest of his life. Some would call it a gift, but Callum sees it as the ultimate curse. Especially after what he witnessed with his parents. And God, Jenny. He lost them all, and the only ounce he has left of them is the house he lives in and the enormous trust they left in his name, with stipulations that he lives there for two years before even thinking about selling or moving away from the house that brings him nothing but nightmares. Imagine walking through the halls of your family home and seeing the ghosts of your past staring back at you. I know he's been counting down the days until he can cash in and move on—only five more months.

His gaze drifts up and down the bar, calculations running rampant through his genius, photographic mind. Ignoring us, he puts his earbuds back in and closes his eyes, peace washing over him. Whatever he's listening to drowns out his worries and settles his soul, but most of all, it takes away the memories of the worst night of his life. There's something about music that lifts us and connects us—whether we're making it or listening to it.

My fingers tighten on the damn steering wheel again until my knuckles turn white, but I offer him a cocky grin—one I don't feel. River fucking Blue. My River is the person we were after this whole time.

"You all should know you guys stood there the whole time," I quip, glaring at Rad through the rearview mirror. He grins back at me and nods, giving me a look.

My stepbrother, Asher, snorts from the passenger seat. "Yeah, it seems like you had a fun time. But did you find what we were looking for?" He raises a brow, turning to examine my face.

Swiping away some of his unruly brown locks, his eyes hone in on the lump I swallow, showcasing my fucking nerves. My dear, stuck-up stepbrother is all business—all the damn time. He never lets up with his serious scowls, grunts, and whatever the fuck is going through his engorged head. He's intelligent, manipulative, and incorrigible at times—AKA—every fucking second he's awake.

His eyes narrow in at me, and I blow out a breath, jerking the car into drive. There's no simple answer for what he wants.

Did I find answers? Unexpectedly, yes. Do I want to do this song and dance with him? No. Yes? Fuck. All I had to do was ask the manager to speak with the man we were emailing from before to get a glimpse of the person we needed in our pocket—River West.

My River Blue. And now it's gone to shit. Total fucking shit. I'm a mean ass bastard, but I still have a fucking heart—sometimes.

But if I think about it, it's only ever beaten for her. The only person who calmed my rage and swallowed my sadness, all at the same time. Fuck. How did I live my life without her for so long? And how could I have forgotten those big, moss-green eyes?

This could be our opportunity. Her being her, we could use that as our in with West Records or her brothers. She's a goddamn West daughter to the man who could sign us to an epic record deal. Having her in our back pocket could be priceless, especially when our goal is to blow out of this town and become rich and famous. The music industry is all about who you know; that person is River West. Her name could get us into any venue on the West coast. No questions asked.

"My dad is mean," she murmurs, holding out an envelope.

"Your dad? Where is he?" I ask, lying back in the grass.

"He won't talk to me. I tried, Knight. I sent him a letter, and he sent it back." Water forms in her eyes when she stares at me, and her hope shatters.

"He doesn't deserve you, Blue," I whisper, setting a hand on hers.

No one deserves her except maybe me. That River is mine. She's always had my name stamped on her ass as Kieran's property. I may have lost her for the past nine years, but now I'm here to reclaim what's mine. And what's mine is her.

"Yeah," I say, pulling out onto the main road. At two a.m., not many cars travel alongside us as we head straight back to our little slice of suburban hell, ten minutes away from the edge of Central City.

"And? Did you find him?" Rad asks with a lazy grin, leaning back into the seat. "You know we need him." He runs a hand through his mullet, massaging his scalp with his fingertips.

I scowl. Whoever told that idiot an 80s mullet was sexy must have been high. But he's been sporting it since I joined him in friggin middle school on the Lakeview side, where his mullet wasn't seen often but never made fun of. They would have been all over him and laughing if he was a Central kid. But not our middle school on the other side of the tracks, a stone's throw away from Central City, but yet so far away.

Hell, his mullet ass was my first best friend, introducing himself to me on my first day at a new fancy school. His grin alone drew me in and helped me feel comfortable after a hard night of shouts and fists in my face. The moment I stepped through Lakeview's doors, I wasn't looking for any friends. Asher tolerated me at best but meeting Rad was a game-changer.

"We have the talent. We don't need him," Callum murmurs, not bothering to remove his headphones, which must be on low volume. Asher scoffs.

Rad continues his mini-rant, blowing out the smoke from the joint resting between his fingers. "I sure as hell didn't see a damn thing except for all the desperate pussy in the crowd. You see Tessa's titties?" He grins at that, looking at Cal, who shakes his head, trying to hide the deep blush reddening his cheeks. "Aw, tiny tots Tessa," Rad barks out a laugh. "As soon as she raised her shirt, I swear little Rad shriveled away." He grunts, patting his junk playfully.

"Yeah, yeah. We had our fun. When will she learn?" I murmur, cringing at the "fun" we had a year back. It's nothing I'll want to revisit mentally or physically. No, my mind only has one prize now.

Callum snorts, not offering anything else as his eyes close, and he settles further into the seat.

Asher rolls his eyes, gritting his teeth so hard I swear I hear them crack. If he doesn't go for a run or fuck some chick soon, he'll implode. I may have suffered under my stepfather's rule over the last ten years, but Asher has suffered his whole life. Since the moment his mom overdosed and slipped into an early grave, Asher has taken the brunt of Nigel's abuse. Pounding the pavement is the only coping mechanism he's been using to soothe the anger surging through him.

Rad sighs. "You know that was the only reason we agreed to play at that shithole. It was your idea to find him," Rad says with a huge grin. "Although, I kinda liked the vibe. It was emo and..."

"Fucking dirty," Asher mumbles in irritation. "It was disgusting there. Do they call that a bar? It smelled terrible. It looked like..."

"God damn, Asher, my man! You're one buzzkill after another!" Rad barks out, slapping Ash's shoulder and knocking him toward the window. "Lighten up! Do you think if we make it big, we'll be playing in anything nicer along the way? We're going to have to work our way up. Unless...." Rad smiles at me in the rearview mirror with a knowing look.

His brows raise, and he nods his head in understanding. He may look like an 80s burnout, but he is as bright as a fucking light with no filter.

Streetlights pass by, progressively getting fancier and fancier the further we get out of the near central part of town. The buildings get enormous and more ornate, letting me know we've officially made it back to the Lakeview District—our slice of hell. I swallow hard, my heart hardening in the center of my chest.

Tonight, we'll make hard decisions—decisions that will stick with us for the rest of our lives. Every day we don't have a plan in place, our desperation grows wilder by the second, and we're liable to do anything to get the fuck out of this shitty town. For years, our parents have waved off our aspirations as if they were mere pipe dreams impossible to achieve. And here we are, ready to prove to them it can happen.

"I sure as fuck didn't see him. Not like I knew who the fuck we were looking for," Asher mumbles angrily, contorting his stuck-up face. "Didn't see much of anyone but a bunch of Central chicks working the bar and front door."

If he wasn't a competent guitar player and a master with his fingers, I'd have left my stepbrother to rot in the fucking suburbs, wallowing in his self-loathing. But alas, he plays like a fucking angel, even when he's a know-it-all fucking tool. Not that he's a bad guy by any means, Ash is cool when he's not bitching. Or being a stuck-up prick, which he does all the time, especially if shit doesn't go his way. But I know, deep down, Asher Montgomery has my damn back like a real brother would. It may have taken us a while to get to this point, but I know he wouldn't lead us down the wrong path or lie to us. We're a damn family, the only family we have.

I sigh, staring through the windshield when we pull into the driveway leading to hell. A light pops on in the living room, and Gloria's pinched face peeks out. Her eyes narrow in on us, and she shakes her head, looking like she's ready to rip us a new one for pulling in so late and disturbing her sleep. Already I hear the slew of words she'll sling in my direction the moment I walk through the door, criticizing me.

Seeing my mom's face is a stark reminder of who I'm loyal to—the assholes in this SUV. They may be loud, inconsiderate, and make me want to punch them, but they're my family. They're the ones I trust with my damn life. Family doesn't have to be blood; family is the people who see you at your lowest and help to raise you, not lower you down. And that's precisely what these dicks do.

River's bewildered face pops into my mind. I cringe, wiping a hand down my face. God, I'm such a prick after a performance. When the high of being on stage fades away, I always need another hit of euphoria. I always crash after the last note plays, and then I need the time to myself. Time to unwind and relax. Fuck! Why did this have to get so fucking complicated? I punch the steering wheel with a huff, throwing myself back into my seat.

I don't know River anymore. Anyone can change after nine years apart. Before, she was an innocent angel mercilessly picked on. And now? She's a stranger to me. So, to hell with it all. I'll do something I might regret later, even though River is consuming my mind.

There's something about River that reels me in like a fish on a hook, drawing me into her orbit. Maybe it's our tainted history together. Those nights spent under the stars, spilling our guts, race through my mind calling me back to her. She's the girl I was forced to leave behind and forget at the hands of my stepfather. There's no way I can get River out of my mind. Not with her moss-green eyes burning through me when her luscious lips pop open. Or maybe it's her banging, tight body and her perfect tits, fitting into my hand, that draw me to her.

Now, I want her back, no matter the cost. This may be the only way I can have her without getting any grief. I'll make her mine.

I swallow hard. "River West isn't some dude," I say on exhale. River West is my River Blue. Mine.

We've searched high and low for an entry into the infamous KC Club in East Point, California, where Seger and Zeppelin West, the famous twin sons of Corbin West and River's brothers, frequent. They're always scouting for new talent to sign to their label. Getting into The KC Club is next to impossible if you don't know the right people, and we don't know anyone in the industry. Not yet at least.

My dick tightens in my damn pants at the thought of her pussy wrapped around me, and her moans echo in my ears. Her sass. Her fucking small curves. Shit, the way her ass bounced against my hips. Fuck. I'm ready to drop these dickbags off and head back to the outskirts of Central City to find River and tie her down. Does she still live in the same apartment from our childhood? Does she still like to eat those disgusting pink peeps dipped in milk? I swallow the obsession bobbing in my throat and threatening to pull me under.

"Come on, boy. You're going onto better things. Leave the trash behind," my new stepdaddy growls, bruising my arm by throwing me into the back of his SUV. "You're onto bigger and better things now."

I swallow hard, pressing my face into the window as the apartment complex becomes a blip and disappears. My heart breaks into a million pieces. River Blue, I need you. I watch until our new neighborhood comes into view, revealing enormous houses and a shiny lake glistening in the sun.

"Welcome home," the man says with a wide, evil-looking grin.

"What's that supposed to mean? We need him, man. He's our one connection. He's our in," Ash says through gritted teeth. "If we don't have West, we can't get in with West Records or the damn exclusive venue. And if we don't make it into West Records, we're fucked. We need River West. Remember our goals? Getting out of this shit fuck town and leaving everyone behind? We need him." Ash closes his eyes, leaning his forehead against the window to calm himself down.

Desperation ebbs from him in waves, and I get it. He's been through hell and back and wants nothing more than to run from this town and start over. Our plan is his saving grace—the one thing that's kept him going. Even if the guilt eats at me daily, I can't disappoint my family. Not now. But what they don't know won't kill them. I have no intention of letting her go. Whatever plan we cook up to get close, I'll keep her closer.

I close my eyes, resting the back of my head against the headrest. "River West isn't a dude, you fucking morons. River West is the fucking manager chick," I say, feeling my heart drop into the depths of my fucking stomach.

"Buzztit!" Rad gasps in mock horror and then mumbles about her forcing the tits into hiding and what a goddamn tragedy it was.

"The chick?" Asher gapes. "That chick is a West?" Once realization settles and the shock wears off, he menacingly rubs his chin.

Wheels turn in the depths of his overused brain, grinding to a halt when he comes to the same conclusion I have. We'll have to befriend her, which means we'll have to be nice. Which shouldn't be too hard for Rad and me, but the other two? They're a different entity altogether.

Callum looks at us with calculating eyes and sits back in his seat, putting away his earbuds. "So, the manager who tore up our check and we watched you bone, is the West chick we need to get to the KC Club?" I nod in response. He sighs, running a hand down his face. "Well, this should be fun then," he mutters.

Something settles inside me, chasing away my demons at the thought of her. I couldn't agree with Callum more. It will be fun, and I'll reclaim what's mine.

"So, K, you got our in? Do you think she'd be down to help? Make the call?" Rad asks, leaning forward with hope glistening deep in his brown eyes.

I run a hand down my face. "You think the chick that ripped up our paycheck because I insulted her will roll over and call her estranged family to get us a gig at the KC Club?" I snark, raising a brow.

"My dad is mean," she whispers again, clutching another sent-back letter. "I just wanted to say hi," she says through a sniffle, wiping away the tears streaming down her face.

"He sent it back again? Why do you keep doing it?" I ask, wrapping an arm around her shoulders and pulling her in. If her mom is

too busy sleeping and won't comfort her, I will. River needs me to help her cope with life, just like I need her.

"I won't anymore," she pouts, growling when she tears up the letter. "That's the last time Daddy will ever hear from me." And from that day forward, I never found River Blue crying over the man who didn't want her in the first place.

Pressing my palms into my eyes, I squeeze them shut, reveling in the vivid memories flowing through my mind. Over the years, I've erased every inch of where I came from—partially due to my stepdad refusing to let me call her or find her across town. Hell, I even tried to ride my bike to her once, but he stopped me within the first mile. Within the first month of living with him, I had a new wardrobe and a brand-new life. Ten-year-old me could never get what I wanted, and River slowly drifted into the past, beaten out of me.

"Don't even think about going back to that side of town," he hisses, heaving his fist in the air. Before I can blink, pain sears through my jaw, and blood spurts from my nose. My mother gasps from the corner of the room, held hostage to witness my punishment. The reality is that she wouldn't lift a finger to help me, anyway. She's here for only one thing—the rich lifestyle Nigel has afforded her.

As I lie motionless on the floor, only grunting when his foot collides with my ribs three times, I promise myself I'll forget about her. If this is what happens when I try to ride my bike across town, I'll never try again. I can't take another fist or kick.

The pain sits with me through the night as I toss and turn, whimpering.

"You can't provoke him," my new stepbrother Asher whispers through the dark. I jolt at his voice, crying out when I sit up. "He'll only hurt you more." Shaking his head, he moves to the side of the bed and sits.

"Yeah?" I whimper, holding my aching ribs.

"Things will go smoother if you just do what he says."

"Is that what you do?" I whisper, earning a scoff.

"I do what I have to do. Now stop making so much noise so I can go to sleep," Ash grumbles, slipping into his bed.

Quiet overtakes the room, the only sound coming from the air conditioning kicking on, blowing across the blinds, knocking them together. Of all the rooms in this house, Nigel insisted we bunk together. Probably to keep a sharper eye on us and lock us together. He didn't count on us forming a deep bond like brothers normally would.

"Kieran?" Asher asks in a soft voice.

"Yeah?" I rasp, wiping away the tears falling down my cheeks.

"You'll be okay. I promise he'll lay off for a few days," Asher whispers, thick with sleep. "Night."

"Night," I mutter, losing all hope I had before.

Seeing River tonight has knocked all the memories loose, and they're running rampant through my mind. I swore I'd forget about her, and I successfully had. Locking her away was the only way I could protect myself from the fury of fists. Eventually, it was like she had never existed, and I moved on with my new life.

The guys all look at one another with questioning gazes, finally landing on the man who apparently has the answers. Ash, ever the man with a fucking plan, grins like the fucking grinch. Too bad there's no way in hell his heart grew three times too big, probably the other way around, shrinking into a damn prune. If Asher has some diabolical plan to enact, it's no doubt evil and crazy.

"We could make her, you know? You already had your way with her. Did she like you?" Ash asks, studying my face with narrowed eyes again.

Fuck. I hate when he plans like this and gives nothing away with his stony facial expression.

Blowing out a breath, I remember our heated exchange. I bite my bottom lip, imagining what River would look like dangling her pussy above my face and me ready for a damn feast. What would she taste like coating my tongue? Probably fire and vanilla all mixed into one explosion of taste. What I wouldn't give to stick my tongue deep in her pussy and make her cum all over my tastebuds. But shit, River isn't one to be pushed around. She isn't going to drop to her knees and do our bidding without incentive. Not now. River Blue isn't the same girl I left nine years ago. She's a fiery fucking treat, and I want another bite of what's mine. And this time, I'm playing for keeps.

"I don't think you could make that girl do shit," I sigh, shaking my head. "She's not the type to sit back and take orders. River needs our trust."

Pinching the bridge of his nose, Rad sighs. "We need this, man. I need out of this fucking place. My mom is driving me fucking bonkers begging me to conform to what Dad wants from me. And I'll be fucked over a pulpit before I do that. I'm my own damn man, damn it." His fists clench in his lap as his eyes drift toward the very house of horrors he escaped and rebelled from when he was just eighteen. Taking one last drag of his joint, Rad tosses it out the window.

Being stuck in a place, financially held hostage by the people who are supposed to love you burns me from the inside out. This car? My phone? My college education? Everything I own, my stepfather taints with his existence, dangling it over our heads. We've tried and tried again to get jobs and further our financial situation. But every step of the way, he's there to knock us on our asses and keep us in his grasp—where he wants us. The only sanctuary we're granted is the music that keeps us alive. According to Nigel, music will get us nowhere in life. Therefore, we can enjoy the ride until our time is up and he needs us to clock into his company—one year. We have one year to get this music thing off the ground, and we're growing desperate.

"I feel your fucking pain," I grunt, gesturing to the woman stalking our every move from the living room window.

Her beady eyes take in every fucking thing we do. Down to the spent joint sitting in her driveway. There's no doubt in my mind that I'll hear about that later through her screeching wails and fucking disappointment. So, yeah—I feel his pain. We all have our reasons for wanting to escape this fucking hell.

"Fine then, we coerce her into doing whatever the fuck we want. I think we can manage that. We're all charming as hell. And we want a gig at her brothers' famous bar, where stars are born. Our name will be in fucking lights. We're destined for that shit..." Asher nods, so fucking sure of himself that we can convince her to help us pursue happiness. Right. Yeah. This will totally fucking work. Considering she probably hates me.

"You left without saying goodbye."

Her words are a punch to the gut. Yeah, I left without a word, basically kidnapped by the man I now call dad. If I could have gone back, I would have. I tried. But he was always there to remind me with his fist that there was no going back to the neighborhood I grew up in.

"And how the hell do you expect to coerce her? She's not exactly the type," I grumble. From the looks of it, she's tough as a fucking nut now and won't take our shit lying down. "You can't make a chick like that do anything but what she wants."

Asher grins over at me, slapping me on the side of the cheek. "Exactly! I've got a plan," he says with confidence, rubbing his hands together. "What's the one thing a woman will do for the man she loves?"

I raise a skeptical brow, looking back to Rad, who shrugs a shoulder. "No idea," I say, looking at Ash, who grins and wiggles his brows. In the low light of the Tahoe, something evil and conniving crosses his face.

"She'll do anything for the man she loves," he says with a sharp nod full of confidence.

"Please don't tell me you're going to say what I think you're going to say," Callum mumbles uncomfortably from the backseat, forcing his Earbuds back into his ears, blocking out the world with murmuring music.

"We'll wine and dine her. We'll make River West fall so madly in love with us that she'll call her family and beg them to hear our music. Imagine the reunion they could have all because of us. It'll be a win-win, but mostly for us."

My mouth gapes open, and I'm not the only one utterly shocked. Rad sputters, choking on his spit.

"Us?" Rad asks with a squeak but quickly soothes his expression. From here, I see the wheels turning in his brain. Wait...us?

"You want us to trick her into loving me?" I gape, shaking my head like it's the worst possible idea on the planet. But a thrill runs through me at the thought. Yes. Let her fall in love with me, and then I'll whisk her away, and she'll never have to live in this shitty town again.

"Where would you go if you left?" I whisper, staring at the stars again, having been kicked out over an hour ago so mom could conduct business. Whatever that is. All I know is a stereo plays so loud, drowning out the weird noises coming from her room.

"I want to touch the ocean," she whispers, leaning into me with a sigh.

"I'll take you when we're older," I whisper, dreaming of the day I can take both of us away from here.

Our dreams will become a reality if I get my way.

"Nope," Ash says, popping the P. "All of us. What better package deal could you get than having her invested in all of us? Our hearts, our everything. We'll all date her, and then, in the end, she can decide who she likes the best."

My gaze snaps in his direction at the thought of any of them touching her.

"I'm sorry, what?" Callum grumbles through the biggest frown ever, still listening to our conversation, not his music. "You want us to seduce her?" His brows furrow, but he looks to Ash for more direction.

"Then it's settled," Ash says, rubbing his hands together with a cocky-as-hell grin. No one could stop him now if they tried. "Operation seduce our meal ticket is underway. Start planning those dates. How long do you think before she caves? A week? Two? Flash some cash, and her panties will fall?" He chuckles, throwing open the passenger's side door with zest. "Hello, Gloria!" he shouts gleefully at two in the fucking morning, waving toward the window.

She scowls again, giving a small wave before stomping away from the window. That's right, and she won't say shit to Asher. But me? I'll get an earful.

Callum mutters solemnly to himself and pushes out the back door with a frown, shutting it behind him. He follows Ash around to the back of the Tahoe, talking to him in a low voice. His arms wave and I can tell his conscience is eating away at him at the idea. But ultimately, Asher will win this fight, and we'll be helpless to do whatever he says. He always does.

Rad's face pinches when he leans forward. "Are we doing that?" he asks in a hushed tone. "Dude, I mean, I'm down for talking to her and getting to know her. But love? That seems kinda...." His lips press together in a tight line, and he shakes his head.

"Demented?" I murmur, throwing my head back into the seat.

This plan is so fucking stupid, but it might just work. We've worked our asses off getting into venues around the big city and building a small following. We only have four hundred followers on social media and a group of people who follow us from venue to venue, buying all our tickets. But if we can get to the venue of our dreams, then we're set. No more parents with expectations. Just music, the road, booze, fame, and River by my fucking side at last. And freedom, the one thing we've craved. No matter the cost, we'll get there.

"Exactly," Rad says, pointing at me.

"You know Ash," I say, swiping a hand down my face.

"Fucker takes it too far," Rad agrees with a sharp nod. "Too fucking extreme."

"Help me watch him," I say, turning to Rad with pleading eyes and curling my fists. "We can't let him take it too far." Not that he'll be able to. River won't have a choice in the matter now. She'll pick me and only me at the end of our time together.

"I'll try." He shrugs, hurrying toward the door. "Who knows, though, this could be fun, right? The four of us, one ballsy chick?" He shrugs and gestures toward my pocket. "How much did we make tonight? It better be a shit ton with all the girls we brought in. Imagine the look on Gloria's face when we make a profit." He's right. We've never managed to make a considerable profit, but with Callum negotiating through email correspondence with River. We got ourselves a golden opportunity with a good chunk of change.

I snort, digging into my pocket and pulling out the check. I flatten it along the center console and turn on the overhead light.

Rad scrunches his face. "Errr, what?" I motion at the check, laughing my ass off. "Dude, she wrote 'To the Whispered Words, you sack of shits, here's the money I owe you.' What the fuck is that?" He groans, shoving himself back. "She didn't even sign it!"

I sigh, staring at the perfect cursive, and rub my jaw. "Well, River gave us the perfect excuse to stalk her." I shrug, shoving the check into my pocket. A thrill of excitement shoots through me at the prospect of seeing her again. Maybe she and I could pick up where we left off.

"Right, dude! She still owes us! Sick!" He chuckles, piles out of the car, and heads to the back of the vehicle.

Huddling together, we plan for the next few months on what we need to do and how we'll reel her like a fish on a hook.

RIVER

I frown, fixing my hair in the long mirror attached to the closed office door. Since Kieran walked out with that possessive look sparkling on his face, I haven't been able to move. Twenty minutes and counting since the last time I laid eyes on him. My mind reels from our encounter, producing more conflicting emotions in my gut. Do I hate him? Like him? Want to smother him? Shit, I don't know.

Nine years ago, he left a cavernous hole in my chest when he disappeared without a trace. It took me years to close the gap and return to myself, even after that night that changed me. And now? Now, he's reopening the wound one word at a time.

I can't do this again. I can't let Kieran waltz back into my life like I mean something to him, to waltz back out.

It was one fuck, and that's it. It meant nothing.

Closing my eyes, I count to ten and release a breath. Chances are, Kieran got precisely what he wanted, and I'll never see his handsome face again. Hopefully. Maybe. Shit.

"We are far from fucking done," he hisses, snapping his gaze to me. *"None of this is over,"* he gestures between us. *"I'll be seeing you, River Blue West."*

His words replay over and over. He promised never to leave me at one point in our young lives. And yet, within a month of his words, he was gone. So, what will it be this time?

I shake my head. Screw these thoughts. How can one guy shake up my entire existence in a matter of ten minutes?

I flip myself off in the mirror and fix my screwed-up ponytail.

Shivers run down my spine at the phantom feel of his fist locking around my hair and directing me to where he wanted me. Shit. Stop it. No more self-pity. It is what it is. If he comes back, then I'll deal with him.

Trailing a finger up and down the outside of my pocket, I feel for my pocket knife, the last gift he ever gave me.

"Take this," he said, sitting beside me on the grass.

"Knight!" I gasp, holding the colossal pocket knife in my hand. "It's a...I can't!" I squeak, closing it and throwing it back to him like it has a disease.

Kieran laughs, throwing his head back. "It's okay, River Blue," he reassures me, flicking open the blade. The bright full moon shines on the reflective blade. "If you look hard enough, your name is here. River Blue," he murmurs, running a finger over the wooden grip where my name sits.

I swallow hard, my fingers shaking when he wraps my fingers around the grip.

"I'll teach you how to protect yourself. One day, you'll need it." He nods, sure of himself, and proceeds to teach me how to use it safely.

My trusty pocketknife has had its fair share of uses over the years, protecting me from unwanted touches and my go-to security when walking alone. Despite its origins, I've kept it firmly in my pocket from the moment he handed it over. It holds more than security in my eyes; it's sentimental.

I huff a breath, wiping a hand down my face. Was the boning worth the pain and satisfaction? No. Maybe? Shit!

All the calmness I felt before evaporates into thin air, and all I want to do is drink, take a bubble bath, and go to bed. I need a goddamn shot before I go home and face the loneliness of my empty apartment. My ma left for work hours ago and always worked through the night. So, it'll be just me, my loneliness, and the ache between my legs—a consolation prize for my consequences.

After cleaning up the office and shutting off the light, I head back into the bar area with my head held high.

"All good?" Leon raises a dark brow, and my cheeks heat when his dark brown eyes take in my messy appearance. Despite fixing my hair and straightening my clothes, he sees right through me.

Fuck.

I grunt, ripping my hair tie out of my hair and throwing it back into a messy bun, sending him a scathing look and daring him to say something. He snorts, shaking his head, and goes back to minding his own damn business. Good boy.

"You were kinda loud," Ode snickers behind her hand, looking at her brother Leon, and they burst out laughing together. Their laughs bounce around the empty bar, filling the room with roaring amusement.

"Ha, ha, ha, laugh it up. But I got laid," I say, pointing proudly to myself through a smirk.

"About damn time, woman!" Leon says, walking around the bar with his hands shoved into his pocket. "I've been saying that you needed it for what?"

"Every day," Ode adds. "He tells me every damn day that you need a little dick to knock the stick out of your ass."

My jaw falls open at the same time Leon curses back at his sister.

"Ode! What the hell? Throw your brother under the bus like that? I never said nothing like that," he says, shaking his head with a grin. Letting me know he has, in fact, said it multiple times.

Some friends I have.

I snort. "It's cool. I needed to get laid after all this promotion business. Plus, I start my first set of classes tomorrow, and I have to work at the record store Monday, too." I blow out a breath, my chest constricting with all the shit I have planned for the next few years.

I have to work two jobs and attend school if I ever want to make it out of this hell-hole city and move on to bigger and better things, like California. I want to see the ocean, smell the saltwater, and push my toes into the cool sand. Most importantly, I want to attend CaliState to complete my Music Business degree. I've had my eyes on the prize since the moment I decided what I wanted to do with my life.

Through CaliState, I can live a full life without worry. After I walk across the stage with my degree, I can go to any record company and live my dream. Managing bands and music has always been my destiny, running through my blood since birth. Even though my father ripped the easy path from my grasp by the time I was two and forced me away. He may be some big musical influencer with more money than God, but give me five years, and I'll prove to him and everyone else who overlooked me that I'm the fucking greatest.

I want what I want, and I can't do that in Central City, where every corner I turn is a constant reminder of who I am here—no one. To everyone walking these streets, I'm the Central City trash living in the slums of income-based apartments with a mom who strips to make ends meet. I want to thrive on my own without assistance backing me up. I can't achieve that here in the middle of Nowhere, Illinois. So, the first opportunity I get, I'm gone. No matter what. By whatever means necessary, even if my mom has to come with me.

"I'm out! See you tomorrow night, college girl!" Leon says with a mock salute, heading out the back door with his keys in hand.

"Everyone else gone?" I ask Ode, and she nods, grabbing her keys too.

"Ya did good, bestie," she says, wrapping her arm around my shoulders and kissing my cheek. "You're the best damn manager I've ever had."

I sigh with a smile, leaning my head on hers. "You think so?" I ask with uncertainty, furrowing my brows.

"Girl, I can only imagine how much your little band brought in. But let's just say I've never served so many damn drinks. So, yeah. Book will see it and give you a bonus for your hard work." She grins, wiggling her brows. "So, how was Richie Rich? Good dick?" I snort, pushing off her, and laugh when she stumbles, righting herself along the tall, wooden bar.

"You're such a bitch," I laugh, leaning over the bar to grab my backpack purse, and set it on the top. "But I don't kiss and tell." I mimic locking my lips and throwing away the key.

Ode gapes, staring at me like I grew another head.

"You won't even tell your bestie?" she asks with a pout and pushes my shoulder. I snort, shaking my head. "Well...those noises you were making gave you away. OHH, RICHIE RICH!!" Her hand slams down on the bar, fake moaning with her head thrown back in false passion.

I groan in embarrassment, feeling the heat travel up my neck and burn my ears. Shit. I forgot how thin the walls of this place were. Just last week, Ode took her on again, off again, hook up, into the bathroom to rock his world. Let's just say we clapped when they walked out of the bathroom, zipping their flies and straightening their shirts.

So, they heard every dirty little word Kieran whispered in my ear as he pounded me hard. My nipples pebble under my shirt, begging for his lips to encase them. Damn it. I need to get the hell out of here and stop thinking about him. Throwing my strap over my shoulders, we head toward the back door and momentarily stop to shut off all the lights.

"Shut up," I groan, shoving her out the door.

She cackles more, straightening her purse. "I'll see ya later, bestie. You think Bessy will start?" She raises a brow when I lock the door and snorts.

"Bessy better start, or I'm trading her ass in." I gesture toward my car, Bessy—who I, in fact, can't afford to trade in or get rid of.

She's my ride or die; well, more the die part. Poor Bes is resting on her last leg. But, hey—she gets me from point A to point B, usually with no complaints. She's big and bad and eats a lot of gas, but I can't complain about my nine-hundred-dollar car and my pride and joy. There's no better feeling than saving up for something and finally getting it.

"Babes, if that pile ever shits out on you, I can take you home," Leon says, leaning against his car with a cigarette hanging from his frowning lips. Taking it from his mouth, he blows smoke into the air. "We're neighbors, after all," he grumbles, shaking his head in disappointment.

"Thanks, L," I say with a smile and wave him on.

"We could be like the cool kids and carpool," he suggests with a grin, tossing his used cigarette to the ground and squishing it with the tip of his shoe. "Think about it. I'll see ya at home. Be safe, yeah?" he says, piling into his car when I give him a thumbs up and drives off.

"Love ya, bitch," Ode says, coming in to hug and squeezing me tight. "I'm going to stay at Ricky's tonight. But I'll see you tomorrow?"

I snort, squeezing her back. "Quicky Ricky again?" I murmur into her neck, reveling in her familiar hug.

Odette and Leon are far more than just my neighbors and coworkers. They are my brother and sister. We may not be blood but fuck that. They're the closest thing I have to a family in this hell hole, and I'll cling to them for the rest of my life.

"Quicky Ricky," she murmurs, confirming my suspicions.

What started as a one-night stand from an internet hook-up app has now turned into a full-blown relationship she's not ready to admit yet. Ode grins when her phone lights up, and another car pulls into the lot a second later. Ode squeals, waves goodbye, and runs to the passenger's side.

"Heya, Ricky!" I shout, waving to him, receiving a small wave out the window before they pull away from the empty parking lot, leaving me there to watch it all go dark.

I sigh, getting into my car with a prayer running through my mind. Immediately, like my momma taught me, I lock my doors and set my purse on the passenger's side, praying to the car gods that Bessy starts without a fight.

Settling into the warm driver's seat, my entire body tingles when my mind returns to the rough quickie. The phantom feel of his fingers tightly gripping my hips sends goosebumps skittering across my skin. An ache between my legs has me closing my eyes and wishing he'd come back for round two.

Oh, the rocking we could do in Bessy. Fuck. I run my fingers over my swollen lips and sigh at the feel of his demanding mouth overtaking mine in desperation. I must be a glutton for punishment if I'm aching for Kieran to come back and rock my world. Is the heartache worth seeing him again?

Throwing my head back, I let out a silent scream. Fuck. Why do I always do this to myself? Huh? I can't get attached. Not again. He'll chew me up and spit me out before I can say, please another, sir, just like last time. From now on, I'm staying away from the entire band for as long as possible until I can get myself in check. No more bands. No more bad boys. I'm swearing them off from now on. No more, I swear.

I shake my head and attempt to start my car, only to receive a worn-down, grinding noise. I narrow my eyes on the dashboard and shove my foot into the gas pedal, pumping it. Again, I try to start Bessy, but she gives me nothing but fumes and sputters.

"No! No! Bessy, don't do this to me now," I grumble, rubbing a hand over the steering wheel. All I get in return is the sound of her slowly dying and nothing. "Great," I mumble, leaning my head back in defeat.

With no other choice, I shove my one working earbud into my ear and begin my journey home in the mid-August muggy heat on foot. Sure, I could call Leon and beg him to come back and get me, but he's probably already at home and settled into bed. I'd hate to drag him out to fetch little old me. Besides, the middle of the night is the most peaceful time to walk.

Sometimes, I need my music, the open air, and nothing to worry about. Sure, there could be a creeper lurking in the shadows, ready to haul me off to his basement, but from the looks of the abandoned sidewalks, there isn't—hopefully. It's just me and the music playing the soothing melodies in my ear, carrying my worries away.

Ma and I have lived in the same two-bedroom apartment gifted by the government since my dad decided he was done with us and kicked us out, forcing us out of Cali and back to her hometown. It was all she could afford on nothing, and we've never been able to leave. It's been good to us and has let us thrive in a bad situation. Ma works her ass off on nights down at the local strip club dancing, but it's never been entirely enough.

Walking down the cracked and disintegrating sidewalk, I let my music take me over. Goosebumps pour over my skin, and I momentarily shut my eyes, allowing the tunes to infect my soul. Music is the life force keeping me going and alive. I'd fade into nothing with no meaning if I didn't have it. It's the thing that accompanies me everywhere; no one can take it away from me, not even money. My greatest joy is looking up at a stage in the distance and feeling every ounce of emotion dropping from their words and notes. It completes me.

I sigh in relief when I make it back to my apartment building in one piece. Without any drama, well—besides my stupid car not starting. Some nights on my lonely drive home, the streets are empty. Some nights, they're full of neighborhood people doing whatever they're doing in the middle of the night. I'd be a liar if I said I lived in a safe area. But my home has always been good to me. And the people? They're just trying to make it in the crazy thing called life. No matter the means.

As I make my way to my ground-floor apartment, I raise a brow at Leon, who rests against his door with his eyes on me. He nods once, throwing the cigarette down, and shakes his head.

"Bess not make the trip?" he asks, reaching into his pocket for his key.

"Thought it'd be a good night for a walk," I mumble, rubbing my wrinkled forehead. Exhaustion sweeps through me when my eyes land on my apartment door. Just behind that barrier are my bathtub and my bed.

"Goodnight, you stubborn ass woman," Leon says, inserting his key into his mother's apartment.

"Night, Korrine," I shout when the door opens, and I grin as her stern eyes set on me, and she nods.

"Night, child. Have a good first day tomorrow. Come for dinner before you go to that second job of yours and tell me all about it," she says in a tired voice, face drooping from the lack of sleep. But God love her. She always stays up to ensure we all come home safely from the bar and still greets the sun in the morning to cook breakfast for the family. She always looks out for us.

"Yes, ma'am," I say, my throat tightening up from all the love pouring from every fiber of her being.

She is my second mother, who took over when my mom couldn't care for me properly. Since Kieran moved away, Korrine has been living next door, raising her three kids after a car accident that disabled her and took her husband's life.

Like us, this apartment was all she could afford atthe time, and she's never left. After my ma started her night jobs, I slept over at Korrine's and became another family member. If it weren't for her all these years, I never would have had big dreams or hope for the future. She pushed her kids and me to succeed when my mother was drowning in grief and financial woes.

She waves me off with a huff and a stern nod, disappearing into the depths of her apartment. With a snick of her lock, the lights turn out, and I head for my own. I suck in a breath, ready for my damn bubble bath and wine, but stop short when a small light shines through the open window. And when I walk inside, my heart fucking drops at the sight of her.

"Ma?" I question, setting my purse down on the kitchen counter. "You okay?" My brows furrow. She usually works until six in the morning and is never home at night.

My mom moves her dark brown hair over her shoulder, sighing, bringing a small glass to her trembling lips, and sets the cup down. Large, dark circles sit under her eyes, and my heart drops when her crystal blue eyes meet mine.

"Fell on stage," she murmurs, kicking out her booted foot. "Broke my damn ankle." Her eyes stay on the floor, observing the cast. "I lost my balance, the room spun, and I just...I fell, River."

"Oh God, Ma. Are you okay? Need meds? Anything?" I take a tentative step forward, cautiously watching the silent tears run down her cheeks. She shakes her head.

"No, baby," she murmurs, running her cold fingers up my arms and stopping at my shoulder. "Barry fired me." When those words leave her lips, my entire body breaks out in a cold sweat.

"F-fired?" I gape. "He can't just fire you because of a broken leg, dammit. You've worked with him for over fifteen years. You're one of his best dancers. You..."

"Yeah, he can. He pays me under the table, Sugar." She squeezes my shoulder with trembling fingers and loses her grip on me. She curses under her breath, reaching for her glass, but it slips between her fingers. Landing back on the counter, thankfully not shattering. Her long fingers run through her curled and primped hair, and a sob leaks from between her lips.

"Ma?" I whisper, swallowing hard. I can tell by her avoidance of eye contact; she's hiding something from me. "What is it?"

She bites into her bottom lip. "I got Multiple Sclerosis, babe."

"M.S.?" I scrunch my face, and she nods when the realization hits me, and dread fills every muscle in my body.

M.S. is something I've seen before in one of our bar patrons. He could walk one day, but then he started to stumble, and by the end, he was in a wheelchair. Last I saw, he had landed in a nursing home because he couldn't take care of himself anymore. He explained to me one day that it was an autoimmune disease that would never have a cure until he dies.

"I got diagnosed," she takes a large breath, fiddling with her fingers on the counter, "seven years ago, and it's only getting worse. I tried so hard to work through the symptoms and the flare-ups. But I can't anymore. I hurt too much, and the club's heat makes it too hard to stand, walk, or think."

I take a step back, gaping at my mother and her admission. Seven fucking years and I never noticed? I run my finger over my clenched jaw, and my chest heaves. All this time, I was so blind to my mother's symptoms because I was a kid caught up in her own life. Shit.

"Why didn't you tell me you had it? I could have helped. I could have done anything to make it easier on you!" I shout, throwing an arm out.

Inside my chest, my heart works overtime, banging against my ribs. My breaths come in short pants as I wrap my head around her confession.

When she looks up at me with her glossy eyes and another sob leaks from her lips, I close in on her, forgetting the anger brewing in my gut. Throwing my arms around her, I pull her into a much-needed hug, and she sags in my grip.

"You have always worked so hard, Riv. I don't know what I did to get such a good kid like you, but you work harder than anyone I know. You got straight A's, worked two jobs, and still managed to be home every night. I didn't want to worry you, Kid. You're my responsibility, and I already failed you once." Every ounce of emotion I know she's buried deep inside her comes to the surface as she sobs into my chest. "I failed you when I couldn't keep your father around. I failed you when I couldn't secure child support from the good-for-nothing Corbin West. I failed you when we had to move back to the middle of nowhere and raise you by myself."

"It'll be all right , Ma. I promise," I murmur, running my fingers through her ratty hair. "We'll get through this. We always do."

Ma pulls back, wiping the tears from her cheeks. "See, Kid? This isn't how it's supposed to be. You're my baby. I'm supposed to rock you and tell you everything will be okay. But I can't anymore." She shakes her head, running a shaky hand through her hair.

"Okay, so Barry fired you. Can you get disability or unemployment? You have to be eligible for something that could help." I breathe, sitting on the stool beside her, trying to think of a solution to our problems.

"No unemployment. It was cash under the table. I never had to claim a cent, so Barry wins this round. But Disability? Maybe," she says, nodding her head. "Korrine will help me make it to the doctor tomorrow and drive me. I'll have more answers tomorrow." She gives me a sad smile and raises her good foot. She hobbles toward her beat-up recliner near the flat screen and sits down with a huff. Our only saving grace through all this is the medical card we've been on since our arrival. If it weren't for that, our medical bills would be through the roof.

"I'll do some research, Ma. There must be something out there for you." I swallow hard, brushing past her toward my bedroom at the end of the hall.

"Night, Kid. Get some rest. You've got a big day tomorrow," she whispers, blowing me a kiss, and I catch it with a small smile.

"You're my big college girl now. I'm so damn proud of you."

"Night, Ma," I say, waltzing into my bedroom with a sigh.

Not only do I have to try and come up with double the money we were making between my job and hers, but now I have to contend with a chronically ill mother, who will only get worse and worse. Then I'll have to put her in a home or try to find a day nurse or...shit, I don't know.

I rub a finger along my forehead and groan at the ceiling. So much for a warm bubble bath and some wine before bed. I have five hours before I must get up and open the store across town. Yay for responsibilities. Yay for being an adult. And yay for walking everywhere! Bessy was our only vehicle, and now....

RIVER

"I'm Professor Webber, and welcome!" I sigh, sitting back in my computer chair, and rubbing my sweaty forehead.

The walk to work this morning was peaceful but fucking hot. I'm sure I have swamp ass and swamp pussy at this point. Who knew the sun would grace us with one-hundred-degree weather at nine in the morning? Next time, I'll look at the bus schedule and catch a ride. Sleep desperately gnaws at the back of my eyes, begging me to close them and rest just a little longer. Just one more hour. Or maybe five, for good measure. I need more coffee. Like a bucket full or in an IV attached to my arm for the rest of eternity. Maybe a fucking nap. Or, and hear me out, another good romp in the hay. I'm just saying; that it could put a rainbow over my day.

I know, I know. You can tell me all day long—River, it's a bad idea to jump in the sack with a guy who will probably disappear soon. And logically, he's a dick. With a good, massive cock, I want to take a three-hour tour of pound town. God. I'm pathetic.

I rub a circle over my temple. Maybe I'm too sleep-deprived to think about this. My body aches in the most delicious ways from his brutal thrusts and dominant ways, and I'm aching for more.

Plus, I need something to keep me sane, right? Because this schedule is going to fucking annihilate me. In the best possible way—I hope. It's all for a good cause. Hurray for furthering my education and expanding my horizons so I can walk off into the sunset with a degree under my belt and far away from here.

Between online classes three days a week, actual classroom time on Wednesdays, and working two jobs split between two shifts daily. I don't know if I'll make it to my next birthday. I might keel over before I turn twenty

Here lies the corpse of River West. Gone too soon after trying to work her ass off.

Yup. That'd do it. Which reminds me... I turn my attention to my computer screen, pretending to listen as he rambles.

The professor, as he insists we call him, wanders around the front of the classroom with his hands behind his back and a stern look lining his face.

"I'd like to welcome you all. As you know, this is a hybrid class. Half of you are here, and half are taking this class from the confines of your homes or other areas." My nose twitches when his eyes look through the camera, and I swear he's looking directly at me.

Yeah, yeah, old man. I'm learning from work. Some of us don't have the luxury of screwing off while in school. I've got my beat-up old laptop propped up on the tall front counter, running on what seems like Windows 8 and half-working earbuds.

This was the only way to attend college full-time and work both jobs. Thank God for Booker's understanding soul. Usually, I'd be at the bar by now, but on Tuesdays and Thursdays, I now open his used record store so I can attend class in peace. It's not like anyone comes here anymore. Most people use The Dot to stream their music nowadays, instead of records or CDs. Briefly, records came back and business boomed, but not anymore. We don't get many walk-ins these days, but we get a good number of online orders from around the world through our website. Thankfully, that keeps this place afloat.

I take out my notebook and pen and take notes on everything he says.

He's apparently a stickler for punctuality, and assignments must be turned in on time: no special treatment—his words, not mine. Again, I swear he looks at me with a disapproving gaze, like he thinks I'll skip out because I'm at home and not physically there.

Despite his asshole, stuck-up face, I keep going and listen to him go on and on. His voice grates my damn nerves with every word he says, and I kind of want to stab him. But hey, I only have a year of this, and then I'll move on to the following year, where he'll hopefully not be.

The bell above the door rings, echoing through the small store.

"Welcome to Dead Records. Look—" I stop short when I meet a familiar pair of icy eyes, filled to the brim with a cocky attitude, possession, and pure sex appeal.

My breath leaves my lungs. Did my rampant thoughts summon the devil himself and his merry band of fuckwits? Probably. This is the luck I'm graced with every day.

"River Blue," he says in a smooth voice, gliding toward the large wooden counter I'm nestled behind and leaning against it. "How many jobs do you have to hold down in this shit town?" His brows furrow with concern, eyeing me up and down.

I sigh, rubbing my temple, hoping to soothe the damn headache forming. My professor drags on, but the entire band of Whispered Words stands in front of me with an expecting gaze. What did I do to deserve this type of punishment today? Is God punishing me? Again?

"Well, some of us can't live off mommy and daddy's money forever. What are you, Kieran? Twenty-one? Have you ever held down a real job?" I snark, barely containing the bitter words on my tongue. His face falls, and his friends snicker as they browse the old records. "Don't laugh. You assholes are in the same boat." I wrinkle my nose when their gazes land on me with narrowed eyes, and their mouths gape. Yeah, dickbags, I called you out. Someone has to.

Kieran blows out a breath and swipes a hand down his face.

"Yeah, got me there," he freely admits, shoving his hands into his pocket. "Listen..." he murmurs in a smooth, panty-dropping voice.

Goosebumps scatter across my flesh, raising the hairs on every inch of my body as he advances with predatory intent. A warm, familiar smile spreads across his lips when he rounds the L-shaped counter and invades every inch of my space.

My breath shudders inside my chest when Kieran looms above my seated frame, hovering there and watching me with a keen eye. His gaze falls on my rapid breaths. Every inhale I take; he counts it in his mind. Every little twitch, he eyes with intent. Every inch of my body is aware of his presence, heating under his watchful gaze. Try as I might, I can't focus on anything but him. Them. All their eyes are on me and invading my bubble.

I stiffen when the faintest touch brushes through the long strands of my brown hair, pushing it to rest over my shoulders and exposing my neck. Shivers run down my spine when his rough fingertips dance across my flesh, taking whatever he wants, inch by inch.

A large lump lodges in my throat, and reality comes crashing in. A panic-fueled storm rages in my belly, and the bile rises. For so long, I've fought off the hazy memories of the worst night of my life, and it's times like these that make them come back with a vengeance. Kieran's too close—too touchy. Ants dance across my skin when their unwanted words rush through my mind. My eyes drift across the boys, connecting with Callum's as his head tilts. Concern etches on his face, and his lips pop open like he's connecting the dots in his mind. Swallowing hard, I stare at the ground, trying to ground myself and forget the world around me.

"She's too drunk, just fucking...."

"Just take them off...."

"Fuck yes...."

Their voices haunt my every waking moment. The feel of their phantom fingers working down my shorts and tossing them and my panties aside, leaving me bare for an entire group of strangers to see. No matter how hard I struggled. No matter how many times I drunkenly said no, these strangers took what they wanted and eliminated my choices when I was only fifteen. My only saving grace was the man with dark eyes and tattoos creeping up his neck.

"Shit! What the hell?" Rad whispers with concern. "Jesus!" he croaks, emotions rising in his throat. "Hey? Hey? Are you okay? Something happened, Sweetness. I think you need to go to the hospital. Hey? Can you hear me?" A light tapping on my cheeks forces my eyes to crack open, and I look around.

The moist grass encases my nearly naked and aching body, and when I peek at the man sitting beside me with tears on his cheeks, I immediately recognize him. Ashton Radcliffe. My classmate and Kieran—my knight's new best friend.

My ma said I shouldn't have gone to the party after it was all said and done. She said I was too young for that side of town, and I should have known the Lakeview kids would have done that. But she never understood my reasoning because she was never there.

I wanted a chance to see the boy who had left me behind and glimpse at the man he had become. Many nights I wished I had stayed home and forgotten about the boy who handed me a weapon to defend myself and taught me about life.

But what I saw was a stark reminder of why I should have given up on that dream because he was a completely different person, lounging by the pool with his new friends, laughing as girls jumped into the pool naked in front of them. That should have been the first clue I was in way over my head, coming to the party with just one friend.

Even when I tried to gain his attention and say hi, he blew me off and pretended not to know me. Hell, as I've gotten older, I don't think he did. Was I so easily forgettable? Or had I changed so much?

In retaliation and with a broken heart, I took my first, second, third, fourth, and fifth drink of alcohol. Something I swore I'd never do. After seeing its effects on Kieran's mom and mine, alcohol was never my go-to. Shit, it still isn't.

I shudder again, trying to tamp the swirling panic roaring in my gut. It's not those strangers. It's not the situation. Regardless of that, the memory plays on a loop. The rest of my patience breaks like a damn rubber band snapping.

Beads of sweat break out in a slight sheen, misting my whole body at the feel of his unwanted hands ghosting through my hair. I learned to set my fucking boundaries long ago, and now it's time to remind them where I stand. Through the years, I've reclaimed my body and pleasure, but on my terms.

I abruptly push from my seat, startling everyone. Before he can move, I'm weaving my fingers through his short, dark strands. Yanking his neck to the side, I snarl, standing on my tippy toes to reach his massive height. If I thought he was enormous on stage, standing in front of him is a whole other story. He towers over me with impressive stature and bulky muscles. Probably put on by lugging amps, guitars, and drum sets around. I huff. Now is not the time to think about his sexy body. Now is the time to show him what I think of him touching me without permission—or anyone for that matter. If these guys think they can follow me around and touch me whenever they want, they've got another thing coming.

I yank the small pocket knife I never leave home without out of my pocket. Flicking it open, I expose the razor-sharp edge and nudge it straight into his cock through his jeans. His eyes blow wide when the tiny tip of my knife nestles snuggly against his balls in warning.

Yeah. It's ball-nicking time, Assface. Feel my fucking fury.

His hands go up in the defense, and I pull his hair tighter, making him wince. River West and no sleep do not mix. But sprinkle over-privileged, touchy pricks into the pot? Makes for an unpleasant morning. For all of us, now, apparently.

"Just because we had one mediocre fuck doesn't give you the right to touch me ever again. Ya hear?" I ask, pulling the strands of his hair tighter in my grip until he answers like a good fucking boy with a nod. Tears collect in my eyes from the fucking anger and fear flowing through my damn veins. I try to shake them off, refusing to let them fall. I'll be damned if these assholes see me cry, even if it's not from sadness.

"Whoa," Rad, the drummer, murmurs in alarm.

As quiet as a damn church mouse, he moves beside me, putting his hands up in a placating manner. A grimace spreads across his face, darting his eyes from the storm brewing behind my eyes and the knife currently two seconds away from plunging into his BFF's dick. Sometimes I wonder if he remembers the girl he found half naked, discarded behind a shed like a piece of trash or if I'm simply a blemish in his memories. Because I often think of the man who helped dress the disoriented, sobbing girl and thank him daily. Not only did he pick me up at my lowest, but he also took me to the hospital.

I grind my teeth, staring deep into the eyes of my former classmate, Rad. The boy who held me close after...I shake my head, ridding my brain of those thoughts again.

"Sorry, River," Rad corrects with a small, understanding smile. "He meant nothing by it. Kieran is a little touchy-feely when he's all hopelessly obsessed." Kieran grunts at his friend's remark but doesn't refute it. In fact, when I look into his icy eyes, I see the fire brewing, just for me—his River Blue.

"Obsessed? What're you, my stalker, now?" I say, staring into Kieran's hooded eyes.

"You kept it," he breathes, gesturing to the knife nestled against his balls with his eyes, not daring to move a muscle.

"I...I..." My tongue sticks to the roof of my mouth as I stare at the name etched into the grip. River Blue.

Butterflies burst to life in my belly, doing somersaults inside me, arousing the beast between my legs. The way he stares at me sends conflicting emotions straight through me. I ache for him to bend me over again and screw me into next week. Hell, even the thrill of his friends watching slickens my panties more, which should disgust me. But it doesn't. And it proves to me more and more how fucked up I am.

Kieran is bad for my health. Bad boy. Rich prick. Can't keep his hands to himself. And looking at me like I'm the answer to everything. Lights burst in his eyes when he looks at me, almost begging to grab me tight, kiss the soul from my body, and claim what's his.

Damn it. I'm spiraling toward poor decisions. Again. I've been down a hopeless road, leading to heartbreak and disaster. If I knew what was good for me, I'd cut his balls off and be done with it. But I never know when to quit. It's my toxic fucking trait.

"I kept it," I whisper, furrowing my brows at my answer.

My breath leaves when I see the desire swimming within the depths of his eyes at my confession like he has me right where he wants me.

Liquid lust spears straight to my pussy, clenching around nothing when his raging hard-on pokes into my stomach. Even with a fucking knife pointed at his balls. He licks his lips, giving me a tiny head shake, and fear overtakes him. Confirming to me all I need to know about the boy who I literally have by the balls. He likes this.

"Not-not stalking you," Callum mumbles, stumbling over his words, carefully flipping through the vintage records nestled in their sleeves.

Callum Rose stands with his broad back to me, flexing every time he pulls a sleeve out and reads the back. He hums to himself mostly, bobbing his head. White earbuds poke out from his ears, obscured by blonde curls hanging over his ears. A deep blush overtakes his face when he peeks back at me, giving me a soft smile, and returns to his findings with vigor.

"And you just happen to work here," Asher Montgomery sneers in my direction, standing with his arms folded across his chest. His lip twitches, looking around the store, and sticking his nose in the air.

"I came to apologize," Kieran murmurs, drawing my attention back to him with the brush of his finger under my chin.

I raise a brow, pulling harder on his hair. He grunts, rolling his eyes back when his boner throbs against my stomach. Interesting....

"For what?" I say with confusion, ignoring the butterflies fluttering in my guts.

Stupid butterflies. Just shoo now. I don't have time for shitty feelings.

"For being an asshole after the show," he whispers with pleading eyes. "I didn't know...it was you." He attempts to shake his head, but my fingers tighten, restricting his movements.

"He also wanted to say how sorry he was for not giving you the orgasm you deserved," Rad hums in a quiet voice, almost so low I don't hear the desire dripping from his words.

But I do. It's the same gut-turning feeling twisting my insides when I peek at him. My hero. My fucking saint. Stepping closer, he's a breath away. A kiss away. No! A punch away. His warmth brushes across my neck, sending shivers down my spine. Every inch of me heats to lava levels.

Stupid, complicated hormones. We're done with bands! Done with guys like this.

I jerk back, narrowing my eyes thick with suspicion. Gritting my teeth, I curse myself. Why these guys? Huh? Why does it have to be them? Why can't it be like some nice guy down the road with a good family who wants a healthy relationship?

This whole situation screams my ex, Donavon Drake. All over again. Why can't I have some nice fella who treats me right and doesn't look at me like I'm their next sex pet? This whole thing will lead to one big, fucking colossal disaster. And they're the damn bomb exploding in the middle. I close my eyes and take several deep breaths and count to ten. If I could afford therapy, I'd have a therapist on speed dial ready to hear the chaos ruling my brain.

"Rad," Kieran hisses between his teeth, grunting as he pulls against my grip. "Don't make it fucking worse, idiot," He curses under his breath when the man, firmly known as Rad, signs his death warrant.

I narrow my eyes when the warmth of a finger hovers above my cheek. "You touch me with that finger you want to stroke my face with, and I'll bite it off. I'm like that llama—no touchy-touchy. I don't even know you," I grit out, eyeing the offending finger like a damn Twinkie. Bring it closer, drummer boy, and you won't be playing with your sticks or dicks any time soon.

"We came for the check you owe us," Ash demands, cutting through the invisible rope of sexual tension hovering above me.

Pushing off the wall, Ash marches toward me with an odd sense of determination. His angular face hardens, and his hazel eyes narrow—my nose wrinkles when he catches Callum's attention and nods in my direction. The tigers are on the prowl, ready to pounce on innocent little me. Callum's eyes roll toward the ceiling at Ash's demand. Placing the record back, he heaves a sigh and follows his leader like the baby duck he is, shoving his hands in his pocket. His gray eyes avoid mine, looking anywhere but at me.

"I paid you," I tsk, shaking my head. "And how did you find me? Do I seriously need to change my address and name?" Shit. I need a security guard or something if these douche canoes are going to be hanging around. Or someone to guard me against doing something stupid, like fucking Kieran again.

"We went to the bar. The cook said you'd be here," Ash says with a calculating eye.

Leon is fucking dead to me. Dead! Gone. I'll dig his grave myself. Ugh! He probably cackled to himself after they left. Oh, yeah. Real fun. Send them to River so she can stress even more on her first day of classes.

"We came so I could apologize for being an asshole," Kieran grunts when my fingers tighten to unimaginable levels, pulling him with my movements.

Rad snorts, pulling my attention to him, and pulls out a crinkled paper from his pocket. His nose wrinkles as he straightens out the crumbled paper on the counter's edge and then holds it in the air with pride. A slight smirk pulls at the edge of his lips when his dark eyes meet mine. My brows furrow when he puts it in front of my face, letting me read the messy print, and it all clicks.

My eyes widen when I read the words etched into the check repeatedly. And finally... I fuckin lose it. A laugh sputters from my lips, and I lose my grip on Kieran and spin around toward the cabinet. Through my fit of laughter, I carefully shut my knife and shove it into my pocket. My husky laugh bounces off the walls and fills the space until I'm practically crying.

"It's not really that funny," Ash says from in front of me with a rigid tone, eyes watching my every move.

"It's kind of funny, dude," Rad says through a chuckle, covering his mouth with his black-painted fingernails.

I stand straight up, feeling the tips of Kieran's fingers brush against my bare legs. Damn, what a day to wear ripped short shorts. Goosebumps erupt, making the hairs on the back of my neck stand on end. This time I don't bother telling him not to touch me. He has enormous balls of steel after I held a knife to his nuts and told him to fuck off. I'll give him a little inch. Now let's see if he takes a mile.

"Come by the bar tonight. I can rewrite this for you," I say, snorting and wiping the tears from my eyes.

"Tonight?" Ash asks, scrunching up his face. "Jesus, you're working tonight too?"

I snort again, shoving the stupid check into my shorts pocket, and shrug. "A girl's gotta eat, Ash. So, yeah, definitely working both jobs today. Like most days." I shrug, swallowing hard when Kieran's hand rests on my leg.

"Wait!" Rad yells with an excited clap, bouncing on his toes. I startle, looking at him with a scathing look. But his joy overtakes everything, and he grins so big the sun shines off his pearly whites.

Sorcha is playing tonight! Isn't she?" His eyes widen with glee. Even making Ash's face go slack as they all look to me for confirmation.

"Yes. Sorcha is playing. There's a cover charge, and it's higher than yours." I give a sharp nod, trying to tamp down my excitement.

Sorcha has the hottest touring independent band in the country. And tonight only, she's stopping at our little bar to play for a room full of her Midwestern fans—me included. It took months and months of back and forth, but I finally snagged a date for her all-woman band to perform. Not only will I see my fucking idol, but she'll bring lots of money to line my pockets.

I stiffen again, coming back to the quiet conversation around me. Kieran's fingers make slow circles on my upper thigh, slipping beneath the fabric of my jean shorts.

"Do you ever sleep, River Blue? Or are you staring into the stars again, asking the man on the moon questions?" Kieran murmurs huskily, causing more goosebumps to pucker at my skin. My breath shudders when I fall into the memories of our past and let myself feel.

"Dear man on the moon. Will Stacey ever stop being mean?" I mumble, angling my head toward the bright stars and full moon.

"Who is the man on the moon?" a voice says from the shadows, startling me from my spot. I should have listened to my ma and stayed inside.

My heart thunders in my chest when a shadowy figure emerges from behind a tree. Blowing out a breath, I narrow my eyes at the neighbor boy waltzing toward me.

"The man on the moon, duh," I say, gesturing to the giant orb, illuminating our quiet space.

"Right," his brows furrow when he sits beside me at a good distance. "I'm Kieran Knight."

"River Blue," I say with a tiny nod, turning back to the moon. "Now, where was I," I whisper, tapping my chin.

"You were asking the moon about Stacey...." Later that week, Stacey mysteriously broke her arm on the playground after a rough round of kickball, and no one knew how. Only Kieran, the Man on the Moon, and Stacey knew the truth.

"What?" I murmur, momentarily stunned by his rough fingertips against my skin.

He chuckles, moving closer. Bold move for someone who just had his nads threatened. But this seems to be his MO. Cocky. Takes what he wants.

"Relax," he murmurs, eyeing the other boys. "I asked if you ever sleep?" I shiver when his fingers roll further up my thigh, almost to my panty line, and then back down again, teasing my exposed skin.

"I can sleep when I'm dead," I whisper, looking back over to my computer screen, trying to ignore the fingers I want to take for a long ride.

My professor still chatters away in my ear, reviewing the syllabus I should listen to. But I can grab it online later and read it over.

The bell over the front door rings again, drawing our eyes toward the two guys casually walking inside. My body stiffens, watching my stupid ex, Van's, eyebrows raise at the sight before him. His wide eyes dart between the four boys standing together and me.

"Well, well, well, Whispered Words," he says mockingly, looking each of the boys over with a snide look.

"Donavan Drake," Ash says calmly, crossing his arms over his chest.

"It's Van," he sniffs haughtily.

Van nods his head at each of the guys in greeting, finally meeting mine. Frantic worry sits in the back of his dark eyes, searing into my soul. Internally, I roll my fucking eyes at the audacity of his stupefied expression. Like a damn deer caught in the headlights. He has no right. He kicked me to the curb. But yet, he still follows me like a lost puppy dog.

"You got the new Hartbraker's album in yet?" he asks, clearing his throat.

Rad snorts, stepping just an inch closer to me, gaining Van's attention. His warm body seeps into my side, and he fucking knows it. He grins like a maniac.

"Hartbraker's bro? Zoe Hart? Didn't she disappear for like seven years?"

Van's eyebrows shoot up into his hairline. "Zoe Hart went into Witness Protection, bro. She almost lost her damn life through it all. She's just now been able to come out and use her real name. She's got a hell of a voice and a hell of a story to tell. This is her first album since she went through that shit in California. Real tragic shit, look it up," Van says, shaking his head.

His brown strands swish with his movements until he swoops it out of his eyes and turns his attention back to me. Just this once, he waits in the winds to hear what I have to say. Of course, he has to, and I don't mind. Music is my fucking life, and The Hartbrakers? They're phenomenal, especially since they came back stronger than ever.

I forget the awkwardness between us and go right into my happy place. Music. The band-aid covers my broken soul, healing me one chord at a time.

"We got the shipment last night," I say quietly, pointing toward the back of the store where stairs will lead him up to the second level. "There's a huge display up there with all her records." He offers me a tight smile, looks around again and then nods.

Van waves his brother along, and they trudge up the stairs, but not before he looks back at me one last time with torment on his face. He licks his lips, looking toward the backroom behind the counter, and then shakes his head.

You know, a long time ago, my ma told me to never, and I repeat, NEVER fuck around with rock stars. She said they were tormented souls who'd screw you over for every penny they could get, and I guess she's right.

Exhibit A: my damn father. But we know all about that.

Exhibit B: Van Drake. The walking, talking sex on a stick, emo, punk rock wannabe who performed at Dead End and stole my heart once in high school. He was the best thing ever to happen to me until his parents discovered us in the back of his rocking mustang. Naked and panting. Thick with sweat. Then he had to look me in the eye the next day and tell me he couldn't be with me anymore. Yeah, how sweet of him, huh?

It turns out, ole mommy and daddy didn't like him hanging out with the trash—me. Can you see why now I want to escape this stupid town and never look back? He comes in here every so often, giving me those big brown eyes, and I fail almost every time. Somehow, we always end up naked and panting, hiding in my boss's office for a quickie.

But not today. And never again.

I'm so tired of being second-rate pussy that he's too embarrassed to be seen in public with. Especially after he tore my damn heart out because mommy and daddy said so. Besides, the person I really want is rubbing his fingers up and down my leg. Even though I threatened him with a knife to the balls, he's still as bold as they come. And I want another piece. You see, I'm not after love or affection because everyone around me leaves me, including Kieran. I'll take good dick, maybe some dinner, but that's it. No love is in the cards for this gal.

"Donavan Drake, huh? So, you're the girl that sent Judge Drake into an uproar?" Ash asks, watching Van pace the second floor.

I scrunch my nose. "Yeah, I'm not discussing that with you," I mumble because I'd rather choke on bleach than open myself up to a room full of bullies I went to high school with.

Rad whistles. "Man, his dad was on a damn rampage a year ago, going on about some Central chick who had trapped his son," he says, moving a piece of hair from my forehead. "That was you, wasn't it?"

I frown, thinking back to the hot and heavy nine months we spent together. Nine months of filthy sex. Passion. And what I thought was love. And then a hole in my heart.

"I don't know how I trapped him," I say, using rabbit ears over the word trapped. "We dated, had a good time, and then he tucked his tail when mommy and daddy said no." My voice lowers when my eyes connect with his from the second level. A paleness takes over his tanned features, and he averts his eyes, looking ill. That's right, buddy, I figured you out. He's in love with me but refuses to acknowledge it.

"Informative," Ash says, rubbing his chin, looking toward the sun beaming through the tall front windows.

"Informative?" I huff back, shaking my head.

"Just like I said," he replies with a smirk, nodding his head to the other boys and gesturing to them at the front door.

"Buzzkill," Rad murmurs with disappointment but quickly produces a smile. "See ya tonight, Pretty Girl! Make sure you make me a nice Pina Colada, my fav." He winks, hopping over the tall counter easily.

"Give me a second," Kieran says in a soft voice right in my ear as the others walk out.

"You can go with them, Knight," I say dismissively, fiddling with my earbud.

Despite the distractions around me, I made it through my first class. Granted, I was barely listening to his nasally voice. I huff, closing my laptop and pushing it aside. I don't have another one until later, so I'll do the same thing then, too. Work while listening, and hopefully, there won't be any distractions.

"I can make my sorry up to you later," he whispers directly in my ear, fingers brushing up the inside of my thigh, daring to go further. I swallow hard when he stands even closer to me, fingers working beneath the tethered ends of my shorts. "Or now," he murmurs.

I clutch the counter's edge until my knuckles turn white and nod my head in agreement. I'm taking back what I want and what I want is his fingers inside me.

"I'd much rather you boss me around and tell me you want to ride my face, but this will do for now, yeah?" he murmurs, flicking his tongue over my ear.

"That's it then, huh?" I gasp when he hits my bundle of nerves with his fingertips. I lick my lip when he nods into my neck, and I sigh. "Then what are you waiting for? You have four seconds to get me off before Van comes downstairs with his brother and sees what you're doing."

"Maybe I want him to see what I'm doing?" Kieran says, rubbing his fingers over my clit in a frantic circle, bringing my orgasm closer and closer to the surface. Fire brews hotter in my stomach, spreading out through my veins. My toes curl in my chucks, and goosebumps erupt everywhere, despite the heat filling every molecule of my body. "You think he'd get jealous? I think he would.

Fun fact, Van never got over the girl they forced him to leave. But you don't belong to Van Drake anymore. The truth is, you never did. He was a pathetic excuse of a placeholder. Naw, my sweet River Blue, you belong to me. Always have. Always fucking will," he murmurs into the curve of my neck with such possession that it ties my tongue into knots. I want to yell at him. I am my own fucking woman, and I don't need him. Not after he left me. But nothing seems to come off my heavy tongue except heavy breaths.

My mouth hangs open, and my nails dig into the meaty flesh of his forearm, gripping him so hard I rip my index nail in half. "Fuck him," I grunt, moving my hips with his movements. "Make me come, Kieran," I whisper with desperation, giving in to the euphoric feeling taking over and leaning the back of my head against his shoulder. "And do it quickly," I beg when his teeth sink into the flesh of my shoulder, creating such a delicious pain stars burst behind my eyelids. A silent scream leaves my lips when the feeling finally wrecks through me.

My pussy clamps around his fingers, and I hold back the scream lodged in my throat. As much as I want to yell it out and let Van hear my pleasure, I hold it back. My breaths come down as soon as their footsteps sound on the metal staircase and head our way.

"Better?" he asks, licking along the wound he created.

"Good boy," I murmur, tapping his leg. "You can go now," I say, eyeing Van, talking to his brother in a low voice. He holds two records in his hands and has a smile on his face.

"I think I'll stay for the show," he says with a chuckle, eyeing the two boys.

"Well, you can remove your damn fingers from my pussy," I say through gritted teeth, earning me another chuckle when he does.

"Van," Kieran says, reaching across the counter with the very hand that was knuckle deep inside me.

My eyes widen in horror at his glistening fingers, soaked to the bone with my pussy juices, grasping onto Van's in a weird bro handshake. They shake for a brief second, exchanging a few words.

"Nice to see you, man. I haven't seen you around the circuit anymore.

Your band not playing anymore?" Kieran asks, moving my long strands from the side of my neck and drifting them down my back, seeming to have any excuse to touch me. Hell, maybe he is a stalker, and I'm the willing little prey eating up his touch.

"Uh, nah. We kind of gave that up a year ago. College and all that got in the way." Van shrugs with a cocky smirk, quickly dropping away when his eyes zero in on the exposed part of my neck. He swallows hard, huffing a breath. "Parents wouldn't stop nagging me to give it up and focus on the future. So, they gave me a compromise." Van's eyes dart to me with uncertainty.

"Compromise?" Kieran asks, leaning against the counter with a lazy grin. He watches with glee as Van scratches under his nose and furrows his brows, staring at a glistening spot on his hand. "Was it over that chick?"

Great. I'm that chick now.

Van shifts uncomfortably, still staring at the spot on his hand when he shrugs again. "Um, nah. Dad handed me a check and told me to focus on my real future. So it was money or the band. Ya know?"

Kieran scoffs, curling his lip back. "You chose money over the band?"

Van scowls. "Yeah. And what would you do, huh? It was take the money and go to college. Or he was going to kick my ass out. Money trumped the band. I needed school. I didn't need the music." He shakes his head, scratching under his nose again, and recoils. With furrowed brows, Van discreetly licks along the wet spot on his hand and jerks back, staring daggers in my direction, but remains rooted in place.

"Any true musician knows the music lives in their souls. It's the fuel for life, man. You can't just give that up for some green. That's like throwing something away you love just because your parents say so." Kieran side-eyes me, and I roll my eyes toward the ceiling, counting down the seconds until Van marches out of here and takes Kieran with him. I got off, and now they can fuck off.

When Van takes a deep breath and his nostrils flare, a twinkle sparkles in Kieran's mismatched eyes. Immediately he turns beet red, stopping the conversation when he shoves the records across the counter.

He pulls out two twenties and tosses them at me without care. "Keep the change," he says through gritted teeth, yanking his confused as fuck brother along. Dillon awkwardly waves over his shoulder, cursing his brother when he shoves him out the door. And once again, I'm left alone with my kryptonite.

Kieran hums, watching them go, and then walks back around the L-shaped counter. He stops in front of my bewildered face and bops my nose with his index finger, grinning like a fucking madman. Which I'm coming to realize he is.

"That was fun, River Blue. We should do it again," he rasps, leaning in to kiss my cheek. The warmth of his lips lingers on my cheek, and my damn body shudders from the contact.

"Don't get too eager. Who says I'll ever let you touch me again? This was a one-time thing," I murmur, leaning my elbow into the counter and inadvertently leaning into his kiss.

He snorts, waving a hand. "See you tonight. But don't make any plans for after your shift."

I scoff. "Asshole, I get off at two in the morning, and then I'm going home." He raises a brow, waltzing towards the front door leisurely.

"Don't make any plans," he all but demands with a possessive growl, spearing right through me.

"Fine." I shrug like he didn't make my pussy fucking gush at the sound of his growl. "But you better up your game, Richy." He scowls at the nickname, shaking his head.

"It's Kieran, not Richy," he mumbles.

"Yeah, I'm River, not your River Blue or whatever other nicknames you can think of. Remember that. In fact, if you are so inclined, get on your damn knees and worship me next time we meet. I'd be highly disappointed if you didn't. How's that for taking charge?" I demand, putting the bills into the register and shoving the change into my pocket.

"You'll always be my River Blue," he says with a smirk. "And I'll make good on that."

And with that, Kieran walks out the door and gets into the passenger seat of the large Tahoe parked on the other side of the road. I watch through the bright windows as they silently sit until Ash's mouth moves, and they start a discussion. I wish I could be a fly on the damn car ceiling to hear whatever they were saying.

My heart aches in my chest at his sudden reemergence. For so long, I told myself to forget about Kieran Knight. Yet, here he is in the flesh, laying down some sort of claim on me like he has any damn right. What's so different now than before? Why is he coming at me so hard with everything he has and stamping his name on my forehead?

I'm pulled from my thoughts as the bell rings over the door again. I frown, staring at the last culprit I thought I'd ever see again. Van comes back through the door with determination etched on his face as he marches up to me.

"Don't trust those assholes," he grits his teeth. "Whatever they say to you, they're lying," he says, slamming a fist onto the counter. "Believe me, they'll screw you over faster than you can count to three, Rivy," he pleads, clenching his teeth.

I nod my head, looking at them through the tall window. They stare over this way. Asher's mouth flaps a few times, and the others stare, waiting in the car, inspecting everything we do with a keen eye.

"Yeah? Just like you, Van?" I hum, leaning my elbow on the counter.

"Yeah, Riv," he sighs, running a hand down his face. "Just like that, trust me on this." His voice sounds urgent, and his eyes plead with me to believe him.

I snort. "Right. Trust you? You're joking, right? Well, I'm a big girl, Van. I've got this. Thanks for your concern."

"Damnit, Rivy, you're too stubborn," he mutters, cursing under his breath. "I'm serious. Whatever they're hanging around for, they're going to use you. That's all they do is use people for what they want."

"Huh, sounds familiar," I say, tilting my head toward the back office, and then I frown.

Shit. I must have a knack for fucking in Booker's offices. First, Van is here whenever he wants to slum it, and then Kieran at the bar. I need to get laid in bed or somewhere normal next time.

Van swallows hard, looking toward the ground. "I... Riv, I...you know..." I hold up a hand, cutting him off.

"I don't need your excuses, but our time against the desk is done. I don't need to be second to anyone. No hard feelings," I say with a shrug, eyeing his shallow breaths.

Ah, it appears that Van doesn't like that answer. No. He wants to keep using me and then dumping me all over again. I don't need to keep clawing at these raw wounds and tearing them open for a man who will never love me. He wants me to beg him to fuck me again so he can leave and return to his charmed life without a second glance.

"I, yeah, um...that's cool," he stutters through his words, rubbing the back of his neck. "I'll still be your friend, though," he murmurs, placing his hand on mine.

At one time, Van's touch made butterflies burst inside my stomach. And for the first time in a long time, I feel absolutely nothing. Not even his big brown eyes could lure me into their spell. It's taken a long time to get over how he made me feel and how he rejected me so severely. But I think I'm finally moving on. And so sue me, it may be into the arms of another rich dickface. To me, it's significant progress on the Rivers' heartbreak scale.

I'm moving on from my first and last love and onto a better dick. And that's it. How's that phrase go? When one dick disappoints, move on to the next one for a better ride? Yeah, something like that.

His fingers curl around mine, and he squeezes once. "I know you're a big girl, way more capable than me. But I'm serious, Riv. They just take with no regard for who they hurt."

"Yeah? And what did they take from you?" I ask, leaning on the counter again.

"Nothing from me, but they'll stop at nothing to get to the top. They want...they want your dad to sign them," he says, swallowing hard. "I've heard them talk about it when we played shows together. He's their rock idol and getting to the KC Club is their ultimate dream."

"Pfft. My dad can have 'em," I say, wrinkling my nose at the thought. But I'm skeptical of whatever he has to say. "So, let's assume what you're trying to say is...these assholes are getting close to me to get to him? Don't they know Corbin West doesn't do shit with his kids unless they're named Seger or Zeppelin?" I scoff at that, envy brewing in my belly.

I vaguely remember my two older brothers from the short time I lived with them. But the one thing I know about them is that they got Dad's attention their whole life. And my dad wrote me off the moment he threw us out. So, to say I'm a little jealous they got his love, and I didn't, is an understatement. Why them and not me? That's always been the question.

"Fine," he mumbles. "But don't say I didn't warn you." He shakes his head, moving his long hair from his eyes.

"You're good. You warned me that if I get burned, that's on me. I don't trust them as far as I can throw them, for the record," I say with a shrug, earning a sharp nod.

Van waves goodbye as he walks out the door with a solemn look on his constipated face before stepping out into the sun. So, the boys think they're getting into my daddy's record company through me? That's laughable at best. But let's see them try. I won't let my feelings get in the way. All I'm here for is a good time.

KIERAN

I lick my fingers as I waltz through the record store's front door, moaning at her taste. Her essence fills my damn taste buds, going directly to my dick. God damn. She tastes as sweet as she felt on my dick, and I can't wait to have another fucking bite of her. River might be the drug I've craved for years now.

Never in a million years did I think I'd reconnect with the girl I obsessed over as a kid. My best friend. The girl they forced me to repress. River was too young to understand how deeply I felt about her back then. I could tell her all day long that I loved her, and she'd never understood the true meaning of my words.

My entire world caved when my stupid stepfather marched into my life, hauled me off to greener pastures, and forced me to forget the life I had before. He effectively erased everything from my childhood memories down to the girl I wanted to rush back to. Through expensive new clothes and a butt load of new friends, he took her from me. By the time I reached high school, River was a distant memory and nothing more than a stain on my existence. If I had passed her in the halls or seen her in public, I wouldn't have noticed or known who she was. I was too consumed with my rich new life to fucking care.

I lost myself for nine years, and now, I've found myself once again. I will do anything to have River by my side, even if it means kidnapping her to wherever we end up. I've only just found her, and I won't lose her. Asher will throw a fit, but—fuck him.

The mid-August sun blares heat down on me like a fucking oven as I walk across the street toward the Tahoe sitting opposite the store. Sweat drips down my back, soaking through my shirt. Man. Screw this one-hundred-degree weather. I could use a dip in the lake. Maybe the boys will want to take the boat out and let loose. A couple of beers, loud music, and a quick dip? Sounds like a dream right about now. Maybe River would want to come to hang out on the lake sometime?

As much as I try to imagine the cool water flowing over my skin and cooling me down, my brain wanders. Memories float, surfacing in my mind, of her moans echoing off the walls and her tight pussy contracting around my cock. Reaching down, I adjust myself. I have no fucking shame. They all know exactly what I did, especially by the stupid expressions lining their faces. And if they have something to say about it, well—they can shove it. I'm doing what Asher instructed and bringing her into our little web, except she's mine. We may use her for her father's influence and gain a little fame. But everything about River West is mine.

Next stop, I'll kneel in her office, awaiting her every instruction. She can grip me by the balls and tell me to squawk like a chicken, and I'd do it if she lets me inside her again. And soon, our plan will all click into place. It's all coming together as I'm coming apart.

Fuck. My dick jumps at that, twitching in my pants, waiting for the moment he can explode to her memory. But I won't touch it until I get to her tonight. I'll make good on my promise and kneel in her office until she allows me a taste and fuck.

I grin when I scoot into the passenger seat of Ash's Tahoe, which is identical to mine. A light feeling falls over me, and my shadows fade away.

"What is Van doing?" Callum asks in a soft voice, eyeing the maniac throwing open the door to the record store with determination on his face.

From here, I can see River's tight expression through the window when he stops in front of her. Concern bleeds from his facial expression as he speaks to her. Fuck him! He left her. He has no fucking right to march back in there like he owns her.

I fucking own her. Those marks on her neck are mine for the world to see who she belongs to. White hot jealousy runs through my damn veins, and I want nothing more than to rip every piece of his throat out and maybe break his face. Fuck him for thinking he could waltz back into her life when he was the dick who fucked her over. No, that's my fucking job. Evil parents forced me away, but now I'm back and better than ever. Van needs to be dealt with.

"Daw look, little Van is trying to get back into her good graces," Rad says mockingly, leaning across Callum to get a better view. He plasters his nose against the backseat window, earning a growl from Asher for leaving marks. Callum pats Rad's back with a sigh as he drapes himself over Cal's lap.

"He still wants to fuck her," Ash says matter-oh-factly. "He could be a problem."

"Not by the look on her face. Oh, snap," Rad cackles, pointing toward them. "He's trying to hold her hand, and she looks like she wants to puke." He snorts at that, howling with laughter at Van's failures.

"I remember hearing about them, just didn't realize it was her until now," Callum says, shaking his head with furrowed brows. Light creeps into his eyes as he stares at her from afar, watching her every move with quiet intentions.

Our buddy may be a budded virgin, but I always know when he's interested in a chick. A look always passes over his eyes, and an interest forms. He'll watch from the shadows, inspecting his crush from afar, but never seems to make the moves. I know his reasoning and why he's held onto his v-card for so long, but I think he'll give it up someday soon. Especially with the way he blushes and stumbles around River. Two down, two to go. Now, all I have to do is get Rad and Asher interested in our little mark, and my plan will come together. There will be no protests when I haul her into my lap and force her to California when we get our big break.

"Bleh. It's hotter than my balls outside today," Rad curses, rearranging his junk in his shorts, probably dreaming of the hour when he can drop them and be free. "Oh, fuck balls, we got a little guest coming." Rad nods toward the figure marching his angry ass toward our vehicle.

"This should be interesting," Asher says in a no-nonsense tone, rolling down his window. "Oh, Van, fancy seeing you here," he drawls in a fake, respectful tone, lazily looking at the fuming man outside our window.

Van shakes his head, a deep scowl forming across his lips. "I don't know what you assholes are up to, but you're barking up the wrong fucking tree. Leave River alone. She's not like these other Central girls," he growls, leaning into Ash's window.

"And have you sampled many Central Girls?" I ask, sitting back in my seat, enjoying the cool air-conditioning pouring from the vents.

He scowls at me, shaking his head. "You know my answer. Leave River alone," he growls again, exposing his gritted teeth like an actual threat.

Pfft. The only threat Van Drake poses is a road bump. He could warn River all he wanted about us and whatever else he might say, but she'd never believe him. From the moment River was born, so was her stubbornness.

"Tell me exactly why you care so much?" Ash asks in an even voice, leaning back in the driver's seat with a relaxed and open pose. Casually, he raises a brow as Van's face comically gets redder and redder by the minute.

"What's so great about her, Donnie boy?" Rad asks through a manic grin, rubbing his hands together. "Why should we stay away? Maybe we need a new toy to play with, and maybe she already said yes."

It's a lie, of course. River isn't just a toy to me, anyway. But by the way Van's face falls from our admission; we've got him on our hook. That's right, back off and eat our lie, fuckhead. My fingers curl into fists when he opens his mouth to speak again. I'd rather shove my fist down his throat than continue this tired conversation. There's nothing on this planet he can do to keep us away from River.

Van scoffs. "You assholes may have this entire city fooled into believing you all are some sort of good guys. But I've seen the shit you used to pull back in high school. You're nothing but users. And as for River? She won't be able to help you in your quest for fame," he growls his words, clenching his teeth. "You know it, and she knows it. Her daddy doesn't talk to her. I know exactly what you're up to. You've had this plan since fucking high school to get the hell out of here. But I'm here to stop you from using another person on your bullshit quest."

Ah, there it is. Not only did Donnie Boy want to continue his own quest into music, but he wants her all to himself. Fat chance that'll ever happen, pal. Kieran Knight is back in town and isn't giving up his River Blue for anything, especially a piss ant like him.

"Tell me, Donnie," Ash admonishes, clenching and unclenching his fists. "Does it eat you up? You can't be with her still? Do you dream of the nights you had to hide her in the back of your Mustang? Stealing her away and fuck her while introducing your parents to Whitley? You know, the girlfriend you have so cleverly hidden in the shadows while you come here and try to convince River to be your fuck toy in the back room?"

Van's paling face completely falls as he looks at Asher in surprise. I'd say my malevolent brother hit the mark.

"What the fuck, man?" he gasps, dropping his arms from the edge of the window. "How..." He peers back at River through the storefront windows, who watches our exchange, kicking back into her chair. I can't make out her expression, but I feel her eyes burning through me. That's right, River Blue—eyes on me, baby.

"I have my ways," Ash says, slowly turning his evil-ass face to look into Van's dark eyes. "At this moment, I have a letter typed up in an email on a timer. If you don't back away now, I will release everything to Whitley promptly. Not that I shouldn't, anyway. What a despicable way to treat the woman you're going to marry."

"What the hell are you, some evil psycho?" Van says, taking another step back.

"Maybe," Ash says with a grin and a shoulder shrug. "You leave River to us. No harm, no foul. We'll both get what we want in the end."

"Yeah? And what the fuck is that?" Van scolds, crossing his arms over his chest.

"We'll get ours, and she'll get hers. Besides, Kieran didn't even need to beg her to fuck him by how loud and responsive she was. It looks like she doesn't need you anymore, Donnie boy. That's all I'm saying...."

"That's right, Donnie Boy," I interrupt, leaning over Asher to get a better view of the laughable rage consuming Van's twisted face. "You see, it isn't your name she screams anymore. It's mine. My fingers were just knuckle deep in her tight pussy as she came all over them. And my teeth mark her skin as fucking mine. You leave my River alone. You have no rights over her. Not anymore. You lost those privileges. She. Is. Mine," I growl, curling my fingers into fists.

Vivid images of pounding his face in as blood pours from his mouth and nose as he begs me to stop hurting him run through my mind. Make no mistake; if Van touched her again without my permission, he's a dead man.

Through his narrow, dark eyes, hate brews toward me, and he snarls, readying his rebuttal, but nothing comes out.

"Now, if you'll excuse us, we're late for a very important meeting." Ash doesn't let Van respond as he closes the window and takes off.

"Meeting, huh?" I ask, blowing at my anger. Now that the danger has passed, my fingers tremble with the leftover adrenaline running through my veins.

"God, you handed him his ass. We left him sputtering and spitting in the middle of the street," Rad cackles more, falling into the backseat. "I bet he'll tuck tail and run back to mommy and daddy with tears in his pathetic eyes."

"He'll keep his hands off what's ours now," Asher declares, narrowing his eyes in the rearview mirror. Shaking his head, he focuses on the long road ahead of us, navigating us back to Lakeview.

The record store disappears from behind us, replaced by the upscale side of Central City. Boutiques and restaurants become blurs of colors, and trees soon line the edges of the road. We may still be in Central City, but you wouldn't know. The Lakeview District has wild hills with trees and tons of wildlife. A large lake sits to my right, expanding over the horizon. Boats putter along, pulling rafts, wake boarders, and skis, looking like a screen paradise. But it is anything but.

"How about a little music therapy?" Callum asks, eagerly leaning forward, tapping his fingers on the center console, aching to strum his bass.

So much better than taking out the boat. Sure, the sun, wind, and water would be a pleasant treat after such a hot day. But nothing compares to the music we're about to create as one unit. I feel it in the depths of my gut. It's the intense need to get my hands moving and create memorable tunes. We all feel it by the sharp nod Ash gives when we pull into our driveway. He throws the SUV into park, strumming his fingers along the steering wheel.

"It's working, isn't it?" he asks with a hint of uncertainty, which is so unlike himself. He twitches uncomfortably, eyeing my smirk.

"Smell Kieran's finger and see if that gives you the answer," Rad says, barking out a sharp laugh. The entire car shakes when he throws himself back into his seat, practically crying with laughter.

Asher scowls. "That's not gonna—" Ash's eyes widen as big as fucking saucers when my pussy-coated fingers slip into his mouth, giving him a taste. He'll never tell Callum and Rad that the tip of his tongue poked against my fingers before he spits and sputters, forcing me out.

"You were saying?" I ask, cocking my head to the side with a feral grin. Nothing makes me happier than riling up my stepbrother. The angrier he gets, the funnier it is.

His teeth grind when he turns his glare directly at me. His nostrils flare wildly, and his fingers clench into a fist until he's punching the steering wheel and grunting curses in my direction.

"I'll be back," he bites out, throwing his shirt off and into my face.

"We'll warm up while you...." Rad says as Ash takes off down the road, jogging toward the only place that calms him down whenever he works himself up like this.

"So dramatic," I mock, throwing his shirt into the passenger seat. "Now, let's get some practice in before he gets back," I say, getting out of the car with the guys on my heels.

"Think he'll be back in time?" Callum asks, rubbing his chin and staring off into the distance. We all wonder the same thing. How long will he run for now? And when will he make it to his destination?

"Give him time," I say, clutching his shoulder and chuckling. "He'll be back. You know him; he always pushes himself to the brink. No matter if it's ten minutes or two hours. He'll be a sweaty fucking mess by the time he gets back."

Asher may like to pretend he doesn't like us, but deep down, he at least enjoys our presence enough to tolerate us regularly.

Walking up to the garage door, I punch in the four-number code with a sigh. This is it. The moment I've been aching for since I woke up this morning. The moment I've been dreaming about through my first classes of the year to finish up my business degree.

As the garage door slowly lifts, our paradise comes into view just as Ash's sweaty form comes back into view. He heaves a breath, leaning his hands on his knees, and shakes the sweat off.

"You good?" I ask, staring down at him when he nods.

"As good as I'll be for now," he mumbles, standing tall. His eyes drift over our setup, and I see the moment the stress of the world rolls off his shoulders. "Just don't fucking stick your pussy fingers in my mouth again," he gripes, pushing my shoulder. "If I wanted a taste, I'd fucking take a taste." And with that, he waltzes into our band space with sweat pouring from every inch of his skin after pushing himself for ten minutes straight. Throwing his guitar strap over his bare shoulder, he begins tuning his strings. Within a few plucks, guided by his natural ability, he's all tuned up and ready to go.

"Why the fuck are you undressing? Again?" Ash asks, turning to Rad, who sits completely naked on his stool behind his drums, minus the combat boots secured to his feet.

"The boys gotta breathe, bro. It's hot, and my balls are cooking inside my jeans," he says, twirling a drumstick in both hands. "Duh." Without another word, he counts us in, and we construct a new song we've felt in the pits of our dark souls for days, flowing out of us with ease.

This is where it's at. The music brings us together, binding us in a friendship that will never fall apart. We may not always like each other. But we're fucking brothers. As long as we have this. The chords. The melodies. And the words, we have it all—even River in the future.

RIVER

Day number two of my manager job at Dead End finds me back at the front door admitting patrons into the bar—AKA my favorite place to be.

When I was fifteen—yeah, fifteen, I know. Probably way too young to be hanging around a bar, but I had good reason. I begged Booker to give me a job. I was desperate to make money and support myself since my mom could barely do that on a good day. Plus, I needed something to take my mind off all the awful shit happening around me. I needed a purpose, and this right here gave me just that.

On the first day on the job, he sat me here and explained what I needed to do. Check IDs, stamp hands, and turn people away when I have to. He was my saving grace. The only adult to look at me and see a responsible girl looking to make a better life for herself.

Nestled on my bar stool with my tiny podium in front of me, I watch the crazy line stretching out the door and onto the sidewalk. Again. Seriously, it has to be a mile long by now. It's the longest line I've ever seen coming into this place. And I fucking did it! I brought these people here. Well, okay. Sorcha's band brought them here to my venue. My hard work made this happen, and I can't wait for Booker to see all the success I'm bringing to Dead End.

Soft murmurs and excited whoops permeate the air, and the growing crowd surrounds our meager stage with such excitement; my fucking heart skips a beat. Packed shoulder to shoulder with their arms touching and their heads leaning back as the lights on stage dim low, leaving us all in the dark. For only a moment, at least.

A sudden cheer erupts through the crowd, their arms bursting into the air. They jump up and down as the band makes their way across the stage, taking their places in the pitch-black atmosphere. Their shoes scuff, and their heels click against the wooden set. And all hell breaks loose when the bright lights flash, and the crowd screeches more when Sorcha herself hits the first notes of their opening song.

Her crazy red curls bounce when she bobs her head, looking back at the three other women playing with her. She grins, turning her pearly whites toward the crowd, and screeches her first line of the night.

"Hello, Central City! Glad to be here! Let's wake the damn dead!" she screams into the microphone before gracefully singing the first notes of their opening song.

Pure ecstasy saturates my soul in waves. The weight of the world momentarily lifts from my shoulders. All the stress. All the pain. Everything I've endured in my brief life leaves me like a bird in flight, hopefully never to return. One day I'll live without this hovering above me, but for now, I'll revel in the music carrying me away. My eyes close on their own, my body swaying to the beat of the heavy drums leading up to the song's chorus. She screeches her words, hyping everyone in the crowd up.

Taking a deep, refreshing breath, I bathe in the atmosphere. This is why I'm here. This is why I do what I do for this place and bring these bands in. They're like sage to the soul; I'd never have it any other way.

Life flashes before me again, and I bring myself back out of the clouds with a renewed sense of determination. Whatever I plan to do with my life after I get my degree in business, I want it to involve music. Maybe that comes from my dad, or perhaps that comes from my dependency on tunes. Whatever it is, I'm determined to make my dreams come true. No matter what I have to do. I'll leave this town behind with one finger raised in the air and a degree in the other hand.

"Ahem! Bitch," a familiar woman's voice snaps me out of my reprieve.

Right. This must be my torture for the evening. Peering up, I put on my polite face and smile at Tessa. Her ice-blue eyes again glare at me, scoffing and tossing her perfect blonde locks over her shoulder.

"I'm sorry?" I ask, raising a brow at the girl standing before me with her hip cocked out in her short as hell skirt. If she swishes, I think her perfectly sculpted butt cheeks would pop out and show the world what she's got cooking under her hood.

"I need a stamp; here's my cover charge," she hisses loud enough for me to hear the venom in her words, practically shoving the money at me. Her eyes dart around the room, and she strains her neck to look over the bobbing crowd.

"Have you seen them?" she shouts over the music to her friend standing behind her when I stamp her hand, and she moves aside.

"No," Sara giggles, shoving fifteen dollars into my hand, a little nicer than her friend.

"Ugh. Their FlashGram said they'd be here hanging out tonight. It's my one chance. They won't be onstage for once," she murmurs, grabbing her friend's hand, and tries to take off into the sea of people.

"Central Trash," her friend says, tilting her head when I wrinkle my nose at the name.

"I have a name," I state with a tight expression, narrowing my eyes at her. Running a finger along my boob, I show the name printed on my shirt for good measure. "I'm River. The manager." I, once again, run a finger over the word manager etched into my tit, earning me a haughty scoff.

Three years ago, they graduated from high school, yet they act like we're still roaming the halls together. This is their ridiculous way of putting me in my place and showing me I'm nothing more than a Central girl, which is laughable. To them, I'm firmly under their fucking sharp heels, ready for them to squish me to pieces.

"Have you seen them yet?" Her friend curses, trying to pull her along, muttering under her breath.

"Who?" I ask, waving the next person forward.

I take their money and stamp their hand, repeating the process with the following people, and check IDs along the way. At least fifty people, okay, that's an exaggeration, come through the door before these two make up their minds. When I look back at the doorway, it's practically empty, and the line has died down. Thank God. It'll give me a second to finally breathe.

"Whispered Words," the girl snarks, leaning forward.

"God, Sara!" Tessa mutters, stomping her foot.

"What, Tessa? She sees everyone who comes through the doors. It's her job," she scoffs, rolling her eyes toward the ceiling. "So, she'd know if they were here. They just played a few days ago!" Tessa nods, staring at me for confirmation.

A deep heat invades my cheeks and ears, remembering precisely what Kieran and I got up to earlier. His fingers were inside me and swirling over my clit while my ex-boyfriend browsed the shop, none the wiser. Rad promised Kieran would deliver the best orgasm of my life, and he did. He really fucking did. I want a repeat, spend a day getting lost in his dick, pretending the outside world doesn't exist and enjoy the man he is now because I've obviously broken my vow about swearing off him. So, why not have some fun?

"No," I state with a shrug, keeping my voice as even as possible. There's no way in hell I'd admit to these two groupies. That has to be what they are, if I have seen them or not.

"See," Tessa scoffs, rolling her eyes again. "We'll find them ourselves. Thanks for nothing, Central Slut," she hisses, dragging her friend into the crowd of people, losing themselves to the loud metal music flowing through the speakers.

"Enjoy the show," I mutter, discreetly lifting my middle finger to their backs.

Who are they going to tell on me, too, anyway? I'm the damn boss right now. I should tell them to shove their judgmental names where the sun doesn't shine, but I like to think I'm a little more professional than that. Well—I cringe, lowering my finger— sometimes I'm professional. I can only handle the whole Central whore/slut, name-calling for so long before I blow a gasket and give them what they deserve.

"Well, hello, Pretty Girl," Rad sings above the music, throwing his arms around. If he wanted to stay small and away from the two groupies asking about them, he's failing miserably by announcing his damn presence. I sneak a peek at the two girls in question and grin when they're caught up in the crowd and unable to make it over. Too bad, so sad for them. Such a shame.

"Well, hello, drummer boy," I sing-song back, cocking my head to the side at the sight of him.

God damn. My momma said don't fuck with rock stars, but it's so hard when they look this delectable and lickable. Seriously! Rad's sporting tight jeans, leaving not-so-little Rad's outline on display. Like holy eggplant in the pants, Batman. I swallow hard, my gaze making it up to his exposed arms coming out of his sleeveless tank, giving me a peek of the tattoo expanding over his chest and into his throat. And finally, his ridiculous curly mullet is perfectly styled, not a curl out of place. But the icing on the cake tonight is the septum piercing glowing in the dark space. His pearly whites pop out when he grins at me again, catching the moment my eyes roamed downwards.

He snorts, leaning against my little podium, grinning like a madman. "I don't know if I've properly introduced myself to you yet," he murmurs, reaching for the stamp in my hand, stamping Callum's and his hand. "Although drummer boy is pretty hot coming from your lips, I'm...."

"Ashton Radcliffe the Third," Asher says in a mimicking tone, strolling through the front door with a smirk plastered on his lips. Leaning against Rad, he places his elbow on his shoulder.

"It's Rad," he hisses, a soft red blooming across his cheeks, reaching to the tips of his burning ears. "I'm Rad, definitely not Ashton," he says, shaking his head and curling his lip. He looks back at me with pleading dark eyes and points. "It's Rad, not Ashton," he argues again, leaning down onto the podium and putting the stamp back into my fingers.

My heart falls when I stare into his sparkling, dark eyes. Although I'm in no particular mood to relive the night, he saved me from the shadows and brought me to the hospital. It's disheartening to hear he doesn't know who I am. I mean, I don't blame them for not recognizing me from high school. So many students from the surrounding area squished into one building that it'd be hard to keep track of everyone. But to look me in the eye and not remember? I shake my head. Maybe he's like me. That night was horrific; if I had come across that sight, I'd have blocked it out, too.

"Okay, definitely not Ashton, who I went to high school with and have talked to before. You've been stamped. Now pay up," I say, holding my free hand out. "It's a fifteen-dollar cover charge per person."

"It's Rad, for fuck's sake," he grumbles to himself, reaching into the depths of his back pocket. "And wait," he says, holding up a finger. "We went to school together?" His brows furrow when he steps around the podium, taking in my short shorts and a tight black t-shirt. "I'd definitely remember you." He rubs his chin, eyeing me with a hunger that makes my stomach knot.

Fuck. If he doesn't stop staring at me like that, I'll invite him into the back room and rock his world with Kieran. No one says I can't have more. Besides, If I'm breaking my vow, I'm going all in.

"There's only one fucking high school in this mediocre town," Asher huffs out, rolling his eyes at our antics like the douchebag he is. I wonder if he ever lightens up or if he's a perpetual grumpy pants?

Sometimes I think that man needs to get laid or yank the giant stick out of his ass. Even in high school, I remember him being a colossal douche to everyone, and he still hasn't changed. Girls used to chase him as a challenge, and he'd wave them off with a scowl, telling them to fuck off. Maybe Tessa and Sara can rock his world and ease the assholishness out of him, or perhaps he can eat eggs and fuck off. Because I'm not touching him with a twenty-foot pole unless he's nicer. Like buying me lots of diamonds, nicer.

"Although, Ashton doesn't sound too bad coming from your mouth. I can see how this relationship is going to go," Rad rambles, disregarding Asher's answer with a grin. Pulling out three twenties and depositing them into my free hand, he wiggles his brows.

"I'm Callum-Callum," Callum says, brushing his blonde curly, shaggy locks from his gray eyes.

A deep blush rises on his cheeks, and he quickly looks away with a bashful smile and moves into the room, wringing his hands together. Looking back, he smiles again, and his blush deepens further. Only this time, he looks me in the eye and gives me a shaky wave, like it took everything inside him to make that connection. With a wink and a wave, I successfully make him blush so hard he resembles a tomato.

"This is so fucking unnecessary," Asher grumbles, running a hand down his twisted face. But again, no one pays attention to him. They simply smile at me with goo-goo eyes and continue their weird introductions.

"That's great," I say with sarcasm, looking behind them.

I wave a hand, motioning the other two idiots forward as Callum and Rad look off into the rowdy crowd. Rad, of course, grins at Callum, muttering something into his ear and gesturing toward the sea of people.

Kieran steps forward with his face tipped down and his mismatched eyes locked on me. His Adam's apple bobs when he finally stops in front of my podium and pulls his hands from his pockets. When he finally lifts his chin, my heart stops at the desperation swimming in the depths of his mesmerizing eyes. They bore into me, and I feel him in my clenching core, begging me to finish what we had started earlier. But correctly this time, and balls deep.

Shit. I need therapy and dickaholics anonymous or something to keep me away from him. At this point, I don't think I'll be able to deny him any longer, and I'll give into his every whim. Would that be so bad?

Heat spreads throughout my entire body, and I flush. Starting at the tip of my ears, working down my neck, and onto my chest. The idiot smirks, knowing precisely what's going through my damn brain. The tips of his fingertips brush against my hand when I stamp it.

Ash growls with annoyance, pushing Kieran out of the way. He grabs the stamp from me, like the asshole he seems to be, and stamps his hand with greater force than necessary. He throws it back at me, tossing his arms in the air at Kieran, and takes off toward an empty booth by himself, pouting the entire way.

"What crawled up his ass?" I mutter, fiddling with the stamp to keep my hands busy.

Rad smirks, watching the entire exchange with his back turned toward the crowd. He saunters over, lazily looking around, and finally stops beside me.

"That's Asher," Rad says, getting into my bubble.

Again.

You'd think he didn't witness his friend's balls getting threatened several hours earlier. But yet, here we are again. Maybe he has issues with stepping into people's bubbles? His breath passes across my neck, making me squirm in my seat when his fingers work up my sides, squeezing me. Surprisingly, his touch sends pleasant tingles all over my body.

I'm about to remind him what happens to men who can't keep their fingers to themselves.

"Just Ash," Asher barks out of nowhere, folding his arms across his chiseled chest. He snarls at each of them and finally settles his evil-looking eyes on me. I swear he's possessed by a demon or something.

"The power of Christ compels you," I murmur under my breath, flinging fake holy water in his direction.

"Did you just?" Rad murmurs through sputtering laughter, doubling over until he's a wheezing mess and wiping tears from his eyes.

Asher cocks his head, etching a deep scowl on his face like it might permanently stay there. Shaking his head, he glares at Rad, who practically rolls on the floor, howling over the music. "We came for the band and the drinks," he barks out, nodding his head toward the busy bar surrounded by people waiting for their drinks. "And to see you," he grits out like it fucking hurts to say.

I crack a smile. "To see little old me?" I ask, cocking my head to the side playfully. He scoffs, flapping his arms around, and stomps off again.

"See you later, River," Kieran mutters, a slight tilt lifting the edges of his lips like he knows something I don't. "I'll be kneeling for you," he whispers, leaning in to kiss my cheek. "I'll see you after your shift. Don't be late." And with that sentiment, he struts off without a backward glance.

I shiver at the thought, picturing him kneeling for me later. His words come back to me, replaying repeatedly. He'll be waiting for me tonight, after my shift, and there's nothing I can do about it.

And maybe I don't want to.

RIVER

My eyes roam the edges of the packed bar, finding the four boys I shouldn't want anything to do with. They'll screw me over, Van says. They'll take, take, take, he says. But what the hell could they want from me? Certainly not my father or his connections. The only thing connecting my father and me is the blood running through my veins. According to Van, that's what the boys want. They can't be serious, right?

My father has been a ghost for nineteen years. Corbin West is a man I know nothing about and vaguely remember what he looks like. All I have is the tiny picture of him holding me as a baby, stashed away in my purse. When I feel like torturing myself, I stare at it, wondering what the hell I did to make him discard me like a piece of trash.

There's no way I can give the boys the connections they're desperate for. I tried for years to write to that waste of space, and he never answered. As a child, I didn't understand what I was doing. All I knew is this man, Corbin West, helped give me life and then abandoned me, and I wanted answers. By the time I was thirteen, I had stopped writing to him, realizing he would never reciprocate my feelings. Every single letter I poured my heart into came back in the same envelope I had sealed. Unopened, with a simple phrase written across the top, return to sender. So, I gave up.

Sinking my teeth into my bottom lip, I blow out a breath. From across the room, a certain man's fiery gaze eats me alive from the inside out, heating every inch of me. One look. One simple stare. That's all it takes to lose my breath and beg for oxygen. Almost as if claws reach through my skin and tear up my insides into a convoluted mess of desire and heartache. The last time I trusted him with my heart, he took off with it down the road without a goodbye. Logically, he was so young; he had no choice, but a phone call or a visit would have let me down easier than just disappearing. Only to reappear years later without a recollection of who I was. I ache for him again, wanting to do all the bad things I shouldn't. It's like his fist grips my soul, entangling us together whether or not I want him to.

Searching the crowd, I instantly find those mismatched eyes checking me out like I'm the prey he's about to pounce on. My damn heart skips a beat when he licks his lips in anticipation. A sultry smirk tugs at his lips, and he nods, saluting me with his beer bottle. Try as I might, I can't force back the smile from my lips.

If I'm going to dip my toes into poisonous water, I had better make it good and fucking hot. I may not honestly believe his intentions are pure, but I'm all about living in the present. Fuck the future. Fuck the past. This is where it's at. He's here. I'm here. And if he breaks my heart into a million pieces, then so be it.

Breaking the intense stare, I huff if I can't handle a look without wetting my damn panties. How am I supposed to handle him kneeling in my office? Shit. I shake my head, turn to the bustling bar, and instruct another worker to stand guard at the door.

"All good?" I shout, leaning over the bar toward Ode. My hips dig into the edges of the bar, and my feet dangle off the floor.

Ode grins, slinging two bottled beers at the men standing beside me. Sweat beads on her brow, but she looks happier than ever with a glow on her cheeks.

"All good," she says with a wink, taking their cash. She smirks when they walk away, stuffing her tip down the front of her bra. "It's been a happening night tonight, boss lady!" she says with a genuine grin. "I can't believe the number of tips I'm getting. You did damn good bringing them in!" She nods toward the ladies rocking out on stage.

Some of the weight eases off my shoulders again, and I swear I can breathe for the first time tonight. Since Ma told me about her diagnosis and how her doctor's visit went, I've felt the entire world on my damn back. Not only do I have to carry our household now, but I have to worry about her health, too.

Ode grabs my hand, squeezing my fingers in hers with affection. The woman staring back at me is not my best friend right now; she's playing the part of my dotting sister. Of course, not by blood—by bond. "You're a good manager, Riv. I swear to God, as much as I want you to stay around, you'll get out of here and live your damn dreams. CaliState, here she comes! You better make room for River Blue West!" A small smile pulls at my lips, and I squeeze her hand in return, letting the terrible full name slide by. Just this time. Because, yeah. I might just live my damn dreams, after all.

"I'll bring ya with me, babe!" I shout back with a giggle, and she releases my hand, taking another order.

"Nah, bitch! I'm good here. You go live your California dream. I'll stay here, living my dream," she shouts back with a grin, winking when the other bartender, Marcus, passes by, giving me a thumbs up.

"Thanks so much for the night, Central City!!" I grin, watching the six-foot-tall red-headed woman banshee screech through the microphone. She stirs up the crowd, promising she'll be back for the second half of her set after a thirty-minute break.

I smile when she approaches the bar and comes right toward me with intent. She taps the bar, grinning with a wild look dancing in her green eyes.

"You!" she shrieks, pointing directly at me. "This place is amazing!" she says, looking me up and down until her brows furrow. "You know, for a manager, you're kinda tiny," she quips with a tiny laugh.

I snort, shaking my head. "Yeah, well, thanks, I guess?"

Pursing my lips, I inspect my five-six self and shrug. "Maybe you're just kinda tall," I joke back, leaning back until I can look her in the eyes.

She barks out a laugh, throwing her curls over her shoulder. "Touché, little manager!"

Sorcha and I met at a May-Field festival at the end of last year. It was the time of my life getting to see so many unsigned bands performing on ten stages in the middle of nowhere. There was nothing but music, food trucks, and tents. Call us hippies or whatever; I never wanted to leave that place. But it brought me something better and the connections I knew I needed. I met with every band as they mingled with fans and took pictures. I got their email addresses and phone numbers, showing them the card I had made up for the event. It was the event that pushed me into the manager's position. It was the same event I saw those four bumbling idiots from Whispered Words playing their songs for the first time. They stumbled through everything, looking like nervous wrecks on stage.

Their music called to me, though. There was something about Kieran's voice that had always drawn me to him. Even under the stars as a kid, he made my insides flip inside and out.

"Hi," his deep voice echoes the large speakers, echoing across the cornfields surrounding us.

The sun beams down on our sweaty bodies, but we don't mind. Vendors line up along the outskirts of the festival, selling drinks and food. People have popped tents up in the fields to the left, hiding from the sun, but still able to hear the various acts performing today.

My breaths shudder in my chest, looking up at the tall stage. I haven't seen any of them since they graduated two years ago and ran off into the sunset together. I had heard they started a band in Kieran's garage, but I never thought I'd see them perform. Let alone here, of all places.

I swallow hard, rooting my feet to the ground. Raising my hand, I block the sun from my eyes, squinting to glimpse the man who was once the stars to my moon—my other half. The boy who played me melodies for the hell of it and calmed my nerves. Here he is in all his rock star glory, waltzing across the tall, curtained stage.

His jet-black hair plasters to his sweaty forehead as the sun beams down. Lifting an arm, he pumps his fist into the air, capturing everyone's attention when he rips his shirt off. Holy mother of pickles on hamburgers—he's ripped as hell.

"We're Whispered Words," Kieran rasps with raw confidence into the microphone. *"I'm Kieran."* His smirk is visible from a mile away. *"This is Asher, Rad..."* My heart pumps double time at the hero sitting half-naked behind the drum kit, waving to the crowd with that glorious smirk. *"And Callum."* Kieran finishes their introductions, twirling back toward the stage. Not once does he fumble over his words, like he's done it a million times before.

"And this is our first ever live performance," Rad interrupts, stealing the microphone from Kieran with a light laugh.

"So, give us a little grace?" Kieran asks, surveying the crowd with a grin.

The crowd cheered, chanting them into their very first bomb of a performance. Kieran had several microphone issues, cutting out his beautiful voice. But they played on, earning whistles and claps after the twenty-minute performance. I knew then they'd become something big.

And that's how they came here. It's how I knew they were playing and garnering attention from the public. And why I secretly used my full name to get them to come. I thought maybe Kieran would see it and recognize it, but he didn't. To him, I was always River Blue—never River West.

"Seriously though, River! You didn't tell me how many people would be here. I swear we've never sold out a show before, and this...this is...beyond my expectations. My guitarist, Libby, swore we shouldn't come here, but I promised her I had met a Kick-Ass representative in you! And see! Libby, you bitch!" Libby meanders forward with a grin, nodding with a chuckle.

"Yeah, yeah, Sore, you really showed me," she says in a sing-song tone, leaning against the bar. "You must be the little manager that convinced this bitch to bring us here. Love this place; it's so unique!" she says, jerking her head to all the décor hung up on the walls and the dark skull wallpaper behind me.

"That is me," I say with a smile, eyeing Asher as he makes his way beside them, examining them up close with the same calculating stare he always wears. "So, what can I get you guys to drink?"

Sorcha bites her lip, grinning when Libby rolls her eyes. "We'll both have a Jack and Coke. It's our on-stage tradition."

"Two Jack and Cokes, you got it," I say, nodding to Marcus as he stands beside me, mixing their drinks before I can even move.

"And for you?" I ask, raising a brow. Asher watches our exchange with indifference. But if there's anything I've come to learn about the elusive frowny-faced jackass is, he's always watching and taking every ounce of information in.

"Three Blue Moons and a fucking Pina Colada, and add theirs to our tab while you're at it," he says, staring into my eyes but nods to the two women gaping at him.

The girls' eyes widen, but they thank him anyway and take a sip of their drinks.

"So, what's next for you guys? You have to be hitting big soon, right? You guys are fucking amazing!" I gush, leaning my elbow on the counter with a grin, soaking in their magnetic presence.

Marcus works around me, prepping the boys' drinks and sliding them one by one to Asher.

"Funny you should ask!" Sorcha says, downing the rest of her drink in one gulp. "We haven't really announced it yet, buttttttt! I figure we can tell you." She grins more, waggling her eyebrows.

"Battle of the Bands," Libby says, taking a little sip.

"In California," Sorcha says with a squeal, jumping in place.

"Battle of the Bands?" I ask, my heart thumping a little in my chest.

Those types of competitions are so damn invigorating. The raw power from every band performing on stage, competing for the title of winner. Sometimes small venues hold the competition. But other times? It's big names calling bands from all across the world to compete for a record deal and a little cash on the side. Each of those bands holds more talent than I have in my pinky. It's stiff competition, but there's no doubt in my mind they'd win. Hands fucking down, Sorcha deserves it.

"Oh yeah! It'll be hot as hell. California and the winner gets a record deal with West Records," Sorcha says, as my heart falls into my ass. "And a million dollars."

"West Records?" I sputter, moving my eyes between the girls as they nod in confirmation.

Thankfully, they don't see me slip up when I choke on my spit.

Throughout our correspondence, with me begging them to come here—they saw my last name. I'd never admit it to Ode or anyone else, but I sometimes use it to my advantage. Only when I want to score the best bands in the area.

"How do you get into that?" Asher asks, with a rigid posture.

A scary-ass smile crosses his lips, and he tilts his head, almost baring all his teeth. Half of me expects fangs to descend from his gums and for him to go on some sort of psycho-killing spree. Asher's fingers flex around one of the beer bottles he's clinging to.

"Invitation," Libby says, furrowing her brows, looking Ash up and down. "We didn't sign up or anything."

"Invitation only, huh?" I muse, trying to keep my voice even. "So, you didn't have to put in an application?"

There's no way in hell I'd tell anyone that my brother's owned that place and that they were the current CEOs of West Records. Nope. No way. People far and wide have already tried that route. They always ask if I still talked to that side of the family or if I had seen my dad recently—what a bunch of friggin' users. Thankfully,

West is such a common last name it never occurs to strangers that I'm a part of THAT family. Well, sometimes.

"Oh yeah, it'll be at the KC Club this upcoming winter in February. They just announced the invited bands a few hours ago online. It's their first, and it'll be the biggest we've ever been to. We got a personal email from The West's themselves, inviting us to compete after they heard us on The Dot and saw a performance on YouTube. I guess playing all these festivals and events has really helped," Sorcha says with a knowing grin. "And this place, of course," she says with a wink, setting her empty glass down. "Thanks for the drinks, but we have a second half to get to now." She and Libby wave at me, returning to the rest of her band on stage.

"Need anything else?" I ask Asher as he stares off at the girls climbing back on stage.

Sorcha's voice again comes over the speakers, almost louder this time. The crowd goes nuts, loving the intro to one of their most famous songs.

"No," he shouts in an even tone, watching the two girls rock out on stage with appreciation. "Thanks, River." I rear back when he tips his head like a gentleman. "For everything." And then he fucking winks at me. WINKS!

"Uh, you're welcome?" I ask, twisting my face when a grin plays at the edges of his lips.

"I'll see you later." He taps the bar, almost sounding like he is flirting with me. Uh? Was he? No. There's no way. He's been nothing but a mouthy jerk this entire time, and yet my stupid heart flutters at his simple thanks and stupid wink. Mmhmm, you stupid organ. Stop fluttering at the sight of that douchebag's smile.

I sigh, leaning my chin on my palm when he gets lost in the crowd and swallowed whole. My family's legacy is something dreams are made of. If I was a part of it, that is. Zeppelin and Seger West are the most influential figures in the music industry right now, running West Records, a company every rock musician hopes they can sign with, better than their father did before them. They've taken the time to add new acts to their roster and have boosted their worth by millions in only a few short years. Or maybe it's their weird relationship with their wife. Yeah—their—wife. I've seen the magazine articles about their poly relationship with her and the two other dudes involved. Who could handle that many guys, anyway?

My eyes drift to the four boys again, huddling together. I wonder what it would be like to have so many guys in one place? And the sex? Jesus, talk about a good time. I've had my fair share of threesomes and added two more dicks into the mix? Yeah, I could totally see that. But a relationship? I wonder how well that would work out. Do they ever get jealous? Enjoy sharing?

I shake my head. There's no time to think about that right now.

ASHER

The surprise in her eyes when I didn't snark back and actually thanked her stalls my steps. Peeking over my shoulder, I watch her with rapt attention, surveying her every move. The crowd around me jumps in place to the music, concealing me from her view and hiding my watchful eyes. I'd be a liar if I said the tiny brunette didn't fascinate me. I couldn't force myself around her if she were anything like Tessa or Sara, who are as unbearable as they come.

Her long brown hair sits past her shoulders, revealing her dainty neck, marked by my stupid brother. A big, red splotch sits in plain view, not unnoticed by everyone. Men walk by, eyeing her like a delicious meal—only stopping themselves from engaging when they see the mark. They could think one or two ways about it. Either she's easy, or she's unavailable. As it is, Kieran watches her every fucking move like a possessive boyfriend ready to defend her honor. I'm surprised the boys kept him seated when I promised them drinks. Since she came back into the picture, he's taken this game a little too seriously. Sure, we need River in our corner to aid us with our bright, famous future. But Kieran's become obsessive, possessive, and any other red flag under the sun, and it's concerning.

"Your drinks," I say, slipping into the sticky booth with a grimace.

You'd think this place would get cleaned every once in a while, but it appears no one has touched the filth in years. Not that I'm a clean freak by any means. Logistically, if they wanted patrons to enjoy their time here more, they'd clean more than once a year.

Kieran's eyes drift toward the bar again, and he growls, threatening to get up as a man approaches her, and she smiles.

Fucking smiles at the guy, and now my best friend is about to lose his shit. His fingers curl into fists at the sight of them.

"Calm down," I say in a monotone voice, holding back the tension rising in my throat.

River's smile lights up the damn room, disarming every man in a fifty-foot radius. My damn heart thunks against my ribs as she glides behind the bar, taking care of everyone's drink orders.

"I'll calm down when they stop staring at what's mine," he grunts, pouring mouthfuls of beer down his throat.

"Ours," Rad reminds him with a drunken grin. "You think she'll let me join you in the office tonight? I can keep her quiet when you rail her from behind. God, just imagine the gag I could make her." I take a deep breath, trying not to imagine the scene he implanted in my head. But yet, my dick twitches in my jeans, proving he's very interested in the tiny annoyance named River.

"Ours?" Callum asks, shifting in his seat. A deep red invades his cheeks when he looks between us with uncertainty and a frown.

Oh, Callum. You have much to learn. We may have never shared before, but it's not something I'm opposed to, especially with her.

"She may be your perfect match, Cally Boy," Rad barks out, laughing.

Callum licks his lips, staring over in her direction. He takes in every move she makes behind the bar until she disappears into the back. One long breath blows from between his lips, and his brows furrow. The gears in his brain work double time until she emerges from the back again and greets more customers. His body physically relaxes, and a slight grin tugs at his lips. In River's presence, he seems to unwind from his usually tense behavior. River appears to be the balm that is slowly unraveling our dear Callum.

"That was our game, right?" I ask, taking a sip of my beer. "Make her fall for us and then coax her into talking to her father for us?" I raise a brow at the boys around the table, who stare at me like I'm fucking crazy.

I am fucking crazy. But I'm so goddamn desperate to get out from under my father's clutches. It's bad enough he's financially holding us hostage and taunting us with the means to leave him for good.

But fuck. Maybe we aren't doing enough. As I stare at the girl working her ass off behind the bar, the realization sinks like lead in my gut. We haven't resorted to any other measure to get out of our situation. Sure, we could get extra jobs and save up that way. We could pawn our valued belongings—even if my father keeps a sharp eye on all our possessions. We could do so much more than we are. But it seems like every solution we've come up with has failed us on every level.

Two years ago, we made a deal. Since most of us are stuck here—Callum and Rad pledged to make the band any spare money we needed while Kieran and I were forced to get degrees. Even if college anchored us to this place with no escape right now, in the future, we'd be out of here with a better future on the horizon. We still have time to make our great escape. We'll be out of here if only we can last one more miserable year under the same roof as our father. My stomach sinks whenever Nigel Montgomery crosses my mind, bringing me back to the darkest days of my life.

"Emergency services. What is the nature of your call?" asks the woman from the other side.

Every inch of me shakes, jostling the phone against my face. Tears well in my eyes and burn down my cheeks.

"My mommy," I mutter into the phone through a hiccup.

"What's wrong with your mommy?" the woman asks in a softer tone.

"She's not moving. She's just laying in bed there...." I roll my lips together, stepping toward the woman lying in bed. "There's something in her arm," I choke out. "Mommy! Wake up!" I shout, forgetting the phone on the ground. "Mommy!" I cry more, dropping to my knees.

That night the men in white uniforms took her away, and my dad locked me in my bedroom for three days without explanation. I pounded and begged him to come back and set me free, but all I got in return was three meals and water bottles. I wanted my mom above all else. I needed to see her and hug her. She had to get okay.

When my dad finally opened my door, it was the day after her funeral.

"You see what happens to bad boys?" he asks, kneeling in front of me with one single rose between his fingers.

"Mommy?" I choke out.

"She's dead, son," he says in a low voice. "You saw what happened?" When I nod, his grin grows across his face, and he nods without further explanation.

The feel of my hair beneath my fingers is the first clue I've zoned out, falling into the terrible tragedies of my youth. Horrific events my father executed under my little nose. Something I had no idea about until I was a teenager. Everything my mother ever owned was burned in the fire pit as he celebrated his win of finally peeling himself away from her. And as for me? I cried myself to sleep every night, earning a beating for every tear I shed. It wasn't until Kieran and his mom moved in; did I get a reprieve from his abuse. He only had more bodies to pound his fist into, instead of mine.

I blink when Kieran stares daggers in my direction, burning holes through my head.

"I'm not playing any fucking games. She's mine," Kieran says matter-of-factly with a sharp nod, exposing his teeth like he'll bite me open if I suggest otherwise.

"Share the goods, bro. River is mine too. I want to splash her titties with my cum and..." Rad grunts when Callum puts his hand over his mouth, shaking his head.

The expression lining Callum's face gives his true feelings away. He didn't stop Rad because he was disgusted with his overly expressive words. It's desire sitting in the depths of his eyes when he peeks at her again with interest, not in disgust. Not with the way his blush deepens, if that's even possible.

Eventually, Callum will decide who the perfect girl is to lose his v-card to, and then he can move on from his embarrassment of sex. Or the opposite sex. Never have I seen a grown man fumble over his words as much as Cal. Despite his good looks, he's been more reluctant than ever to reach out to women and talk to them the older he gets. I suppose his past may play a part in his decisions.

"Oh my god!" I cringe when Tessa and Sara squeal beside our booth, trying to squeeze in with us.

"Not tonight," I bark, taking a swig of my beer.

"But, Asher, baby," Tessa purrs in my ear, rubbing her hand over my shoulder.

"I said not tonight," I growl, catching her wrist and peeling her away. "Not in the mood."

"It's that Central slut, isn't it?" she hisses, earning a growl from Kieran.

"We're not interested. And I'd suggest you not call River names if you know what's good for you," I say, narrowing my eyes at her until she grabs Sara and huffs away.

One day, Tessa will understand we're no longer interested in her company and haven't been for a long time. Somehow, she's been too oblivious to understand, but I feel she'll get the picture now that we have our sights set on the woman across the room. Tessa has run through every person on this planet, hoping to get a little extra. It's girls like her who make my teeth clench at night. They're always looking for something extra like marriage, kids, and a bank account to go with it.

"So long, tiny tots!" Rad calls after her over the music.

After another hour of Sorcha's band playing, the other squeaky bartender jumps on stage, taking their place. Looking at my watch, I frown at the late time and shake my head. We've been cooped up in this corner for so long that I almost forgot what Sorcha spoke of at the bar. Battle of the damn bands. Maybe if we make it through that avenue, we won't need River to help us. But peeking at Kieran, Rad, and Callum again—that will not happen.

"Last call!" the bouncy bartender squeals through the microphone on stage. Throwing her mess of curls all over the place with every step, she grins down at the patrons. "Get your last drinks and pay your tab. You don't have to go home, but you sure as shit can't stay here. Say it with me, folks..." she says, pointing toward a sign above the stage.

"Get the fuck out!" the remaining crowd chants as one unit. They lift their glasses in the air and drink the last of their drinks for the night.

I blink at the small stage at the back of the bar. Dark curtains hide the small backstage, where I'm sure Sorcha and her band of women converge, cooling off after a show well done. My heart pounds when I remember the rush I felt jumping on that stage. It's the one place I can let go of my rising tension and need to flee. It's either that or running away from my issues on foot toward the only woman who ever gave a damn about me. I grind my teeth, taking a deep breath. Every worry in my life piles higher and higher on my shoulders.

My calculating eyes drift across the room toward the object of our newfound obsession—our ticket out of here. And the only reason I even agreed to come to this utter shithole tonight. Her. The girl with the perfect last name. The girl with our way out of this town and into the arms of a record deal—hopefully.

When Sorcha mentioned West records, I watched River's nonexistent reaction. Her facial expressions barely moved, but I caught the slight twist of her face and the hate firing behind her mossy green eyes. If I had to wager a guess, River West hates her family with a fiery passion, which doesn't bode well for us and our plan. If we expect to use her connections, then I don't think we're going to succeed. Not that way, at least. There has to be another way.

I can practically taste our future success on the tip of my tongue, and the cravings come back tenfold, churning in my gut. We need to leave and get out as a band of brothers running toward success. All before my father gets some bright idea about me taking over his company when I graduate from college in May. There's no way in hell I'll ever settle into a nine-to-five—but it's what he's depending on and what he's been grooming me for since I was born. I'm his only son, and in turn, I'm the only person for the job. But I'll be fucked if I step foot inside his business. It's not going to happen. The moment my college degree hits my hand after graduation, I'm gone. But it's never a bad idea to have a fallback degree if shit hits the fan with the band. Wherever I'm going in the future, I'll be prepared.

My only solution...is well...her. Some way, somehow, we're going to utilize her in some capacity. Even if Kieran has to propose to River, drag her to California with us, and throw her at West Record's front door. I frown, thinking about our escape plan. We've saved through the years from each of our gigs in an effort to escape this hellhole, but we've never had enough to execute our plan, even with Rad and Callum running a dirt bike track and taking bets. It never seems to be enough to write home about. One day we'll fucking get there. But today is not the day.

With fascination, I watch her from across the room, talking with patrons and laughing with them. One gentleman steps forward, handing her a wad of cash, and she grins, flirting back with the flutter of her eyelashes. Her brown hair hangs past her shoulders now, swaying when she laughs, throwing her head back. From here, I can hear the happy rasp in her voice when she knocks the guy on the shoulder. He nearly falls over from her push but rights himself and grins at her too. I take a drink of my beer, but I'm really drinking in my newest conquest.

"What the fuck?" Kieran hisses again as Rad holds him down. "Let me fucking go. I'm going to murder him. He's touching what isn't his," he gripes, getting wrestled back into his seat.

Now, how do I make the one girl who won't look my way fall for me? Or slip into bed with me? I think about the quirk of her brow and the confusion earlier when I thanked her for the drinks. Honestly, I'm not an insufferable asshole all the time. Just sometimes. I run my fingers across my forehead, mentally groaning. Okay. I'm an asshole, but sometimes I can't help it. It just comes naturally to me whenever I'm not playing or listening to music. Music is my freedom, and being surrounded by it eases the tension in my chest. I can be wary about River but still execute our plan. Right?

I eye Kieran, the hopeless romantic. He'd do anything to have her as his possession. The image of him hand-feeding her strawberries and swirling whipped cream all over her body comes to mind. It's pleasant imagery, and I'll give him that. Somehow, I don't think Kieran will ever give her up. Not without a fight. But for now, his behavior benefits us. She may want to hate him, but she can't keep her eyes from us. And that's what I wanted all along.

I bite my bottom lip, looking at Callum, who sits back in the booth with his eyes closed and earbuds in, ignoring our presence. Every few minutes, he peeks his eyes open, staring at her like a magnet pulling him in.

Tonight, it was like pulling his molars to get him to come out instead of staying on the couch and playing Xbox with Rad. They've had some sort of weird competition going on with some game called Angel Warrior for weeks. But now, I think he's glad he ventured out. He's not the type to hang at bars with crowds of people.

Rad talks a million miles a minute, the rum hitting him harder since starting his fourth damn drink. He grins and laughs, talking to people behind us, around us, and to anyone who will listen to his stupid stories. Rad never stops talking. The only time he seals his lips is when he's macking on some chick and has his tongue down her throat.

And my dear stepbrother can't stop his fascination from festering to the surface by keeping a keen eye on the short and demanding little manager flitting around the bar.

A loud snort pulls me from my musings, and I turn, looking toward the band sitting behind us. Sorcha and her merry band of women converge after a long, kickass set. They laugh and drink in celebration of a show well done. They're a well-oiled machine, playing together like one person, and their music proves it. They have merch on a table near the back of the bar. They're on the damn Dot app and have the most crucial person supporting them. A manager. Someone to schedule these things. Someone so organized, he got them a gig here and with West Records. We have Callum. He does most of our gigs. But to have someone else work on it as we make music would benefit us immensely.

I clench my jaw, pulling out my phone. Battle of the Bands. Hosted by West Records. Skimming the instructions, I take it all in.

Invitations have been sent to fifteen select bands from across the country. Submitted entries are being accepted for any unsigned bands starting September 1st—November 1st. We will select only five bands from the entries, and only twenty will compete. A one-million-dollar prize will be awarded, and a three-year record deal. December 15th, the Battle of the Bands will kick off at the KC Club in East Point, California.

Qualifications include: music present on the streaming app The Dot in the form of an EP, performance footage available on YouTube, a healthy following on ClockTok, and a prominent social media following.

I scroll through our meager social media pages and growl at the low number of likes on each of them. How are we supposed to bring those numbers up in just a few months?

My body jolts up when a loud bang draws my attention to the middle of the empty floor, and my brows raise. River scowls at the broken glasses littering the floor and shakes her head. She's two seconds away from telling the drunken idiot off but takes a breath, holding her professional composure. I have to commend her for tongue-holding abilities.

"Watch where you're going, bitch."

I'm on my feet before I know what I'm doing and marching over there before Kieran can climb over Callum. A yelp and curses happen in the booth I vacated. My eyes narrow on the polo-wearing douche canoe standing before River, looking at her like she's the scum of the earth, when he was the one who knocked drunkenly into her; his body sways on the spot.

"Fucking Central Cunt," he hisses again, slurring his words and rocking back and forth with unfocused eyes.

"The fuck you say?" I growl, scooping the man by the shirt and bringing his face directly into mine. "Did you just say what I think you just fucking said?" I spit, shaking him with every word.

The stench of day-old beer and cigarettes sends bile up my throat and knots in my stomach but realizing who this douchebag is knocks me back. Bradley Bradford. Stupid name for a stupid cunt. His father's the lovely mayor of this town, who conveniently keeps his rap sheet buried deep. I continue to hold him by the scruff of his shirt.

"Is that any way to talk to a lady?" I snarl, exposing my teeth.

"Down, Killer," River murmurs from beside me, furrowing her brows. The warmth of her hand lingers on my chest when she holds me back. My breath shudders in my chest when her warm fingers dig into my flesh, and goosebumps erupt. An instant connection puts my hair on end, and a ringing fills my ears. Her glassy green eyes stare up at me in warning. "I really need to invest in holy water. Did your demon disappear?"

My eyes pop wide when she suggests...I've been... "I'm not possessed, you little brat," I hiss, ignoring the tingling on my chest from her touch, igniting something deep in me, but I shake it off. I have a douchebag to obliterate for thinking he could even speak to her like that.

My attention snaps back to the scumbag currently turning fifty shades of red and fuming. Bradley's fist raises shakily in the air until I toss him on his back, rejoicing in the useless air pouring from his lungs.

"The power of Christ compels you," she murmurs, side-eyeing me with furrowed brows. "Christo!" she hisses, leaning close enough to examine my eyes. "You didn't flinch...." She cocks her head, a grin exploding across her lush lips. "Worked for Dean." She shrugs.

I fight the smile threatening to pull at my lips and swallow my laugh by looking away. Me? Evil? Have I been that much of an asshole over the last few days? Fuck. Yeah. I have been. My lips pop open, ready to retort and apologize for my actions. But Kieran swoops in to save the damn day. This could have been my chance to show her I'm not the demonic assbag she thinks I am. I suppose I'll have to rectify that one day at a time.

I'm not an insufferable asshole all the time, just occasionally. It's the facade I put on to deal with the world—especially my father.

Show an ounce of weakness, and he picks it apart. His fist alone taught me too many hard lessons to soften to the world. But there's something about River West that softens my resolve and makes me want to throw caution to the wind and unwind. And that's what terrifies me.

"You okay, River Blue?" Kieran asks, wrapping an arm around her shoulders and pulling her into his chest.

I sigh, wishing I was the one comforting her. But what do I have to offer, anyway? Kieran has a rapport with her. Being his long-lost friend, my asshole father brainwashed him into forgetting and all. She'll fall to her damn knees again for him. But for me? She'll light me on fire just to get warm.

"Bradley Bradford," Rad whistles, standing above him with his arms crossed. "And my favorite lady," Rad says through a drunken, dreamy smile, looking at her with envy, nestled in Kieran's arms. "Don't worry, Sugar Tits! We'll kick this piece of shit to the sidewalk." Rad scrunches his nose, grinding his teeth.

Informative. Rad doesn't get angry quickly, but at the sight of this man—he's infuriated. To the naked eye, you wouldn't be able to tell. But to me? Well, his curled fists, rigid muscles, and silent snarl tell a very long story. Bradley Bradford did something wrong in Rad's eyes, and I'll get to the bottom of it.

"Piece of rapist shit," Rad hisses, grabbing Bradley by the shirt, causing him to stumble over his drunken feet, and dragging him toward the front door. He grunts, trying as hard as he can to drag the flailing idiot out. But all two-hundred and fifty pounds of Bradley protests. Rad tosses his hands in the air with frustration. "Help?" Rad says, narrowing his drunken eyes at us. Looking around, I eye the surrounding area looking for the bouncers I know exist, but I find none for help. Some fucking good they are they can't even protect the one person they should. Well, fine, it's our duty now.

"Ugh. I don't need you guys to do this. You!" River snipes, removing Kieran's arm from her shoulder, and points directly at Bradley, who is trying to stand on his wobbly feet. I bite back a smile when a wet spot forms on the front of his jeans. He groans, slumping against the front of the stage. That's right, you utter waste of space, pee your pants like a child. "Get the fuck out of my bar, man."

Bradley chuckles like he has a chance and stumbles forward directly into my arms. "Get the fuck off me," he slurs, pushing against my chest.

"Not happening," I growl, dragging his thrashing body out the front door and literally tossing him onto the sidewalk.

"And don't come back here," River says, shaking her head. A paleness takes over her face when she pushes past us and waltzes back into the bar without a word of thanks.

"If I ever catch you talking to, touching, or even thinking about her, I'll rip your scrotum in half. Fucking leave before I do it," Kieran hisses, popping his knuckles directly above Bradley, who groans, rolling around on the sidewalk.

Well, that's one way to threaten a guy who touches the girl you're currently obsessed with.

"Fuck, I'm going to see how she is," Kieran grumbles, swiping a hand down his face.

"She's a big girl," I say, raising a brow. "I'm sure she's fine."

"She will be in a minute," Rad says, rubbing his hand together. "I'm about to gag her into next week," he cackles, running back into the bar like a kid marching down the stairs on Christmas Day.

Kieran stares after him, shaking his head with a frown.

"Before you go to pound town," I murmur, pulling my phone from my pocket. "I wanted to share a little tidbit I picked up today. It was just announced at like 2 a.m." I grin, shoving my phone into his waiting hands. I can tell by the sour look on his face that he's not impressed that I'm holding him up. But it blows into a grin when he reads the rules of Battle of the Bands. "To qualify for Battle of the Bands, we need an EP and an entry video, and having our own merch would help our chances." Excitement spears through me at the chance to finally get there.

"Battle of the fucking Bands," he muses, scrolling through my phone, and nods.

"Imagine we get her to help with all this," I murmur, gesturing toward the list of requirements.

Callum nods and licks his lips, abashedly looking toward the bar with a red tint enveloping his cheeks. "We get all that; then we can get the hell away from here."

"And her?" Kieran asks like the knight in shining armor he is.

I raise a brow at his meaning and shrug. "What about her?" I ask calmly, but I know exactly what he's going to say.

We went after her for a reason; we can't abandon ship now. And hell, maybe I don't want to jump into the churning sea without a safety net to catch us in the end. But there's something about River that draws me into her flame, burning me whole.

"If she gets to know us and falls for us, she can help us achieve all this, and then we make it to the Battle of the Bands? What next? What if we get signed? We can..." Kieran trails off, biting into his bottom lip with unease.

He doesn't want to leave her here in the dust. With his obsession growing every second, he wants to take her with us. I can see it in his pleading eyes. And who am I to deny my brother? Even if it's just soothing him until the time comes. From a mile away, I can see the distraction River is going to bring to us in the future. She'll pull my brothers apart as they eat away at her attention, begging for more bones.

"You want to what? Bring her along, then?" I ask, rubbing my chin, placating every worry he has inside of him. Kieran hyper-fixates on things, obsessing until it's all he can think about. And that's what River is—a hyper fixation. "I suppose it could work. Imagine showing up to West Records with an actual West," I chuckle, but if anything, I placate myself.

We can continue this charade with those facts in mind. River West will serve us well either way. Whether on her glorious knees, sucking cock... I shake my head. Fuck. She's infecting me, too, but maybe I want to be full of her poison.

Callum shrugs, trying to look as nonchalant as possible, but he fails. A spark ignites in his gray eyes as he looks back toward the bar again, and a grin spreads across his jovial face.

"She's our ticket out of here," Callum whispers with sincerity. "From what I've observed, she's organized. She works two jobs, goes to school, and completely manages this bar. If we can gain her trust, then she'll want to help us organize on her own." He nods, rolling his lips together with guilt.

My lip twitches when he narrows his eyes on me because he stole the thoughts directly from my mind.

"Exactly," I say, pointing a finger at him. "That's exactly what we can offer her, too. A way out."

"You're staying?" I raise a brow, a red glow lighting up Kieran's cheeks, and he nods.

"You bet your ass I'm staying," he says with a grin, rubbing his hands together. "I made a promise, and I'm going to deliver on it." With that, my brother glides off through the front doors, presumably in the direction of her office again. Only this time, we won't barge in and disrupt their time together.

I wave, taking a deep breath. I can't leave Kieran and Rad here. "You want me to drop you off at home while I wait for them?"

Callum's cheeks tint a darker shade of red, and he shakes his head, clearing his throat. "I have to go to the bathroom," he rasps in a low voice, pointing toward the bar.

"I'll be in the Tahoe then whenever you're done," I murmur when he scurries away into the bar without a second glance.

Funnily enough, I don't think he's going just to use the bathroom.

Turning on my heel, I march to the Tahoe parked across the street and climb in, patiently waiting for my friends to get done with their fuckfest and come home with me. I'll try not to think about Kieran and Rad sharing her. Just the mention of Rad gagging her has my dick hard and pressing against my jeans.

Fuck blue balls, man.

KIERAN

"Get on your damn knees and worship me." Her voice hums through my mind on repeat, exciting me even more. A deep ache pulsates in my balls, begging me to touch and release the pent-up tension that has been building since yesterday. My dick stands hard and heavy inside my jeans, begging to spring free.

But I don't dare relieve myself. Or move from my position on my knees, digging into the uncomfortable floor.

Closing my eyes, memories flood my mind from the last time I angrily barged my way in here and took all my after-performance frustrations out on her body. Anger fueled my decisions, but desire held me here.

She held me there.

My River Blue.

How could I have forgotten her for so long? It's like Asher's dad swooped into my life and erased everything before the age of ten. Only now, after seeing her again, do I remember my time in the shitty apartment I was raised in as a kid. The time we spent together under the stars as we hid from our moms.

"When is she coming?" Rad whines, interrupting my peace.

Shifting in her office chair with his eyes closed, his forehead leans against the wood desk. All the alcohol he consumed comes back to bite him in the ass.

Secretly, I hope he falls asleep long before she walks into this room. She's mine. All fucking mine. I'll tattoo my name on her ass if that's what it takes. The last thing I want to do is fucking share her with anyone else. But I know Rad. A little too well.

The prospect of having her command my every move has me aching in my jeans. But it excites Rad more. Don't get me wrong; he likes to participate. But watching from a distance and getting himself off will suffice.

After seeing the knife against my junk, I'm sure he locked himself in his room for hours, pleasuring himself to the image. He moaned "Oh, River," more times than I can count. Not that I was listening or anything. But that's what happens when we all hang out at their house, shooting the shit.

"Hopefully soon and on my face," I mumble, shifting my knees and trying to get comfortable.

It's only been five minutes since she waltzed back into the bar, and we came here.

"Mmm," he hums, "just like she did at the record store. God, that was the hottest thing I've ever seen. I can't wait to take her out in public and make her come around my cock."

My head jerks back at his comment. I'm two seconds from bashing his face in for even thinking about her like that. The imagery of him and her in public tingles my damn balls. She's mine. But maybe not just mine. River will go where I go; I'll make sure of that. I'll leash her if I have to and shove her in my damn trunk, kicking and screaming. Maybe Asher had a point with the whole—make her fall for all of us—thing. If she does, then she'll willingly help us and come with us whenever we can make it out of here.

"Just be careful," I mumble, keeping my eyes on the carpet.

"Always careful," Rad assures me with a sleepy yawn. "Can't scare her off yet. Ash's dumbass obviously has some plans for her."

"Yeah," I huff. "And as much as I don't want to admit it, his plan is pretty solid. But he didn't account for one thing."

"Yeah? And what's that?" Rad asks, stifling a yawn behind his hand.

"Me," I say in a demanding voice, curling my fingers into fists.

Rad chuckles. "Yeah, that's my Kieran," he says softly. "We'll make sure our pretty girl doesn't get heartbroken. She'll come with and give me a shit ton of Radalicious babies."

I snort. "Babies, dude?"

"You heard me," he slurs, tripping over his tongue. "Just imagine her tits." He sighs like he's dreaming about the day he can knock her up, and fuck, it's not a bad idea.

"We're not knocking her up, dickbag. That's just...." I trail off when images of her in my bed with my cum leaking from her pussy, and my fingers pushing it back in. "Fuck," I mumble, palming myself through my jeans.

"See," he says, barking out a laugh. "It's hot as fuck."

I don't raise my eyes when the office door opens and shuts, keeping my eyes on the carpet.

"Heya, Pretty Girl, fancy meeting you here. You ready to get naked?" Rad says with such enthusiasm I can't help a snort. He must be awake now at the sight of her.

"I didn't order an audience," she says through a tired sigh.

"You're tired," I say, keeping my voice soft when her beat-up chucks come into view. I nearly cum in my pants when her fingers lightly brush through my hair, and shivers run down my back.

"And you're kneeling," she says, testing the waters and giving my hair a yank.

"Are you staying?" she asks Rad, but her voice only gives away the aching exhaustion she must be feeling.

"Oh my, Pretty Girl," he purrs softly with excitement. The chair makes a squeaking sound, and his footsteps come toward us leisurely. I'm sure not to scare her off. "Only if you'll have me," he says in all seriousness. "Only if you want me to watch or touch you or whatever you want." I can hear the grin on his lips and the sincerity in his voice. He'd leave if she wanted him to. He'd do anything she asked, and never without permission.

"Let us take care of you," I mumble, pushing into her fingers. They tease through my hair in soft and gentle strokes, relaxing my entire body.

"Okay," she whispers without hesitation.

Bravely, I sneak a peek through my lashes, watching as Rad overtakes her mouth and shoves his tongue down her throat, claiming what is his. Fury should build in my gut watching them together, but it doesn't. Watching him take what he wants turns me on even more.

River moans, tightening her other hand through his ridiculous mullet, pulling him flush against her body.

"Ah, Pretty Girl," he murmurs against her lips with a pant. "You taste better than I'd ever imagined."

I get harder when his hand drifts toward her tit, and he gently massages it through her shirt, earning small, sexy noises from her throat—the tip of his finger's circles over her achingly hard bud, punishing it between his fingertips. Something I wish I could do right now, but I let her take the lead.

She moans, leaning her forehead against his with heavy breaths. "Fuck," she curses through her swollen lips, tightening her hold on my hair.

"Use us, River," I demand in a deep voice, feeling it the moment her mossy green eyes spear through me with intense heat, boiling my insides to molten levels. "However, you want," I beg, palming myself, trying to keep my dick from showing how desperate I am for her to ride my goddamn face. "Ride my face," I practically moan, wishing she'd take her shorts off and stick her pussy in my face.

She swallows hard as her pupils dilate, nearly blackening her entire eye. "Take off your clothes," she demands with a hunger building in the back of her darkening moss-green eyes.

"And me?" Rad practically begs, palming her tits again with fascination. His dark eyes twinkle with desire, dilating with the need to fuck her senselessly.

Same dude. Same.

"No touching," she says, glancing back at him with authority. Letting us know she's the one in charge and no one else.

He drops his hands and nods with compliance when she says it. Rad would never take a woman against her will or push her limits. He respects everyone. Especially after the girl he helped save years ago, he's been traumatized ever since knowing what she went through and so brutally.

"You only get to watch right now." His Adam's apple bobs, and he nods with understanding, taking a step back.

"You're the queen of this domain, Pretty Girl," he murmurs, taking a step back toward the desk, leaning against it with a cool, relaxed expression. But his eyes zone in on her every move.

I lift on my knees, lifting my shirt over my head. "On your feet," she whispers, putting two fingers beneath my chin. I rise to my feet at the command, nearly coming in my pants, when she flicks the button of my jeans open.

My abdomen jumps under her touch as her fingertips play in the dark happy trail leading to my throbbing dick. If she touches it, I'm going to come in her hand. Jesus. Get a grip, K. You have to last longer than three seconds in her presence. But I guess If there was one woman to take me that far, it'd be River. I'd happily let her destroy my dignity in one stroke. Even in front of Rad. I'd never hear the end of it but fuck it.

"Don't come," she whispers, staring directly into my eyes as she reaches into the depths of my pants and strokes me with heavy pressure, squeezing when she reaches the tip. Her thumb brushes over my weeping slit, spreading my precum.

Fuck.

Yeah. Don't come. Easier said than done. A tingle works down my spine, and I swear my balls tighten when her grip tightens around me. An inhuman noise bubbles in my throat, and I can't help when I toss my head back, and it falls from my lips. Fuck. Shit. This isn't good. I'm going to spew into her hand. Think of something else. Anything else but her hand wrapped perfectly around me....

Earlier today, I made her ride my fingers until she came harder than any woman I've ever met. Her pussy squeezed, clamping down, and marking my fingers as hers to use. The moment I got into the SUV and got home, my dick ached with the most extreme pain, begging me to touch him. He wanted to come in my fist with her memory on my mind. But I refused. I wouldn't come until I was nestled deep inside her cunt.

I grit my teeth when she cups my balls with her other hand in the tight confines of my jeans. My breaths come in short pants, and I swear my balls tighten toward my body, and pre-cum drips from my tip like a faucet. Fuck. Hell. I'm going to blow.

Using my precum, she spreads it all around as her mouth attaches to my nipple and sucks it between her teeth. The sensitive shit lights me on fire, and I jerk in her hand, desperate for more friction.

"If you don't want me to come, you're going to have to stop that," I gasp; my hips thrust forward into her hand repeatedly until I'm basically rutting into her warm palm.

Stars burst behind my eyes. The world around me melts away, leaving just the two of us in this compromising position, with her hand around my dick and that mischievous smirk pulling at the edges of her lips. Every muscle tightens in my body with anticipation. Waiting and waiting for her to make her next move. Waiting and waiting for her to give me permission to finally fucking come.

I heave a heavy breath of disappointment when she pulls her hands away. When her warmth leaves me, I'm begging for more like an addict. My lips pop open, a whine on the tip of my tongue about to beg for more of her touch when she mumbles something, pulling my boxers and jeans down my legs, leaving me to work them over my shoes and toss them aside.

She bites her lip and dips her head, running her tongue over my tip. I blink, staring at the water-stained ceiling, and count to one hundred. If I concentrate on the end of her tongue tracing every protruding vein or the way her lips pop over my tip and suck it into her mouth, I'll cum—everywhere.

"Fuck," Rad rasps from behind me, groaning when she takes me deep in her throat.

I grit my teeth harder, probably cracking a damn tooth in the process. Her throat relaxes and tightens around my tip, and she hums her approval. Fuck. Her forehead meets my abdomen when she takes me in the back of her throat, leaving it there as she hums a damn song.

Hold your shit together, Kieran. Don't let that tempting fucking throat ruin the fun you're about to have.

Her mouth detaches from my dick with a pop, and she stands before me with a heavenly smirk. Her chin glistens with saliva and precum, dripping from her swollen lips into the floor and creating a small wet spot. Her tongue darts out, licking it all up, and she swallows hard.

"Lick it up," she whispers, pointing to the spot on the floor with lustful eyes, awaiting my answer.

My body shivers at her command, goosebumps puckering across my flesh. My eyes flash, darting to the small spot on the ground. Without a second thought, I glide my tongue across our mixed essence and suck it up.

"Good boy," she murmurs, rubbing her fingers through my hair and tightening her grip. With force, she yanks my head back. "Get on your knees," she whispers, lust swimming in the depths of her voice, making it husky with need. "And you stay there." She points to Rad, who hasn't moved a muscle.

"Yes, Pretty Girl," he rasps. "Whatever you say."

I sink to my bare knees again, placing my naked ass on the heels of my shoes.

"On second thought," she says, flicking her eyes to Rad. "Undress me." Rad doesn't have to be told twice when he comes into view behind her, running his hands along the edges of her work uniform. She cranes her neck, allowing his lips to graze her flesh when he pulls at the ends of her shirt and lifts it over her head.

"Jesus," he mumbles, running his fingertips from the middle of her lacy bra, and tracing them back toward the clasp. He visibly swallows when the clasp releases, brings it down her arms, and tucks it into the pocket of his jeans.

"My shorts," she says, kicking off her chucks. They land in a heap near the door, but she never takes her eyes off me.

I bite my lip, my dick throbbing even harder, turning red and purple with need.

"Yes, my Pretty Girl," he murmurs against her skin, flicking the button of her tiny booty shorts and pulling them down her legs. He bends with them, brushing his nose against her bare ass, and groans. "I'm keeping this too," he says, pulling her tiny white thong down her legs and stuffing them into his pocket.

"So fucking gorgeous," I say, brushing a finger up her creamy thigh and around her belly button, deliberately skipping over her dripping pussy. An eye for an eye is what I always say. And in this case, I can't wait to have her begging me to fuck her.

Goosebumps erupt all over her flesh, and she shudders from my touch.

"What do you want to do?" Rad asks against the flesh of her neck, testing the waters when she cranes her neck, allowing him access. Her eyes roll back when he sinks his teeth into her flesh and softly moans. Her hips instantly rock, seeking the pleasure she's about to receive. "You want to fuck him hard? Fuck his face? Hell, fuck my face for all I care. Let us take you to pleasure town."

If I weren't so turned on by the sight of her naked form, I'd roll my eyes at his stupid phrases. Idiot.

"You say the words, and we do it." He emphasizes every word with the squeeze of her tits, fitting perfectly in his calloused hands.

"Kieran," she moans my name like a prayer, and I know this moment will be etched in my memory forever.

"Yeah, River Blue?" I whisper, eager to hear her answer.

"I want to ride your face. Make me cum." And she doesn't have to ask again when I lurch forward, burying my face between her thighs. I groan when the taste of her tangy pussy crosses over my tongue. And if I wasn't an obsessed addict before, I am now. There's no way this woman is ever going anywhere else again. I'll chain her to me and drag her to California. Fuck Ash and his plans. Fuck everything else.

This pussy?

Mine.

This ass?

Mine.

Fuck, she's mine, and I don't even fucking care. My protective, obsessive side flares to life, and a shrine erects, dedicated to her in the back of my mind.

"Kieran," her stifled moan hits me right in the aching dick. I circle my tongue around her throbbing clit and then back to her pussy, plunging it in over and over again. I want to bathe in her juices, and fucking own them all at the same time.

"Here," Rad says, tapping my head, and I back away with a scowl, hating how he interrupted my meal. He nods, showing me what he's doing, and I grin when she squeaks. He lifts her into the air by the backs of her thighs, spreading her pussy out for me just like a dessert. "Good?" he asks her when her head lolls against his shoulder, and she nods with a dreamy grin spreading across her face.

"Yes," she whimpers, reaching to grab my hair. She gently forces my face between her thighs again, and I go to fucking town. I lick and suck, taking everything from her until she's a muffled, screaming mess coming on my tongue. I sit there, licking her clean until her breaths shudder, and she pushes me away.

She swallows hard, closes her eyes, and taps Rad's hands. He gently puts her to her wobbling legs, holding onto her shoulders when she takes a deep breath. I watch with rapt attention when she sinks to her knees and sits before me. Her cheeks flush, and her eyes blow wider than before.

"Fuck me," she whispers, reaching for my face. "Fuck me," she demands again, slowly coming forward until our lips meet. I wrap my fingers around her hair, pulling her harder against me, and moan into her mouth.

She tastes herself, diving her tongue in and out.

"Turn around then," I demand this time, looking deep into her eyes. "Turn around and let me fuck your pussy until you come again, but we have to let Rad watch, yeah?" She swallows hard, nodding at the switch I've given her.

I can be demanding, or I can be submissive. Whichever pleases me, but right now, I need to take control of her. I need to fuck her until she has to use Rad's dick as a gag to stop her from yelling out our names.

She nods to me one last time, letting the exhaustion from the day settle on her face. I see it in her eyes as well, but she still turns around, showing me her perfectly-shaped, round ass. I knead them in my palms, only taking them off when I reach into my pocket and pull out a condom.

"This will be fast and hard," I say through gritted teeth, rolling the condom on my length. "I don't know how much more I can hang on.
You're a fucking goddess. But don't think this will be the last time my cock sinks into your pussy." I groan when I push myself to the hilt, trying to think of anything but her clamping around me. "Now, are you going to leave him hanging?" I ask, stilling before I thrust again.

Her eyes bounce up toward Rad when he sinks to his knees on the carpet. "I can watch if you want," he says, running a finger down her jaw when she digs her fingers into the floor. "I may be an asshole, but I'd never force you to..."

"I want to," she says with demand. "You're going to have to gag me anyway."

Rad's eyes widen at her demand, but he lets her undo his jeans and pop his throbbing cock out. She gives a few tentative strokes, licking his tip, then shoves forward, taking him into the depths of her throat. I take that as my sign, praying to whoever I don't come in five seconds, but I'm pretty sure that's where we're headed.

My hips slam into hers hard and fast, just like I promised. There's no mercy here, especially with this burning need scalding down my spine and tightening my balls. With every thrust I give, it forces her forward, spearing Rad's cock down her throat. Rad's eyes roll into the back of his head when he grabs ahold of her hair and fucks her face with all his might. His hips pound against her gagging face, and saliva falls to the ground, pooling on the floor.

White bright stars take over my vision, and my mouth hangs open, frozen in place when I spill into the condom. My hips continue to rock against hers, savoring the feel of her wrapped around me until Rad groans. He throws his head back, stilling with his dick shoved deep in her mouth. No doubt, spilling himself down her beautiful throat, and she takes every bit of it.

He swallows hard, looking deep into my eyes. And I know the moment his mind goes to "We're super fucked if we have to leave her behind" because it glazes over his eyes, and his jaw sets.

Our plan is solid. We've lured her in. Almost too well. And we've become the suckers.

I shake my head. We're not leaving her behind. She's always on my damn mind like an obsession I can't escape. Soon I'll be waiting outside her apartment with binoculars, making sure no one fucks with her, watching her undress from afar, and jacking my shit in the trees.

Rad licks his lips, gently pulling his length from her mouth. He swipes his thumb along her bottom lip, leaning down to kiss her plump lips gently.

"You've given me a little taste, and now I want the whole menu," he whispers against her lips as I reluctantly pull out of her pussy. Removing the condom, I throw it into the trash.

"Maybe," comes her breathy reply when her body gives out and she curls up on the ground. "But later," she snarks, waving a tired hand in the air. Her eyes close, and she sighs.

He grins, searches the room for his clothes, and gets dressed.

"I only have like two bras, give that back," she says, pointing a finger to the bra dangling from Rad's pocket.

His brows furrow. "Fuck no, Pretty Girl. These souvenirs are for me now." He snorts, shoving them further into his pocket, and bats away her hand.

She frowns, rolling her eyes, snatching the bra from his pocket. Crossing her arms over her bare chest, she shakes her head at him when he yelps, attempting to tackle her. With a laugh, I put a hand on his chest, shaking my head with a grin.

"Just this once," he says with a lazy grin. "Next time, don't wear one; then, I can feel your pretty titties whenever I want." He hums at the thought and nods like that's the best solution.

"Pretty titties?" she mutters to herself, getting to her wobbly feet, and stumbling a bit. She groans, leaning against the wall.

"River Blue," I murmur, coming to her side.

"Give me just a minute. I, uh, have to go to the bathroom," River says with a huff, marching out the door as quickly as she can like her ass is on fire.

A door slams next to us, shaking the walls. Rad wrinkles his nose, staring at the door with big, puppy dog eyes.

"You, uh...think she's okay?" he asks in a low voice, fiddling with the bottom of his shirt. "I didn't push her too far, did I? Man..."

Shaking his head, he runs his trembling fingers through his hair. "I never want to push a girl too far. After that one chick—" He swallows thickly with a solemn expression lining his face.

"River asked you to, dude. And she didn't take it back. I think...." I stare off in the opposite direction of the bathroom, right next to us. "She'll tell us." With a firm nod, I putter around the back office and collect my clothes. Reluctantly, I pull my shirt over my head, find my boxers and jeans, and put them on.

Once fully dressed, I take a deep breath and reflect on what just happened. As it went down, it didn't fully sink in that I had her again. My obsession begs me to grab her up right now, take her home, lock her in my room for days, and not resurface until next Saturday. I run a hand down my face, sighing.

"I bet they're getting antsy. Let's say goodbye to our girl, and yeah—our girl—and head out. Because knowing Ash, he'll leave us here." Grinning, Rad slaps me on the shoulder, shoving me toward the door.

Rad cackles, throwing his head back. "I can't wait to see the look on Asher's face when we...."

"God, River!" A guttural moan roars through the walls.

"What in the fuck?" I growl, marching through the door, and rip open the bathroom door. My heart beats triple time, and my lips pop open at the sight before me.

"Holy shit," Rad laughs. "No way."

CALLUM

Leaning my head against the puke-green stall, I take a deep breath and center myself. Music plays through my earbuds, drowning out the world as I finish my business in the isolation of the bar bathroom.

After drinking a few beers and enjoying the live show, it hit me when we stepped outside to take care of Bradley—the biggest douchebag in town. In high school, he was the absolute worst person, bullying everyone in sight—including me. I was the quiet kid who barely spoke and relied on my friends too much. To him, I was an easy target. How he treated River after crashing into her was more than despicable. No one deserves that amount of hate, no matter what side of town they're on. My fists clench at the memory of his hate-filled eyes looking up and down her body like a meal. No matter what words he used to describe her, in that drunken moment, there was only one thing he wanted to do with her. I should have clocked him in the jaw when I had the chance and filled my memory with something worthwhile to look back on.

I shudder, remembering River's exact face when he crashed into her and uttered those terrible words. Her lips turned down, and her breathing picked up. All the color drained from her face, and her eyes dilated. She claimed she didn't need our help and could have taken care of it herself, but her expression said it all. River was terrified of Bradley. But why? Sure, he was scary at that moment, snarling in her face and calling her names. But why did River's face fall into oblivion, and her lips tremble before him? The others may not have noticed, but I caught every down-turned lip and every quiver of fear.

The entire night, I watched her out of the corner of my eye, checking her movements like a stalker. No one else noticed my newest fascination festering under my skin. I don't know what it is about River that pulls me in and won't let me go. I'm a transfixed moth flying straight into the roaring flame, praying I don't get burned. We all are. There's something addicting about her that reels us in and begs us to stay.

I mutter a curse under my breath when my music unexpectedly cuts out, leaving only the ringing in my ears to accompany me. The silence stretches out around me, drowning me in the nothingness I can't seem to outrun.

Flushing the toilet, I frown when I yank my earbuds out with a huff. Checking my phone, I note the battery percentage sits at 0%. Thinking back; I forgot to put them on the charger last night when I crawled into my cold bed. Shoving my earbuds into my pocket in defeat, I shake my head at my incompetence. I need the noise to filter out the world. So I don't fucking remember. I never want to fucking remember.

My teeth grit together when all the noise around me returns, and my brain works double time, filing everything away for later. Water drips. The wind blows outside, shifting something in the building. Voices mutter in the distance. Even dogs bark somewhere near the bar. The noises will forever be cemented in my memories without an erase button.

Some call what I have a gift. Everything I see, taste, hear, and fucking touch—I remember forever. It never goes away and is never forgotten. If you ask me to quote what I did three years ago on a random day, I can reach back into my brain's filing cabinet and perfectly recall it without missing a beat and explain it in vivid detail.

Kids envied me in school, calling me a cheater for my perfect scores. Teachers grew concerned I wasn't being challenged enough and wanted to speed up my learning. Little did they know I had this horrible secret weapon blooming inside me. I wanted nothing to do with the gift bestowed upon me.

And me? I call it a heavy ass burden to carry. Something I didn't ask for. Being able to remember every event in my life is torture on repeat. The good. The bad. And the extremely ugly. No matter what side of life it is, I can't push it from my brain, and it will forever lie in wait, forcing me to remember.

"Callum! Help me!"

"It's so cold, Cally," she whispers, crawling over me. My breaths shudder as warm blood coats my front and seeps into my skin. Helplessly, I cling to her, begging God to spare us from the wrath of death.

"I love you, Jenny," I murmur, stroking a shaky hand through her damp hair.

"Love you too," she whispers in a small, quiet voice—leaving me only two minutes later.

Her tiny voice screams in my head. Those cries for help, begging me to rescue her from a situation I couldn't get us out of. Fuck. I fumble with my phone, needing something to take away the sound of grinding metal, screams, and the feel of warm blood pooling on my chest.

I grunt, slamming a hand into the side of my head twice, trying to knock my brain around. Without the music blasting in my ears, her tiny cries echo on repeat. Make her voice leave. Make it fucking stop haunting me every day. I slam my hand into my head again, silently screaming into the void, pushing saliva out of my mouth and dripping onto the floor. I lose my fight, slumping on the toilet and leaning my head back against the tile again. Lightly, I knock the back of my head against the wall, begging for the phantom noises to disappear forever. If I could just fucking forget.

Shaking my head, I try to focus on my surroundings and center myself on the here and now. My therapist swears this grounding method will keep me focused on the present, but sometimes I have doubts. A door hangs off the hinges of the stall, which refused to close when I tried. Didn't matter, anyway. No one else is left in the bar except Kieran, Rad, River, and me. Doors close in the distance, offering goodbyes and laughs to River, and she offers them back in return. As her light footsteps walk past the bathroom, I hold my breath, hoping she doesn't peek in and see the mess huddled on the toilet, barely hanging on to reality.

My fists curl at my sides until she walks right past and into the room next to the bathroom. In the same room, I watched Kieran and Rad disappear into the moment we separated, going to two different places.

Murmured voices rise through the walls with such clarity I hear every word they speak, as if I'm standing in the room. Heat encases my cheeks when the first moans roar through the walls, projecting into the small, echoey bathroom. They're breathy and begging, yet she's the one in charge. Every sound she makes comes through, and my imagination takes off into a fantasy world where I'm a suave, smooth talker who never stumbles over my words.

My breaths pick up as her moans grow louder and louder, and I swear my cock stands at attention in three seconds. All the blood whooshes through my ears and goes straight to my dick, making it jerk in my fucking pants.

With shaky fingers, I close my eyes and undo my pants, bringing the zipper entirely down. With just one tug, I could have my cock out. Only stopping for one second when my conscience barrels in and begs me to stop. This is their private time together, and I'm an intruder listening in like a creep. But the sounds she's making drive me fucking insane. No one has ever gotten me this hard before. Sure, I've kissed a few girls, but none gave me the sparks in my belly like River.

River West will either be our ruination or our fucking salvation—I haven't decided which yet.

Looking down, I move the elastic of my boxers and bring my aching cock out. I swear the tip is purple by the time I rub my thumb over the tip and swipe along my crease, spreading my clear pre-cum. Fuck my conscience. For once, I want to come to the live sounds of a woman getting what she needs from my two best friends. Temporarily, I'm not Callum Rose, the idiot who blushes at every look River throws at me. No. I'm Callum Rose, the guy getting off to the sounds of her orgasm blasting through her. Her screams break off like someone has captured her lips with theirs, thrusting their tongue in her mouth. I shudder at the image of Rad shoving his cock down her throat, gagging her like he said he would.

Fuck. Wrapping my hand around my cock, I stroke up and down, using what little pre-cum I have as lubrication. Eventually, the friction becomes too heated, and I spit in my palm several times, lubing myself up.

A loud groan leaves my lips when I pick up the pace, fucking my hand with the same intensity they're fucking her now. The slap of skin bleeds through the walls. Deep in my mind, I imagine I'm sitting right before them, locking eyes with the girl I'm desperate to touch. I throw my head back, my balls fucking tingling and teetering on the edge when I see the dilation of her moss-green eyes staring heat into mine in my mind. I'm so fucking close to spilling my damn cum all over this bathroom stall. Heat descends my spine, heading straight for my rock-hard cock, twitching in my hand with every stroke. So fucking close....

My body jumps, and I stop all movement when the door beside me crashes open and slams closed with heavy force. Rad and Kieran murmur in low voices, so low I can't hear them anymore. I hold my breath, not daring to move a muscle until she walks by the door.

Please let her walk by. Please don't let her come in here and see that I'm fucking my hand to her.

The men's bathroom door slams open and closes with the same hurried intensity. Only her heavy breaths fill the room. I roll my lips together, fighting the feeling taking me over. I've edged myself so far now that I need to fucking cum, or the pain will overtake me. Fuck.

"Fuck," she murmurs, a light banging happening against the door, which I can only imagine is the back of her head tapping it. "Fuck..."

I swallow the whimper in my throat when I'm forced to stroke myself lightly. The scent of sex wafts off her body, infecting the bathroom with their combined scents. In turn, my heart beats a million miles a minute, filling my ears with persistent thumps. My dick gets impossibly harder, and I suck in a breath, trying to remain as quiet as possible. She'll hear everything in this quiet bathroom if I move a muscle or tuck myself into my pants.

"Who the fuck is in here?" she says in a quiet voice, making my heart drop into the pits of my stomach.

I lick my lips, covering my dick with both my hands. Closing my eyes, I say a brief prayer and do the only thing I can to make her stay away.

"It's me," I whisper, hoping she'll stay by the door and not come any further.

"Yeah? And who is me?" she growls in a harsh tone, but it does little to ease the desire rushing through me.

Fuck, what I wouldn't give to have her on her knees in front of me, begging for me to come on her tits. My lips pop open when a familiar heat races up my neck to the tip of my ears. I swear I'm in a perpetual state of blushing.

Clearing my throat, I utter, "Callum." Instead of coming out in a normal tone, it comes out in a deep rasp, alluding to what I've been doing in the back stall of the bathroom.

"Oh," she breathes, her tiny feet stepping closer to my reality.

"I wouldn't," I plead, begging her to go back out the bathroom door and pretend she didn't fucking see me sitting here jacking my shit to the sexy sounds of her.

But it's too late.

As she steps in front of me, I clench my eyes shut, not bothering to hide anymore. I feel her gaze working up and down my body.

"Callum," she whispers in surprise, a tiny gasp escaping her lips. "What're you...were you?"

I blow out a breath; the heat intensifies on my cheeks. I'm sure turning me a dark shade of red. I can't peel my eyes open and face the disgust that will be on her face. Because I know it'll be there. It's always there.

"I'm sorry," I rasp. "I came to use the bathroom, and then..."

"You heard us," she whispers in a soft voice. No judgment sits in her tone, but I still refuse to open my eyes.

"Y-yes. A-and I'm-I'm sorry," I whisper, stumbling over my words with my heavy tongue. Everything tingles on my body, but yet, my dick stays hard and refuses to fucking leave.

Read the room, you prick. She'll definitely shun you after this. I probably just ruined all our chances...

"Did you get off?" My eyes pop open at her question, and I swallow hard.

There standing before me, River cocks her head. Her long brown locks look ratty from overuse, probably Rad shoving his fingers through her hair. Her pink, swollen lips glisten in the shitty bathroom light. A small smile pulls at the edges of her lips when lust fills her eyes and her bare chest heaves. Before me stands a tiny fucking goddess. The fresh, just-fucked look suits her well, and I will forever remember the look in her eyes as she takes me in.

"I... I...." My eyes bug out of my head when she steps closer.

"Start again," she says in a soft tone.

"Wh-what?" I gasp, tightening my fist around my throbbing dick. I shake my head. There's no way I'd be able to perform in front of her.

"You heard me," she barks again, but softly, so as not to alert the two idiots still having a conversation on the other side of the wall. "Stroke yourself, Callum."

I heave a breath, reluctantly removing my left hand, and reveal myself to her completely. Like in my imagination, I lock eyes with her, and she nods with encouragement. Tentatively, I stroke myself, letting myself fall back into the rhythm I had before. Up and down, I stroke my cock. Like she's not standing before me in all her naked glory and watching my every move.

"Good job," she whispers, taking a step closer. "Do you care that I'm this close, Callum?" she whispers, and I shake my head.

"N-no, you're fine... I..."

"Do you want to come on my tits?" she whispers, softly touching my leg. More heat pours across my flesh at the imagery of spilling my seed across her tits and marking her as mine.

I nod, biting into my lower lip. There's no way I'd ever admit that to anyone else.

"Then do it," she says, falling to her knees onto the bathroom floor, waiting for me to finish.

"You-you're serious?" I whisper frantically, stroking myself harder and harder until the need to come rears its beautiful head again, and I'm ten seconds away from blowing all over River's chest.

"I wouldn't have said it if I wasn't. That's all you're comfortable with, right?" I nod because, yeah, as much as I want to jam my cock down her throat and paint her with it, I can't do that yet. My stupid mind holds me back. "Then I want you to cum all over me."

Without another thought, I let myself revel in the feeling of her kneeling in front of me. My balls tighten. Heat descends my spine, straight into my balls. The tip of my dick tingles, and my orgasm hits its peak.

I throw my head back, grunting when the feeling finally overtakes me, and I let go of every fucking thing around me.

"Oh, River!" I shout, spilling everything I have on her awaiting tits.

"What the fuck?" Kieran shouts from the other room, filled with rage.

"You did good," she whispers with encouragement, putting a hand on my knee.

"You really don't care that I did that? What—what about them? I..." I trip over my tongue again, feeling the heat on my neck. But relief comes when I stare into the depth of her bright eyes.

"It's okay," she says with a shrug, staying on her knees until the bathroom door cranks open and shuts with a thud.

Their footsteps pound toward the back stall. This time, without embarrassment, I let it all hang out. Bliss overtakes me, and I don't care what they think or have to say about it. I finally let loose and let myself feel something right in front of me.

"Holy shit," Rad laughs. "No way." Shaking his head, he leans over and examines the mess I left on River. His dark eyes sparkle with pride when he grins at me.

"What're you guys doing in here?" she asks, narrowing her eyes when she climbs to her feet.

Slowly, I tuck my dick back into my pants and zip myself in. Even if the sight of her with my cum dripping down her tits makes my cock stir again. My breaths shudder when I climb to my wobbly feet.

"We came to see what prick shouted your name. Fuck."

Possession seizes Kieran's voice when his eyes find mine. Instead of the ire I thought I'd receive, a smirk pulls at his lips. He nods at me approvingly and turns to grip River by the hair.

"Now, before we go, be a good girl and tell Callum thank you," Kieran demands in a low voice, sending me a knowing look.

I swallow hard, my heart thumping through my damn chest when she turns to me, sporting a smirk. Shivers run down my spine, and my mouth pops open at her glistening in my jizz. Sliding a finger down her cum-soaked chest, she swirls it in my essence, almost playing with it. I track her movements when she swishes it around her erect nipple, painting it like a masterpiece. Fuck. Making eye contact, she sucks her finger into her mouth, hollowing out her cheeks and moaning.

"Thank you, Callum," she rasps, effectively leaving me and the other two idiots dumbfounded and unable to utter words.

My tongue sticks to the roof of my mouth, twisting when she winks, letting me know I did a good job.

Holy fuck. What a woman.

"Uh, we uhh, we came to say goodbye. Asher is probably losing his shit by now," Kieran finally spits out, leaning in to take her lips hostage.

"Fine, goodbye," she mutters breathlessly, shoving at his chest.

"We'll leave you to get cleaned up, Pretty Girl," Rad says with a megawatt grin, lighting up the entire room.

She shrugs with a tired sigh, rubbing at her temples. He gives her a quick peck on the lips and pulls back.

"Give me a minute," I mutter, nodding for them to leave.

Immediately, they take the hint and head toward the door with their shoulders back and smiles on their faces. I haven't seen my friends this happy in a long time, and it's all because of her. Maybe Kieran and his obsession make sense because I'm falling down the same rabbit hole. Asher won't know what hit him when we bring her along when we get into the Battle of the Bands. Because we're getting in, there's no way around that. It's our one and final chance to drive off into the sunset.

"We'll wait by the front door," Kieran says just as they leave the room, leaving River and me alone.

I give her a soft smile as I walk to the sink and start the water. Reaching up, I grab a few brown paper towels and wet them.

"I'll... I'll clean you up," I whisper, stumbling over my damn tongue again. Swallowing hard, I avert my eyes to the ground as anxiety grabs hold.

"You can look at me," she whispers, lifting my chin with her fingers.

Once my eyes meet hers, my breath shudders. Everything seems to click into place, and I nod, gently wiping away my essence from her chest.

"It's hard to make eye contact sometimes," I mutter, throwing the towels into the trash and reaching for more.

"With me, you don't have to worry. I mean, you came on my chest, Cal. I think we're a little past not making eye contact," she says with a small laugh, pulling a chuckle from my chest.

I blush again, instinctively wanting to look away. "I'll work on it," I promise, smiling down at her when I pat her chest dry.

"Now you're just feeling me up," she quips, pointing to my hands as they dab along her tits.

I rip my hand away, looking down at the ground again. "Just trying to make sure you're dry." I quickly throw the towels out and beeline toward the door. I've been brave enough for one day—my heart pounds when I throw the door open, stopping when she calls out my name.

"Callum!" she laughs, strolling forward with a wad of clothes in her hands. "I was just teasing. Now, go with your bros and back to greener pastures." She grins about it, but a deep-seated fear rests in the back of her moss-green eyes.

I lick my lips, stepping up to her. My palms are slick with sweat, and my heart fucking pounds harder than ever. My head swims in anxiety, but I push through it, pressing my lips against her supple cheek. I linger for longer than necessary, soaking in the feeling of her warm flesh beneath my lips.

"We aren't him-him...Van," I whisper against her flesh, taking in her scent. When I pull back, her lips pop open, and her brows furrow.

I'll see you later. Th—thanks for uh...."

"Letting you come on my tits?" she asks, coming out of her stupor with a quip.

Heat retakes my cheeks, and my eyes fall to the floor. "Yeah-yeah, that. See you," I quickly breathe, rushing from the hallway and out the front door.

"There he is!" Rad says with cheer, wrapping an arm around my shoulder. "The man of the damn hour! How'd it feel, bro?"

"Leave him alone," Kieran cuts in with a laugh, shoving Rad off me.

A smile creeps across my face, and I swear I blush more.

"Finally," Asher gripes, starting up the Tahoe with a yawn. "Did you all have a fun circle jerk?" he quips with an eye roll.

"Better than that. You should have sat in the corner...or the bathroom," Rad says, grinning when he eyes me.

I roll my eyes, shaking my head, but don't utter a word. The last thing I need is to spill the beans about River and me to Asher.

"You too?" Asher asks, raising his brow.

My blush deepens, and I look away, focusing on the outside. "I don't kiss and tell," I murmur in a shaky voice.

They can talk about their sexcapaids all they want, but my lips are sealed for eternity.

"Well, he didn't kiss he...." I grunt, slamming my hand over Rad's mouth. "What?" Rad gripes, trying to peel my hand away.

"Shhh," I grumble, shaking my head.

"Fine," he says into my palm with a huff and folds his arms.

"Such a baby," Kieran mocks, sitting back in the passenger's seat with a smile.

My brows furrow when a familiar figure emerges from the shadows with an earbud dangling from her ear.

"Is she walking?" I ask in outrage, looking toward the clock. "At three in the morning? Here?"

Ash clenches his fists around the steering wheel, eyeing her with narrowed eyes as she walks by without looking in our direction. He lurches the car forward, slowly following right beside her. The whirl of the window goes down, exposing us to the warm, damp air. She doesn't bat an eye.

"Get in the fucking car," Asher growls out the opened window.

She looks at us and rolls her eyes, walking faster down the cracked sidewalk. Ash snarls again, revving the engine, and speeds ahead of her. Our bodies bounce when he hops the curb, pulling right in front of her on the sidewalk, forcing her to stop.

"Get in the car, River," Asher says in a no-nonsense tone, eyeing her like he's about to snatch her off the street.

River sighs. "Listen, Assfaces. Great to see you again, but I'm capable of making it home without interference. Thanks a bunch." Without a second glance, she walks around the back of the SUV and starts walking down the side of the road without a fucking care.

"Where the fuck is her car? Does she have one?" Rad says, looking behind us, and shakes his head.

"Why she gotta be so fucking stubborn?" Asher grunts, slamming the car into reverse and then into drive. Our tires squeal when he hits the gas pedal harder and drives toward her with a sparkle in his eye.

"Jesus, man! Slow down; you're going to run your meal ticket over," Kieran shouts, hanging onto the oh-shit bar with a grimace.

"Do not make me get out of this car, drag your ass in here, and then spank it raw for being so goddamn defiant!" Asher snarls out the window, throwing the Tahoe into park, and opening the door with a growl. "If you make me get out of this car, I will punish you."

River's eyes pop wide when she turns toward him, defiantly putting her hands on her hips. Raising a brow, she stands her ground, not giving in to his demands. She doesn't even flinch when he jumps out of the SUV, Kieran yelling after him to stop being an asshole.

Asher stops right before her, giving her one last chance to comply.

"You are a goddamn psycho. Don't you know no means no, Assbag? I've walked this way before. Thanks a bunch for...." Her words are cut off when she screams bloody murder, slapping Asher when he heaves her over his shoulder. He grunts, hitting her ass hard, and then throws her into Kieran's lap.

Asher's breaths heave in his chest, and he turns his vicious stare to the woman staring him down with murder in her eyes. Kieran quickly holds down her arms, knowing precisely what she was about to go for, and chuckles at her attempt.

"Next time, listen," Asher growls, throwing the car into drive and slamming on the brake. Taking hold of her jaw, he leans in with a vicious glare, declaring one last promise. "Or you'll receive more than an ass slap, baby brat. I'll make you sorry for ever defying me."

"I. Will. Fucking. Stab. You," she growls with such malice my balls shrivel in my pants.

Asher laughs, leaning in more, and examines her hate-filled eyes. "Maybe I'd like that, brat. But for now, I'm taking you home." He lifts a brow when she snarls at him, egging him on more.

With those parting words, he presses the accelerator again, and we take off down the abandoned road.

"I swear my dick just throbbed and shriveled at the same time. Confusing ass woman. But fuck, I think I'm in love," Rad stage whispers to me, eyeing the woman in question who fumes in Kieran's arms.

"I said I was fine," she sighs, pulling her arm from Kieran's grasp, and pinches Asher's nipple through his shirt in punishment.

He flinches, catching her wrist in his hard grasp, grunting through the pain. A familiar smirk twitches the edge of his lips, and he forcefully pulls her face forward with a jerk. In the middle of the road, like a psycho, he pumps the brakes, and we halt. Again. We'll never make it back to her apartment with Asher at the wheel.

"Psychopath," I mumble, pulling myself from the floorboards with a groan. Pain radiates up my tailbone, and I shake my head, locking my seatbelt. "Seatbelts," I reprimand, tugging on my belt.

"You're testing my limits, Little Brat," Asher hisses, rubbing at his chest.

"Settle," Kieran grumbles, pulling her closer.

"Fine," she says, shaking her head.

River huffs, looking out the window, and then watches us out the edge of her eyes. I nod, and her body relaxes into Kieran's as she gives me a warm smile that I commit to memory. When my haunting nightmares surface, I'll look at this moment and seek salvation in her warmth.

"Now, where do you live? I'll do my gentleman duties for the night and escort you home. I can't have my future girlfriend dying at the hands of that guy," Asher growls, waving a hand at two men smoking against a building, watching us with a sharp eye.

"You drew attention to yourself when you fucking kidnapped me!" she growls, staring out the window and paling.

It isn't until her entire body tenses up the moment she lays eyes on them, and a tremble works through her body, do I take note it's Bradley from before. He leans against a building, talking with two more men I've never seen before, smoking cigarettes.

Mentally, I take note, vowing to ensure her safety from here on out. From the corner of my eye, I notice Kieran taking in everything being said and the men outside. Catching his eye, he heaves a breath and nods, knowing exactly what I'm thinking, too.

"And girlfriend? Are you insane?" she gripes again, resting her head against Kieran's shoulder. With a sigh, she points down the road. "Just down the way," she mumbles with less fire, settling into Kieran more. Fuck, how I wish it were me that held her close instead of him. "Central Apartment Complex." She sighs when she says it, leaning her head back, and shuts her eyes.

I exchange a look with Asher, and he licks his lips, knowing precisely what neighborhood we're pulling into and what danger lurks there, especially for pretty girls like her. She shouldn't be on the streets alone, let alone on this one. Central City isn't known for being safe at any time of day. Crime runs rampant in these parts compared to our slice of heaven in Lakeview. It's night and day between the two.

The street blurs by as we drive the eight blocks from the bar to her apartment complex. It's not a long drive—short and sweet. But the walk would have blistered her feet and taken at least forty-five minutes.

Her apartment building stands in the distance with dark brick and barely any street lights lining the parking lot. Three more units lay in a semi-circle around her building, with their own dimly lit parking lots filled to the brim with an assortment of cars.

"Over there." She points to a unit in the middle of the complex, bringing me out of my thoughts.

Ash directs the Tahoe toward the middle unit, eyes darting around the filled-up parking lot. He pulls up next to a Toyota, which looks like it's seen better days. I look back at River, slumped against Kieran with even breaths. Her eyes flutter open and shut, and if she trusted me more, I'd carry her to her bed. Or force her into mine for the night. I'd tuck her in and never let her leave.

"Thanks for the ride," she mumbles, rubbing her eyes.

"No, no, thank you!" Rad says with enthusiasm, reaching between the seats. He pulls her tired face toward his and kisses her again, shoving his tongue down her unsuspecting throat. She groans, pushing him away, and wipes the spit from her lips, giving him a death glare.

"Asshole," she mumbles, opening the door, and jumps down. She lingers a moment, staring into my eyes, and doesn't shut the door until I give her a nod.

We watch with rapt attention when she walks to the ground-floor apartment and pulls out her keys. Unit 7—I take notes, remembering the information for later.

This obsession crashes down on me, and I can only think about her now. Her and our music. I let it settle beneath my skin and take me over. The more of her I have, the fewer nightmares I'll experience.

She opens the door, not sparing us a glance or a thank you, and shuts the door quietly.

"Fuck," Asher sighs, hitting the steering wheel with an open palm, letting all his frustrations leak through. There's no hiding the interest he holds for our little River.

"Yeah, fuck. Fuck me," Rad reiterates, staring at the door as she disappears behind. "Ah, shit," Rad murmurs, holding up a beat-up old iPhone with a split screen.

I frown, grabbing it from his hand, and holding it up to examine it. Ouch. It's definitely seen better days. Maybe I could buy her a new one with a better case using the trust my parents left me. It would more than accommodate a new phone, or maybe I could lend her my old one. It's just collecting dust. I bite my lip, thinking about all the things I could shower her with. Not like she'd want them, anyway.

River is making her way through this world. That much is obvious. But what is a little present here and there? Besides, if she is going to date us or be our girlfriend, she needs a better phone to communicate with us. And...hmm. Yes. That will be perfect. I grin to myself and nod. Ah, yeah, that's it. A giddy butterfly erupts in my gut at the thought of throwing a new phone at her with a little something extra.

"That hers?" Asher asks, raising a brow at the sight of the poor, abused phone.

"Appears so," Rad whistles under his breath and then snatches it from my hand. "Time to find out where my new favorite girl lives." I choke on my spit when he leaps out of the car, stumbling over his drunken feet, and marches toward her door with large amounts of liquid courage.

"Shit," I yelp, jumping out and taking off after him at full speed and stopping when we come face to face with her weathered door, with the number 7 on it. Kieran breathes heavily when he joins us at the door and frowns.

"You have to be careful, man," he growls, looking around the complex, and his shoulders sag. "You can't just run out here at night. Never know who's waiting around the corner." Kieran swallows hard, eyeing the surrounding buildings with a sharp eye.

Rad grins again, wiggling his brows, completely disregarding Kieran's concerns. Instead, he obviously thinks he's going another round with her between the sheets. Fat chance. Asher would storm the damn castle and yank them out by their dicks.

"For fuck's sake," Asher gripes, running a hand down his face when he finally catches up to us and locks the Tahoe. "Can't have you, idiots, leaving me in the car again."

The door bursts open with a frightened-looking River standing on the other side, and my hackles rise. I growl, looking her up and down, noticing the tears she's frantically wiping away and trying to hide.

"What's going on?" Kieran asks, stepping protectively up to her. He grabs her shoulders, forcing her to look at us. Terror and pure panic rest in the back of her eyes when she stares back, and my heart drops.

"Help," she murmurs, staring us in the eyes with a bewildered look. "I need your help."

And every instinct in my body tells me to drop everything and help.

RIVER

Do not fall in love with these assholes. Just. Don't. Don't think about their big dicks sliding inside you, giving you a better release than anyone ever has. Don't think about how powerful you felt pushing Kieran to do as you said, as he gave into the demand in your voice. Don't think about how he filled you up; then, his friend did the same to your mouth. Don't think about Callum's face when he finally had the courage to come and how he cared for you afterward.

Just don't do it, River. Definitely don't think about their friends doing the same and rolling around with each of them to find your pleasure. And most definitely, don't think about going on a date with them or cozying up to them or whatever else your twisted little mind can think of.

I'm in such deep shit. They're all I can think about as I saunter through the nightly air, immediately sweating from the intensity of the heat. Even if the sun went down hours ago, a mugginess drifts in the air.

A rogue thought smacks the smitten feeling right out of me, and I frown. This is one hundred percent the definition of a whore. Right? Shit. Am I a whore? I shake my head, answering my own stupid question. Nah. You know what? Fuck the stereotypes. I'm not a whore. I'm a girl with needs who fucked two guys simultaneously and loved every second of being in their grasp. One to fuck me, the second one to gag me, and the third to cum all over me.

By society's standards, I'm one hundred percent a whore. But you know what? Society can suck my dick for all I care. And I know, I know. People love to remind me I don't have a dick, but I'm not talking about the flesh flute hanging between my legs. I'm talking my soul dick. The dick that lives deep inside of me, not literally. So, suck my aura dick, society, and leave the name-calling out of your mouth.

That's just the deep-seated hate women get for enjoying the same sexual experiences men enjoy without the label. I fucked two guys at once and let their other friend cum on my tits. And you know what? I liked it, and I'm damn proud. And I'd do it again.

Use us, River. We'll do whatever you want.

I shiver as Kieran's words roll around in my brain. More vivid memories flash in rapid succession, like a movie on repeat in my mind. Heat envelopes me, going straight to my core and begging for more of Kieran, Rad, and Callum. Hell, throw Asher in there, too. A nice hate fuck, where he bosses me around, and I'm the defiant brat, sounds like a good time. God, as fucked as it sounds, I can't wait for the day when Asher punishes me for every minor infraction. He could bend me over his knee, spank my ass raw, and then fuck me in it.

Yup. I'm fucked.

I sink my teeth into my bottom lip as I unlock my front door. Heaving a breath, I feel the echoes of their stares burning through me and holding me prisoner. It doesn't cease until I shut the door and block their view. Finally, I can take a full breath without them breathing down my neck—without them suffocating me with one heated stare.

Pulling fresh oxygen into my lungs, I step further into the darkened apartment and stare at my mother's empty chair. Since she got fired from her job and broke her leg, she's been chair bound.

Nothing has fucked with my mom's depression more than being stuck in her recliner with her leg in the air, unable to do a damn thing. I peek around the apartment and sigh again at the mess filling the sink and the grime on the countertops.

How the hell am I supposed to help her when I have two jobs, schooling, and four weirdos trailing after me? I know Korrine has been checking in on her and sitting with her for lunch, ensuring my mom's fed. But I can't rely on my neighbor forever. She has her own life, and my mom needs me. But I'm so damn busy taking care of myself and this house. I don't know what I'm going to do with her holed up as essentially a child. My mom is the most important person in my life. I don't know how I will cope with all this on my own at nineteen.

"Ma?" I ask, looking around the deserted apartment.

My heart rate spikes when she doesn't respond. Swallowing hard, I move toward the running water sound coming from our tiny bathroom.

"Hey, Ma? You in there? You doing, okay?" I lightly tap on the wood door.

Once again, she doesn't respond. Normally she hums or sings as she prepares for work, drowning herself in long showers. I search for the comfort of her voice, but it's nothing but emptiness. The shower is roaring down on the tiled tub, filling the space with its noise. Placing my ear against the wooden door, I listen further, still getting nothing in return.

"Fuck, Ma! I'm coming in. If you don't answer, you're about to scar me for life," I shout, twisting the knob, and my heart drops way into my ass at the sight before me. "Ma!" I gasp, dropping to my knees.

Blood drips from the gash on her forehead, pooling on the ground and matting in her hair. Sprawled out completely naked on her back, she's unresponsive, not flinching when I shake her. Yelling out to her again in broken sobs, I try to rouse her, but she doesn't stir. Her broken leg is wrapped in plastic, sticking over the side of the tub where the water rains down. Shaking her again, I get the same response. Nothing.

"Shit, shit, shit!" I curse, covering her naked body with a towel, and shutting off the water. What the hell do I do? How do I? "Fuck," I growl, my hands shaking, looking down at her pale body. What the hell do I do? What the hell? Hospital? Ambulance? Chaotic thoughts take over my brain, spinning like a damn tornado. "Shit. I need Korrine," I gasp out in desperation.

She's a former nurse, only quitting to raise her family many years ago. My hands tremble more when I run them through my hair and get to my feet, but not before checking her pulse. It's strong and beating against my fingers. So, I know she's okay there. Just injured. Severely. And—I pale at the blood sticking to her skin. My stomach churns, threatening to send up the contents of my stomach.

My heavy heartbeat pounds against my chest, and oxygen refuses to enter my lungs. A tight rubber band constricts around my chest, hellbent on suffocating me before I can get the help my mom needs.

I run out of the bathroom in a haze, gasping for breath and throwing open the front door. I only stop when Kieran, Callum, Asher, and Rad stand before me with my phone dangling in the air and confusion etching across their faces.

"What's going on?" Kieran asks, stepping protectively up to me and grabbing my shoulders firmly.

For whatever reason, I slump into him like he's the best protector I've ever had and will shield me from the dangers surrounding us. Maybe it's the familiarity he offers and seeing him shoves my panic to the deepest pit. His scent overtakes my senses, confusing every bit of me, but also calms the raging inferno inside me.

Sincerity and concern bleed through his gaze when he stares me up and down, checking for wounds. For some odd reason, I think he cares for me and maybe my well-being. Quickly, I wipe my tears away, refusing to show them my weaknesses.

"Help," I murmur through a gasp, staring at him with pleading eyes. "I need your help." My heart beats out of control when their faces fall into determined looks. Each of them steps up, awaiting my words. Even Asher looks around, evaluating the apartment from the outside and searching for the culprit of my panic.

"What is it?" Kieran pushes past me, waltzing into my apartment.

Callum ushers me in with his arm tightly wrapping around my shoulders and pulls me into the side of his body. His warmth spreads through me when they all stand in my messy apartment. Someone shuts the front door, cutting off the outside world.

"Pretty Girl," Rad whispers, standing before me, and cups my jaw. "Tell us what's going on, okay?" I shiver under his touch, my body trembling more.

Kieran looks around, snarling when he doesn't see the threat sending me into shock, and jerks his gaze toward me. Eyeing me up and down, he repeatedly looks me over like blood should be pouring from every orifice.

My teeth chatter together, filling the room with their constant noise. Static takes over my brain, and my thoughts work through a thick sludge, slowing it down until I can't form words. Shit. Think. Fucking think! I'm a fucking manager, for Christ's sake. I should be able to figure out disasters without falling on my ass. No matter how often I chant that in my head, I'm stuck in a phantom mud.

Asher snarls, throwing Rad out of the way and standing before me, taking my jaw forcefully in his grip, clamping down on me. Pain spears through my jaw and onto my cheeks, forcing my eyes to his angry stare.

"River West, tell us what's going on!" His demand lands like a whip against my ass, kicking the panic out of my brain long enough for clarity to take over.

"My mom!" I force out through my chattering teeth. Asher's brows raise into his hairline when I snatch his hand from my jaw and lead him toward the bathroom. "My mom, my mom, has MS; she fell!" I gasp, standing in front of the bathroom door, unable to get oxygen into my lungs.

"Shit," Rad hisses as footsteps pound behind us.

"River Blue," Kieran says, turning me to face him and cupping my cheeks. "We'll help, okay? What do you need us to do?" His mismatched eyes examine my face, and my mind goes fucking blank.

B-l-a-n-k! The fuck! I'm supposed to know what I'm doing. But I'm frozen by the sight of my mom's fucking blood on the ground and in her hairline. She's motionless, barely breathing on the bathroom floor.   And who knows for how long? Is she still alive?

"I need to get her back in her chair.... God, I can't call an ambulance; that would cost too much money. We can't afford that. I..." Tears burn the back of my eyes, and I'm not too proud to admit fear is coursing through me mixed with indecision. Do this? Do that? The fuck do I do first.

"River, why don't you get your mom some clothes?" Asher demands in a calm voice, leaning over my mom's still body. He checks her forehead, finds gauze under the sink, and puts it on her bleeding wound. "You might have to take her to the ER, just in case. This gash is pretty bad." Asher gives me a pointed stare. "Now is not the time to defy me, River. Go get your mother some clothes." Again, he demands, and it snaps like a rubber band against me, immediately sending me into action. If there's one person to tamp my panic with demands and get me moving, it seems to be Asher. I swallow hard and nod at his words. "Good girl," he says, praising me when I take a step back, following his directions.

If the situation weren't so dire, I'd slap him across the head for his praise. And I'd definitely never admit to him that his words do something odd to me, sending goosebumps down my skin and lightness taking me over.

Turning toward her tiny bedroom, I gather some fresh underwear, shorts, and a fresh shirt. Once they're bundled into my arms, I step into the bathroom, sliding my mom's panties up her legs and shorts on as the guys turn around for privacy.

In the back of my mind, I know the emergency room will cost an arm and a leg. We just have to convince our state insurance to cover the bill. But whatever we can do to save her fucking life.

Rad quietly calls 911 for me, explaining the situation to the dispatcher calmly and precisely. I swallow hard when I put my mom's shirt on, careful of her head injury, sliding her arms through the sleeves and pulling it over her stomach. She still doesn't stir when I'm done, and tears leak from my eyes. She looks dead, barely breathing, and has a giant gash on her fucking forehead.

Callum pulls me into his chest again, letting his shirt soak up my stupid tears. He whispers soft words of confirmation in my ear, reassuring me she'll be okay. With every word he speaks, my panic slowly drains out, and I slump into him. I wrap my arms around his body, soaking up his warmth and the safety he offers me when the world around me is so chaotic.

Thank God they came back to...well, why did they come back? My brows furrow as my thoughts slowly come back to me at a rapid pace. If they hadn't been at the door while I threw it open, I would have been lost. Sure, Korrine would have jumped at my pleas for help and come over, but I hate to rely on her so much. She's already done so much.

"Hey, Pretty Girl, they're on their way, okay?" I swallow hard when Rad wraps himself around my back, sandwiching me between them. "Everything will be okay. I promise," he whispers, gently kissing the side of my head.

The moment his warmth hits my back, and his words sink into me, I fucking lose it like a baby, uncontrollably sobbing as I've never done before. Usually, no one gets to see this side of me. I hold it all in. No one takes an over-emotional woman seriously because, well—society is fucked.

Fear tightens every inch of me at the thought of losing my mother to this disease, dragging her down. Ever since she told me, she's folded in on herself and barely talked. It's only been a day, but it feels like my mom has all but given up. I've got to do something to help her get out more and help her get healthy. But what can I do? I work two jobs to feed us and keep us warm and cool. I go to college to better our future. When I am trying to better my life to better hers, I can't stay home and watch her. I could quit everything and just become another statistic, but I refuse. In ten years, I don't want to be here. Instead, I want to work for a record company or manage a business dealing with music and take my mother with me. I want to give her the best care she can ever imagine. I have to stick it out.

Another warm body presses into our sides, whispering kind words when he wraps his arms around the three of us. Together, the boys create a solid circle around me, protecting me from anything that comes our way. Kieran kisses the back of my skull, nuzzling into me with such care I know I'm fucked. So fucking fucked. Because the moment his lips meet my hair, he has me right where he wants me. I'm falling hard and fast, even though my brain screams it's a bad idea. Like, I don't know already.

I've learned this lesson before with Van. But Van never came over here. He never volunteered to drive me home and ensure my safety like they did. Van let me walk home when my car died, or he'd drop me off a block away. I should have seen the giant red flags from a mile away, but I was too blinded by the look in his eyes and how he made me feel. He never came to see me at the bar, only the record store, or hang out. Why does this feel different? But it gives me the same feeling at the same time. I'm so damn conflicted about how I should feel about them and how they just showed up in my life like a hurricane.

After a moment, I pull away from them when someone pounds on the front door, yelling about being EMTs. Wiping my eyes, I avert my gaze toward the ground, giving them a tight smile—a red tint blossoms on my cheeks when I peek at the wetness covering Callum's shirt.

"Thank you for the help," I say through heavy emotions clogging my throat. Walking out of the bathroom at a quick pace, I try to get to the door as quickly as possible. Probably looking like I'm scurrying away like a little mouse, desperate to get away from them.

"Anytime, River Blue," Kieran says, grabbing my shoulder and stopping my retreat. Turning me to face him, he cups my cheeks again. "You can reach out to us at any time, okay? Especially with something like this. If you need help, we're here." He gives me a firm nod, something in his eyes telling me he might somehow relate to this entire situation. Leaning in, he softly kisses my lips, reaffirming his feelings for me.

Behind me, the front door opens, and Rad graciously shows them to my mother. Callum and Asher stand beside Kieran as he continues to hold me through all the movement in my apartment. Eventually, Kieran escorts me to the bathroom, where I explain the situation to them.

They quickly assess her and help rouse her to the land of the living. She comes to slowly with wide eyes, frantically looking around with confusion. Once she's calmed down, they patch her forehead up, run some tests for a concussion, and clear her.

They advise her not to shower alone again and to go to the ER if any more symptoms pop up. I agree to monitor her as they guide her back to her chair and set her down. They go on their way, waving when they walk out the door.

Kieran, Rad, Callum, and Asher stay by my side through the entire ordeal, helping to center me through my panic. Rad clutches my hands and murmurs sweet words of encouragement. Something about his pretty words centers my whole being, and I settle. My mind comes back online just in time for the four boys to stand around me after the EMTs leave.

"Thank you so much for everything you've done tonight," I murmur, running a hand across my forehead. "I kind of panicked." I look away, wincing with embarrassment. A heat takes over my cheeks and runs down my neck.

Yeah, it's cool; River, just go ahead and show these assholes your vulnerabilities and weaknesses. Just tell them your entire life story, why don't ya? Shit. I have to be more careful about what I share with them or anyone else. I have goals, and sure, they're massive amounts of fun. But I can't afford to get stuck here or with them.

"No probs, Pretty Girl. What're friends for, right?" Rad says with a grin, shoving his hands in his pocket.

"You'll be okay with her for the rest of the day?" Kieran asks, furrowing his brows at my mom, who slumps in her chair, watching some channel that sells jewelry.

"Yeah, it'll be fine," I say through a breath.

Yeah, I'd be fine. I'd have to skip school and the bar, but I'd make do. Right? Right? We'll be okay. Shit, I need to talk to Korrine and see if I can set up nurse visits or something to help me.

"What's your number?" Kieran asks, holding out his phone. "If you need anything, call, okay?" I nod, sending them on their way after putting my number in his contacts, and collapse against the door when they're finally out of view.

Outside, the sound of an engine coming to life echoes through the parking lot and then takes off down the road.

"They seem like good boys," Ma says, settling into her recliner with a sleepy look. I'm not sure why it took me so long to put two and two together, but she's been opting to snooze in her chair over lying in bed.

"Yeah," I breathe.

They seem like good boys—too good of guys for me.

After making sure my mom is okay, I head to bed and attempt to sleep for what feels like the first time this week, forgetting my responsibilities. Tomorrow, I'll deal with work. Tomorrow, I'll deal with school. Tomorrow, I'll deal with the fallout of this whole mess.

Quickly texting Booker about my night, he tells me to watch my mom for the day and not worry about work. Thank God he's a night owl, or he'd have a hell of a message to wake up to in the morning. I quickly change into an oversized shirt, sans pants, and panties, and crawl into bed with a sigh.

RIVER

Laying in the darkness of my room, I stare at the glowing stars I stuck to the ceiling when I was five. Ma hated them, but Booker helped me stick them up there. I smile at the memory of him setting me on his shoulder so I could stick the little stars myself. After that night, I was never afraid of the dark again as long as I had the stars to guide me.

I roll to my side, watching the trees blow through the sliding glass door of my room. Many moons ago, I'd sneak out through that door to avoid the noises coming from my mom's bedroom. She'd try to cover it up with music, but it never worked. Or I'd sneak out when she left for work, leaving me alone in the tiny apartment.

"Dear Man on the Moon," I mumble, finding the brightly lit moon beaming down on the earth, preparing to leave for another night. Soon the sun will shine, and my day will start all over again. "Will you watch over us again? Just this once, I need my life in order and for everything to go right. Just this once. I need a damn miracle." I sigh and nearly jump out of my skin when a small knock from the sliding glass door shakes me from my pity party.

I furrow my brows, throwing the sheet from my body. Who the hell could that be? It's four in the damn morning. I need to sleep, not company. With caution, I peek out the hanging blinds, and my eyes widen at the darkened figure standing just outside the door. His gray eyes take me in, and he offers me a small, inviting wave. A soft smile pulls at his lips, and every worry flees from my body. Without a thought, I open the sliding glass door and lean against the frame, letting the warm night into my room.

"Callum?" I whisper with confusion at him, standing outside my bedroom at almost four in the morning.

"Could I... Could I...." He blows out a breath, shaking his head when he stumbles over his words. "Can I come in? I thought after tonight; you might want some company?" he murmurs with concern taking over his face. He cocks his head to the side like an observant puppy, watching my every move. Here I thought Asher was the observant one, but Callum seems to take it all in, too. Maybe more.

The prospect of having someone hold me until the sun comes up appeases me to the point I never thought. I'm not the cuddling type or the hugging type. I'm the fuck me and then leave me alone type. But my body preens at the thought of him wrapping his long arms around me and holding me until we fall asleep. Something soft and sweet about Callum pulls me into his orbit. He's like the stars shining above us, dazzling me with his presence, giving me no other option because I can't seem to say no to him right now. Not when he graces me with that slight grin and hope in his eyes.

"Yeah," I whisper, swallowing the lump in my throat. "It's not much, but this is my room." I gesture for him to come in, and he nods, waltzing into my room with his hands in his pockets.

A heavenly smile graces his soft face. "I think it's perfect."

I huff a quiet laugh, shut the sliding glass door, and fix the blinds so it won't disturb us when the sun rises. There's nothing perfect about my tiny room, only housing my bed and a small standing dresser with my few pieces of jewelry sitting on top. There's no TV, only my stars—it's just my space I sleep in and nothing more.

"Any plans today?" I ask, raising a brow when he meanders to the opposite side of my queen-sized bed and shakes his head.

"Only this," he whispers, planting his ass on the edge of my bed and removing his socks and shoes. "Do you mind if I take off my shirt and pants? I-I can keep-keep them on if-if you want me to."

I smile as his nerves get the best of him, and his eyes fall to the worn-out carpet, not meeting my stare. Even with the darkness of my room, a red tint takes over his cheeks. Callum's presence, I realize, is disarming in a way. He's taking down the walls I've carefully erected over the years as a defense—brick by brick.

"As long as you don't mind that I'm not wearing panties under this long shirt," I murmur, climbing into my side of the bed.

His gaze jerks to my bare legs, working up them with a shuddering breath until he meets my gaze. Through the dark, I see the dilation of eyes and more red-tinted cheeks.

— 156 —

"Maybe I should keep my clothes on," he quips with trembling fingers, working his shirt up several times before he finally pulls it over his head and throws it aside.

My breath halts at the multitude of tattoos lining his chest and sides, covering what looks like deep scars running across Callum's body. You'd never guess what lies beneath his shirt, especially not this.

Without thinking, I run the tips of my fingers across the deep scars that, to the naked eye, would be hidden under the array of colorful tattoos. But I see the wounds like I try to see everything else on him.

Callum doesn't flinch when I trace them toward his chest, only stopping me when I get near his nipple.

"You can ask," he whispers, leaning back on the bed with his jeans intact. A distinct dick imprint pushes at the material, letting me know he's keeping himself in check by keeping the pants on.

"Only if you want to tell it," I say, leaning my head on my hand.

Callum's expression doesn't change, but I see the ghosts haunting him through his glazed-over eyes. "As long-long as you keep touch-touching me." He swallows hard, clamping his eyes shut. His hand squeezes over mine, holding it hostage on his chest.

"Odd request, Cal. But sure, I'll keep touching you," I quip, trying to lighten the mood for him.

I succeed when a soft smile tugs at his lips, but the haunted look remains.

"It was almost two years ago," he whispers, shivering like the memories are coming back in full picture. "I was in a plane crash. My parents and my little sister Jenny...they-they died-died beside me." I swallow hard, lean into him, and hug him with all my might. "The only thing I have left of them is my house, everything inside it, and the trust they left in my name for bills."

"I'm sure you hear this all the time, but I'm so sorry you went through that. I can't imagine the pain...." my words trail off when he nods.

"There was nothing I could do. I severely broke my leg from the impact. My little sister crawled on top of me, told me she loved me, and then passed away in my arms. Ever since... Without music, I can't keep the nightmares from taking over." Realization hits me like a truck, and I note all the times he had his earbuds in, seeming to ignore the world around him. But it wasn't because he was rude. It was to drown out the ghosts trying to haunt him. He looks at me, curling a piece of my long hair behind my ear. "Since the accident, only one thing has kept me sane. Until today, though, I've discovered there are now two things that chase away the monsters haunting my mind and grant me peace."

"Yeah?" I whisper as he leans in close, bumping his nose against mine.

"Yeah," he confirms, brushing his lips against mine and holding my body close. "You," he whispers with a shaky breath, breaking me with his confession. "And music."

My heart drops into my stomach when he swoops in and steals the breath from my lungs with lazy kisses. His tongue prods at the seam of my lips, and I grant him access, moaning into his mouth when he rocks against me. Pulling back, a sparkle reignites in his eyes, and life seems to reinflate inside him.

"Now, can I ask you a question?" he whispers, keeping me close when I pull the sheet up, covering us together. His confession weighs on my mind, but I nod, snuggling into him. Despite what I've felt before, this is the most comfortable I've been with another human being in almost four years. Since....

"Why were you so afraid of the guy at the bar? Bradley?" I quirk a brow at his bold question, searching his eyes when my heart picks up speed.

"How did you...?" I shake my head when he nods in confirmation.

"I tend to notice things others don't. You froze when he called you those awful names and slammed into you. The vein in your neck pumped double time, and your nostrils flared. But the paleness that took over your face really solidified what was wrong." For the first time since interacting with the quietest member of Whispered Words, he keeps eye contact and stays confident with his speech. It's like he's evaluated the entire situation and knows exactly what happened four years ago.

Heat brews beneath my skin, and I shake my head. "It's nothing...."

"It's something," he whispers. "But I won't pry into your personal matters. I respect you, River. And...I kinda like-like you-you." With a deep breath, he closes his eyes. "I don't want you to talk about anything you don't want to."

I close my eyes, leaning my head on his chest. The deep, thunderous pound of his heart echoes in my ear, soothing all the fear inside me. Maybe Callum and I have a weird connection after all. If I soothe his nightmares and he seems to soothe the anxiety always begging to ruin my life, we're meant for each other in some fucked up way.

"Four years ago, I went to a party when I was fifteen. That night, after seeing someone who I thought would recognize me—"

"It was Kieran?" he asks in his oh-so-observant way, and I nod. "Sorry, I didn't mean to interrupt."

Remorse clings to his voice, and he holds me tighter, giving me the comfort no one has offered my entire life. Van sure as hell never held me after we had sex or listened to me when I spoke. Again, all the red flags were present; I just didn't see them.

"Kieran used to live here; one day, he was gone. Asher's dad, I'm assuming, started coming around. I... I knew Kieran would be at that party and wanted to see him. He was my best friend, and... Well, let's just say he had no idea. To make a long, boring story short, I drank too much and found myself at the hands of Bradley and his friend."

Callum gulps a breath, kissing my head when I shudder in his arms. Why is it so easy to spill this secret to him? I haven't told anyone since the police waved me off and practically blamed me for the entire situation. I tried to go forward with my life and ignore the injustice I had been served, but seeing Bradley tonight stirred up all those old, foggy memories.

"They took advantage of me, if you can imagine. Then...." I close my eyes as the memory of Rad's soft, dark eyes looking down on me resurfaces. The comforting words he uttered when he picked me up off the ground and put me in his car.

"I'll find those fuckers for you," he said in a soft but demanding voice. "I'll beat their asses. Who was it?" he whispers, starting up his car. But I just shook my head, tears streaming down my face, and I refused to look at the man who saved me. "Please talk to the cops. Let them know everything. I know something bad happened. Someone at that party...took what wasn't theirs, right?" he asks when he pulls up to the hospital, staring at me when I nod in confirmation.

"Rad has always had a soft spot for you, you know? When he found you like that, it fucking broke him. He went to the cops and told them he found you to corroborate your story, but they...."

"Laughed him off like they did me?" I ask with a shaky breath, shaking my head. "I'll always remember how he took care of me."

"Will you ever let him know it's you?" he asks, stroking a hand through my hair, causing my eyes to close.

It feels like the world lifts from my shoulders at his validation. No one has ever told me it wasn't my fault, or that I didn't deserve it. Even my mother looked down at me and rolled her eyes when I called her from the hospital.

I shrug, unable to speak through the lump in my throat. "I think I need to get some sleep. It's been a long ass day," I mutter, burying my face into his chest.

"Avoidance at its best, but that's okay, my Little Star," he murmurs, snuggling into me. My heart fucking soars at the name, and my eyes find the green neon stars shining on the ceiling. "Let's get some rest."

Taking one last, long breath, Callum and I drift off to sleep in each other's arms, sinking into the best dreams I've had in years.

The first thing I notice when I wake up in the morning is the blaring sunshine beating through the sliding glass door, which I swore I had secured the blinds better than that.

The second thing I notice is the second warm body squishing against me, heating my back. Sweat coats every inch of my skin from the ovens surrounding me and....

"What the hell?" I shriek, pushing the second body away from me with my fist to their hard chest as panic takes over.

He grunts, rolling onto the floor with a loud hiss. If we had downstairs neighbors, they'd be pounding on the ceiling out of frustration.

"Wh-what is it?" Callum asks in a raspy, just woken-up voice, rubbing his eyes with urgency.

Peeking over the bed, my heart hammers in my chest when I meet the gaze of the intruder rolling around on the ground. He groans, holding his chest and wincing through the pain. Huh. Apparently, I punched him harder than I thought.

"Pretty Girl, it's not nice to punch people out of bed. You interrupted an amazing dream. You and me and the rest of the guys naked on the beach with sand in places we shouldn't speak of. But you were about to give me a sandy pussy sandwich, and then you pushed me out of bed," he groans through his entire speech, finally rising to a sitting position. His big brown eyes peer at me with mischief.

"First off, I don't even want to know what a sandy pussy sandwich is," I say, shaking my head. "Second off...."

"How'd I get in your room?" he asks with an enormous grin, climbing to his feet. "You all ask the same questions. How'd you get into my room? Why're my panties in your pockets? Which they're not, by the way. No panties in here," he says, lying through his teeth when he pats his bulging pocket. "But the answer is always the same. You summoned me with your mind." He grins, tapping the side of his head.

"Are you high?" I ask, furrowing my brows. "Wait, don't answer that. It's way too early in the morning."

"It's noon," Rad says, climbing back into bed beside me. He grins, pulls his phone from his pocket, and shows me the screen. "But you two were the best snuggle buddies. We should get rings made. Snuggle Buddies activate!" he howls, thrusting his fist into the air.

I blink a few times, processing what the fuck is going on. I'm too tired and way too grumpy to deal with his optimism—which he should kindly choke on until I get more sleep. But noon? Seriously? I haven't slept this late since.... Well, forever. I've been up at the butt crack of dawn since I was fourteen, busting my ass at work.

"Is he serious?" I stage whisper to Callum, who pulls my body into his and huffs into my neck.

"Unfortunately," he grumbles, sounding half asleep.

Rad frowns, bumping his own fist, and sighs. "You all left me hanging. It's rude. So, what are we doing today? Obviously, my girlfriend is not killing herself at work. So...what should we do?"

I sigh, putting an arm over my eyes. "I'm not your girlfriend, Rad."

"You can say that and believe it, but no matter what you say, you're mine. If another man besides my best friends even approaches you, I'm gouging their eyes out and wearing them as trophies," Rad says with a smug expression, leaning in closer to me to boop my nose.

"I am a biter," I remind him, closing my eyes and trying to go back to sleep. "And very sleepy," I mumble.

Rad grumbles under his breath, slinking up to me and pressing his front against mine. "But, Pretty Girl, we could have so much fun today on your day off! I brought my dirt bike! We can go for a ride down at the track. I can show you a thing or two," he says through fits of fucking giggles.

"You are too damn chipper in the morning...."

"It's noon! The sun is shining and..." I put my hand over his mouth and peek an eye open, glaring at him.

"If you're not careful, she's going to kick you out," Callum mutters the warning into my neck.

"He's got a point," I say, raising a brow.

"Pfft. Don't worry, Pretty girl. Me and your mom, Stella, had some breakfast from the donut shop. I fed her coffee, and we watched the news. She's taking a nap, and then she's got a home health nurse for the day." Rad grins like this is common knowledge, and my lips pop open.

"Who are you?" I ask, slumping into the bed with a groan.

Rad snorts. "You were worried last night, babe," he says in a softer tone, running a finger down my jaw. "I wanted to make it better. I didn't realize this guy was here, though." His warm, dark eyes light up when his best friend huffs.

"I was-was worried, too," Callum says through a frustrated sigh. When I peek back, a red tint takes over his cheeks again.

"But I should have guessed where you were headed the moment you walked out the front door. You didn't even tell me goodbye or invite me to the slumber party, which is rude, by the way," Rad whines, fake pouting. "Next time, it'll be at our house!" he says, wiggling his brows again.

I strum his lip and scoff. "Too early," I mumble again, going over his words. "Wait, you said home health nurse?" My eyes pop wide at his words, making my heart skip a beat.

Rad grins from ear to ear, and he nods. "Your mom is super chill. I like her. She requested donuts every morning, so I guess you'll see me around here a lot. I kind of dig this place. Anyway, I called my mom..."

"You called your mom?" Callum asks in disbelief. "But you…" Rad waves him off, shaking his head before Callum can continue.

"Yeah, through the church, she has a lot of connections. So, I asked her for a favor," Rad says, grimacing. "She still calls me occasionally, to see how I'm doing. We don't talk much, not since my dad kicked me out, but it was worth it this time. There's a company that does this sort of thing and can come to take care of your mom five days a week. She'll never be alone, Pretty Girl."

Rad took every worry from my mind and fixed it overnight. Leaning in, I don't think and press my lips to his in appreciation. I groan when he takes advantage, thrusting his tongue in my mouth and overtaking me. I'm breathless by the time we come up for air.

"You don't know how much that means to me. But the cost, Rad?" I whisper, searching his dark eyes that light up with me so close. "You know I can't afford to pay…"

"Don't worry. It's covered," he says, kissing the edge of my lips. "Now, since I granted you a favor…." He waggles his brows as he jumps out of bed, dragging my reluctant body with him.

"Callum, help," I pout, crossing my arms.

I sigh when Callum stands tall, stretching his long arms above his head. Every inch of his body stretches, pulling his muscles taut and extenuating them. I nearly drool at the sight of all his tattoos until he throws his shirt on and covers them. A small smile pulls at his lips when his gray eyes meet mine.

"He's pretty hot, right?" Rad says, throwing his arm over my shoulders. "You'd never guess all those tats were hiding on that virgin body." I stiffen, but Rad continues his rant. "He's had a needle before he's had pussy; it's a tragedy. Will you fix that for him, Pretty Girl? Will you be the first penis fly trap to grab hold of his trouser snake…" I slap my hand over his mouth, shaking my head.

"Do you ever shut up?" I gripe when he grins beneath my hand. "And seriously, a penis fly trap? What in the… Never mind, I realize that with you, I don't even want to know." He waggles his dark, bushy brows, staying silent beneath my palm.

"Damn-damn it, Rad," Callum curses, throwing his socks and shoes on. He groans, rubbing a hand down his face, hiding the redness taking over his cheeks. "And-and no, he never shuts his trap." Callum sighs, avoiding my eyes when he stands. Shoving his hands in his pockets, he takes a deep breath, probably centering himself from all the embarrassing shit Rad just threw out.

"There's nothing wrong with being a virgin. It just means you were saving your experiences for something better," I say, trying to lighten the conversation. "Besides, virginity is an outdated way of saying you just haven't had sex. It's our stupid society that created it." I roll my eyes at the world we live in, hoping it offers Callum a small light at the end of the tunnel. "Nothing to be ashamed of," I add again, and he nods, finally letting my words sink in.

Callum slowly lifts his eyes from the floor, searching me for honesty. Licking his lips, he nods. "Thanks, Little Star," he whispers.

"Little Star?" Rad asks, removing my hand from his lips and locking our fingers together. "I kinda like that. You are a little star, aren't you?"

I sigh. "I need to get dressed and check on my mom. Maybe wait until the nurse...."

"Oh, she's already here. I let her in at nine. She's pretty cool. Your mom took a shower while I did the dishes and... Why're you looking at me like that?" Rad asks, looking between Callum and me with raised brows, taking in our varying expressions.

"You-you did the dishes? And-and organized the nurse?" Callum asks through bewilderment.

Rad scoffs. "You act like I don't do anything domestic! How do you think our dishes get done? The laundry? Who picks up your rock sock and makes sure it's clean for your next round of taming the snake? I mean, come on, dude! I'm not incapable."

"I'm ignoring the rock sock comment," Callum says, giving Rad a scathing look. "And the tame the snake comment."

"Hold up," I say, lifting a finger. "You two live together?" My head jerks back when Rad stares at me like I'm an idiot.

"My house," Callum murmurs, shuffling his feet on the floor.

Rad shrugs, pulling me toward my closet. "Of course we do. We always live in roommate bliss. All right, Pretty Girl. Time to get on those sexy booty shorts and a tight shirt. We're going to the dirt bike track so I can show you off. And if anyone asks, you are my girlfriend.

Slimy fuckers will try to steal you away. I even have a sign that says, *'I suck Rad's dick when he wins'* for motivation," he rambles more, rifling through my closet. "Because that would definitely make me smoke those suckers. The last thing they'll see is my ass when I beat them."

"For the last time, I'm not your girlfriend," I mutter, tossing my hands.

"You say that now. But what's mine is mine, and you're fucking mine. You know Kieran suggested putting a tattoo on your ass, and I'm kinda agreeing. It'll say Property of Rad. The other three can fight it out for you." He shakes his head like what I said was ridiculous, and I give up.

"I could think of other places to put that tattoo," Callum whispers, lifting the hairs on the back of my neck.

I shiver, looking back at him when he shyly grins. "So...the track? What the hell is he talking about?" I ask, folding my arms over my chest. "And I'm not holding a sign that says that." I shake my head when he turns, giving me a disarming grin.

"There are three things you should know about me, Pretty Girl. I like you, drumming, and racing my dirt bike. In that order, too," he says with a wink, pulling out a black, lacy shirt from the back of my closet and thrusting it at me. "Now, put that on! We have lunch to eat and races to win."

I blink a few times when he throws himself on my bed, giving me an expectant look.

"Should I be worried?" I ask Callum out of the corner of my mouth.

He snorts. "With him? Always."

"Wonderful."

RAD

Nothing gets my blood pumping more than riding my dirt bike up and down the dirt hills at Racoon Run, nestled deep in the woods and hidden from the authorities. If they knew what we were up to out here, they'd haul us all in and slam the book in our faces.   I'm too pretty to go to jail.

But out here, it's just me, five solid acres of woods, winding dirt paths, and the privacy to compete against the other fools stupid enough to go up against me. Pfft. Like they'd ever win.

Throwing my head back, I cackle despite the heavy helmet weighing on my head and threatening to send me off my rapidly accelerating bike. This is the fucking time to be alive! The wind in my hair. The stiff competition. And the hottest girl in town is waiting for me on the sidelines. Since she wore me as a gag, I haven't gotten her out of my head. She's like this sexy little bug living in my brain, constantly screaming at me to follow her around and be her damn boyfriend.

Adrenaline pours through my veins when I peek behind me, hearing the telltale sign of the other assholes gaining. Their engines whine and rev up, steadily coming around the last turn I came around three seconds ago. Whenever I think I've taken the lead and relax, they catch up. Someone's upping their game, and we can't have that. I'm the reigning champion and intend to keep it that way. They've been a pain in my ass for the last three laps, and now it's time to smoke their asses.

"Eat my tires, assmunchers!" I shout, holding the clutch; I lightly use my left foot and change gears, darting further away from the competition.

Looking back, I grin. Suckers. They always think they can take on the great Rad, but they never can. I haven't lost a race in two years and don't plan on losing today. Especially not in front of my Pretty Girl—my girlfriend.

As ridiculous as it seems, I have to remind her a lot that she's mine. Fuck. I guess ours. Right? I mean, we made a deal to share her affection and gain her interest. I don't know how I will pound it into her head more...maybe pound her pussy? God, I can't wait to have that girl again. Shit. *Now is not the time, Little Rad. We have important things to do, like win this race so I can claim my prize and my girl.*

Speaking of...

I grin, rounding another turn and climbing the last rocky hill. Every bone in my body jostles at the dangerously high speed I'm rolling with. Pushing it faster and harder than before, I make it to the top, overlooking the trees and people waiting along the rocky dirt road. As soon as I come down the hill, there she is with a grin a mile wide, jumping up and down with excitement at the bottom of the valley. Cal grins down at her like the love-sick dope he is and hoots when I pass with his fist into the air, cheering me on. After so many months of moping around and feeling guilty, I finally see Callum's joy return. And it's all thanks to the bouncing Central girl beside him.

When I cross the finish line—first as always—I turn circles with my bike, kicking up the dust around the losers, finally trickling in.

"Holy shit!" my pretty girl says when she walks forward with a smile. God damn. That tight, lacy, black top I had her wear makes her boobs jiggle with every step. The stark image of my face, motorboating her titties, comes to mind, and I know what I'm doing tonight.

That and teaching Cal a little thing or two in the bedroom. Tonight, I'll cook dinner on the grill like a sophisticated gentleman and then motorboat my girl. Hashtag—goals. Hashtag—adulting.

"You were amazing!" she shrieks again, jumping up and down with a beautiful smile.

My pride blooms even bigger at her compliment, and I grin, pulling her close once she's in grabbing distance. If I had my way, I'd ride off into the sunset with her clasped behind me, holding my waist tight. But I rarely get my way, so holding her against my body is as good as it will get.

"I had a good luck charm here today," I say, throwing my helmet off and into Callum's unsuspecting arms. He grunts, narrowing his eyes at me with a shake of his head, securing the helmet on the bars of my bike. "It was all you, Pretty Girl. Oh, and the panties I stole from your drawer this morning. I'll keep them forever in your honor," I chuckle, tapping my pocket where a black, lacy thong sits like a good luck charm.

"He's never lost. Don't let him fool you with those pant-panties," Callum says, turning beat red at the prospect of her panties being in my pocket.

Her brows furrow. "You actually stole my panties, you psycho?" She gapes at me, staring at the bulge in my pocket, which I'd love to say is little Rad happy to see her.

You know, I've tried for years to get Callum in on my shenanigans and to loosen up. But the man is like a brick wall and never wants to play. Such a pity before, but now seeing him with our girl, well—things are changing in Callum's world. Actually, in our world. I know Kieran is fully invested in this River thing, and now we are, too. The only person sitting on the bench is Asher. He'll continue to fight with himself until he gives in and sinks his teeth into our girl. And boy, I can't wait for that day. Not only will he loosen up and get the large stick out of his ass, but he'll also finally get laid.

Callum is finally opening his horizons and seeing how easy it is to talk to her. When I walked into River's bedroom this morning after breaking in through her sliding glass door—which reminds me, I need to punish her for leaving her door unlocked. A wicked grin splits my lips. I guess that's what my handcuffs are for.

Anywho, the image of them snuggled so closely and the peace on his face I hadn't seen in over a year was heart-stopping. So, I took a picture. And backed it up several times. If they ever get ahold of it, they'll castrate me. She more than him, but I like my family jewels and would prefer them intact. I've seen what she can do with a knife, and I'm good.

"Once again, you're unbeatable," comes a deep voice behind me, causing River to stiffen against my body.

No, damn it, she was just warm and pliable against me. Now she's as stiff as a board, glaring at Van with so much hate. Finally, she relaxes in my hold, rolling her eyes toward the sky in annoyance at his presence.

Van eyes River like a prize he wants to claim, but too bad for him. She's fucking mine. Stupid, jealous idiot. It's like if he can't have River to himself, then no one can. But I have news for him.

I almost forgot old Donnie Boy started coming down to the track after he had to dump his Central girl into the gutter. Too bad for him. I scooped her right up, and now she's mine and onto bigger—yeah, bigger—and better dicks. Except we have much nicer personalities, too. We're the whole damn package, and Donnie is the trash panda begging for scraps.

"Ah, Donnie Boy," I greet with a smile, pulling a resistant River further into my side.

I frown when she's still stiff, barely breathing in this toxic idiot's presence. Don't resist my love, Pretty Girl. Go with the flow. I'll never let this idiot touch you ever again or hurt you.

"Fancy seeing you here." I grin again, tilting my head when his jealous eyes turn to River, who frowns at him with unease.

His eyes light up, jealousy taking him over. If he were a monster, he'd turn green with envy, snatch her out of my arms, and carry her to his kingdom. I'd be the gallant knight with sword in hand, ready to defend my girlfriend's honor.

"Rivy," he whispers, furrowing his brows. "You're here?" His voice dips low in warning, like he's secretly trying to tell her something.

"Yes, my girlfriend is here. With me," I say, goading him with a friendly grin.

His eyes widen a smidge, and his head jerks back. Hook, line, and sinker, fucker.

Keeping my hands on her waist, I squeeze her into me, loving how her body feels against mine. God, I can't get enough of her. I'd eat her... WAIT.... I will eat her all up. But later. Maybe I'll tie Van down and force him to watch as he kicks and screams, and I give River the best orgasm ever.

I love the way Van's jaw ticks when he glares at her in disappointment and shakes his head.

"How much of a wager did you put on this one?" I ask, once again poking the Van bear for my entertainment.

His jaw ticks, telling me all I need to know. He's squandering away what his daddy paid him to step away from River and stay in college. I bet he never told River a thing. I wonder how he did it? Did he just walk away from the precious jewel in my arms like she was nothing more than toilet paper? I bet he did.

His nostrils flare, and I want to cackle at his stupid fucking face. "Callum," he greets, ignoring me entirely while still watching River with an interested eye.

"Van," Callum says in a deep voice, inclining his head in greeting, taking a step closer to River. The back of his fingers lightly skims against hers, drawing her into him.

"Congrats on the win. I guess I'll see you at the neighborhood cookout next week," Van says, thinning his lips. His beady, evil eyes fall on Callum and River's pinkies hooking together.

I grin triumphantly when he balls up his fists. I live to piss this juvenile prick off. Nothing grinds my gears more than some idiot laying down and doing what their mommy and daddy told them to do. You know what mine told me to do? They told me no tattoos and piercings, and the moment I turned into an adult, the band was done. Fat chance is what I told them. No one takes away my band. They're more family to me than the people who raised me.

In turn, they raised their haughty eyebrows at me like I was still their sweet little Rad. The son who didn't move a toe out of line. Little did they know I had plans for freedom. The night of my eighteenth birthday, Cal brought me to his tattoo guy and helped me celebrate with the musical notes on my chest.

"I'm home!" The door slams behind me, louder than necessary, announcing my arrival.

"It's ten-thirty!" my mother hisses, drying her hands on a towel in the kitchen.

"It's Friday," I retort without an ounce of emotion and grab a drink from the refrigerator.

The cold liquid slides down my throat, giving me the necessary courage. Throughout the entirety of my tattoo, regret sat in the back of my mind. My father's words constantly played on a loop as I lay there, suffering through the pain of the needle. But it was what I wanted. I've been subjected to my father's iron fist for so long. He may not have ever hit me, but I was done being subjected to something I didn't quite believe.

Locking everything inside, I turn to face the man of the house. Wrinkles mar his older-looking face, tinting with disapproval. His dark eyes, similar to mine, rove over my neck, covered in protective plastic, and his entire body locks up.

You know, I could have gone the safe route and gotten music notes behind my ears or hell on my ass. My parents wouldn't have seen those. At least, not right away. But why go small when you can go big and all the way? For years, my parents have warned me time and time again that every inch of my body is God's temple. Every scar or scratch, they'd tsk me into being ashamed of falling off my bike or breaking my damn arm.

"Your body's a temple, Ashton. Treat it like one. No tattoos or piercings are allowed under our roof." Yeah, right. Okay. Sure.

"What did you do?" he shouts, inching closer with a snarl lining his wrinkly face.

I hold my breath in my lungs when he inches down, eyeing my tattoo closely.

"Ashton!" my mother yelps, coming to inspect my newest piece. "What have you done?"

I shrug. "What I wanted to do," I say in a low, warning voice. "This is my body; I wanted something to represent myself through."

It's the only piece of me I have. My parents have restricted every ounce of everything I've ever taken an interest in. Video games, TV, and even the band—limiting my time with each. They've thrown them to the wayside when it became too much. Hell, I couldn't even watch The Wizard movie I wanted to when I was twelve because of magic. Their entire logic makes my eyes roll into the back of my head.

With this tattoo, I took back a little piece of what made me, me.

"What you wanted to do? Do you know how expensive that is to get removed?" my father spits, standing straight.

"I'm not getting it removed," I tell him simply, staring straight into the abyss of his darkening eyes.

"Then you're not staying here," my father spits, crossing his arms over his chest and lifting his chin.

"Ashton," my mother begs my father with pleading eyes. "He's only eighteen. You can't just kick him out." She swallows hard when his burning gaze turns to her, and she shakes her head. I swear I've never seen my mother cry, but in this instant, tears stream down her cheeks. But she should have seen this rebellion from a mile away.

"Get out of my house until that abomination is peeled from your skin," my father says, waltzing toward the front door and throwing it open.

"Call me," my mother whispers, kissing me on the cheek. "Don't hesitate." I nod when I only want to scoff at her hypocritical face. How can a woman stand by while her husband throws out their only son?

As the door slams behind me and all the lights disappear from the house, I realize how fucking alone I am. It isn't until Callum's mom steps out from the shadows and offers me her hand.

"Callum may have spilled what you two have been up to today," she whispers, leading me across the street toward their house.

I swallow hard, on the verge of tears when she pulls me into the lively house and sets me down on the couch.

"You have a home here for as long as you need, Rad. Okay?" I nod with gratitude, washing away the tears from my cheeks.

"Thank you," I whisper, receiving the tall glass of water she hands me. Silently, I promise myself that I will never let another person stifle my wants and needs. I will never live under a cloud of bullshit.

I swallow hard, coming out of the memory with a shaky breath. There's nothing like winning a race and immediately being thrown into the wolf's den. My parents and I aren't exactly on speaking terms, especially my father. Occasionally, I talk to my mom and update her on my life. But for the most part, they're living their life, and I'm living mine. I guess that's why Callum was so surprised when I called my mom asking for any home nurses in the area.

"The cookout?" Callum groans quietly, shaking his head. "I hate that tradition."

Yeah, me too, buddy. It's the one day a year our parents all get together with mimosas, margaritas, and catered barbeque ribs, all in the name of neighborhood unity. We're forced to stand in the scorching sun, watching as they gossip and flitter around while stuffing our faces with the catered food that they were too lazy to make themselves. Fucking Gloria and Nigel Montgomery and their ridiculous traditions of unity. Unity, my ass. They want to wave their money around for the world to see in the form of social events and rub their neighbor's noses in it.

"Me too," Van grumbles. "But they make us go."

Van is so fucking hopeless. I snicker when I lean down, plant a kiss right on River's lips, and overtake her in front of him, shoving my tongue down her throat. He curses under his breath, huffing and puffing. There's nothing this idiot can do to stop this from happening.

Nope.

Instead, he walks away with his pride bruised and his dick hard—hopefully. I want him to drown in the misery River has felt all this time; we'll build her back up and take her away from this place.

Her breaths heave frantically, and her hand swats at my chest over and over like she wants me to stop shoving my tongue down her throat. I pull back, squeezing my eyes shut as I catch my breath. Her mouth tastes as good as I remember, and I want to live inside it for eternity.

"That was my prize," I murmur, nudging my nose against hers, fluttering my eyes open, and staring into the abyss of her green eyes.

Think we have some time to play before practice?" I wiggle my brows at Callum, who turns beat red, averting his eyes to the fallen sticks around us.

"It's only three," he murmurs, looking at his phone. "They don't get out of class for a few more hours."

Right. Kieran and Asher were forced into university after high school. So, while they suffer getting their degrees, Callum and I make the cash for our band. One day, we'll save enough and hightail it out of here. But first, we need to secure as much as we can. With their college degrees in hand, we'll safely be on our way to the top, far away from here.

"All right, Pretty Girl. We'll take you back to our house and handcuff you to the bed. It's about time Callum learned a little something about cunnilingus." I grin, rolling my extra-long tongue out, creating waves with it.

Her eyes widen at the length, and she nearly chokes, staring at it when I scoop her up and force her legs around my waist. Digging my fingers into her pert ass, I grin, mounting my bike with her wrapped around me. Those delectable fingernails dig into the back of my neck, breaking through the skin.

Trembling, her eyes dart around as she pales.

"Rad," she hisses, staring frantically into my eyes.

Furrowing my brows, my heart rate doubles at the sight of her distress. Yeah, I'm not fond of that at all. I want to ease her tension, not cause it.

"You good?" I ask Callum, and he nods with a roll of his eyes.

"I'll see you at the house," he confirms, waltzing into the woods with his hands in his pockets.

Before he passes a large tree, he stares back at us with longing. A small smile touches his lips, and then he's gone—lost to the trees surrounding us.

"I gotta get my prize, and then...it's tongue town for you, Pretty Girl. I'm going to suck your clit so hard you're going to cum in my mouth," I murmur in her ear, starting up the bike. "I can't wait to taste you."

She shivers against me and shakes her head. "Rad, I've never been on a bike."

Anxiety sparks in her voice when her worried eyes find mine again. A drum pounds in my ears and my brows furrow as a deep-seated need to keep her safe overtakes me. I tighten my grip on her waist and kiss her cheek, lingering longer than necessary. She shudders against me, clinging tighter to my body.

"You'll never have to worry with me, Pretty Girl. I'll fight off the monsters and keep your brains in your head," I murmur, shoving the helmet over her head.

She grunts when I fasten the strap under her chin and wiggle the helmet to ensure it's secured properly. Like her, I'd rather she not get injured on our ride home through the woods.

She side-eyes me and probably frowns under the helmet. "I'd appreciate it if my brains didn't hit the pavement," she says in a shaky voice, looking toward the ground.

"Have no fear. Your Rad boyfriend is here," I whisper, starting the loud bike as the sound fills the woods, and she scoots closer to my front.

People wave and cheer as we slowly make our way through the small crowd, lingering against trees and discreetly drinking out of flasks. Down in Raccoon Run, no one seems to follow the rules. It's the one place we can disappear and hide from expectations. We drink, have races, party, and have a fun time.

"Good race, bro."

I grin, stopping in front of my most trusted track manager—Reese. We met him a few years back in school. He's always been a financial god and a trustworthy individual—well, for a drug dealer. Now, he helps around the track, taking bets and selling what he wants. You'd never guess his parents lived in Lakewood, and he did, too. For a time, that is. Then he found his crowd in Central City and moved there to continue growing his empire.

"Thanks, man," I say, taking the plastic bag filled with a mixture of crisp and crinkled bills. AKA—my winnings for being the badass I am. "How much?" I ask, cocking a brow when he grins.

"Eight hundred," he says, side-eyeing the surrounding people, and I nod. We exchange a few more words before he returns to handing out more winnings to the people who put their money on the safest bet—me.

"All right, Pretty Girl. Let's go to my house," I say, revving up the engine again and kicking off with a cackle.

I peek behind me, meeting Van's steel gaze and flick dirt in his stupid face, laughing with glee when he sputters and bends at the waist. Asshat. You can stare at me like you want to kill me all you want, but it's not going to happen. River will never be yours again.

River is mine.

Okay, fine. She's ours. I mean, I've never had to share before. But what can I say? I'm a marvelous and caring lover who enjoys sharing. Just this once.

After a five-minute drive through the woods using my trails, I pull up to my backdoor with a grin. Looking down at my girl, I smile; she lights up my whole damn life. Not once did she try to jump off the bike or yell at me or smack me again. Instead, she pulled herself closer and closer to me, pushing her center against my raging hard-on.

I set both feet on the ground, balancing the bike and shutting it off. I rub my hands up and down her back, slowly working toward the helmet, weighing her down. She huffs when I gently pull it off her head and hang the strap on the bar where it sways in the light summer wind.

"If you enjoyed that ride, I'll give you an even better one in the next twenty minutes," I say, grinning with a wink.

"I did not enjoy the ride," she huffs, running a hand through her wild long strands and blowing some out of her face.

Moving some hairs from her face, I stare down at her again. I'm so fucking smitten with this damn girl, and my damn heart flutters out of control. Even when she gives me the stank eye, probably plotting my death.

"How about another one? Maybe on my bed as we roll around on eight hundred bucks?" Her pretty, pouting lips pop open, and her green eyes bounce to mine in shock. I grin more, holding up the plastic bag I had shoved in my pocket. Her eyes dance across the multiple crinkled bills. "After we pour this on the sheets, I'm going to lay you down," I rasp, nipping at her jawline.

Her breaths pick up, her chest heaving against mine. The feel of her fingernails ripping into my flesh has me grinding myself against her center, begging to rip through her shorts and fuck her until she says my name.

"And then what?" she whispers when my tongue swirls down her neck, and I suck her flesh between my teeth.

She groans, letting my hand wander between our bodies to the soaked, promised land I can't wait to live in. Do you think she'd let me sleep with my cock buried inside her—hard or not? I shiver at the thought, moving her tiny shorts and panties aside with my fingers.

"You good, Pretty Girl? Can I stick my fingers in your pussy and make you come on my bike?"

What I don't tell her is I want her to christen my winning bike with her pussy juices so I can continue to win fat stacks of cash to fuck her on.

Shit. My dick rages inside my jeans, begging to punch through and fuck her right here. But If I fuck her first, I can't show our precious Callum how to use his tongue correctly. Soon, he'll be an expert. First, though, I need to prime her and get her juices flowing, so he has a juicy fruit to sink his teeth into.

"Yes," she moans as I shove my fingers inside her, basking in the feel of her contracting inner walls seizing around my fingers.

"Good girl," I whisper, slowly pumping my fingers in and out. "You're so goddamn wet, Pretty Girl. Did you really not like the ride? Was it the vibrations that got you going?" I murmur, nipping at her neck again and leaving my marks behind on her flesh.

Mine. Fucking mine.

"Shut. Up," she gasps, hiding her face in the crook of my neck. "Harder, Rad."

Well, she doesn't have to tell me twice. Grunting, I pick up the pace, enjoying my name on her lips. Her moans ring in my ears like music until she cries out into my neck, squeezing around my fingers as she comes so hard her damn body trembles.

"You are fucking exceptional," I whisper, kissing her cheek.

Her warm breath brushes across my skin when she pulls back, staring at me with glossed-over green eyes—a small smile tugs at her lips when she looks my face over. Dare I say, she seems impressed and likes what she sees.

"You're not too bad yourself," she murmurs in a daze, leaning her forehead against mine.

Her breath picks up again when I wiggle my fingers, still nestled inside her. I contemplate leaving them inside her but decide against it. Bringing my soaked fingers to my mouth, I suck them in. Her taste explodes on my tongue. And yup. I'm keeping her forever.

There's no doubt about that. I'll lock her on my bed or tie her up in my closet.

"God, you taste so damn good. I want to put this in a jar and keep it forever and..." River puts a hand over my mouth with a shake of her head.

"You're really disgusting sometimes, but I'll forgive you just this once because you gave me an orgasm," she huffs, but my damn pride blooms, and I lick her hand.

"The best one ever, right?" I say with a grin, lifting her off the bike and setting her on her wobbly feet. I jump off, kicking the kickstand down so the bike rests. "Now, let's throw some cash around and teach Callum a thing or two."

"Teach him?" She raises a skeptical brow but still follows me through the back sliding glass door into the spotless kitchen—my domestic work of art. "What would we teach him?" Her skeptical voice echoes through the room, turning to me, awaiting an answer.

"Well, definitely not science or math, Pretty Girl. I'm talking...." I stick out my long tongue again, loving the way her eyes dilate at the sight, and wiggle it around. "Butt stuff, pussy stuff, tongue stuff.... Any type of stuff, really." I shrug, walking further into the house with wild ideas running through my mind.

Ideas like River sprawled out with her pussy in the air and my mouth on it while he fucks her mouth, and then we take turns fucking her until my cock can sleep inside her. Shit. I discreetly adjust my cock inside my pants, watching her from the corner of my eyes.

Her nose wrinkles. "Butt stuff? Really? What are you, an alien?" Her eyes roll toward the ceiling.

"I could dress up as one if you wanted! I could paint my skin blue and probe you all night long." My grin spreads when she shoots me a scathing look, shaking her head. "Well, in that case, welcome to Casa Callum and Rad," I offer, spreading my arms wide and highlighting the beautiful house we own together.

"You two?" she asks, running a finger over the countertops. "You weren't kidding about your domestic duties, were you?"

"I am the man of this house," I proclaim with a grin, pulling my pants up further on my hips.

"Second man," Callum mutters, moseying into the kitchen with his hands in his pockets. The telltale sign that he's nervous as fuck, having a chick in the house. But not just any chick, our River.

His eyes light up when she turns toward him and grins, offering him a little wave.

"Did you like your ride?" he asks quietly, never lifting his head. His eyes drift over the floor, studying the damn tile like it's more interesting than the beautiful girl standing before us.

She side-eyes me, mischief sparkling in the depths of her green eyes, and shrugs. "Meh, it was okay." I nearly sputter at her but decide to bite my tongue.

He smiles softly, finally lifting his eyes and meeting hers. Hearts explode over his head at the sight of her. "So, you hung-hungry?" he asks, taking a deep breath. I've never seen him so damn flustered before, let alone talk to a girl.

She shrugs again, once again looking around our place. "I could eat..." she trails off, looking off toward the small living room. "This place is nice," she murmurs, offering him a warm smile. "How'd you two?" I jerk my gaze to Callum, who looks off toward the small living room again, getting lost in his head.

"After my parents kicked me out, I came here," I say, fondly looking around. I've only lived here for three years, but this has been more of a home for me than my other one ever was.

The environment my parents cultivated behind their four walls was more than toxic; it was downright deadly. My father, the beloved pastor of the Lutheran church, ruled that house with an iron fist. They placed rules upon rules on me, their only child, for years. No one ever knew the moment he stepped into the church, a firm mask fell into place. He became the man he thought the world wanted to see. Father of the year, if I say so myself. The moment I could escape, I did.

"Why'd they kick you out?" she asks, brows furrowing in concern. Her fingers work up my arm, eventually stopping to massage my shoulder. I lean into her touch, taking comfort in her.

"They're assholes," I say with a big breath. "I got some tats, and they didn't approve, so I moved in here with my boy Callum."

"My parents invited him to stay after they did-did that," allum whispers, peeking at us. "They were the best. They really liked him."

"How?" River laughs. "Seriously? They liked him?" My mouth opens at her insult, and she giggles, making Callum's face light up.

"Somehow," he quips, "but yeah, they did. He lived here with us when...." My heart falls into my ass when the ghosts of his past, grab hold of him, but before I can do anything, River's on him with a giant hug.

"You don't have to say it," she murmurs into his chest, rubbing her hands up and down his back. Relaxing in her hold, he puts his cheek on the top of her head, sighing with contentment. Every worry leaks out of him with her in his arms.

Shock takes me over at her words. My jaw hits the ground. He fucking told her the tragic story of his parents and sister. Callum doesn't tell anyone what happened, instead keeping it bottled up and reliving it every day in his genius mind. I never thought I'd see the day when he opened up to someone besides us. River's done the fucking unthinkable and grabbed his attention.

He whispers something in her ears until she pulls away, staying at arm's length. His fingers run through her hair, curling it behind her ear. Love emanates from his gray eyes, pouring out to her. It would break his fucking heart if we had to leave her behind in this shit town. And we won't.

River West is ours to keep.

Leaning down, Callum tentatively presses his lips into hers with uncertainty. Tangling her fingers in his blonde locks, she holds him there until their tongues dance together, and they're left breathless. Callum groans into her mouth when his shaky hands find her ass, and he squeezes it, pulling her closer.

"All right," I say, wrapping my arms around the both of them as they pull away from each other with swollen lips, eyeing me like I'm up to something. "I'm feeling a little left out of the fun. Let's teach our boy some tongue tricks."

Callum sucks in a breath. A blush takes over his entire head, turning him into a strawberry. I expect River to give me sass, but that cute smile she loves to toss around crosses her lips. She shrugs, getting to her tippy toes. Her soft lips kiss the edge of his, trailing down his neck. He groans, running both hands through her hair and holding her there.

"You-you don't have to," Callum stutters through the tremors shaking his body. "I..." He loses himself in the feel of her fingers roaming over his chest, slowly guiding down to the bulge growing in his jeans. She squeezes him, earning a full-blown moan from him.

That's right, Callum. Let loose. Let our River guide you into a den of sin.

"So, shall we go?" I say, wiggling my eyebrows, and gesture to the bedroom.

"Lead the way," River rasps, holding out her hand.

We stare at Callum, waiting for him to decide. Because ultimately, it's up to him whether he wants to participate.

"You—you'll teach me?" he asks softly, refusing to look at her.

"I'm fine with it," River proclaims with a shrug. "You, him, and me? Hell, yes."

And that's all Callum needs. With as much confidence as he can muster, he grabs her arm and leads her to my bedroom down the hallway. Dare I say there's a little pep in his horny step and pride swelling his chest.

"Well, this should be fun!" I whoop, ripping off my shirt and tossing it on the couch when I pass, heading down the hallway.

RIVER

"And eight hundred," Rad sing-songs, placing the last twenty-dollar bill onto the white sheet.

Stepping back, he nods a few times, fixing a few bills until they're straight. His arms are wide, showing off his newest masterpiece with pride, just like he promised—a bed full of money ready to roll around on.

"Was that really necessary? Like...you seriously want to screw on money?" I raise a brow, grasping for his logic, but come back empty-handed.

Rad doesn't seem to have a lot of logic to his actions, but I can't fault him for that. Secretly, I like him just the way he is—weirdo tendencies and all. In my eyes, he will always be the kind-hearted hero who scooped my broken body off the darkened lawn.

He turns his energetic smile toward me and winks. Warmth fills my chest at how he smiles, looking at me like I'm already the light of his life, and he can't wait to get boned on a pile of money.

"You christened my bike. Now, you have to christen my money. For good luck!" he proclaims, tossing a fist in the air and doing an odd dance by twirling in a circle and whooping.

I groan, wrinkling my nose. "You know, that money could have been in some dude's ass last night after he stripped and his sweaty balls got stuck to it," I quip, raising a brow when his face brightens even more, and he laughs.

Looking down at the pile of money, he shrugs, waving my comment off. Sometimes I think the guy needs something to calm him down. But other times, he turns me into a mushy, giggling schoolgirl with his antics. Fuck. What is happening to me? I've kept people at arm's length for years, and these assholes march in like they already own my heart. And I'm giving it to them willingly, without a fight. Here, take my heart into your palms and promise you won't crush it. I can't deny the heart of gold Rad seems to have and his caring yet odd nature. Between saving me and saving my mom, my heart flutters in his presence. Maybe I've spent too much of my life guarding my heart. For good reason, I suppose. But fuck it if I don't want to give in.

"You've won-won every race for two years in a row," Callum stammers, keeping his wide eyes on the money, refusing to look at either of us.

"Facts!" Rad says, pointing at Callum. "But what's a little extra pussy juice for good luck?"

Callum sputters, turning beet red, and turns away with a huff. Hiding behind his head, he releases a deep, calming breath before turning toward Rad again.

"Ra-Rad, for fuck's sake."

"Come on, man, we've lived together for three years now." Rad's grin grows when he places a hand on Callum's shoulder and leans in. "You should be used to me by now." Rad laughs when Callum shoves him sideways with a grunt, tossing him onto the pile of money.

Rad doesn't seem to mind the assault as he rolls around on top of the money, collecting some bills in his hands and then throwing them above his head. The green bills slowly fall and land on his chest and stomach like snowflakes floating through the winter breeze. His grin never breaks when he rubs it all over his chest with a menacing chuckle, turning all of his attention to me.

Rad may not be as intense as Kieran or even Asher, but the look he levels me with has my heart pounding. All the care and love he can provide shines through, and there's no doubt about how he's feeling.

"Am I sexy like this, Pretty Girl?" he asks, playfully wiggling his brows.

I lick my lips, eyeing his lean body when he props his head on his hand, turning to his side. Something dangerous lurks in the depth of his dark eyes, promising nothing but pleasure in my future.

My eyes trail from the tip of his curly mullet soaked in sweat to the ink blotting his chest and neck. Music notes curl over dark black ink, crawling up his neck and only stopping on the right side near his skull, where more music notes dot his skin. He smiles up at me so brightly it's almost blinding. I suck in a breath, staring intensely at his tattoo, losing myself in the lowest part of my life, brought on by the memory of what I endured.

"Don't," I warn, frantically trying to kick him off. "Please," I whisper, gasping for breath, kicking a foot out and landing my kick somewhere on his body.

What a night to leave my knife behind. From now on, I will carry it everywhere. No exceptions.

"Hey," he whispers softly, running a soft finger down my wet cheeks. His touch momentarily calms my nerves. I heave a breath. "You fell asleep on the way to the hospital. I'm not them, remember? We're at the hospital now." My eyes roam over his concern-filled face when he crouches in the opened passenger's side door. The warm breeze of August swirls around us, lifting my long brown strands. I shiver as they tickle along my back, and memories of those monsters' hands grabbing and pulling make my stomach turn.

Behind Rad rests the four-story Central City Hospital. Flags wave and lights blink on and off in the night sky filled with sagging clouds thick with moisture. The smell of rain hits my nose, and my chest caves in. Chaos runs free through my mind at the thought of stepping foot in the hospital. Behind those walls rests my salvation— the answer to the pain radiating from between my legs. It throbs and aches with every move of my body.

The softness in Rad's expression makes more tears trail down my cheeks and fall to the leather seats. With a quivering lip, I shake my head.

"I'm sorry," I gasp out. "I...." Without a second thought, he brings me into his arms, holding me close when he stands at full height, closing the door behind us.

For one split second, I panic at his touch. My mind begs me to thrash and save myself, but the adrenaline that once coursed through my veins ebbs away—leaving my muscles tired and my brain in a foggy existence. I sag into him and realize he's holding me tight and secure without really touching me. Not sexually, no. He's touching me protectively like I'm his little injured bird needing a rescue.

"If you ever want to name names, I'll kill them for you." His voice wavers for only a second, something arctic taking over like he's plotting my revenge on the walk through the front door. "My name is Ashton Radcliffe," he says in a rare moment of vulnerability, swallowing a large lump in his throat.

If I were in a better state of mind and not slowly drowning in the grief of my rape, I'd have told him I knew who he was, that we go to the same high school and have all year. But he didn't seem to recognize me, and that was fine. I hold my tongue, feeling oddly comfortable in the arms of my savior.

The heat of his gaze staring down at me with curiosity seers through me. He doesn't utter another word until we're standing in front of the emergency room desk, refusing to let my feet hit the floor.

"Can I help you?" the nurse says I'm sure looking us over with an inspecting eye.

"I..." he begins, but his beautiful face twists, and his dark eyes dart to mine for permission.

I swallow all the hurt, aches, and pains, burying them in the pit of my stomach. Tears burn the back of my eyes, and my nose tingles against his shirt. If I could stay covered and protected in his arms, I would.

"I was raped." And those words hit me harder than anything my life has brought me. It's real now. I've said the words, and they carry a heavy weight. The truth of my situation now hangs in the air.

"I found her. We were at a party. They..." He takes a shuddering breath.

"Pretty Girl," Rad whispers, cupping my cheeks, grounding me in the present. "Why're you crying?" Two seconds ago, he was light and happy, rolling on his side in the money he insisted on laying down, and now he's sitting on the edge of the bed with me nestled between his legs. I hover above him, planting my feet on the ground.

Wetness coats my cheeks and chin. Shit. I'm really fucking crying right now. How'd I get so trapped in the past that I didn't realize what was happening?

Seeing his tattoo brought everything I had buried for so long back to the surface. When I opened my eyes after the rape happened, it was the first thing I saw hovering above me. I should have been frightened, but something was soothing in his words and gentle in his touch when he placed his coat around my exposed parts.

"I'd never force you to do anything," he whispers with concern, taking over his tone, "Pretty girl. We can watch a movie. We can..." I lose his voice in the vivid memories of my past. His lips keep moving, but nothing registers in my mind. Nothing but the words he's uttered before flash through my mind.

"You'll never have to worry with me, Pretty Girl. I'll fight off the monsters."

His words hit me hard in the chest, knocking the remaining oxygen from my lungs. My lips pop open, fighting to bring much-needed air into my body. Fighting the memories floating through my mind evades me, and I once again fall into their depths as Rad strokes fingers through my hair and Callum rests at my back. He whispers encouraging words into the nape of my neck, seeming to know exactly where my brain went.

Nervously, I peek around the empty school hallway, standing before Rad's locker. Hearts and other notes decorate the outside.

Every inch of me trembles at the prospect of him catching me standing here with a tiny note clutched in hand—a small message filled with the two names I never wanted to see again.

After returning to school a week ago, their faces were the only thing I saw. When they passed in the halls, they discreetly checked me over—even being as bold as cornering me and reminding me of what they could do as punishment for opening my mouth. Every detail plays like a damn movie.

The police refused to do anything about the situation. Instead, laughing me away after I had given them their names and showed them their faces. My innocence was lost, and it'was nothing but a joke. Who wouldn't want to lose their virginity to the star football player? Or two? Even better. Now, I have no other options.

No one else is on my side.

With one last breath, I shove the note through the top holes of his locker, silently begging that he finds it. And then finds them. I don't know what I want to accomplish with this, but I want justice.

"I never told you thank you." My voice breaks in half as my fingers trace over the musical notes on his chest.

"Oh, Little Star," Callum whispers with encouragement, wrapping his arms around me in gentle support. "Tell him." Rad's brows furrow in confusion, darting his eyes between the two of us.

"Thank me?" Rad asks, shaking his head. "Today was..."

"Not for today," I whisper, my voice full of unshed emotions I let no one see. Callum tightens his hold on me, burying his face in my neck and helping me breathe evenly.

"Did you hear?"

"Oh, my God!" Tessa says in a hushed voice, turning toward the front doors with Sara right beside her.

They continue to whisper until Bradley and his best friend Kyler march through the doors with matching black eyes and limps. I hold on to my gasp, watching with wide eyes as they walk by without passing off another threat.

"A long time ago, I slipped two names into your locker, and you...." I roll my lips together as his thumbs brush across my cheeks. "And you..." My heavy tongue refuses to cooperate, but Rad picks up.

"My locker?" He looks down, scrunching his cute button nose. Losing himself in his thoughts, he finally stiffens when realization smacks him. Jerking back, his lips pop open, and he stares at me in disbelief, shaking his head. "We beat the ever-living shit out of those assholes. Kieran, Asher, and me...we cornered them and made them regret what they did to...to.... Wait...." More realization swiftly takes over his paling face, and he clasps my cheeks tighter as if I were about to run away from him.

The night of the party, he could have turned the other cheek and walked away, leaving me exposed to the world. He could have had his fun, too, and I would have had no power to stop him. Instead, he cradled me in his arms and took me away from the party like my personal protector.

"You?" he breathes. "No, I would have remembered. I looked everywhere for you." He shakes his head. "I would have recognized you anywhere." But he didn't, because I didn't want him to. That night, he may have been my hero, but I wanted to shrink into the shadows and pretend it didn't happen.

Tears stream down my cheeks when the first cut snips off ten inches of hair, landing in a spiral on the bathroom floor. They used my hair as a weapon to hold me down and inflict pain. Now, I'm ridding myself of the weakness that caused me so much harm. By the time I'm finished, my brown locks lay lifelessly by my jaw, framing my face with uneven strands and imperfections. But I don't give a shit. I raise my chin, eyeing my new stony exterior. No one will ever get something over on me again.

My fingers run through his curly mullet, tracing down his neck and onto his chest. The warmth of his skin bleeds through my fingers tips, taking away the darkness of my memories. Bad things happen to everyone every single day. It's what you do with those dire situations that count. I drowned in my misery for an entire year, blaming myself for everything. If I hadn't done this.... If I hadn't done that.... But it happened. And it wasn't my fault. Through shitty therapy provided by the reluctant state, I made it through to the other side. I embrace who I am now and who I was. We're one and mentally stronger than before. Sure, I've had my fair share of hurdles, but I always make my way through them.

"I cut my hair after it happened and wore big clothes." I swallow hard, keeping eye contact, but my fingers still wander down his flesh. Callum squeezes my waist in support, holding me as I talk through it.

"Why don't I remember?" he whispers, seeming pained that he can't remember me or my face.

"Because I didn't want you to," I whisper with a break in my voice, cupping his crestfallen cheeks so tinged with hurt his eyes water.

"I went to the police," he says, swallowing his emotions. They..."

"They laughed me away. How dare I accuse the two starting football players of something so heinous? Their words, not mine." Rad gently wipes the remaining tears from my cheeks with understanding.

"I wanted to disappear, Rad. I wanted.... To forget about it. They haunted me...."

"And when you saw him at the bar?" he questions, tensing up.

"It was like seeing a ghost from my past, but that's it. Nothing more," I murmur, vividly remembering the terror I felt when Bradley bumped into me that night, shattering glasses from my tray. And then again, down the road where he stood next to another man draped in shadows.

"Oh, Pretty Girl," he urgently whispers, putting his forehead on mine. "You saw him, and then you.... God, I didn't force you into anything that night, right? I didn't...." My desperate lips pounce on him, shutting down his train of thought until I pull back breathlessly. Wild, nervous eyes inspect mine.

"I decided a long time ago to take my body back. I didn't want the memory of those assholes holding me back from doing what I wanted. Trauma healing comes in many forms, and I took mine by the horns." I search his eyes, hoping he understands my meaning.

I've never thought twice about the men I sleep with. As long as we're safe and clean, I take what I want and give my body the pleasure it deserves. Some might say it's too much and I shouldn't heal in the arms of another. But what do they know?

Leaning in again, I lay my lips on his, waiting for the moment he gives in. His fingers softly roam, not daring to delve into other places. Tracing softly up my leg, he leaves goosebumps in his wake with the tiny circles he rubs against my skin.

"I'm not a breakable doll," I whisper, nipping at his bottom lip. Securing it between my teeth, I nibble more, forcing a groan from the back of his throat.

"I know you're not, Pretty Girl," he whispers, bravely cupping my ass and squeezing until he pulls me into his lap. "You're the bravest girl I know."

I fall into his kiss, letting him overtake my mouth. My fingers rake through his hair. He touches me everywhere except the places I need him. I pull back, panting when his mouth descends my jaw toward my neck, nipping the whole way.

"I'll leave you two," Callum whispers behind my ear, kissing me one last time.

"Wait," I say through an exhale, my breaths shuddering in my chest when I reach for him, grasping his forearm. Warily, I look at Rad, who stops his kisses on my neck with one last loud pop.

A slight smile picks up the edges of his lips against my flesh. "Yeah, dude. You can see the live show this time. No more hiding behind walls." I roll my eyes, squeezing Callum's arm in reassurance.

"Stay," I murmur, staring into the abyss of his gray eyes, darkening with a maddening lust at the sight of us together.

"Ok-okay," he murmurs, stumbling over his words as a red tint fills his cheeks and stains his neck.

Callum stays close when I remove my grip from his forearm. Licking his lips, his eyes drop to mine, and I seize the moment before he can think anything about it. Gently, I press my lips to his, savoring the shudder that runs through him. His tongue dives into my mouth as Rad's hands wander down my body, pulling at my shirt.

"Pause the tongue town session, and let's get our Pretty Girl naked," Rad murmurs, forcing Callum to break his kiss. Callum pants against me when Rad pulls off my shirt and tosses it aside.

"I'll be over here," he whispers, pointing to the beat-up recliner in the corner.

"Oh, no, you don't. This is a teachable moment, dude. Lay down," Rad says, pointing to the bed.

"But-but, I...." Callum turns such a dark shade of red I almost swear he's going to run away.

"No buts, well, maybe hers," Rad chuckles, and I swat him in the chest. "Just lay down. You want to learn the logistics of fucking? Then you need to be deep in the trenches when I fuck her," Rad says in a no-nonsense tone. "Watch as I fuck our girl and learn a little something."

"It's okay," I say with an encouraging grin, nodding toward the middle of the bed.

Tentatively, he sits on the edge of the bed, keeping his distance, staring with such intensity I swear my skin is about to go up in flames. Every caress of my skin lights me up until I'm completely naked, sitting in Rad's lap. Callum sits back with wide eyes, staring like a deer in headlights. From here, I see the tension lining his face and the enormous bulge pressing against his jeans.

"Touch yourself," I demand softly, aching to see his hand stroke his length.

Callum's Adam's apple bobs with a heavy swallow, and his teeth sink into his lips. Nervousness takes over his trembling fingers when he tries three times to grip the bottom of his black t-shirt. Finally, with one last frustrated huff, he throws his shirt next to him, exposing his beautifully toned chest and stomach. His tattoos come to life with every move he makes. And I want nothing more than to lick every inch of him if he'll let me.

"Pants too, dude. Show our girl your dick," Rad snickers, rubbing up and down my body. "Again," he adds, causing Callum to cover his reddened face with his hands.

With one last curse, Callum slowly undoes his jeans and shoves them down his legs. Sitting back, his long fingers curl over his dick, trying its hardest to come out from his boxers.

"Now sit back and watch the show. If you're lucky, maybe Pretty Girl will let you come all over her titties again." Rad wiggles his brows playfully, turning his attention to me. His large, brown eyes take me in, and it's as if a switch was flipped when his fingers caress my cheeks with deep concern etching across his face.

"You're seriously good with this?" Rad whispers, pressing light kisses on my lips. "We can stop. You just told me a lot of heavy shit, Pretty Girl. And I'm a damn gentleman."

I smirk against his lips, forcing him back into the bed. Money lifts into the air when his back lands against the mattress, and he grins at me, running his hands down my bare sides. His thumbs swipe across my nipples, and shivers roll down my spine, causing goosebumps in their wake. Over and over, he swipes against my sensitive nipples until their painful buds beg for the warmth of his mouth.

"Maybe I don't want a gentleman right now." I cement that fact by leaning down and running my tongue over his hard nipple. His sharp intake of breath eggs me on, and I pull it between my teeth until his moan and whimpers fill the room.

"River," he moans my name, thrusting himself against my center with desperation, seeking friction.

My hand runs down the length of his lean body and over his jeans, still secured around his waist.

"Why aren't you naked?" I whisper, rolling my tongue down his chest and over his abdomen, nibbling near his pants line where his muscles flex and tense from the sensation.

A deep groan vibrates his chest when he lays back, putting his hands under his head. With glazed-over hooded eyes, he watches my every move. Piece by piece, I remove his leftover clothes, tossing them aside with haste. Saliva pools in my mouth when his dick springs free from his boxers, begging me to taste it. Precum drips down the side of his engorged and purple tip, pulsating with need.

Rad moans when my fingers wrap around his shaft, and I pump a few times, marveling at the feel of his smooth, warm skin beneath my touch. Leaning down, I lick the sweet curve of his dick, slightly leaning to the right. Running my tongue from base to tip several times, I lick him like I'm eating my favorite ice cream. Faintly, I taste the vanilla I crave so badly and continue sucking his tip into my mouth and running my tongue along his weeping slit, swallowing his pre-cum. Nothing beats the desperate sounds Rad makes when I take him into the back of my throat and squeeze around him. He writhes beneath me, silently screaming, with his head thrown back and fingers pulling at my loose hair.

"Pretty Girl, I'm desperate," he moans, tossing his head back again and arching his back. His cock throbs in my mouth, on the brink of spewing into my throat. Anticipation settles through me when I use my tongue, swirling around the base. A tight grip grasps my hair, pulling my mouth away. "I need you," he reaffirms, guiding me on top of his body and my legs straddling his hips. "I need to be inside of you now." Rad reaches over to his bedside table, flicking through the contents. Pulling out a condom, he carefully rolls it down his length and grips my waist tightly. "Next time, Pretty girl, I'm going raw. This time, we'll be careful," he murmurs, sucking my nipple into his mouth and swirling the tip of his tongue around my hard bud. "I won't have a barrier between us from this moment on." Something wicked sparks in the depth of his dark brown eyes, sending shivers down my spine when he surges forward and enters me with one thrust. His words ring through my mind on repeat. Raw. Nothing between us. Fuck. My pussy flutters around him, and he groans. "Yeah, Pretty Girl. You like that, don't you? I want my cum dripping out of you and down your legs."

Relief floods through me the moment he thrusts into me over and over. Pleasure sensations roar through me when I lift my hips and slam back down on his length, jamming him further into me. Stars brighten my eyes, and my brain turns to mush.

"I'm on birth control. I have been for years," I gasp out, tossing my head back and letting my hair cascade down my back. The white ceiling comes into view when my eyes flutter open, and I swallow hard.

Memories try to come through, but I force them down. There's no way in hell I'm thinking about that right now. Not when Rad is taking me away from this world thrust by thrust. I swear I see stars when he grunts, pounding into me from underneath. The sweet curve of his dick hits that spot deep inside me perfectly, making me want to let go.

"Thank fuck," Rad gasps, thrusting up into me. "You feel like a goddamn angel wrapped around my cock. I'm going to live in your cunt any time I can," he confesses, groaning when I lift my hips and slam back down.

"You don't feel too bad yourself." That's a lie. He feels fucking amazing. The curve of his dick hits right inside me. I'm two seconds away from orgasming and exploding all over him.

"Well, let me make it feel even better," he grunts, pulling out with a gasp. "On your hands and knees. Maybe we should include our watcher."

My eyes find Callum immediately when I get to my hands and knees. His soft, pink lips part in ecstasy as he pumps his hand up and down his shaft, swiping the pre-cum from his slit for friction.

"Scoot closer, bro," Rad demands, beckoning him with a finger curl.

Callum settles closer, brushing his thigh against my fingers, curling in the sheets. Lust brews deep behind his stormy gray eyes as he watches with an intense stare, taking in every touch Rad lays against my flesh.

Rad's hands settle on my hips when he gently reenters me from behind with a long, drawn-out moan.

"Seriously, I'm never leaving. I'll sleep with my dick inside you if I have to," he groans, resting his forehead between my shoulder blades.

Reaching around, his hand grips my breast again, squeezing hard. All the breath leaves my depleted lungs when his hips snap forward harder and harder, driving into me like a man on a mission. Until he stills, laying his front over my back, leaning against me. Soft fingers swirl over my clit, beckoning my orgasm closer to the surface. And then backs off. Repeatedly, he swirls his fingertips over my clit until it's a throbbing mess and backs off.

"Rad, please," I moan, rocking into the sensation threatening to take me over. Every swirl has my eyes rolling into the back of my head and moans spilling out.

"River," he rasps in a low voice. "You're so fucking beautiful. And you're mine," he grunts the last part quietly, easing into his thrusts again. "Should we invite him to join? I think he wants a repeat. Maybe you should ask him?"

Callum's eyes widen and ragged breaths spill from his lips when his hand stops pumping his length, and he swallows hard.

"Callum," I moan his name, blindly staring in his direction as my vision blurs.

Callum's movements stop completely, frozen by his name on my lips, and he stares when I wiggle my finger, beckoning him forward more. He stumbles, scooting even closer. A deep red tint takes over his cheeks and neck and spreads on his chest. Lust swims deep in his eyes when he sits on the edge of the bed, staring at Rad and me with a curious but watchful eye. With every drive of Rad's cock forward, Callum watches closely.

"What-what do you want me-me to do?" His beautiful gray eyes dilate when Rad moves his hips, and my eyes roll into the back of my head.

"Whatever you want," I moan breathlessly, digging my fingers into the money and sheets beneath me.

He licks his lips again, staring at mine with raw desire.

"Either kiss her, come on her tits, or let her suck you off, bro," Rad directs, squeezing my tit in his hand, breathing heavily into my neck. "Because I won't last much longer," he whispers, snapping his hips forward several more times, grunting my name.

Callum stays close, dryly stroking himself from base to tip. His eyes never stray from Rad's erratic movements, dilating when Rad picks up the pace, shoving his cock further inside me.

"Rad, stop," I gasp out, and he instantly stops, pulling out.

"Shit, you okay? Sorry! Did I hurt you?" he asks with desperation, grazing his hand up and down my back.

"I'm fine," I insist, looking over my shoulder at his twisted face. "But Callum needs some lube," I say, raising a brow.

Rad's gaze finds Callum's dry hands rubbing his dick raw. A slow smile spreads across Rad's lips, and he nods. "For Callum, of course. Come here," he says to Callum, beckoning him forward.

Callum trembles, crawling to my side, close to where Rad resides. Looking over my shoulder, my gaze connects with his dilated eyes. Nodding, I give him a soft smile when his fingers brush over my ass cheek.

"Right here," Rad says in a soothing tone, taking hold of Callum's wrist and directing him to my dripping pussy before stopping. "Are you good with this? I'm not trying to push, man."

Callum licks his lip, sinking his teeth into his bottom lip. "Yes! Oh-oh, Jesus," Callum groans when he brushes against my pussy lips. "Oh God." His eyes roll back when Rad directs his fingers into me.

I groan when he shoves his long fingers inside me and twists them around, gathering my juices with Rad's. Four fingers from two different hands push the boundaries of my fluttering pussy walls.

"Feel that, man? She fucking loves it. She's going to cum all over them. And then you're going to finish yourself with her cum. Okay?" Rad asks through the fog of my mind, and I hear him moan in the distance.

Fire spreads throughout my limbs, and everything trembles as Rad and Callum pick up their pace, slamming into the depths of my cunt and turning me inside out. A moan lodges in my throat the moment my pussy contracts, and fireworks explode behind my eyes. My pussy clamps down on them, earning more groans from behind me.

"Fuck, River," Rad grunts, stilling inside me.

"Oh, f-fuck," Callum gasps, pulling in and out with urgency, staring at the wetness coating his entire hand with wonder.

"Use it, bro. Slather her pussy juices all over your dick, and then come on her ass while I come in her pussy." Rad doesn't waste a second when he buries himself deep in my cunt and pounds harder than before.

Callum moans, confidently putting the tip of his dick against my ass cheek, pumping as hard as he can. I watch his every move through my limited view of him over my shoulder. His head falls back, and his mouth drops open in ecstasy, lathering his dick with my juices.

"Come for me," I rasp, staring into his gray eyes. "Come, Callum." Heavy breaths pour from his mouth until every muscle in his body locks tight. Deep moans pull from his chest when he sprays his cum all over the flesh of my ass, dripping down my crack and toward Rad's chaotic thrusts and mixes.

Leaning over in desperation, Rad buries his teeth in my shoulder, spilling his seed into the condom with labored breaths and moaning.

"You're goddamn amazing," he murmurs, licking the wound on my shoulder. Rad kisses my shoulder, moving my hair from my neck. "Don't move. I'm staying here," he rasps.

I roll my eyes, wiggling my hips. "You can't seriously stay inside me. We have lives to live."

He snorts. "You underestimate my commitment," he murmurs, slowly pulling out with a groan. "But for today, I'll let it go."

For one brief second of silence, Callum's wide eyes stay transfixed on the cum sliding down my flesh, through my crack, and mingling with my juices. I shiver when his finger bravely runs through the line, swirling it into me.

"Come-come on," Callum murmurs, grasping my hand with a blush, pulling himself from the visual. "Let's get cleaned up." I swear he sounds breathless when he helps me off the bed. My legs wobble when I take my first step, but Cal is there to catch me when I tumble.

"I'm going to take that stumble as a win," Rad says with a tired grin, throwing the condom into the trash. Sighing, he throws himself back into the bed with a groan. "Thanks for christening my money, Pretty Girl. You're officially my good luck charm." Warmth fills me when his earnest eyes find mine, and I see nothing but honesty reflecting. For some reason, he truly believes I'm his good luck charm.

"Any time," I quip, clinging to Callum as he leads us into the oversized bathroom fitted with a large tub, stand-up shower, and a nice-sized closet connected to it.

Leaning down, Callum runs a bath and plugs the drain. He stands, collects the shampoo, conditioner, and body wash, and places them around the edge of the tub with care. His fingers brush through the rapidly rising water, and he nods, approving of the temperature.

"I think it's ready-ready," he says, taking a deep breath when he stands back, gesturing for me to climb in.

He helps me ease my legs over the tall bathtub with gentle hands until the water laps at my calves and feet. I sigh when my feet envelop in warmth, tingling my toes and legs. When I turn, Callum watches me with an intense stare, watching my every move as I slowly sit down in the water's warmth.

"Are you coming?" I ask, raising a brow and gesturing to the spot behind me.

His eyes widen for a fraction of a second, and I think he's about to tell me no until he marches forward with determination on his face. Deep down, I think Callum fights with himself and what he wants. Something holds him back from jumping into the fray and getting his too.

Settling behind me, he gently eases my back to his front and carefully wraps his arms around me. Resting his hands on my stomach with trembling fingers, I can tell he's trying not to touch anything he shouldn't.

Resting my head against his shoulder, I savor the warmth and protection he offers me. Callum is a gentle soul, and I never want anyone to take that from him. This world is a cruel, evil mess, and he's the only goodness left to bring me light. Besides the other two, I've seemed to have fallen for them in a short time. Sometimes I can't stop my heart from falling for the wrong people.

"Can I ask you something?" I whisper, running my wet fingers up and down his tense thighs on either side of me. His hardening dick rests at my back, but he makes no move to do anything about it. In fact, I'm sure he's ignoring it.

"Sure-sure," he says, stumbling over his tongue again. "You can ask me anything."

"What holds you back from sex?" Turning, I peek over my shoulder at his red-tinted face. Worry lines the creases in his brows, and he nods like he knows this is coming. "I'm not trying to pry, Cal. You don't have to talk about anything if you don't want to," I murmur with encouragement, turning back to face the wall.

I'd never force him to tell me anything. We all have hidden secrets, guidelines we live by, and boundaries we like to keep. Some people can't stand to be touched because of sensitivities. Some people are saving themselves for the right moment. And some haven't found the perfect person to connect with. Whatever the reason, he's still a virgin. That's up to him.

He leans his forehead against the back of my head, laying a sweet kiss on my hair. His shuddering breath blows across my wet neck as he composes himself to answer. Deep down, I suspect he's again hiding the embarrassment from his face.

"I want it to be right," he murmurs into my hair. "It probably sounds-sounds so stupid, but I want the moment to be something that I'm proud to remember. I..." He stops himself, taking a deep breath. "I never forget a moment."

"Never forget?" I ask, trying to look into the depths of his eyes, but he hides again and nods.

"Every life event. Every day. If you asked me what I did on March fourteenth two years ago, I'd be able to tell you in great detail how my day went," he murmurs, almost ashamed at what his mind can do.

Absentmindedly, I rub my fingers along his, tracing the wrinkles on his knuckles, trying to ease the rising tension. His muscles bunch, and his breaths grow haggard behind me, attempting to hold back all the frustrations that must come with his unique ability.

"So, what did you do on March fourteenth?" I quip with a smile, tugging at the edges of my lips.

Finally, after a few seconds of silence, he snorts, lifting his face from my hair. Those gray eyes connect with mine, filled with relief, spilling everything without saying a word. People must judge him when he confesses what his mind can do, expecting a lot from him. I could never imagine having the ability to remember every moment of my life. Our brains are meant to forget and ease away from painful moments.

He hums under his breath and closes his eyes. I wonder if the memory is right there in reach, and all he has to do is open a file and view it, much like a computer. A slow smile spreads across his lips, indicating it must be a wonderful memory.

"Woke up as usual at seven a.m., had cereal without milk, drank a cold coffee, and then celebrated my little sister Jenny's birthday." His eyes squeeze shut, and he takes a deep breath, reliving the memory vividly.

"And July second?" I ask, raising a brow, secretly knowing the answer.

"Woke up, had cereal with no milk, drank a hot coffee with two packets of sweeteners and a splash of vanilla creamer, and then went to the May-Fair event out on route seven. We had one of our first gigs. Kieran stumbled over his words while singing. Rad got so hot and sweated so much that he threw his stick off the stage. My string broke. And Ash's dad scolded him for embarrassing him in public," he rambles in detail about the first day I ever saw them perform on stage, but my brain neglected to remember the chaos of their first performance.

"Ah, I didn't think you guys sounded too bad," I say with a shrug, nestled deeper into his tight embrace.

"You were there?" he asks in a soft voice, leaning his head on the edge of the tub.

"How do you think I knew to email you guys? I mean, you handed me your card," I ask with a laugh. "Although I didn't remember you guys messing up too much, I remember being enamored by you all." Enamored was an understatement. Like before, they drew me in with their magical voices and strumming fingers. They hypnotized me every step of the way, leading to now. Perhaps our unions are inevitable, and fate brought us together.

"It was me, wasn't it, Pretty Girl?" Rad asks, waltzing into the bathroom, still naked and swaying his hips—among other things. He marches toward a door next to the tub, proceeds to pee without shame, and reemerges, washing his hands.

I scoff. "The world doesn't revolve around you, Ashton Radcliffe." He grins, splashing water on my face, causing me to yelp from the sudden warmth.

"Be nice," Callum murmurs, splashing Rad back with warm water.

Rad scowls, pulling back to dry off his face. He rests by the tub for another few minutes and helps Callum wash me. They run shampoo and conditioner through my hair, washing it away. Soon I'm scrubbed clean with Rad's body wash, which he smugly rubs into my skin, promising he'll get me a bottle, so I smell like him at all times. Plus, he swears it'll piss off Kieran to no end.

Soon enough, we're all out of the tub, dried off, and lying covered in Callum's bed. We don't bother to get dressed, instead lying lazily around and cuddling. Callum nestles into my back, draping an arm over my stomach and Rad stays to my front, looking deeply into my eyes.

"Well, how was your day off, Pretty Girl?" he asks, brushing my wet hair behind my ear.

I smile. "It was one of the best days I've had in a long time," I freely admit, letting the happiness settle in my gut.

I'd never tell them I haven't had this much fun in years. I've always had to worry about work and school and never had downtime, never ridden on a bike, gone to the races, or hung out just to hang out. Especially now with my mom, her illness, and her dependency on me. I'll never have another day like today. So, I'll savor it forever.

Rad hums happily under his breath, softly putting his face on my neck. "Just lay here with me. I see the exhaustion in your eyes and the hurt in your bones. Lay here with me, and feel my warmth." Rad sucks in a breath, reaching for something on the shelf above my head with urgency. Cranking my neck, I see the moment a dark notebook lands between us. "I need to write this down," he mumbles to himself.

"Lyrics?" I ask, scrunching my nose.

Rad grins, not breaking his concentration by repeating the lines repeatedly.

"Lyrics come from the heart, Pretty Girl. Unexpectedly. Beautiful. Raw. Lyrics appear out of nowhere," he murmurs, scrunching his brows.

A light flickers above us, highlighting Rad like a spotlight when he uncaps a pen with his teeth. Pages ruffle when he turns to a blank page and sighs in relief. Writing this down is the most important thing he's done all day.

A sparkle of excitement lights up his dark brown eyes. No one else in the room exists. Not me. Not Callum. These are just the words he casually said. Watching him scribble lyrics down fascinates me. One day they'll be someone's favorite song, sung worldwide, and it all started here in this tiny bedroom.

I take the unexpected chance to take all of him in, in his most vulnerable state. His dark, curly mullet sticks up from our romp in the sheets. His bare shoulders and chest, splattered with his tattoo, are tanned from his time in the sun. Freckles dot the tops of his shoulders and sprinkle down his tanned arms.

"There," he says victoriously, putting the notebook back above our heads and settling in. "Let's nap now," he grumbles with a small yawn.

I nearly jump out of my skin when a piano riff echoes through the room until I realize it's my phone sounding off with a message. I swallow hard at the ominous sound, knowing precisely who's texting me this time.

"Your-your phone," Callum mumbles, blindly reaching behind him and grabbing it on the end table.

"Pretty Girl, that thing is so damn cracked and beat up," Rad says, closing his eyes with a yawn. "We'll get you a new one...." his voice trails off when his hand brushes up and down my thigh, slowly stopping when Rad completely conks out and snores.

"Fat chance," I mumble, unlocking my phone. Peeking behind me, I make sure Callum's face stays buried in my neck, and he slowly drifts off with even breaths.

Swiping on my cracked screen, I bring the message up and wrinkle my nose.

Van: I need to talk to you.
Van: Why won't you talk to me anymore, Riv?
Van: You're like a stranger.
Van: Please talk to me.
Van: I saw you go to Callum's, Rivey.....

I shake my head and silence my phone. I don't need Van in my ear, whispering things I don't want to hear. He broke my heart. He's the one who left me because his parents couldn't stand the fact I was who I was. And now he's suddenly crawling back on his hands and knees, begging me to talk to him?

Hell no.

Van Drake can drown in the depths of the misery he put me through.

KIERAN

If I never had to step foot into a classroom again, I'd be fucking ecstatic. Why can't I move on with my life without the hassle of a degree in hand? I would have rather gone to trade school and learned to weld. Then, I would have been at work, already making my money. But instead, I'm stuck in a prison of expectations and no way out. Leaning my head back against the side of the Tahoe, I soak in the late summer sun and close my eyes.

"It's important, Kieran!" my mother hisses in my ear the moment Nigel tells us we were attending college right after high school graduation. And given the fact I didn't apply to any sort of college; it meant Nigel stuck his nose in something he shouldn't have. He was probably using the green lining of his wallet to get us into the college of his choosing—sans applications. Standing under the blaring May sun, a warm breeze passes over us. I haven't even taken my robes off. I had no plans to attend regular college. In fact, they knew I wanted to leave. Maybe live on the other side of the country, but they've again tied my hands financially. "This will give you a much better life than I had. Don't dive back into the gutter I got us out of."

"Yeah? By what? Spreading your legs to that monster," I hiss back, earning a sharp slap across the face.

"I will not let you fail. No way, no how. Nigel made us a good life here," she says in a haughty tone, lifting her chin.

I eye every inch of her overly made-up face and scoff, counting the marks lining her cheeks and under her eyes. Deep purple bruises shine under the sun, letting the world know what goes on behind closed doors.

"Yeah? And at what cost, Gloria? So, he can hit you every day? Hit me? And Asher? What about Camilla? What will you do when he lays his hands on my little sister?" I step up to her, towering above her with gritted teeth.

Her face falls, and I know I've hit a nerve, but she backpedals, waving a hand like it's not a big fucking deal that he does what he does. She has no idea I hear the awful words he shouts at her behind the bedroom door. How can she act like this is all okay? How can she sit there and pretend he's not the bad guy? Fuck. I thought graduating high school would get me the fuck out of here, but now I'm even more stuck than before.

"Don't be so obtuse, Kieran." With that, she spins on her thousand-dollar high heels and struts away toward the man who has become nothing more than a nightmare.

I grit my teeth at the raw memory resurfacing from absolutely nowhere. The last thing I want to think about is the man I'm bound to because my mother purposely got pregnant by him years ago.

Through the years, he's molded her into the perfect wife and Camilla into the perfect, dutiful daughter. Asher and I have silently resisted every command he's given at every damn turn. I'll be damned if I become his perfect stepson. And Asher feels the same. That clawing desperation closes my throat when the man in question peeks out the upper-story window, watching us as he always does with a sharp eye. He scowls when Cami bounces on her toes with excitement, staring up at Asher and me like we're saints. Big blue eyes meet mine when she stops in front of us and gives us a toothy grin.

"Cami," I murmur, watching my sister jump excitedly in front of us with a large pink bouncy ball in her hands.

"Kieran. Ash," she says in a small voice, shrinking in on herself when she peeks up at the window looming above us, and suddenly, our warm and happy sister disappears.

"It's okay, Cam," Asher whispers, reaching out and touching her arm. She relaxes at his touch, scrunching her face when she sighs, looking up at the window above us again with apprehension and nodding. "He's in there. We're out here. We'll always protect you, right?" She nods, nibbling on her bottom lip, knowing it's the truth. I'd protect my sister to the ends of the earth, even making sacrifices I shouldn't. Whatever those might be.

"How'd your project go?" I ask, sparking a light in her big blue eyes.

"I turned in my project today at school and got an A+!" she says with a beaming grin, pride puffing out her chest.

"Good job! See, you did it all on your own," I say, ruffling her long brown hair until she playfully swats me away with a little grunt.

"Good job, Cam," Asher says with encouragement, squeezing her shoulder.

"Better go play while you can, okay? We'll be back later. You have more homework?" I ask, discreetly watching the old prick glaring down at us. To him, it's like having a good time is a fucking crime, especially on his own lawn.

"Yeah," she says, furrowing her brows. "It's science." Her face scrunches when she says that, but she quickly gets called by one of her neighborhood friends and takes off, leaving us with him and the weight of his intense stare beaming down on us. I swear my skin catches fire when he shifts in the window, putting his hand in his suit pockets.

"Get a life, old man," Asher grunts quietly, leaning against his Tahoe and shaking his head.

"Only a few more months, man," I murmur, clapping him on the shoulder. "We've survived twelve years under his shoe, and we can do it for a few more."

"The moment that letter comes in with our invitation, we're out," Asher grumbles with confidence, swiping a hand down his face.

"Or the moment we get our diplomas, right? We can't put all our hope into that fucking gig. There are how many bands applying for this spot? We have to think about the worst-case scenario," I surmise, turning to Ash, who nods in agreement.

"Either we get the letter, or the moment that fucking diploma touches our hands, we're gone. We need something to fall back on, and that degree is it. We've been saving for years. You, me, Rad, and Callum are out," Asher growls, throwing a hand around in anger as he speaks. "Callum even mentioned selling the house to help pay for our trip to California. And then you and I can work, play in the band, and wait for our break far the fuck away from here," Asher says, rubbing his chin. "So, when his trust ends, we can get out." A small smile takes over his lips. "Then it's just the four of us against the world.

"Hell, we can get out," I murmur, rubbing my hands together. No matter what—we're out of here. The moment my diploma touches my fingertips, we're leaving this place before my father can sink his claws into me.

"Yeah. We'll talk to the guys about that. What do you think they've been up to today?" They've been silent throughout the day.

Rad had a race to raise money for our band fund, and Callum usually looks through venues, contacting managers hoping to play. Obnoxiously, they typically keep us updated throughout the day on their activities. But today? They've been silent as fuck. Which is suspect at best. But I suppose we'll know exactly what they've been up to in twenty minutes.

"Six sharp for dinner! Don't keep your mother waiting!" Nigel yells out the window with a growl. "Not a second later! Don't give me more reason to pull the plug on your little side project. Such a waste of time," he huffs with a snarl, perpetually hating our band with a passion. He thinks it's a waste of time and it'll take us nowhere in life. Just because he had nothing exciting in his life besides work doesn't mean he gets to bash ours.

"Yes, sir," Asher and I say in unison without missing a beat.

We've figured out how to stay under his nasty radar this long. The last thing we need is for him to take away our freedoms. We may be twenty-one and adults, but he's made sure we depend on him every step of the way.

Our vehicles? His. Our phones? His. Our clothes and allowances? His. Our college education? His. His insistence that we do not get jobs—all his. And we're powerless in all situations. Nigel has us right where he wants us, needy and dependent on his dime. So, when the time comes, and he offers us some big wig job within his company, we'd be dumb not to take it. Well, at least that's what he thinks.

Nigel Montgomery has tainted everything we own, hoping he can twist our arms into running his company alongside him. As much as it pains him to have his sons at the bottom, he knows he can mold us like he has everyone else. The only thing he hasn't accounted for is our waste of time hobby, which has made us our own money this past year. And he can't touch it. Our band is ours: our home, our family. And there's nothing Nigel can do to stop it.

Once we enter the Battle of the Bands and hopefully gain entry, we're gone. We'll buy vehicles under our names and drive to California without a second glance.

Nigel steps away from the window, grumbling loudly about our laziness and being unappreciative of his kindness. In his eyes, we're never enough, and I can't live the rest of my life like that.

"Let's get out of here while we can," Asher mumbles, grabbing me by the shirt. "We'll bring up the competition and what we have to do. More live shows to film, a recording of our music as professional as possible, and a social media presence are what we need. We can't let this shit slip through our fingers, bro. We need this or...." He side-eyes me, swallowing hard. I see the wheels turning in his big ass brain, and I know precisely the subject of his thoughts.

"She doesn't know her family, bro," I murmur, regret seizing my heart. "She can't get us into the KC Club any better than we can waltz in there. The Battle of the Bands is our best hope." I shake my head, remembering the plan Asher came up with, which has blown itself out of the water.

I'm way too deep with her, drowning in my obsession. There's no resurfacing from this as the same man I was before I met River West again. Mine to keep. Mine to hold. Mine forever.

There's no way I'm letting Asher use her to get to her brothers' record company or venue. From my memories, she hasn't had the best relationship with that side of the family. They abandoned her. And I won't force her to see them again.

"It was worth a shot," he grumbles, wiping his face. "You think she would ever reconnect with them?" I shake my head immediately, blowing out a breath.

"I don't know, man...."

Asher stops on the sidewalk a block away from Callum and Rad's house, putting a hand on my chest.

"You've got her in your grip," he says with an odd glint sparking in his eyes, making me frown. "She's your old bestie from the bad side. You've..."

"I'm going to punch that shit out of your head and laugh while you bleed. River West is not a toy to use in some scheme to get to her family. Sure, we thought that before we got to know her, but it ain't fucking happening. She is not someone we fuck over. Ya hear?" I growl, curling my fingers in his shirt to get my point across. "She. Is. Mine. Asher." I punctuate every word by dragging him closer and closer until our noses touch.

But my message doesn't seem to compute in his thick head. His eyes roll toward the sky in exaggeration, and he mutters angrily under his breath.

"Are you sure about that?" he says, cocking an eyebrow at me.

"Yes," I grunt, shoving him away.

His teeth grit again when he finds his footing. "I see how she looks at you and them," he hisses, pointing down the street.

"So?" I gape. "You think I didn't know what I was doing when I let Rad in on our little moment? He's fucking obsessed with her, just like me. And Callum? He's ten seconds away from pouncing on her. Thank God. Besides, that was your whole fucking grand plan, right? Wine and dine her and make her fall for all of us. But maybe she doesn't have to choose in the end. She gets us all. Well, except you." His eyes widen a smidge, but he quickly covers his surprise and hurt. "You could be a little fucking nicer," I quip.

That's right. Asher may seem like he wants nothing to do with her, but he wants her, too. His only complaint is that he can't reel her in with his assholeness, and he has to try. Before with other women, he's just kind of grunted, went along with their plans, and got what he needed. But with River, she's an entirely new breed of woman he's never experienced. But fuck, it's fun to watch him struggle. The way I see it, Asher will flounder for months until he's crawling on his knees and begging for her forgiveness. He'll be so in love with her that he'll insist we take her with us. I can see it now in vivid imagery. Now, we have to get to that point where he digs his head out of his own ass and gets on board with the rest of us.

"Fucking nicer," he mumbles, walking away in disbelief. "I'm fucking nice!" he yells offhandedly in disbelief.

"You're a perpetual grump!" I shout after him, finally catching up and throwing my arm over his shoulders.

"Grump this," he quips, shoving me away with a soft chuckle.

"Just don't be a dick for once, okay? River is cool. River is..." I smile, thinking about the way she feels when I'm nestled deep inside her. And the way she lights up when I walk into a room. God, she's extraordinary, and I never want to let her out of my sight.

Asher grunts in response, rolling his eyes at my expression and digs his keys from his pocket once we reach the bright red front door of Rad and Callum's shared home. It's a quaint ranch-style home nestled on the edge of the neighborhood. Heavy woods surround the backyard and side yards, leading to Central Lake glistening in the evening sun. The house itself is off on its own, giving us the privacy we crave. It's the one place we love to come to when we need to get away. It's our space—our home.

"Let's discuss what we need to do with the Battle of the Bands and how we're going to get there in the first place." Asher shakes his head, shoving the front door open to a quiet house. His nose wrinkles when we step inside, shutting the door behind us.

"Well, they weren't playing Angel Warrior all day," I mutter, noting the dark TV and living room.

On any given day, that's where we find them—curled up on the couch in an intense battle between the angels and demons. They'll yell and fight after a long day of making money any way they know how. Recently, we've gotten income from Rad's dirt bike races and the few gigs we find here and there from our performances. Callum brings money in through stocks, which doesn't give us a lot to go on because he invests it straight from the leftover cash of his trust. The same trust that pays his house bills and gives him a little spending money which has never been enough to get us out of this stupid town and away from Nigel... But we're saving as much as possible and as fast as we can.

"There aren't even dishes in the damn sink," Asher mutters from across the room, looking down at the shiny sink with a wrinkled nose. "His bike is outside." He peeks out the back door window, furrowing his brows.

"Maybe Cal took his car?" I mutter, peeking in the large dining room off the kitchen, and note an empty table still decorated for the last Christmas Callum's parents spent here almost two years ago. A heavyweight presses on my chest at the sight.

Callum's parents were the best of all of ours. Caring. Kind. Loving. They let us come here and hang out, fed us, and ensured we were okay, never knowing the extent of Nigel's temper against Ash and me, but they could tell we needed a place to hide and regroup. They supplied a sanctuary for us while they were alive, and now, they still are.

When they died, a trust kicked in for Callum, paying his monthly bills and house payment. It provides everything he needs to keep the roof over his head, but nothing more.

It feels like a century ago that they left this world and shattered our reality. At the same time, it feels like only yesterday when we visited Cal in the hospital after the accident. His leg was broken, and his soul was shattered. Somehow, by some miracle, we pieced him back together one day at a time. All of us. Together. Here in this house. It took months to help Callum out of the shadows of his depression. Music has always been our go-to, and his especially. He's poured himself into his bass every day since.

"Fuck. I'll go check the damn boathouse," Asher grunts, pulling the back door open and walking through the woods to the tiny boat house nestled near the lake and dock where Callum's parent's boat still hangs, ready for use.

Fond memories resurrect in my mind. Of all the times spent hiding in the boathouse with a fifth of vodka and a can of coke as a chaser. We've spent our lives down there and grew up together here.

I roll my eyes, walking down the darkened hallway toward Callum's room, keeping my ears open for any noises in the silent rooms. It isn't until I'm right outside the door do I hear two distinct snores echoing through the room—my brows furrow when I push the door open and stop dead.

A grin explodes on my face at the sight before me, and I glue my eyes to her. Even sleeping soundly, she draws me in like a moth to a flame, threatening to burn me alive. Fuck. I'd gladly let her at this point.

There, squished between my two best friends, is the woman I had dreamed about all day. Her chest rises and falls under the thin blanket. My fingers itch to touch her skin and caress what's mine.

"My fucking River Blue," I mumble quietly, walking on my tiptoes toward the bed and hovering above them. "So, this is why you two were finally entertained all day?" I whisper above their heads, watching their every move.

"Yes, now go away," Rad grumbles, pulling River into him. "She's mine now. I live inside her." River doesn't stir when he tucks her head under his chin and soothes back her long brown strands until her peaceful face is all I see. Tiny freckles dot her cheeks, and her pouty lips turn down into a frown—the only sign she's listening.

"Sharing is caring," I murmur, slapping him on the back of the head until he jerks completely awake.

He frowns, finally opening his dark eyes, and glares at me with a venomous stare. A big, toothy smile takes over my face just to piss him off more. Rad is a happy-go-lucky guy, but if you wake him up, he's rather testy and often threatens murder.

"Why?" he groans, holding the back of his head. "I'm telling on you," he whines, shutting his eyes again. "Asher, come collect your brother. He's being a douche again."

"You two are annoying," River rasps in a sleepy voice, staying snuggled into Rad.

I long to see the warmth of her green eyes staring up at me, but they remain closed. It's only then that I feel a hint of jealousy spear through me. I want her wrapped around me and snuggling into my chest. Not his. Mine.

"They're not in the fucking boathouse!" Asher shouts, slamming through the back door and shutting it with a loud thud. "Where the fuck are they?"

Rolling my eyes, I reach over and flick Callum in the ear. Stormy gray eyes find mine when his body jolts awake, and he looks around with confusion, furrowing his brows.

"Band meeting. We have shit to discuss," I announce, leaning over Rad and kissing River's cheek.

"You all have fun," she mumbles, burying her face deeper into Rad's neck with a whine. "I'll hold down the fort in bed." I snort, pulling the blankets off all of them.

"Whyyyyy?" Rad whines. "This is the rudest wake-up call in history. Can't we sleep for five more minutes, Dad?"

"No," I chuckle, reaching over him, wrapping my arms around River, and kissing her again.

Fuck. I can't get enough of her soft skin beneath my lips.

"What the?" Asher stops at the threshold, glaring at the four of us in bed. "So, this is what you guys did all day?"

Rad scoffs. "I won eight hundred bucks at the races all because of my good luck charm. Now, get off me," he grunts, shoving me away from the warmth of River, who groans into his pillow. Rad glares at me the entire time he rifles through his closet, throwing on a shirt over his naked body, glaring more when he picks out a long shirt for River and throws it at her when she sits up without shame, catching it and putting it over her head.

"Band meeting," Asher announces in a sharp voice. "We've got some business to discuss." His eyes narrow on River, who wrestles to put on a long shirt she's in, securing it over her ass when she sits on the edge of the bed with a scowl. Blinking wildly, she looks around the room, meeting Asher's eyes.

Callum and Rad reluctantly peel themselves from the bed, knowing Asher means business when he barks orders. Without hesitation, Rad and Callum get dressed, throwing on comfortable clothes.

"Here," Callum mutters, handing River a long pair of sweatpants from his drawer.

She murmurs thanks, pulling them up and securing the pants around her slim waist. Seeing their half-naked bodies and her wearing their clothes sends jealousy through me again.

Fuck.

That should be my shirt and my sweatpants. It should have been my hands all over her. I shake my head, tamping down the green monster threatening to burst through my skin. There's no room for jealousy between us. I haven't asked River to be only mine. Not that I could now. The way Rad grins at her when she tosses her hair into a messy bun and frowns at our existence has his eyes lighting up, and he's as obsessed as I am. His whole face screams joy and happiness, and I couldn't take that away from him. Or Callum. His entire being vibrates and simultaneously bursts with red cheeks. He's absolutely smitten by her. Just like I am.

River isn't just mine, no matter how badly I wish she were. She's ours.

Asher stands rigid in the living room, watching us as we make our way into the room. River shuffles in behind us, mumbling something about coffee and possibly stabbing us.

"I'll get you some," Callum offers, squeezing her hand before heading into the kitchen and heating a cup of coffee. If I asked, he'd tell me to fuck right off and shoo me from the kitchen. But with her? He fucking lights up, pouring the cup.

I smirk when she hums into the warm mug sitting in the middle of the couch. Sighing, she sips her coffee as we all crowd around her, sitting on either side—Rad on her left and me on her right. Callum sits at the other end of the couch, keeping a distance from us. But his eyes don't stray from her for too long.

"Can we do this now?" Asher growls, pulling his phone from his pocket.

"Someone grab the salt and draw a circle around him," River mumbles into her cup, watching Asher with a mischievous spark lighting up her eyes.

His eyes snap to her, but he shakes his head, thinking better of saying anything.

"So, what's going on, boss?" Rad asks, sitting back on the couch with a sigh.

"We have an opportunity," I say, taking the reins of the conversation.

"Go on," Callum softly says, rolling his wrist for me to continue.

"West Records is holding the Battle of the Bands at the KC Club," Asher announces, opening a checklist he created on his phone.

The room falls into silence. Even River stiffens between us, eyeing our every move.

"It's an application process, and only five applications will be selected. They invited the rest of the bands competing. So, it's stiff competition. All we have to do is have certain things checked off, and then we can submit our application through their website," I say, leaning my elbows on my knees.

"We need more live shows," Asher says, staring down at his phone. "We need to record a few songs and have them available on the Dot...."

"Like Sorcha does?" River asks, tilting her head to the side.

Asher's calm eyes find hers, and he nods. "Exactly like she does. We have to figure out how to digitally get our music on there."

"First, we have to figure out how to record the shit," Rad mumbles, running a hand through his hair before dropping his head back. "There aren't many recording studios in a hundred-mile radius, let alone one that'll let us do it for cheap." He shakes his head and worries his lip. "Maybe..."

"Um, Central City Community College has a recording studio. It's part of the music business associates program," River says, looking around the room warily. "I know a guy." My ears instantly perk up at 'know a guy,' and my fingers curl in my lap, more jealousy running through my veins, ready to attack this so-called guy.

"Know a guy?" Rad asks, raising his head to meet her gaze. I snort because he beat me to it. The same jealousy sparks in his eyes, and images of us pounding our fists into the guy I don't even know has a smirk pulling at my lips. Oh yes, we'd pummel him into next week for even thinking about talking to River. Shit. We're hopeless and semi-toxic.

She instantly rolls her eyes and takes a sip of coffee. "Yeah, as in, I know a guy. Like we went to high school with him, and he's the student head of that department right now. Meaning we need that guy to rent time to get to the studio. Meaning, you can't kick his ass or whatever meat-headed ideas you have running through your caveman brains," she says, shaking her head.

"Pretty Girl, I'm offended you would even consider me a meathead. I wasn't...." Rad says with his hand on his chest.

"I see it in your eyes, Assface," she grumbles, shimming out from between our bodies. I almost don't let her go but grin when she plunks down on Callum's lap, and he engulfs her with his arms. "I'll be with my new favorite over here until you two decide to play nice."

Callum's cheeks turn a deep red, and his eyes widen. "Fav-favorite?" he murmurs through a heavy breath. She grins, nestling further into him.

"Am I going to have to make a rule about no chicks at band meetings?" Asher snarls, gaining all of our attention. "We still have more shit to discuss."

"No, please go ahead, Evil Ash," she says with a smirk, sipping her coffee. "I won't interrupt with my brilliant ideas again."

"Bro!" Rad says, throwing a small couch pillow at Ash. "She just said she could secure us a spot at a legit recording studio. Don't bite the hand that feeds you, dickweed."

"Now say you're sorry," I antagonize, nodding my head at a grinning River, who squirms in Callum's lap.

Asher closes his eyes like an impatient parent and blows out a breath. I know it's taking everything in him to keep his shit together, but it's too much fun fucking with him. He's like a loose cannon. One day, he'll explode, and I can't fucking wait to see it.

With one last deep breath, he refocuses on her with a grateful smile. "Thank you for the suggestion. We'd appreciate it if you could kindly point us in the right direction."

River snorts. "Who knew Evil Ash could be so kind?" she snickers into her coffee but nods. "I'll text Rion today and see when the studio is available. I'll get it all set up and let you know."

Rad jumps in the air and whoops. "You're the best, Pretty Girl."

"What else do we have to do?" I ask.

"Performance videos, social media presence, we need to build up our audience, and maybe get some more venues under our belt." Asher worries his lips, swiping through his phone. "And we have to submit all of this before November 1st. Submissions start on September 1st. So, we don't have very long to get all this done." He gives one last nod before looking at our smiling faces around the room. Even River feels the excitement humming through us.

"It's time to make our dreams happen," Callum says with a grin.

"We're going to be famous!" Rad whoops, throwing his fist in the air, and shakes his ass.

"We're really going to do this," Asher says, letting his excitement come through.

"We are," I agree, rubbing my hands together.

"I can give you the hook up to more venues around Illinois. I've been in contact with people from The Umbrella Club and The Barn." My eyebrows raise to my hairline when she mentions the two best venues around Central City. "Hell, I can get you more gigs at Dead End if you want."

Looking around, I see the awe in everyone's eyes. River may not be able to introduce us to her family like we initially planned—which, in hindsight, was dumb. But she's still our best bet at more gigs at other venues.

"You're like our sugar band manager," Rad quips.

"A sugar band manager? Are you high?" she asks, setting her coffee cup on the end table. "But yeah, I can help you in that area. As long as we have one thing understood," she says sternly, raising a brow.

"Yeah? And what's that?" Asher asks, shoving his phone back into his pocket.

"My father abandoned me years ago. I have no contact with him or my brothers. I can't help you with connections. But..." She bites her lip, looking down at her lap, looking more vulnerable than I've ever seen her in front of us. Sure, as a kid, she spilled her guts and tears, but that was just for me. This is for all of us. She's opening herself up to the room instead of just one person. "But I can help you with this if you want me to."

Callum leans in, whispering in her ear as his hands work up and down her arms.

"Nah, Pretty Girl. We never expected you to do that," Rad whispers, guilt tinging his tone.

"I'm going to pretend you didn't lie to me," River says in a light tone, leaning into Callum. My heart kicks up at her words. Did she know that's why we initially tracked her down at the bar? Shit. I hope not. "Anyway, I'll help you. But when you go, I want to come with you." She rushes her words, nervously licking her lips.

My heart seizes at her confession, and her eyes stay firmly in her lap.

"I want to see California...." She'd never admit she wanted to meet them, but her brothers are there, and we'd be there, too.

"Well, that saves Kieran from having to kidnap you then," Asher says in an oddly vibrant tone. "All right, let's get to work. We got lots of shit to cover before we're ready." Asher claps, marches toward the basement door, and throws it open. "I'll meet you down here," he says one last time before disappearing into the depths of the basement. The sound of his guitar coming to life filters through the house, and one string at a time, he tunes it.

"You heard the man," Rad says with a grin, climbing to his feet.

You coming, Pretty Girl. We can give you your own private concert."

Callum rolls his eyes and kisses her cheek. "He tends to get naked."

"Well, in that case," she says sarcastically, climbing off his lap and plunking down on the couch.

"You'll stay?" I ask as the other two meander toward the door, but look back with hopeful looks. Leaning down, I get eye level, staring into the abyss of her moss-green eyes.

Her nose wrinkles, and she nods. "I'm calling my ma and making sure she's okay. Then, I'll text Rion and get you a spot at the studio. But yeah, if everything is fine there, I'll stay," she says, blowing out a breath. "But don't get used to it." A slight grin picks up the edges of her lips, and I laugh.

"River Blue," I murmur, leaning forward and pressing my lips to hers. "Be a good girl and stay here. I'll reward you later." I grin when her cheeks flush, and her eyes dilate wide, letting me know she will enjoy the reward I give her later.

Images of River coming to California with us rush through my mind. Us at the beach. Her at our concerts, egging us on from the sidelines. It's a beautiful image of a beautiful future I can't wait to explore.

As band practice continues, River slowly makes her way down and rests on the ratty old couch in the corner while playing on her phone. We each watch her with different intensity levels, but she seems to bring out the good in us. Our music gets heavier and better. A new song emerges from the flames of our fingers, and we dive into a new chapter of our lives.

One with River in it at our side.

Forever.

RIVER

So, this is what suburban hell feels like. Hot sun. Barbeque roasting. Loud country music. And hoity-toity moms and dads looking down their noses at me when I pass by with a plate full of food in one hand, Kieran's arm around my shoulders, and Rad on my tail as the latter talks a million miles a minute. Sometimes I don't think he takes a breath to speak. Is he even human?

As we pass people, Rad loudly introduces me, without shame, to each and every person and lets them all know I'm his girlfriend. I'm constantly reminding the fucker that we're not in a committed relationship. We're—well, whatever we are. Fuck buddies? Having a good time? I mean, the way he looks at me gives me butterflies. But still. Do we need an actual label to put on ourselves?

He seems to think so because he's constantly reminding me that we are in a relationship—I just won't admit it. In Rad's mind, we're probably married by now and have two kids and a white picket fence.

It's only been five days since we rolled around on Callum's bed and had some of the best sex of my life. Since then, we've taken advantage of our time together. Any chance I get, I'm at Rad's, watching him and Callum play some game called Angel Warrior while doing my homework. I'm falling into a weird routine with them: they pick me up from home, take me to work, and then take me back. Every step of the way, they're there. Always following me. Their faces are all I see, and I'm beginning to get used to it halfway, expecting them to be there every turn I make. Rad, Callum, or Kieran make an appearance every night outside my sliding glass door, begging to crawl into my bed. Some nights we rest together, but most nights, we have our wicked ways with each other until the sun comes up and I'm exhausted. It's gotten to the point where I rarely lock the door, opting to leave it open for them to slip through.

"I can't believe we're going to be in a recording studio in a month," Kieran murmurs with a grin, squeezing my shoulder with happiness.

Wednesday, the one day a week I make it on campus for classes, I signed the boys up for a recording session after talking to the guy in charge. Come October first, they'll be nestled away in the recording studio, making their dreams come true. And mine. The more and more I've thought about it, the more excited I get for the adventure to California with the guys to watch them perform.

Come December, I'll be walking the cold beaches and shivering in the waves. Something I've always dreamed of. You crave change when you've lived almost your whole life in one town surrounded by bean and corn fields with no ocean in sight. I want to breathe in the salty waters and watch as the waves crash down. I want to walk the beaches without any stress.

And maybe...just maybe, I'll find my father and brothers, too. It can't hurt, right? They may have forgotten about me for the past nineteen years, but I haven't forgotten them, even after all the rejected letters I received. It's a tough pill to swallow, but I'll know for sure when I meet them face to face.

"Yeah, and my only reward for being such a big help is these ribs and wings," I quip with a grin, nudging playfully into Kieran's ribs as he chuckles at me.

My mouth waters at the sight of the delicious BBQ ribs and wings filling up my plate, and on cue, my stomach erupts with growls begging for the food. I haven't had anything this good since my ma took me out for my birthday at the local buffet, where I ate anything and everything I wanted. And now is no exception. No matter the judgy eyes following me around and watching my every move. What do they think? That I'll steal their TVs while they're outside or something? Sheesh. They need to cool their jets. I'm no thief. I work for everything in my life. Just because I come from the other side of town means nothing. So, they can shove their judgmental glares and whispers up their tight assholes and go back to minding their own business. I've got food to demolish. Finally, we make it to a picnic table set up in the middle of the cul-de-sac, fit with a white tablecloth, salt, pepper, and even a fancy napkin holder set up in the middle.

The warm breeze blows through my hair as I watch the cookout in full swing and marvel at their dedication. They've literally blocked off the entrance to their block with police barricades and a sign that says, road closed to traffic. How they pulled that off, I'll never know.

People meander around, carrying plates. Their gossiping whispers and wandering eyes pierce through me, but I don't give a shit. I'm eating homemade ribs dripping with barbecue. And I'm in heaven. Screw their mean glares and noses in the air.

"K!" I raise a brow when a cute little girl throws her arms around Kieran, hugging him tightly and nearly knocking him over.

A marvelous smile lights up his face, chasing away any ounce of darkness bringing him down when he happily chuckles at her antics. He doesn't hesitate, pulling her into his lap and wrapping his arms around her little body. When she pulls back, a huge grin lifts her lips.

"I didn't know if you'd make it," she says in a small voice, her big, blue eyes dancing around the cookout. "I thought maybe...."

"Nah! We made it, Cam," he murmurs, straightening out her perfectly curled brown locks. "Cam, I want you to meet my girlfriend, River." My heart pounds double time, nearly melting, when she turns to me and politely offers me her little hand. "River, this is my little sister, Camilla."

"Nice to meet you," she whispers, biting her lip when we firmly shake hands.

"Nice to meet you, too," I say with my heart in my throat, watching the two of them interact with each other in such a loving way. With every word Camilla says with excitement, Kieran leans in and listens attentively. He doesn't take his eyes off her until she skips away when her mother calls Camilla over to her.

"She seems sweet," I mutter through another bite of food, nearly coming from the glorious taste hitting my buds. I swear, if the boys tasted half as good as these BBQ ribs and wings, I'd never leave them alone.

"She is," Kieran mumbles, rubbing his chin as something odd sparks across his pensive face. Something darker brews between Kieran and his parents, judging by how his eyes narrow in on the man moving toward Camilla and her mother.

"You having fun yet, Pretty Girl?" Rad asks with a grin, putting an arm around my shoulders when he settles into the seat next to me with a big plate of food.

"You kidnapped me on my day off. I'm just here for the food," I groan, ripping a bite off the ribs like a damn animal.

So. Damn. Good. Fuck what I thought about these assholes before. They can cook. Well, the people they hired can cook, that is. They've been milling around, filling the pots with more food in their white chef outfits. I swear I've seen the guy on TV somewhere.

Probably one of those BBQ competition shows. Because damn, this is good food!

So they get a River-approved gold star. Only for the cooking, though. Their hospitality is lacking in several departments.

"Kidnapped you?" Kieran says with a raised brow. "You willingly got in the car." I glare at him when he grins more, tilting his head to watch me savagely bite into another wing.

"Yeah, Assface..."

"Oh, we're back to Assface now?" he quips, biting his bottom lip. I swear his eyes light up, giving me his undivided attention.

I frown. "Yeah, Assface. As I was saying. You tricked me into your vehicle by using him." Callum stiffens when I point to him. He sits across the table with a blush so deep sweat drips from his brows.

"I-I...it was them," Callum says with an accusing glare, shaking his head.

Poor Callum. They sent him into my room as I lay in bed watching the damn ClockTok app on the new phone Kieran insisted I have. I put up a good fight, but at the end of the day, it was a gift—an expensive gift, but one nonetheless.

"Your new phone," Kieran says with a smug grin, puffing out his chest when I take the device from his hand and shove it back.

"I'm not a charity case," I snap, tossing the phone back at him from the backseat of the Tahoe and nearly laugh when it bounces off his big head and lands on the floorboard of the driver's seat.

"I never said you were a charity case, River Blue," he grumbles, picking the phone off the floor and wiping it on the tight black shirt stretching across his defined pecs. "But Callum doesn't use it anymore. It's collecting dust. And your fingers are fucking bleeding from swiping." I frown, looking at my fingertips.

"Do not," I say, shaking my head. "My phone does just fine. Seriously."

"Seriously, nothing, Pretty Girl. Take the phone! You'll need it anyway. I started a group chat." To prove his point, Rad sends eggplant emojis on repeat at least fifty times.

"Could you not?" Asher snaps, turning in the passenger's seat with a scowl, glaring at Rad. "Last time, you bombarded my phone with pictures of your dick. And they don't make water hot enough to get those images out." He fake shivers and shakes his head with disgust.

I snort at Rad's fallen face until he snatches my broken phone out of my hands and tosses it to Kieran. Traitor!

"You're supposed to be on my side!" I hiss, slapping his chest, but he catches my hands.

"I'm always on your side, Pretty Girl. That's why I want you to have this phone," he mumbles, leaning in so fast and shoving his tongue down my throat as a distraction. I moan into his mouth, pulling him harder against me, and DISTRACTION! Rad snorts, grinning at me when I pull back, all flushed with puffy lips. "Teamwork, bro," he says, high-fiving Kieran, who turns to me with a smug, victorious look.

A smug look I wish I could punch from his face. Do you think he'll miss his nose when I push it through his skull for being such a prick? No? Okay, then. Worth a shot. I grit my teeth.

"It wasn't a request. It's a gift that you're keeping," Kieran demands as he tears my broken phone apart, digs out the damn SIM card, and places it in the other.

"Don't fight it, Pretty Girl. It's either that or he spanks you," Rad says, wiggling his brows. "Although, I'm down for the spanking." I shiver at the image in my mind of pink butt cheeks and the burn it leaves behind.

"Or me," Asher says in a low voice that turns my insides into knots.

I swallow hard, catching the slow smile spreading across Asher's lips. If there's one thing I can say for the guy, he'd be an excellent hate fuck. Like, pound me into oblivion, hate fuck. He'd be good at it, too. Too bad he's an asshole and not touching me with a twenty-foot pole. Yet.

"Mmhmm," Asher hums, snatching the new working phone from Kieran's hand. "Now, be a good little brat and use this phone."

"Jesus," Rad murmurs, adjusting himself. "You gonna spank her? Or should I? Bend over my knee, Pretty Girl," he says jokingly, tapping his lap.

"Like fuck," I quip, snatching the phone out of his hands. "Thanks for the phone," I murmur, looking over the sleek screen and four camera lenses in the back. "I guess." I shrug, shoving it into my pocket with a calm demeanor.

But I'm anything but calm. No one has bought me anything like this before. I've paid for everything out of my own pocket. Van didn't even buy me flowers or chocolates. The only thing Van brought me was heartache. And yet, these four guys have already come to my house, set up a home nurse for my ailing mother, slept with me every night, taken my mind off my shitty circumstances, and got me a new phone. It's a longer list than anyone had ever done.

Later that night, Callum snuck back through my sliding glass door, stripped to his boxers, and held me all night. My new phone played soft melodies, and we drifted to sleep in each other's arms. He seems to be sleeping better since he started crawling into my bed and rarely wears his earbuds anymore.

When Callum walked through my sliding glass door with an innocent grin, I instantly lit up. I was still in my pajamas when he innocently convinced me to get dressed in shorts and a t-shirt because we had somewhere to go. I thought we were going to hang out. They had other plans. So, here we are at the Lakeview neighborhood cookout, eating everything under the sun.

"Now, now," Kieran says, shoving another BBQ wing into my fingers. "He did good. He got you here so we could show you off."

"Show me off," I scoff, ripping into another wing and moaning at the taste in my mouth.

"Right," Rad rasps, staring straight at my mouth as I bite into another wing like he's hypnotized by the way I eat. "You just keep eating, Pretty Girl. I'll hide this boner somehow. Unless you want to sit on my lap and talk about the first thing that pops up." He doesn't take his eyes off me even when I set the cleaned bone on my paper plate.

"Then we could play just the tip. Or hide the hotdog. Or maybe...." He wiggles his brows, letting that charismatic smile fall across his lips.

"Mmmm, maybe," I moan into my fingers as I suck them one by one, getting the remnants of the sweet barbecue sauce off my fingers. Seriously. How do they get this shit so sweet but tangy? I could drink a gallon of this stuff or bathe in a pool full of it.

"For fucks sake, Little Brat," Asher huffs, yanking my fingers from my mouth and holding my wrist hostage in his tight grip. He shakes his head, lust swimming in the depths of his hazel eyes. I suck in a breath when he leans closer, a breath away from kissing me, and mumbles, "This is a family event."

A protective growl vibrates through his throat when he gestures to the older males standing around and staring in my direction. Some of them shift away, hiding their interest. And by interest, I mean their old man dicks standing at attention for the first time since Regan was president. Perverts. Talk about losing my appetite.

I snort, shrugging. "Better watch out, Asher. I might just become your new mommy," I quip, digging into the remaining ribs on my plate with zest.

"I need a drink," he hisses, adjusting himself with a grunt. Narrowing his eyes at me, he stares at me like I might do something else wrong. Asher huffs, trying to cover his boner.

Me? Do something bad? I would never march over to the grill and demand more ribs or cause a scene if I don't get any.

Asher leans closer than before, brushing his lips against my cheek. My breath leaves my body entirely at the sparks flying from his touch, heating my entire being.

"You're trouble with a capital T, Little Brat. Be a good girl, and stop licking your goddamn fingers in front of them. You really want to give them something to jack off to tonight?"

My nose wrinkles, and I cut my eyes to the old men standing in a circle across the party. Some of them look this way but quickly stop when they realize I'm watching. Asher's breath brushes against my cheek when he chuckles.

"Will you?" I ask suddenly, jerking my face to his and nearly kissing him.

He swallows hard, his eyes dilating. "That drink," he barks, marching away.

"Yeah! That's right, get your drink. By the time you get back, I'll be..." A hand covers my mouth, settling their warm body beside me, chuckling.

"I wouldn't finish that sentence," Kieran says with a grin, shaking his head. "Asher will blow a gasket, and he really will bend you over his knee."

"That's hot," Rad groans, running a hand down his face. "We gotta stop being so sexy out in the open. My dick..." he trails off, shaking his head.

"Ashton Radcliffe!" Bellows an angry woman from across the cul-de-sac. "Come here this instant!" Her demands echo through the neighborhood, turning everyone's attention this way for one brief second.

"That's one way to make a boner disappear. Thanks, Mother," he mumbles, pushing up from the seat with a frown. "Fuck my life, man," Rad hisses, running a hand through his hair. "I'll be back. And don't you dare move."

"Aye, aye, Ashton," I say, saluting him as he walks away. Only looking back once with a storm brewing in his eyes, promising me of the things to come later.

"For someone who didn't want to come, you're enjoying yourself," Kieran says with a grin, watching as I gobble down my last rib.

"Well, you should have started with the food is top-notch, River. Then I wouldn't have put up such a fight." I chew through the pieces of meat, reveling in the melt-in-your-mouth deliciousness on my tongue.

Screw sex, bands, rock and roll, and anything else in between; I'd die in the depth of these barbecue ribs any day just to get another taste. Shit. When I reach down to grab another, all I get is a cleaned-off bone.

"I need more," I hum, nodding to my plate. If I'm going to be here for free food, I might as well stuff myself until I want to puke. They invited me, so I'm taking advantage. Besides, he wants to show me off, right? Well, take that, Kieran Knight.

Kieran cracks a grin. "I'm going to remember this moment forever." He barks out a laugh and straightens his spine. His smile melts away into a grimace until he's standing behind me and places a firm hand on my shoulder. "Go get your ribs and whatever else you need. Apparently, our parents are having a tizzy fit."

"A tizzy? Over what?" I ask, looking around the party, taking it in. And what I see sends my heart into a frenzy. Of course.

Like every other parent on this side of the green grass, they're concerned about their boys hanging around a Central girl. Oh, right, that's me. The Central girl, who they think is too stupid to make any good decisions and will convince their sons she needs a baby or will rob them blind. I'm just here for the food, and well, their dicks are nice, too. But no babies for me, thanks. I have life aspirations that don't include children until I'm at least thirty.

"Got it," I mumble into my empty plate when Kieran gets up and waltzes toward the woman glaring daggers at him.

Her face wrinkles when Kieran approaches with his hands in his pocket, murmuring a few things to him and shaking her head in disappointment. If they only knew I wouldn't be here unless these assfaces had dragged me here kicking and screaming. It was a kidnapping. Whatever. Nothing I can drown my sorrows in more food.

"I'll be back," I tell Callum, pointing toward the food.

"You-you want me to come with you? I don't have parents to disappoint," he says, cracking a smile when I snort.

"Nah. I got this. You stay here."

I march my happy ass toward the long row of potluck food. The entire neighborhood chipped in, bringing a slew of homemade goods that would make Martha Stewart jealous. Chicken and noodles, with those thick noodles, mashed potatoes, beef and noodles, pulled pork with bbq sauce, and finally, the glorious bbq ribs stacked high. I nearly come when more gets added to the platter, fresh, hot, and ready for my mouth. I'm practically drooling by the time I grab a clean plate and pile it high with ribs, adding mashed potatoes and even a little potato salad because nothing says hello Midwest, like cold potato salad on a hot day or any kind of cold salad, for that matter.

"I know what you're up to." a menacing voice says from beside me, breaking me from my rambling potato thoughts.

I clutch my plate, and my heart races in my chest. Shit. I almost dropped my food at the sound of his deep voice. And that's a goddamn tragedy. There are hungry people all over this city who'd die to get a taste of these ribs and the seven different types of cold ass salad that doesn't involve lettuce.

"Wow, you caught me. I'm just grabbing a bite to eat," I say, my voice dripping with heavy amounts of sarcasm. There's no way I'd show this man any amount of respect.

Every time I'm face to face with this pain in my ass, he's nothing but a walking, talking dickhead. I cock my head, imagining his bald head into the shape of a dick, and wouldn't you know, he's not as intimidating.

He snarls at me, lifting his upper lip. "First, you poison my son Van with your filth, and now those four? You're really moving through them, aren't you?" Disgust fills every molecule when he steps up to me, letting me feel every inch of his over-inflated body.

Reading between the lines, I see exactly what he's throwing down. Whore. Slut. Trash. Yeah, I've heard it all. But screw him and all these people who look at where I come from instead of looking into my heart. I know exactly who I am and where I come from. The fucked up thing is, if I had even some of my dad's money, I'd be richer than all of them. How ironic is that?

Wrinkling my nose, I pick up my plate and take a big bite of my rib. "It's funny you think that," I say with a shrug, moving to walk past him, but he grabs my arm with lightning speed, squeezing tight.

I narrow my eyes at the fat fingers holding me captive. I could tell a cop when he leaves bruises, but big and round Judge Drake is just that—a goddamn judge. No one would believe the poor Central girl over the reigning judge of Central County. Besides, I've been down this road before with the police. They laughed at me then, and they'd laugh at me now.

"I don't think so. I know so. We all know how you tramp Central girls work. Trap a nice, hardworking Lakeview boy, and then you have a cushy future." His teeth grind back and forth when he speaks. I'm surprised he doesn't break a tooth.

I nod, taking another bite of my rib without care, working around the hand holding me hostage.

"You know, I shouldn't explain anything to you because, in your mind, I'm nothing more than this idea you have. But let me clarify it for you, Judge Drake." Van's father's eyebrows raise when I use his formal term with venom. "I work two jobs, more than your precious little angel Van ever has. I go to community college to better my future. I literally don't give a flying fuck about anyone on this side of town. I want out of this place. Now, let go of me." I bite into my rib again when his fat fingers finally peel away from my arm, and he wipes them on his pants like I have a disease on my skin.

What a twatwaffle.

"Don't think their parents will sit back and let them continue this little pipe dream of theirs, which doesn't include you. Go back to the hole you crawled out of and leave this side of town," he growls his entire sentence, shaking his head in disgust. "I'll make sure they know all about you." At that moment, I see the first glimmer of a wicked plan developing in his pea-sized brain.

"River," Callum says in a tight voice, coming to my side and placing an arm around my shoulder. "You okay?" he murmurs, staring daggers at the Judge, lifting his chin.

"We were just chatting," Judge Drake says with a crude smile. "I'd watch yourself if I were you, son. She'll bring you nothing but a damn headache."

Callum cocks his head to the side. "I happen to like my headache," he says confidently, squeezing my shoulder. "Come on, let's go sit." I nod in confirmation as we take a few steps from the stupid judge and stop in front of the large trashcan.

Great. Just what I need, pissed-off parents coming after me for no reason. I sigh, looking down at my delicious plate of food, and grieve with a broken heart that splits in half and cries. Lead sits in the pits of my stomach, threatening to send my already delicious ribs back up. I have a feeling they won't taste as orgasmic the second time around. There's no way I'll be able to inhale this food like I wanted to after all his words sink in. I'm only human, after all, and sometimes the words people throw at me do stick. I'm not worthless or whatever because of where I come from. I'm trying my best, but no one will ever see it from this side of town. They only see a Central girl clinging to their kids with stars in her eyes.

With a heavy heart, I mean seriously, my heart hurts when I toss my full plate in the garbage, thinking about all the hungry souls out in the world begging for a full plate of food just like that—what a waste. But I can't imagine biting into that food without it tasting like ash in my mouth. Grabbing a few napkins, I wipe all the sauce from my sticky fingers and mourn the loss of the delicious food staring back at me.

I shove my hands into my shorts pocket and peek around the party again with Callum at my side. The parents mingle, drinking their martinis and whatever fruity shit they have in their glasses. Judge Drake stands close to Kieran's mom and another man I haven't seen before, discussing something. Or someone.

"How-how about a walk?" Callum suggests, nodding his head toward the sidewalk.

I wrinkle my nose, flipping them off from my pocket, as we start walking through the party. Looking around, I don't see the others who dragged me here anywhere. How can they abandon me in the depths of Hell like this?

"You're still my favorite," I mumble, leaning my head on his shoulder for support.

"I won't-won't tell them," he whispers, kissing my hair with such love my heart pumps double time.

"Good, because they're seriously trailing behind," I grumble when we make our journey up the sidewalk away from prying eyes.

A soft chuckle vibrates through his chest when he kisses my head again and hums. Every day I swear he breaks out of his shell more and more. We haven't done more than kiss—oh, and what we did in bed with Rad. Callum's taking things at his pace, doing what he needs to do, and I'm waiting on him. Whatever my sweet Callum needs, he'll get.

"Can I ask you something?" Peering beneath my lashes, I glance up at Callum, who shrugs.

"Sure," he says through a breath, furrowing his brows.

"Your house," I mumble as our walk slows. "I..." Callum's lips pull up into a tight smile, and he shifts uncomfortably to my side, nervously peering around the neighborhood. "No. You don't have to talk about it. I'm just nosy," I say, playing it off with a laugh.

"What do you want to know?" he asks in a deep voice, slowing our steps to a stop at the edge of the party madness as we overlook everyone milling around with plates of food in one hand and an alcoholic beverage in the other.

"How?" I ask, nibbling my bottom lip. "It's just you and Rad with no jobs and no school. You guys play in a band and barely make enough to get out of here. So, um...how?" I ramble, spitting out my question as fast as possible.

He nods, eyes falling to the large crack in the road's asphalt and studying it intently. For several long seconds, he doesn't say a word. I'm almost to the point of apologizing again and dropping my nosy question, but then he speaks, stunning me into silence.

"When my family died, they left all their bank accounts, life insurance, and assets in a trust with their lawyer," he heaves a trembling breath, finally peering at me with bloodshot eyes. "It pays my monthly bills and leaves me with a little spending money to get by, but nothing substantial. At the end of December, the trust will be completely signed over to me, and I'll be free to do what I want. My parents wanted me to go to college and get a degree. So, they stipulated that if they passed before I was a certain age, I'd have to hang onto the house for that long. I don't-don't think they realized it would be like living in a tomb," he wheezes the last words, clamping his eyes shut.

I swallow hard, pulling his face down into my neck, letting him cling to me for dear life. His fingers dig into my ribs as he pulls in deep breaths of oxygen. "I'm sorry," I whisper, running my fingers through his blonde locks and twirling them in my fingers. "I didn't mean to upset you like this."

"It's okay, Little Star," he mutters into my flesh. "I rarely-rarely talk about them anymore. Sometimes, I need to let this out, and I'm...I'm glad you asked. I want to tell you everything," he whispers, lifting his face from my neck. Staring deep into my eyes, I see all the vulnerabilities swimming in the depths of his gray eyes as they soften more. "Once I can leave, have access to their money, and sell the house, we'll have enough to invest more into the band. I-I don't know what our plans are. But you'll come with us, anyway. Right?" he whispers the last part, making my heart fall into my churning stomach.

"More than anything," I reply without thinking about the future's implications or consequences. I'm living in the present, and I can't think of what will happen come December when they walk away and live their dreams. Will I go? Or will I stay home with my ill mother? Only time will tell.

RIVER

After our talk, Callum gently leads me between two houses and out of view from the party, and we settle ourselves in the grass between two big houses. Callum's brows furrow when he looks at me and leans in, kissing my cheek.

"I gotta-gotta..." His lips roll together when he stands, gesturing to his house down the block. Swallowing hard, his face flushes. "Go to the bathroom," he mumbles with embarrassment, shoving his hands in his pockets. "You want to come with or...."

I smile at him and shake my head. "I'll stay here and away from the predators," I say, pointing in the party's direction.

He nods. "Stay and be safe. He...he looked at you with so much hate. I kind of wanted-wanted to punch him." I smile even wider at the imagery of his fist hitting Judge Drake's face.

"Don't mess up your hands," I say, shaking my head.

Callum nervously waves as he jogs toward his house with urgency, leaving me to fend for myself. I pull out my new phone, enjoying the privacy the homes provide for me, and scroll SpaceFace aimlessly, looking for anything to entertain me while I wait for the assfaces—totally renaming their band that whenever they win the Battle of the Bands—who left me here to fend for myself. Seriously? How can they just walk away with their heads hung low and their puppy tails tucked, leaving me up against the damn lions circling me. My stomach churns with the similarities between them and Van. I mean, Van never would have brought me here in the first place, but still. He left me because his mean daddy said so. Oh well, I'm better off without him.

"River."

I sigh to myself, leaning my head back against the cool siding of the house. Speak of the devil. It's like I summoned him to join me in my hiding place. I squint, looking up toward the towering figure looming above me.

"Van," I say in an equally ominous voice, shoving my phone into my pocket. To equal the playing field, I jump to my feet and wipe away the grass clippings from my ass. "What brings you to my little oasis?" I ask with scathing sarcasm dripping from my tongue.

He rolls his eyes toward the sky, shaking his head like he can't with me. "I saw you got cornered by my dad, and I wanted to make sure you were okay." He swipes his foot along the manicured grass, looking at me coyly through his eyelashes.

Fucking boys and their beautiful eyelashes. How'd they get so damn blessed? And me. I have to apply fakes to achieve what they get just by waking up and greeting the sun.

I scoff. "Okay? No, I'm not. Your dad made me lose my appetite." I shake my head in disgust, mourning the food I had to throw away. Ugh. The feeling of his slimy fingers wrapped around my arm linger on my flesh, and I want to hurl. No one should touch anyone without permission.

He snorts. "Sorry about him. He was just surprised to see you here. Me too, actually." He shrugs nonchalantly, but I know Van better than he thinks I do. He's fishing for answers from me in his usual way.

"Oh, yeah? Surprised to see me? I'm always at these barbecues.

What're you talking about?" I quip, earning myself a scoff of disbelief.

"Why're you here, Rivey?" he asks, narrowing his eyes, using the nickname I never wanted to hear from his lips again. It's the one he used to seduce me into the backseat of his car and the one he moaned when he thrust into me.

"I'm here for the food," I snark, rocking on my toes. I mean, it's not a lie. "Delicious by the way." I point fingers guns in his direction, earning another scowl. I live to piss this guy off.

"No," he grits out, stepping up to me, effectively entering my personal space. "You're here with them. Aren't you?" His brows furrow like he's constipated, and I almost suggest adding some prune juice to his diet. But I bite my tongue because he knows the answer. He apparently watched me go to Callum's a few days ago.

I frown. "And what if I am? What is it to you?" I bite back, putting my hand on my hip.

Here we go. Another lecture from someone I don't want a lesson from. I trust only five people in this world enough to listen to their lectures, and it doesn't include this assclown.

"I thought I warned you away from them, Rivey. Seriously! What are you doing with them? They're users. They only want you for one thing," he growls, caging me in against the house. His eyes dilate when he presses his entire body against mine, relaxing into me. My whole body stiffens beneath his chest, and the worst thoughts roar through my mind. We're alone, and he's a lot stronger than me. Plus, the wild look in his eye doesn't promise a happy ending. I swear my throat closes, and my heart pounds in my ears when he leans down, getting into my face. "They are going to use you and then throw you away. Mark my damn words," he hisses between his teeth.

"What? Like you did?" I seethe, clenching my teeth.

I cock my head, running my fingers over the wooden grip of my special knife in my pocket. Since my rape, I've never left without it. It has protected me on many occasions. And right now? Yeah, I'm half tempted to sink it deep into his balls and watch him scream in agony and rue the day he ever warned me and tried to run my life.

If Van thinks he can corner me like this and put his face directly into mine, then he's way too fucking comfortable with me. Like everyone else, he deeply underestimates me, thinking he can pin me against the wall and tell me what I can and can't do or who I can fuck. He's way out of line, and I'm about to show him the error of his ways.

"You didn't like it when I called you daddy when we screwed. So, what makes you think you can act like my daddy now?" I seethe, fitting my closed knife against his balls. In one flick, I could have him flayed open and begging for the hospital. "You have some balls on you, Van. I'll give you that. But you're about to lose them for overstepping if you're not careful. We've established that I'm a big girl and don't need my ex-boyfriend to protect me anymore. So, what will it be? Balls? No balls? Your choice. With the flick of my damn wrist, I could relieve you of them." His Adam's apple bobs when his eyes dart down to my fingers wrapped around the handle of my knife. I swear all the blood rushes to his face, and he shakes his head.

"Rivey," he grumbles, hanging his head in defeat, and takes one step back. "You'll thank me one day for giving you..."

"The fuck you think you're doing?" A low, menacing voice comes from beside us with such possession, I swear my nipples pebble under my shirt, showing their approval.

In the blink of an eye, Van is pushed off of me and stumbles backward with a stunned expression lining his face. Kieran charges him again with flaring nostrils and tight fists like a damn wild bull on the loose.

"Kieran," I say in a low voice, scanning his face and trying to stop it. "He's not worth it." His eyes flick to the knife in my hand, hanging loosely without the blade protruding.

"You felt threatened," he hisses, nodding toward the knife. "What the fuck were you saying to her, Donny boy?" he asks, flexing his fists. "You looked like you were getting fucking cozy with my girlfriend."

"Again, with the girlfriend remarks!" I hiss, tossing my hands up in exasperation.

It's like they think if they keep saying it over and over again that I'll finally believe it. But there's no way I'm their anything. Nothing but a good time and...whatever else I have to convince myself of.

Kieran shifts his weight from foot to foot, cracking his knuckles like a crazy man hell-bent on defending my honor. Great. He's going to kick Van's ass. Not that Van doesn't deserve a good-ass whooping, but still. At a family cookout where their parents already hate me. It's not what I need right now. What I need is a stack of ribs, a damn strawberry milkshake, and no damn drama. Is that too much to ask for?

"Kieran," I warn with a growl, stepping toward him.

"What's it to you, Knight? Huh? Her pussy that good that you're going to punch me in the face?" A redness takes over Van's face when he steps up to Kieran, facing off with him with a snarl.

I frown. "Leave my pussy out of this. You know what? You're all jackasses." I throw my hands in the air when Kieran grabs him by the collar and holds him close. Idiots. They're all fucking idiots. I shake my head, stuffing my knife back into my pocket. They can keep their balls and have fun beating the snot out of each other.

"Nah. You're just a jealous asshole," Kieran spits through gritted teeth. "It tears you apart that the girl you're in love with is on my dick, not yours. But that's your fault, isn't it, Drake?" Kieran cocks his head as Van seethes in his grip, shaking with anger. His eyes cut to mine, and I fucking sigh at the situation. Who knew my Knight would argue and defend my pussy against my stupid ex-boyfriend who broke my heart. It'd be romantic if he weren't being such a dick.

"You shouldn't have her," Van grits out, shoving against Kieran, and knocks them both to the ground. Van lands on top of Kieran and raises his fist, letting it dangle.

"God damn it!" I hiss, marching toward them and grabbing his hand. "This isn't cute, romantic, or whatever the hell you two think you're fighting over. This is fucking barbaric. Get. Off. Of. Him." I grunt, trying to pull Van's lean body off Kieran, but he doesn't budge. He stays on top of Kieran, glaring down at the smirking asshole beneath him who eggs him on with a sparkle in his eyes.

"Do it, Van," Kieran says in a low, gruff voice. "Punch me like you want to."

"You're not helping, Assface," I huff, trying to pull Van's hand back, but it backfires when I stumble over my feet and land hard on my ass. As soon as my hand releases from his fist, he throws it into the side of Kieran's laughing face.

"Oh God, yes," Kieran shouts when Van wails on him repeatedly, pounding his fist into his face until blood spurts out of his nose. He laughs, thrashes around, and soaks up the pain every fist inflicts.

"Van, you asshole!" I hiss, getting into the mix and launching myself at my stupid ex, who couldn't leave it alone.

"What the hell?" Rad's voice rings through the fray of fists, and he forces Van off and helps my aching body off the ground. "Dude, seriously?" he asks Kieran, who jumps to his feet, wiping the blood from under his nose. He loosens his neck and grins with bloody teeth in Van's direction.

"Feel better?" Kieran asks in a condescending tone and cocks his head.

"Loads," Van grits out, popping his knuckles.

"Go the fuck back home, Van," Asher demands, strolling between the houses with so much fucking confidence it chokes the air. "You've said your peace. Now get the fuck out. She doesn't want you. We don't want you. Run along." He flicks his wrist with an arrogant attitude.

"I'm just trying to keep you safe, Rivey," Van says, cutting his eyes to me. "They're going to hurt you." I swear his eyes mist over when he looks at me, pleading with me to heed his words.

"Just like you did?" I say, letting all my vulnerabilities shine through.

His lips roll together, and his eyes drop, dripping in shame.

"Yeah," he mumbles. "But I'd never make that mistake again." He shakes his head, snapping back when a new voice comes toward us.

"Van, baby! What are you doing?"

I jerk my head when a beautiful brunette strolls up with her hand on her chest and shock on her face. But that's not what draws me in. Nope. It's the giant diamond glistening on her left hand—an engagement ring. Correction, a massive engagement ring. Jesus. That has to cost more than my yearly salary. "Did you...did you fight?" She takes his hand, examining the blood on his fist, and then looks at Kieran's face. "Oh, no," she gasps.

"Heya, Whitley," Rad greets, tipping his head in her direction with a small, knowing smirk.

"Rad," she greets with a frown, taking the crowd in until she gets to me. Her face hardens, and her ice-blue eyes cut to Van, where guilt is written all over his face.

"I see," she huffs and turns to walk away.

"Whitley, wait!" he shouts, running until he catches up to her. "It's not what it looks like, I promise."

"And her?" She points her manicured nail directly at me.

I groan, running a hand down my face. Jesus. I just need one day where I'm not put in this kind of situation. Just one! That's all I'm asking for.

"It's nothing." His words would have cut like a knife a few months ago and bled me dry, but today I'm thankful I can smile in his direction and not feel a damn thing. Thanks for that, Van. You've been a real treat. But I've moved on to bigger and better things.

"Don't worry!" I shout, waving an arm at her. "He was only warning me away from their dicks! Not his!" She gasps, slapping Van across the face, and takes off with choked sobs.

Am I an asshole? Sure. But I won't let anyone spread lies about me right to my face. If I didn't mean a damn thing to him, then he would have let me go completely. He's just mad I won't let him sneak into the record store office with me anymore. I'd say he's pussy deprived. But that would be a lie. He's obviously been hiding a girlfriend—no, scratch that—a fiance away. The question is, when did he start dating her? And was it while we were screwing around? If there's one thing I don't stand for, it's fucking cheating.

"Oh, Pretty Girl." Rad barks a laugh, wrapping his arm around my shoulders and turning my face toward his. "Don't listen to him, okay?" he asks, wrapping his fingers around my jaw and directing my mouth to his.

"Get off me, you sweaty asshole," I grunt, pushing his body away. He cackles as he stumbles, only righting himself when he bumps into the side of the house.

"He's such a fucking dick," Kieran explodes, grinding his teeth.

"Takes one to know one," Callum offers with a grunt, strolling towards us with his hands in his pocket. "You-you okay?" he asks, coming to my side and taking my cheeks in his palms. With worried eyes, he looks me over and nods, kissing my forehead.

"I'm fine," I mumble, leaning into his embrace even though I'm anything but fine.

"Fuck sakes," Asher mutters, running a hand down his face, shaking his head. "I'm going to kill that guy." Yeah, me too, pal.

"Welcome to the shit show," Rad says with a grimace, looking me over too. "Where every year our neighborhood cookout turns into a Real Housewives drama."

I wrinkle my nose. "You've watched Real Housewives?" I ask, raising a brow and burst out laughing when his cheeks turn pink.

"*Real Housewives. Laguna Beach. The Hills.* Any old-school reality drama you can think of, Rad loved to indulge in," Asher says dryly with an eye roll.

"Dick," Rad mutters, swiping a hand through his mullet.

"Well, listen. As much as I've so loved being forced to live through this hell, I'd appreciate it if someone could take me home. I have homework, and some of us have to get up and go to a job in the morning," I say with a pointed look.

"Grab your things, Pretty Girl," Rad says with a pout, nodding toward his house, reminding me I left my backpack at their house because I was under the impression we were doing our usual couch dates. "I'll take you home," he says through a defeated sigh, clinging to me like he doesn't want to let me go.

Before we can manage a step, Asher huffs, crossing his arms over his chest. "Little Brat will have to wait. My father has requested our musical presence," he says through gritted teeth.

"What?" Callum murmurs, knitting his brows together when Asher heaves a breath.

"Musical presence?" I snort, nearly jerking back when his heated gaze finds mine, overflowing with a wave of fiery anger he can't seem to contain.

"He wants us to play?" Callum asks, cocking his head to the side, inspecting Asher's agitated state.

"He never wants us to play," Kieran confesses, scrunching his face. "Why?" His Adam's apple bobs when he swallows hard, looking intently at Asher, studying his reaction.

"Yeah..." Asher says with confusion, shaking his head. "Fuck. I don't know. It's weird... The entire party wants to hear us." He shrugs, moving a hand through his hair.

"You'll stay?" Callum murmurs in my ear when we meander back into the house, standing an inch apart in the living room.

"Sure," I say, offering him a tight smile, despite wanting to run as far away as I can from Van and his weird, psycho bullshit.

With a few more murmured words, I sit my stuff down and help the boys move their equipment to the center of the cul-de-sac, prepping for their impromptu performance for the entire neighborhood crowding around. The crowd's drunk voices rise into whistles and hollers the moment Asher hits the first note of the evening.

ASHER

L eaning forward, I put my elbows on my knees, gripping my
phone. Heart after heart floats up the screen, accompanied
by comments of praise and admiration. My breaths shudder
in my chest, ballooning with elation and pride.

Wow! Following you guys now!
You guys sound amazing!
Holy hell! They're hot as hell!
Wow! @whisperedwordsband! Who are you? You sound so
good!

Fan for life!

My eyes widen as I scroll through the comments, and I flush.
If this is what even a sliver of fame feels like, then I'm fucking blown
away. All these people are lining up to get a piece of us and begging
for more videos and performances. Some are local people. But most
are scattered across the country and overseas.

Holy shit.

The list goes on with more intrusive questions just as our
newest video hits one-million views on ClockTok. Disbelief slams
through me as the numbers climb and climb with each passing
second.

We'll be internet sensations before the night is through, and
everyone will shout our names. Now, we need to deliver more
performances to the masses before we fade into obscurity before
the competition.

It's hard to believe that just yesterday, my father forced us
to play an impromptu concert for the neighborhood. Begrudgingly,
of course.

Never in a million years would he actually want us to live out
our little fantasy, as he calls it. But when the public wants something,
my father will deliver.

My father's talk from yesterday rattles in my mind when he pulled me away from the cookout and threw me into his office with such force I landed on my ass with a grunt. The pain seared up my tailbone, letting me know the kind of mood he was in.

"Stay away from the trash, son. You're a fucking embarrassment," my father hisses, sending a fist into my gut as we stand in his brightly-lit office.

All the breath leaves my body when I double over, counting to ten. Desperation to remove myself from here clamps my tongue down. I refuse to say a goddamn thing and inflict more pain on my body when I could simply shut my mouth and walk away. One day, I won't have to endure his angry fists—but that day is not today.

"Stand up straight," he barks, grabbing me by the collar and yanking me up despite the pain of his blow knotting my stomach.

My lips pop open when he releases me and leans against his mahogany desk in a relaxed pose. River teases me that a demon resides in my body, but the actual devil stands before me with black eyes, a cruel smile, and a wicked right hook.

"Enlighten me on why the trash is eating my food. Judge Drake seems to think she's nothing but a whore, luring you in for money," he says in a smooth voice, straightening his ten thousand dollar suit he insisted on wearing to the catered cookout. "And we all know what happens when a whore lures a man of our status in with her pussy." He raises a brow, alluding to the woman he married and now loathes.

My father may be a good business owner, making more money than anyone in a ten-mile radius. But as a father? He's shit. It's no wonder my mother buried her anguish in a needle and slowly poisoned her veins to leave his tight grip. Some days, I wish I could do the same. Financially, though? I'm stuck, rooted in the spot with nowhere to run.

"She's not luring us in for money," I say in a small voice, locking my hands together in front of me. I keep my eyes down low and my body locked tight. The last thing I want to do is provoke the devil even more, but I have to tell him something believable. "We're the ones using her."

She may not be after our money, but there's something about River West that makes me want to either fuck her or run her off. She's dangerous for us; I don't know to what extent. Something is nagging in the back of my mind warning me to watch my back and my boys.

They're my family, and I'll be damned if one chick swoops in and ruins what my family has built for the past five years.

My father scoffs, checking his watch. "Right. Using her?" Great. He wants me to elaborate more than I fucking should.

I clear my throat. "River is Corbin West's daughter. He owns..." Ding. Ding. Ding. For once in my short life, I've uttered the correct words he wants to hear. His eyes light up and widen, and his body puffs up with pride.

"I know who he is and what he owns," my father barks in a deep voice. Bravely, I meet his eyes. His lips purse, and he nods, something churning in his mind. "That man is worth more than this entire neighborhood combined and more than Montgomery Inc." He opens his lips to possibly say more but rethinks it when he shakes his head, redirecting the conversation. "The neighbor, Susie, specifically requested you boys to put on a show for the neighborhood. She says you sound really good for a waste of time and would like a live concert."

"A show?" I ask, my heart pounding against my chest at the prospect of playing in front of the crowd.

"Get your fucking guitars and shit and bring it out. You and the boys are performing tonight." He steps forward, towering over me with a twisted face. "Don't fuck this up and embarrass the family, Asher. Make it good."

"Of course, sir," I say quickly, taking a step toward the door, aching to escape the oppressive atmosphere putting pressure on my chest.

"Impress me, boy," he mutters from his desk. "Prove to me it's not a waste of time." My eyes widen when I leave the office and head out the door, trailing Kieran and Rad just as he pushes Van off River.

That conversation was all the permission I needed. I felt lighter than I had in days, elated at the opportunity to impress my overbearing and relentless father. If I showed him what we could do, even for a night, we'd have a better shot at making it all real.

That night, we blew everyone away with our raw talent, drawing praise from the drunk housewives and stuffy old men. My fucking father even nodded in my direction with a sense of pride swallowing him. He didn't utter another word to me that night, instead locking himself away in his office. Even Gloria stood stupefied by the closed door and retreated somewhere in the house.

For one night, the man who always disapproved of our actions left us alone.

Turning my attention back to the screen, I smile. There we are with the sun to our backs, barely beaming down. Dusk settles in, leaving nothing but a pink sky as our backdrop.

Kieran leads us into the beginning of our set list, starting with *Midnight*. His voice rings through the microphone, and his piercing eyes follow the camera as it moves in front of him, getting a close-up. The smirk that lights up his face and the sparkle in his eyes makes my heart drop into my stomach. As she moves, his eyes follow like a predator watching his prey, ready to pounce.

River leans the camera over Kieran's shoulder, capturing Rad's intense grin. His arms pound the sticks into the snares several times before crashing them into the cymbals and back down to the rest of the kit. Rad's tongue pokes out from between his lips, and a look of concentration crosses his face. But when his eyes find River standing before him with the camera, he brightens completely and watches her as she backs away, turning to Callum and then me. Throughout the rest of the performance, their eyes follow her every move, never straying from her presence.

"Dude! It's fucking amazing!" Rad whoops, slumping down on the couch beside me with a dopey grin. Bringing a beer to his lips, he takes a long swig and then sighs when he pulls it back.

"One million views and counting," I gape, shaking my head in disbelief. Who knew this many people would want to see us perform?

Jesus. Images of our future shine brighter and brighter in my mind, and genuine excitement starts to settle in—us on the big stage with big lights shining down on us as the crowd chants our name over and over. People fall to their knees to get a taste of the music we've bled for. Staring straight ahead, I get lost in the fantasy that could one day be our reality. To leave this place and never see my father again lifts a massive amount of pressure off my chest. I've always ached to see the rest of the world from a tour bus, and the closer we get to making our dreams come true, the lighter I feel.

My only worry... My only concern holding me back is our little sister, Camilla. Her little face pops into my mind twisting in grief as our father strikes me down to the ground, raining blow after blow after he had a rough night of drinking, forcing her to see the consequences of my actions. Forcing her to see what her life will be like if she doesn't bend to my father's every whim and desire. She's seen it a million times—his fists hitting us and tearing us down. For every punishment we receive, she's there to witness our downfall with tears in her eyes and a distraught expression.

If I leave her behind, what will happen? Will he threaten her with a sharp tongue and swift fists? Her cries from over the weekend plague my nightmares. Camilla shouldn't have to go through what we do—ever. Somehow, I need to get Camilla and Gloria away from my father for good. But how? I have no idea.

I swallow hard, returning to the murmured conversation going on around me between the guys, snapping me back to the present instead of sucking me into the past. The boys mill around Callum and Rad's house—our home base.

"She did good, yeah?" Kieran asks with pride, referring to the camera woman in charge of filming our entire show.

"*Little Brat,*" *I murmur, motioning for her to come to me with the curl of my finger.*

As the drunken crowd of suburban moms moves closer, creating a circle around our setup like sharks circling blood in the ocean, they still. Their glazed-over eyes light up when Kieran tunes his guitar, quietly listening for the right notes. It's like they're hoping to relieve their shitty teenage years with booze, bands, and... Yeah, I'm not finishing that disgusting thought. Even Gloria straightens her spine in the crowd with a glass of red wine perched in her hand, quietly assessing the band. We've never played for anyone in this neighborhood, instead hiding in our home base's basement, trying to conceal our sound.

Per her usual, River raises a defiant brow a few steps away, refusing to budge until I'm huffing mad. And fucking hard. One day, I'd love to pound the attitude out of her ass until she's panting and begging me to stop the punishment, which I wouldn't. My little whore would tremble before me after coming so many times...I... Shit. Why does she take my mind there?

No one gets a rise out of me like this. Not even Rad, who tries his hardest. The longer I'm around River, the more I want to bend to her every whim and then bend her to mine. Something deep, dark, and dangerous hides in River. Calling to me to release whatever it is. A wildness she never sets free. The tears she refuses to shed. I want to be the one to tame her and then hold her, letting her know everything will be okay. A sliver of darkness filled with unresolved trauma rests behind the spark in her eyes, hidden from the world but not hidden from me. I see behind the tough mask she presents to the world, and one day, I'll pull it off. I close my eyes, groaning at the serious hold she has on us. It's borderline dangerous.

Knocking the dick-hardening thoughts from my mind before I mount her in front of everyone, I watch as she places her hands on her hips. Then, and only then, does her magical grin spread across her luscious lips, making me wish my lips were on hers. Fuck me.

"Yes, Evil Ash?" she asks in a sarcastic tone, batting her lashes playfully at me, hoping to get a reaction.

I lick my lips, wanting to confront her about that stupid nickname. But I think better of it and huff.

"Take your phone from your pocket and record us."

It's not a question. It's a demand for her to comply. If there's one thing about my little brat, she loves to poke the bear—aka—me. Brats like River need swift direction, not options. Her lips pop open, exposing the argument on the tip of her tongue. I roll my eyes.

"Please, River," I bark, placating her with the niceness everyone else offers her. Kieran always says I'm a perpetual grump, which must be true, judging by how she stiffens.

"Did that hurt?" she quips, digging her brand-new phone from her pocket.

"No," I growl, clenching my teeth. Here she goes again, winding me tighter than I was before. One day, I'll fucking explode and grab her by the hair. But that's not today. Not when the crowd closes in even closer than before.

She shrugs, clicking a few things on her phone, and nods. "All right. This will be good for your ClockTok account."

"We don't have a ClockTok account," I deadpan with a grimace, thinking about the ridiculous video-sharing app everyone obsesses over.

"You do now, boss man," she says with a grin, shoving the stupid phone in my face.

My teeth clench when a picture of the four of us pops up in the little window, accompanied by the username: whisperedwordsband and a little bio about who we are and where we're from. There's even a link to all our social media profiles—the same profiles we barely use—at the top. Fuck.

"You've thought of everything, haven't you?" I ask, blinking at her. Who knew a Central girl could be so damn useful with these sorts of things.

"Sometimes, I think you underestimate my abilities. It's kind of offensive, Evil Ash. Now, play your little show, and I'll capture it all." She grins one last time, stepping back and settling herself next to Gloria.

I swallow hard, watching Gloria lean in, whisper something into River's ear, and back away. Their faces give nothing away, but I know something out of left field was said when River's lip curls, and she shakes it off. Something to ask her later when we're alone, and I can force the words from her lips.

FUCK!

I blow out a breath, running a hand down my face when Kieran walks by, swiping the phone from my hand as he passes by. "Jesus. There are like forty thousand comments!"

"It's about how hot we are, isn't it? Cuz we're fucking smoking!" Rad explains with an even bigger grin.

"Nigel gave me permission to do that," I say in a monotone voice, keeping my eyes forward, refusing to meet his bewildered expression.

Kieran chokes on his drink, snapping his head at me. "He what?"

"He said impress me," I blurt, running a hand down my face.

What I don't say is, judging by the non-existent interaction we had with him last night, that I succeeded in impressing him.

"Impress him?" Kieran mumbles with confusion.

I shrug. "No idea. But he seems semi-on board. So we can head to the competition without issue whenever the time comes."

Without issue would be a dream come true. But I'm a realist. At the drop of a dime, my father could change his mind. Not that he has any real say. If I want to leave this place with my life intact, we need to be smart about it.

Kieran snorts, knowing exactly what's going through my mind. "Right," he mutters, throwing my phone back to me.

"Looks like we need Pretty Girl to get us more shows so we can keep feeding the fans," Rad says with a lazy grin, putting a joint between his lips and lighting it. "Speaking of. How was she today?" he asks Callum, who turns a deep shade of red.

"Fine," he mumbles, settling back on the couch.

"Just fine?" Kieran asks with an ounce of protectiveness leaking into his tone.

Callum snorts and rolls his eyes. "She wasn't expecting me. I had to force her into my car, and even then...."

"She bitched the whole way?" I gripe, earning a smack to the back of my head.

"Bitch and her do not belong in the same sentence. Have some respect," Rad says with a frown as I nurse the pulsating pain in the back of my head.

"She was fine," Callum continues with a stronger voice. "I took her home, and we hung out with her mom for a little while. Then, I took her to the bar for work."

"She works too goddamn hard," Kieran mumbles in awe.

I couldn't agree more. River works herself to the bone day in and day out, looking increasingly more exhausted as the days go on. Sprinkle school she's putting herself through without help from anyone around her, and she's killing herself for a better future. Seeing such a young person balance so many things in life is odd. Not only does she work two jobs, but she goes to school and somehow cares for her mother in the process. My heart aches at how much she does for everyone else but never seems to take time for herself. River really does deserve better than four assholes who started by using her for her last name and wanting a better future for themselves. Fuck. How did we get down this fucked up rabbit hole? Guilt gnaws away at my insides, churning my stomach.

"Does she have a car?" I ask, looking around the room as they shake their heads.

"If she had a car, then we wouldn't be able to drive her around or force her to come over," Rad gripes like a psychopath, grinning at the win.

"Not when we're around," Kieran says in agreement. "If she has one, we can fix it as slowly as possible."

Callum snorts. "I'll keep taking her anywhere she wants to go," he mumbles with satisfaction, pride puffing out his chest.

I shake my head at their obsessive tendencies. Jesus. I may have rogue thoughts about fucking her into oblivion, but I'm no caveman.

"Then she doesn't walk alone anymore," I declare, earning nods of approval.

"We're her road to safety!" Rad whoops, throwing his fist in the air.

I sigh when our phones ding, indicating the only other person in our group chat needs us. Anticipation roars through my veins when I dig my phone out of my pocket. My heart rate skyrockets when the words flash across the screen, and I jump to my feet like the others.

River: Fuck. I need your help. Can you meet me at the bar?

Rad: What is it? That fucker again? I'll rip the skin from his dick, fry it, and shove it down his throat.

I throw him a look, eyeing the cold fury passing over his face. There's something there he hasn't told us. Sure, Bradley is the biggest waste of space in the universe. But Rad's expression says there's more to River's story that we don't know about. Kieran may not have caught on, but I sure have.

River: Wow, ever the romantic. But no... I...you know what? Nevermind. I can handle this.

Kieran: Nice try, River Blue. But we're already in the car and on our way. We'll meet you there in twenty minutes.

She thought she could dismiss us with a few words. Yeah, that shit doesn't fly. Before we know it, we're in the damn car, flying down the streets of Central City until we pull into the parking lot behind the raging bar. Music spills from every orifice, and people stumble on the sidewalk.

RIVER

The worst things in life come in fours. More specifically, the four bumbling idiots I texted out of desperation. Commit me now because I don't know what ran through my mind when I pressed send. Too bad I can't take it back. I'd give anything to have a time machine. Then I could go back in time, smack myself over the head, and throw my phone. It's too late now, though. Here they are, pushing into the bar like wild animals stampeding over anyone who gets in their way.

"Bitch, you've got them wrapped around your finger," Ode leans in awe, watching intently as they stumble through the door with feral looks. "They look like they're about to rip this place apart for you. My god..." She whistles under her breath, looking at them with disbelief and fanning her face with a nearby menu.

I sigh, watching Kieran stomp his way through the rowdy crowd with a stone-cold expression. I swear everyone jumps out of his way when his eyes look around the room for the threat.

Said problem lurks in a booth at the back of the bar, hiding in the shadows, watching our every move when Kieran locks eyes with him and growls, planting his feet. Rad pushes through people with a grin, setting his sights on me.

"There she is," Rad proclaims with glee, breaking through the rising tension.

Coming around the bar, he wraps his arms securely around me and squeezes me into his chest. The scent of his body wash filters through my nose, and subconsciously, I know I'm safe. Every ounce of tension melts away when I breathe in his scent and bask in the warmth of his hug.

"Here I am," I mumble into his chest, gripping the back of his shirt and keeping him there within my reach.

Ashton Radcliffe may be outspoken and unable to hold his tongue, but he was my hero once. My knight in shining armor who continues to protect me from the dangers threatening me.

Tipping my head back, I gaze into his sparkling brown eyes, tinted with concern. With a content sigh, I press my lips to his, savoring the flavor of his tongue dancing with mine. He groans into my mouth, pushing me back into the bar. Warm hands encase my jaw, holding me firmly in place.

"Is that what you needed?" Rad asks breathlessly when he pulls back, cocking his head and examining my flushed face until I nod. "Good," he murmurs, rubbing his hands over my shoulders, relaxing me even more.

His dark eyes search the bar with predatory intent, finally landing back on me with a frown. "Why is Van here? Fuck. I thought maybe that other fucker had shown up again to harass you." Worry lines crease on his face when he looks at me for confirmation.

"No," I murmur, running a thumb over his cheek. "He hasn't been back since you kicked him out. And hell, that was the first time I had ever seen him here."

Lakeview residents rarely show up to Dead End unless they're desperate. They've got fancier, nicer bars on their side of town without the crime rates surrounding it. Besides, Van has never come here before. Hell, he practically refused to come and meet me on this side of town unless it was at the record store. So, to see him so out of his usual territory has me on edge.

"Why the fuck is he here?" Kieran questions with a growl, curling his fingers into a fist. Glancing at Van again, he frowns more, baring his teeth at the threat. Van, in return, lifts his beer and salutes the guys tauntingly. "I'll kill him," he mutters, tightening his stance and squaring his shoulders. "I'll fucking murder him if he fucked with you. Did he do anything to you? Talk to you? Touch you?" A wild shift happens in his eyes as his voice raises with every word he speaks, pulling back his lips into a snarl.

"Is this why-why you texted?" Callum asks, blinking rapidly.

Stepping forward with a hardened face, which is so unlike himself, he looks over his shoulder. Every inch of his body tenses up, pulling his shoulders into his ears when his eyes find Van and his friend lounging in a booth, drinking their beers. Callum sighs, slumping into the bar stool. Shaking his head, he runs a hand down his face in frustration.

I nibble my lip and nod, not willing to admit he's shaken me up as much as he has. It seems like everywhere I go, Van's face pops up. The cookout. The record store. Just last night, after Callum had settled into bed with me, I swear I heard someone outside my sliding glass door rustling the leaves and tapping on the windows. I thought maybe it was Rad coming for a visit. Through the darkness, I couldn't make out any shapes lurking outside, but I felt it. The eyes searched me out in the night, sending goosebumps down my arms and raising the hairs on the back of my neck. The only way I could shake off the feeling was by snuggling into Callum more and ignoring it until I fell fast asleep. In Callum's arms, I felt more protected than ever.

"Is he bothering you?" Asher asks, settling across from us on a bar stool with a deadly expression tightening his beautiful face. If he weren't such an assface, he'd be handsome as hell.

"No, and yes," I sigh, shaking my head. "I don't know, I felt.... Fuck, he makes me feel uneasy, okay?" I spit out, rushing my words together. My stomach turns at my admission, and my eyes fall to the floor, avoiding their stares.

Rad picks up my chin with two fingers, forcing me to face the twinkle in his eyes. "We got you, Pretty Girl, okay? That's what boyfriends are for. And lucky for you, you have four."

"You are not my boyfriends. How does that even work?" I say, shaking my chin from his hold. "There's four of you and only...."

"Three holes? Yeah, we've discussed that. But you have hands, too. It's like a fivesome for all, and we're all satisfied." Rad grins, pride puffing out his chest.

"That makes no sense, jackass," Kieran quips, shoving Rad to the side. "And you are our girlfriend. You have no choices in this discussion."

I frown. "Again, with the demands, Assface. I am my own fucking woman. I swear to God, you're asking for a dick punch tonight."

"The good kind?" Rad asks, wiggling his brows, and then his face falls at our sour expressions. "Okay, so not the good kind?" he questions again with furrowed brows.

Asher huffs. "There is literally no such thing as a good dick punch, idiot. For fuck's sake," he grumbles, running a hand through his hair. "I'm surrounded by idiots every day," he mutters, along with several more unintelligible words.

"I take offense to that," Rad says with mock hurt, rearing back.

"Shut up," Callum grumbles with a snort, effectively shutting Rad up, who still grins like an idiot.

"Anyway, we'll stand guard, Little Brat," Asher says with a shrug, sitting back on the stool. Looking over his shoulder, his eyes connect with Van's in a challenge like a dog staring down a perpetrator ready to bite.

"We got you, Pretty Girl," Rad says with conviction, turning around and grabbing three beers from the fridge, opening them, and handing them out to the boys. "Now, can you make me a Pina Colada? I'm aching for some sweetness, which I'll get from you later, but I need liquid sweetness," he says, punctuating his words with a butt slap and grab.

"Sure, just help yourself," I quip, throwing my arms in the air and promptly shoving my new bodyguards out from behind the bar before they destroy something—like my sanity.

"I got it," Ode says with a sigh, mixing his drink for him and bringing it back. Rad grins when she sets it down in front of him and hums when he takes a sip. "So, are you boys stepping up and protecting my girl here?" she asks with a grin, throwing her arm over my shoulders and squeezing me into her side. Leaning her head on mine, she sighs.

"Anything for her," Kieran proclaims with a slight smirk, bringing his beer to his lips.

I flush, sweat breaking out on every inch of me. No matter how often they tell me they're my boyfriends or get that funny, protective look in their eyes, I have a hard time thinking they'll stick around. Every important male in my life has walked away without looking back. So, what makes them so different? They can have my body over and over again. But my heart is a different story.

"These ones?" Ode whispers directly in my ear like she's seen inside my brain and knows exactly what I'm thinking. "These are the good ones. That one over there? He's bad news. Should we kick him out?"

My eyes stray to the man himself, sitting back in the booth, discreetly watching me with interest. Should I kick him back to his side of town? Probably. But he hasn't done anything to warrant these feelings tumbling inside me. There's just something about him blaring warning signals in my mind.

"He's been steadily buying beers for himself and his friend for the past two hours. He's not really doing anything wrong," I murmur nervously, twiddling my damn thumbs.

"You say the word, and we'll destroy his existence," Asher says in a—fuck with me and find out—tone, pulling my eyes to his. "No one fucks with what is ours." He raises a brow, daring me to argue.

Fuck with what's ours? This again? I swear to God I'm going to wake up with a tattoo on my forehead that says Property of Whispered Words, and then I'm going to start throwing hands and breaking balls. Sinking my teeth into my tongue, armed with a retort, I sigh, deciding better of it. They came all this way to help me, and I should be grateful they dropped everything—which I am. So damn thankful they dropped everything to be with me. But sometimes, when they chip away at my independence, I want to bite their heads off. Is it irrational? Fuck yes. But I'm a strong, independent woman who just happened to need her men to fight her battles.

"I'll keep that in mind. Thank you," I say, blowing out a breath and earning a satisfied smirk from the jerk in question.

"Looks like your little stalker needs a refill. I got them," Ode says with reassurance, clapping me on the shoulder. "I'll be back."

"You're not allowed to go over there," Kieran demands with narrowed eyes, following Ode's every move as she speaks with Van, who smiles up at her, lazily swirling his finger over the edge of the glass beer bottle.

I blink a few times, staring at him. "Did he just say that?" I ask Callum, who nervously grins at me and nods in confirmation, scooting back in his seat. "Look, I'm grateful as hell you guys came, but you can't put me in a damn corner. I have no intention of walking over there. But you can't tell me what to do." I raise a brow when Kieran whips his head toward me and gapes in surprise.

"What the fuck?" he growls, discreetly moving his free hand over his dick for protection. "Then don't make me tie you to the damn bar because I will," he growls, shifting in his seat. "And then throw him out with the trash."

"Sounds like a plan, Big Guy. I like the part where we throw him out with the trash," I quip, rolling my eyes. "But the controlling part? I'm a big girl." Leaning forward, I snarl in his face. "Don't tell me what to do. Got it?"

"If you're such a big girl, Little Brat, you wouldn't have texted us to come here and save the day," Asher snarks, raising a brow and sipping his beer when I whip my snarling face toward him.

"Not-not helping," Callum warns with a shake of his head.

"I am a big girl. But I don't need someone telling me what I can and can't do. You're not my daddy," I growl, inching closer to Asher, who grins wider.

"Yeah? And who says I'm not?" he huskily asks, knocking me back to my feet. I swear my face heats ten million degrees, and then he fucking winks at me. "Call me daddy, Little Brat, and see what happens." His reply is laced in a threatening manner, but an edge sits in his words, warning me that if I do, in fact, call him daddy, he'll explode. Most likely in his damn pants.

"Now, what about the tying down part? I've got rope at home. We could..." I grunt, putting my hand over Rad's mouth until he's grinning behind it.

"Leave it," I grumble with a shake of my head, pulling my hand back and wiping it down my jeans.

A pounding headache knocks on my skull, begging for entry. Ugh. Could this night get any worse than it already is?

"Incoming alert," Ode hisses, hurriedly coming toward me and nodding toward Van leaning against the bar, watching me with a mask of indifference lining his face. In reality, he's anything but. His beady, dark eyes catalog the guys' interactions with me, down to the wink Asher sends me again.

I spoke too soon.

Awesome. Here we go. Just what I needed. Kieran growls, aching to jump to his feet. Release the damn psychos. Next time I'll rethink this whole River needs help scenario and maybe do it all myself. Who needs overbearing boyfriends, anyhow? Wait! Not fucking boyfriends. Just boys I fuck on multiple occasions and spend lots of time with when I'm off work.

You're our girlfriend, whether you like it or not.

Shit. I think I am. And it's totally against my will. When the fuck did this happen? And why the fuck am I halfway okay with it? Not that I'd ever admit that to them. That'd give them way too much satisfaction.

I lick my lips, locking eyes with each of the boys for good measure, letting them know who the boss of the situation is. Always look the bulls in the eyes to show dominance. Or maybe not. Kieran huffs, flaring his nostrils, attempting to get up. Asher rolls his eyes, clamping a hand down on Kieran's shoulder as he struggles.

"For the love of God, don't fucking move. I'll take care of this," I hiss under my breath, running my fingers across my throat threateningly because I will cut them if they move an inch. That's not a threat. That's a goddamn promise.

"Is this foreplay?" Rad asks, leaning on the bar and winks. "Do the sexy thing with my throat again. I love it when you suffocate me with your pussy!" he says louder than necessary, leaning over to glare at Van standing ten feet away. Heat envelops my whole body when I bury my face in my hands with a groan.

Van's entire body locks up, and his fingers curl into tight fists on the bar top. Clueing me into how much Rad's words affected him. But that's the only indication he heard Rad's words.

"Go before you unleash the beast," Rad murmurs, narrowing his eyes at Van like he wants to slap him upside the head.

Me too, pal. Me friggin, too.

"Van," I say, raising a brow. "How can I help you?"

Van bites his lip, looking around the bar. "So, this is the other place you work?" His fingers drum along the top of the bar with impatience as he peers around, finally looking at the four idiots who glare daggers at him.

I scoff. "Yeah, the whole time we dated, you knew exactly where I worked and never visited. What is up with that?" Not that I'm bitter or anything, but still. He can't just waltz into my place of business months after we broke up and expect me to fall back into his arms.

He frowns, scrunching up his face. "I was always busy. You know that." He waves a hand, once again staring in their direction, just asking for a damn beat down.

"Busy, right," I mumble, rubbing my temple in irritation. I've been working all day, plus school, and I don't have time for Van Drake's shit tonight.

"So, you're really hanging out with them?" Van asks, leaning against the bar and tilting his head. "Like for real?"

"I don't have the mental capacity to deal with your shit tonight, Van. Yes. I like them. Are they assfaces? Absolutely! But I enjoy their company. Get that through your thick skull," I say with a groan.

"I'm just...I'm just looking out for you, River. I'm trying to keep you safe. I don't trust them." He shakes his head, running a hand down his face. "I'm just...." I hold up a hand, meeting his desperate eyes.

"Once again, thanks for your concern. But you have to let it go, Van. Like...are you following me to work? Watching me? You're becoming kind of stalkerish."

He rolls his eyes. "Right, me looking out for you is stalkerish? One day, Rivey. You'll see, and then you'll thank me for it. Until then, I'll be around," he says with one last long look and then walks out the front door with a huff.

"So fucking weird," I mumble as Ode comes to my side and shakes her head.

"What the hell is up with that?"

"No friggin idea. He's been acting weird since I started hanging with them," I say, jabbing a thumb over my shoulder, aiming at the boys.

"Well, you might get back. Booker is here and talking their ear off. He's probably asking them if they're treating you right and wrapping it before they tap it. Then he'll go into the whole spiel about you being the daughter he never wanted, and if they hurt you, he castrates them and mounts their dicks on the wall," Ode snickers when my face falls, and I swivel around to face the horror show.

Somehow in the past two minutes, the owner of Dead End has snuck in without being detected, setting his sights on Whispered Words. I watch in horror, my jaw falling open as they listen to Booker intently, nodding their heads to whatever he's saying. No fear crosses their faces. Instead, they smile and high-five each other with excitement.

"Hey, Booker," I say with a slight wave, interrupting their chatter.

Booker's dark eyes meet mine in amusement, nodding in greeting.

"Hey, kid," he says in a gruff voice, running a hand through his long dark hair and pulling it over his shoulder. "I was talking to the band that packed the place a few weeks ago." Something evil sparks in his eyes, and my stomach drops.

"He says we were good, Pretty Girl," Rad says with a grin, easing some of my tension.

My cheeks flare red when Booker raises a knowing brow. "They were pretty good," Booker reaffirms with a nod. "That's why I just offered them the Celebration stage in a month."

My eyes widen at his offer. Not just any band gets to represent Dead End at the Celebration Street Festival. That stage is usually reserved for bigger names, drawing the crowd to our tiny little section of the festival. We have a tent, a stage, beer, and lots of food to sell to the thousands of people walking the streets and enjoying the festivities.

But we're not the only attraction drawing people in. Food vendors from around the country, musicians, crafts, the carnival, and so much more line the ten-block downtown area for one weekend a year. It's our biggest investment and the biggest moneymaker. It's make it or break it. So, seeing Booker invite Whispered Words to our little corner of the world is shocking.

My eyes widen. "The celebration?" I question through a breath, confirming I heard him correctly. "Wait! What happened to Break? I thought the times were full?"

"Break took off to New York," Booker says, scratching his scruffy chin and pulling at his beard.

"So, now we're going to fill their shoes!" Rad throws his fist in the air with excitement. "We'll be high on the stage in front of thousands of people!"

"Calm your tits," Asher grumbles, pulling Rad down. This evening, Asher has been nothing more than a glorified babysitter. "Excuse my friend, sir. We appreciate this opportunity. We've gone to the Celebration street fair every year."

"We always wished someone would take a chance on us. So, thank you," Kieran adds with an earnest grin, saluting Booker with his beer.

"Well, I saw your video on ClockTok. It seems to be doing very well. Besides, River has been gushing about you guys for months now. She's been so excited to have you guys perform. I haven't heard the end of it." Ope, yup. There it is. That's why he couldn't stop smirking at me, letting me know he was up to something.

My entire body becomes a cooked tomato, heating my flesh with embarrassment. I give Booker the stink eye, and he chuckles, tapping the bar top a few times.

"The gig will pay. We'll give you twenty-five percent of our earnings that day. My advice would be to start letting everyone know where you'll be now. There are no tickets necessary and no charges. Unless they want to buy food, and that's where your money comes in. Most bands that come through have merchandise they sell: t-shirts, mugs, and EPs. But that's up to you, boys. If you have any other questions before the festival, River can fill you in." Shaking their hands one last time, Booker smirks when he walks by me. "They're better than the last one. All of them, though?"

"Jesus fuck," I mutter, meeting his stare. "What the hell did you guys discuss in the two friggin minutes I was gone?" I hiss through clenched teeth.

"Enough," he mutters with a fake shiver of disgust. "Now, you'll be in charge of their appearance on our stage. I'll handle the food and the booze. Come October tenth, they're your complete responsibility. It'll give you a little taste of what band management is like." He smirks, patting me on the shoulder before walking away toward his office with his hands in his pocket. He greets a few patrons here and there, shaking their hands, and finally disappears.

"So," Asher begins, tapping the bar. "Looks like we've got a lot to plan before that show."

For the rest of the evening, and every night after for the next three weeks—they come to the bar and plan out their set lists, hyping the future performance. Throughout the nights, they drink, eat, plan, and—my favorite—send Van the stink eye.

If I thought Van had gotten the message before, I shouldn't have. Every night he sits in the same booth with a different friend, drinking while keeping an eye on me. And every night, the boys escort me out, drive me home, and Callum or Rad—or both—stay with me. Somehow, they feel the anxiety crawling under my skin and soothe me by never leaving my side. I'm still a strong, independent woman, and I happen to have four very protective bodyguards. The more I get used to their barbaric ways, the more my walls come down.

RIVER

"Holy shit! I can't believe three-hundred and sixty-thousand people like us enough to follow us," Rad gapes, marveling at his phone from my right.

Swiping up, he clicks through all the stitched and duetted videos of their performances. A pang of jealousy hits me square in the chest as these beautiful women grace the screen with their reactions, going on and on about how charming the guys are and what they want to do with them.

I cringe. God, they're gorgeous girls. What will happen when Whispered Words are famous? And I'm me? Shit. I can't think like that. They're mine for now—in the present. But who knows what the future holds?

"FlashGram, too," I say, tapping the screen a few times until it pops up. "It's almost the same amount. You guys need more pics," I murmur, scrolling through the hot action takes I took over the weekend at Dead End. Nothing beats standing on the bar and snapping pictures as they perform. It gives me the best height advantage and the best snapshots.

"Jesus," Callum murmurs from my left, wrapping his arm around my shoulders and tucking my head under his chin. Shivers roll through me from the proximity of our bodies. Day after day, Callum gets more and more comfortable in my presence, always finding ways to hold my hand or touch my body. One day, I'll corrupt this boy into doing the one thing I know he wants. "I can't believe it," he says in awe, with his eyes glued to the screen.

"Well, believe it," Asher says with a cocky grin, startling us from our huddle. "Whispered Words is taking over the damn world one stage at a time." Asher tips his head back, admiring the back of the main stage we're nestled behind, concealing us from the growing crowd beyond. The largest grin I've ever seen slithers across his lips. And this time, it's not so damn scary.

Joy lights up his face, chasing away the massive amounts of shadows plaguing him. I don't know what Asher's home life is like, but every time he holds his guitar and strums the strings, he's a different man—a lighter man. Music seems to have the same calming effect on Asher as it does me, and it draws me in.

"And it's all because of you, River Blue," Kieran says, stalking toward me with predatory intent. Warm hands grip my cheeks, tearing me from Rad and Callum's grip as his lips graze mine, entirely devouring me in a matter of minutes.

Jesus. I'm panting by the time he lets me come up for air. Oh, and soaked, too. I swear my shorts are sticking to my damn vagina. But maybe that was his plan. By the look crossing his smug as fuck face, I'd say he did what he set out to do—claim me and make me horny.

"I didn't do much," I breathlessly say, panting to regain my breaths against his lips, melting into his grip.

"Don't sell yourself short, Little Brat. You're the reason we have videos on ClockTok. The only reason we were able to record our EP last week. Our downloads on The Dot are through the damn roof. And now, here we are," he says, spreading his arms out, aiming his chest toward the large stage looming before us.

"Let's start unloading," Kieran says, nodding his head toward the Tahoe parked a few feet away and dropping his hold on me.

I wrinkle my nose, ten seconds away from asking him to unload in me instead. With a few choice words inside my head, and a lengthy lecture from myself, I think better of it. They have so much to do before their performance in two hours. And Asher would throw a fit. I'm going to Rad and Callum's after the show, anyway. Speaking of...

River: Ma. You doing good?

Mother: Just peachy, kiddo. Korrine brought me a nice dinner. I'm feeling a lot better.

River: Glad to hear! I probably won't be home tonight. The bar is closed, but I have lots of work to do at the Celebration.

Mother: I figured. You've been a busy girl lately. Keep up the good work. Don't worry about me.

I snort. Right. Don't worry about her. That's all I do. If it wasn't for the nurse and Korrine sharing the responsibility of caring for her, I'd be drowning in it all.

Looking back, I take in the boys who have clawed their way into my heart as they huddle around the Tahoe and slowly unload their gear.

Thankfully, the street festival workers let us drive it back here and back it up to the stage. Or we'd have had to walk a mile through the enormous crowds and back for more. Asher and Kieran pop the doors on the Tahoe and begin unloading it.

A blush takes over my cheeks, and I look away, focusing on the flapping curtain dangling backstage. In two hours, Whispered Words will put on the show of a lifetime for a roaring crowd of eager fans who came from across the country to see them. Since their ClockTok fame, their fan base has grown exponentially.

My heart skips a beat, anticipation shooting through me. Every time I see them perform, it never ceases to amaze me. Their music. Them. It all clicks in my soul like this entire thing we're doing is meant to be, and fate brought us together like this.

Over the past three weeks, their social media presence has blown through the damn roof. Like an elevator exploding through the ceiling and flying into space, type of boom. The boys have recorded their EP at the school, uploaded their music to The Dot, and successfully invested in merch. All in a short period. It's like all they needed was for me to light a fire under their ass and get them going with these goals. My chest puffs with pride watching my little worker bees make their dreams come true. I'd say I'm a proud mama, but that would be awkward. I'm the proud woman, standing on the sidelines, watching as their empire grows with every song they sing.

"Jesus, it's hotter than Satan's asshole out here," Rad gripes, tugging at the collar of his new shirt. I'm sure he can't wait to tear it off. "I'm sweating like a whore in church," he whines more, puffing out his bottom lip like a damn child.

"You are a whore in church," I mutter playfully. "But the shirts, huh?" I ask with a grin, slapping his hand away and plucking his lip.

He groans, catching my wrist. "Yeah. They're cool, Pretty Girl. All fancy with our band name on it, but I'm so restricted." Rad leans in closer to my ear. "It feels like a damn lake in my pants. My balls are so sweaty, babe," he pouts, begging me with his eyes to give him permission to strip them off and air out his dangly bits.

"Keep your pants on, Cowboy. You can't scare away the crowd. You can air those out later tonight, in private," I say, smoothing out his shirt that sticks to his skin. His lips pop open in retort, but he's cut off.

"The sun will set soon, and it'll cool down when it does," Asher grunts, rolling his amp down the ramp attached to the back of Kieran's SUV. "Please keep your dick in your pants." He scowls in Rad's direction. "We're in public," he mutters the last part with a headshake. "And there might be children present. The last thing you need is a trip to jail."

Rad recoils at the thought of jail but continues his rant anyway. "But it's hot now. Can't I strip?" Rad whines, pulling at the ends of his shirt, attempting to take it off.

"You heard Evil Ash. There's definitely a no stripping rule on stage," I say, fixing his shirt and earning a scoff. "But I do have an idea."

Rad's eyes widen when I whip out my knife and flick it open, exposing the sharp blade gleaming in the sun.

"Pretty Girl," he says with apprehension. "I might be into a little stabby-stabby in the sack, but uh..." he trails off when I pull the sleeves away from his skin and yelps when the blade tears through the fabric, eliminating the sleeve. I swear his body sags in relief when the slight breeze blows through, cooling him off. "Ah, finally. Fuck. I think I love you, Pretty Girl. Will you marry me?" he asks breathlessly as I do the other sleeve and even cut down the sides to expose his ribs.

"Evil Ash?" Asher huffs, amusement pulling the edge of his lips. "We'll discuss that later." I roll my eyes at his attempt to discipline me.

We definitely won't be discussing that later. What is he going to do? Spank me? Bend me over his knee and tell me I've been a bad River? I shiver. Okay, so it doesn't sound like a bad idea to me. He seems like the—take control in the bedroom—type. I'm down for that only if he's ready to take on a brat.

Over the last three weeks, Asher and I have grown a little closer. We aren't besties by any means, and sometimes I want to smash his skull in the doorway, but we're getting there. Just recently, we've gotten into this push-and-pull sort of relationship mixed with heavy amounts of sexual tension. One day, Asher will blow his lid and take me like I know he wants to. So, I'll keep pressing his buttons and getting on his last nerve.

"Fine." Rad frowns, looking up at the back of the stage, losing his pout.

A closed, dark curtain cuts off the audience's view, separating us from the growing crowd beyond. Our stage is nestled in the back of Central Park, settled just past the large fountain and facing a blocked-off street. Several businesses line the road, towering above us. People drunkenly walk the streets, free to roam without worrying about traffic. It's street festivals like this that I live for. The atmosphere, people, and smells of food—make it perfect.

People hoot and holler as they roam the blocked-off streets of the Celebration. Police barricades sit at the end of every downtown road, forcing traffic to avoid this area. Not like they'd get through the crowds or people, anyway.

The Central Fall Celebration started over fifty years ago. Street vendors who offer food, wood carvings, toys, and anything you can imagine line the streets. Bands play on five different stages, placed around the ten-block radius. It's practically a holiday for the people of Central City. A time to let loose, drink, eat, and socialize with everyone in their path. It's the only time both sides of the city come together and celebrate as one unit, bringing in the new season with a bang.

"Sounds like-like a lot of people are here already," Callum mumbles, hanging tight to his bass case with wide eyes, white-knuckling it. A large lump bobs in his throat when he swallows hard, frantically looking around.

"It's your fans. You go on in two hours, but everyone is already lining up at the front of the stage." I peek between the curtains. "Yup, there's already two or three rows of people."

Even Tessa and Sara sit front and center as usual with their tits pushed up to their chins and fake smiles on their faces. A gaggle of girls surrounds them, moving their arms excitedly around, anticipating the boys getting on stage. Great. Just who I want to deal with all night. The boys have already dismissed them repeatedly, and I'm not sure how they're not getting the hint. Maybe I need to jump one of the boys on stage and claim what's mine for them to get the message to fuck off.

Asher's grin grows when he stops beside me, peeking out. "Fucking hell," he mumbles in awe. "You got us somewhere, Little Brat." Color me shocked when he places a hand on my shoulder and squeezes. Dare I say he's happy and proud? "This is the best thing anyone's ever helped us accomplish."

Meeting his eyes, I offer him a soft smile and tap his hand resting on my shoulder.

Something odd happens inside my body when his praise hits my ears. I stand taller. My chin juts out, and my heart pounds with excitement. If Asher happens to call me good girl, I might drop to my damn knees and suck his soul from his dick.

"You almost sound proud of me, Evil Ash," I quip, swallowing the odd feeling bursting inside me. "Is Daddy proud?" I bat my eyelashes, poking the rigid bear.

Ash's eyes widen, and a little red tint takes over his cheeks as he sputters, collecting his breaths. His eyes slide to mine with a knowing look, most likely remembering the words he spoke a few weeks ago.

"For fuck's sake, Little Brat," he gasps, tightening his grip on my shoulder. "You remember what I said, right? What happens when you call me daddy?" he murmurs, inching his face close to mine.

Asher looms over me, bringing our bodies closer and closer together until my back hits a wood support, and he cages me in, examining my eyes. I don't know what he sees behind them, but he grins, exposing all his teeth.

"I am very fucking proud. Maybe you'll get a reward later," Asher murmurs, inching closer until his soft lips land on my cheek, awakening the butterflies in my stomach. "But stop calling me daddy," he says against my flesh, verbally pleading with me. "Or you won't like the consequences." Shivers roll through me when he pushes away and walks toward the SUV.

"Okay, Daddy," I taunt, watching as he halts his steps before making a mad dash away.

"You've gotta stop winding him up, River Blue. Especially before a performance," Kieran chuckles, wrapping a sweaty arm around my shoulders.

"Um, what's the fun in that?" I laugh, shrugging off his heavy arm. "You boys have two hours until the show. It gives you time for sound check and all that fun stuff."

"And you?" Callum asks in a small voice, making his way onto the back of the stage with his bass. Standing high above me, he tilts his head and examines me. "You're staying, right-right?" Big puppy dog eyes greet me when I look up at him, drenched in the shadows of the stage.

Offering Callum a soft smile, I nod. "Of course. I'll be out there setting this up. Let's see how much your fans love you," I say, picking up a box full of shirts.

He grunts, setting down his bass, and jumps off the stage. Landing with a soft thud, he yanks the box from my hand. As we walk from behind the stage, we finally glimpse the full view of the crowd lining up to see them.

"That has-has to be the biggest crowd we'll ever play for." Callum shudders, placing the box on a table set up to the right of the stage. He swallows hard, surveying the crowd with awe, and reaches for my hand, squeezing tight.

"You'll do amazing," I whisper, squeezing his hand back.

His cheeks darken at my compliment, and he nods. "Thanks, River," he murmurs, kissing my cheek.

"No problem. Now, go get ready. You have a raging crowd of four hundred people to impress. And hopefully, sell lots of merch," I say, nodding toward the box full of their new merchandise.

I shoo Callum away with a grin, watching his retreating form. He only looks back once, reddening at the sight of me, and offers me a little wave.

So, as the boys do their thing backstage, getting their equipment set up, I do my thing at their new merch table, setting everything up.

After planning a design and chatting with the printer, we got shirts, pins, and postcards with their band name for a reasonable price. Everything's coming together for them in the past three weeks since they sat down and got to business. It's the first time I've seen them hunker down and put effort into their future as a band. Sure, they've played at a few venues but never invested in themselves.

Scooting the long plastic table next to the stage, I set out their merch. A few people meander over, looking over the shirts, and buy a few before the boys go on stage, explaining they can't wait to see the show. As two hours tick by, I hear the boys' hushed conversation behind the curtain protecting them from view. If I leaned back far enough, I'd have a clear shot of them murmuring in each other's ears and braiding their hair.

"Telling secrets?" I quip, pulling a piece of the curtain back to reveal the boys standing in a circle. I lean my elbows on the stage that comes up to my chest and raise a brow.

"You're nosy," Asher deadpans, grabbing the curtain from my hand. "Back to your table, Little Brat." I snort when he pulls the curtain closed, blocking my view of them.

"Secrets don't make friends!" I shout, taking a few steps back to my table and plopping down on the lawn chair I thankfully remembered to pack.

My eyes roam the ever-growing crowd, mesmerized by the mass of people forming around our small area. Every year we invite popular bands to this stage, and every year they draw sizeable crowds. But nothing like this. This crowd is massive, swaying together in anticipation.

As my eyes look over the rest of the crowd, I groan at the sight of my high school enemies. Fuck. A few girls around Tessa and Sara stare in my direction with narrowed eyes before leaning in to whisper to one another. God, it's like we're back in high school. Hello, bitches—we're adults now.

Each and every one of those girls was a dick to everyone else, especially me. Their fucking plaything for two years. And now, it seems I'm their target—once again. Yippy. Little do they know, I won't roll over and be a good puppy anymore. I have more bite than bark. The sooner they realize that, the better. Because if they keep coming after me, I'm going to rip their annoying faces off.

The curtain behind me draws again, revealing a smiling Rad, glowing with pre-concert jitters. I swear he's the damn sun beaming down, and I'm the little planet, soaking it in. Crooking a finger, he pulls me toward the stage with one finger flick. I raise a brow, leaning against the wooden structure, staring into the abyss of his dark eyes that twinkle in the dwindling sunlight.

"Pretty Girl. I've got a new shirt for you," Rad says, trying and failing to hold back his grin while holding up a dark shirt that says: Property of Whispered Words.

I blink rapidly, taking in the meaning of the words scrawled across the black shirt waving in the warm breeze. Once it settles in, I narrow my eyes at the possessive fools standing above me on stage.

"Really? You want me to wear a shirt like that?" I raise a brow when Rad looks at the crowd mixed with women and men. Without hesitation, he nods with enthusiasm—or maybe it's possession hiding behind his intentions.

"Uh, huh. Yup! Now, put it on," Rad demands, holding it in front of my face with expectation. "Put it on, beautiful! I want to see our band name stamped over your pretty titties for the entire world."

"It's to keep the other vultures away," Asher says with a noncommittal shrug. "They'll know who you belong to."

"Wear it to work, too," Kieran adds, placing his guitar strap over his shoulders and settling it across his body. His fingers tweak the strings a few times, tuning it by ear.

"Then everyone will know not to talk to you," Rad adds, freeing his grin.

"No talking to other boys," Kieran barks with possession, curling his lip back, and eyeing all the people wandering the streets with drinks in their hands. Slowly, his eyes move over the crowd.

I blink. "Excuse me? Did I hear what I think I heard?" I huff, putting my hands on my hips. There's no way in hell they can tell me who I can and cannot talk to. No fucking way.

"He's right, Pretty Girl—no more boys. There are four of us. How many more dicks do you need? None. That's the answer," Rad says, shaking his head. "Don't let them look at you. Here, put this damn thing on." Rad grunts, forcing the Whispered Words shirt over my head, no matter how hard I struggle against him. Kieran chips in, jumping down from the stage after setting his guitar down, forcing my arms through the sleeves, and chuckles when I curse at them, threatening their lives.

"What the fuck, Rad?" I hiss, pushing him away as he cackles, falling onto his ass. Placing his hands on his knees, he grins more, eyeing the words across my tits.

"Perfect. Property of... It has a nice ring to it, doesn't it, K?" Pride puffs Rad's chest out, and he grins with satisfaction.

Kieran tilts his head when I cross my arms, giving him my meanest scowl. "Yup. Property of Whispered Words. Find a marker, and we'll print our names on her tits. Then no one will talk to her," he grunts, looking out at the crowd again from behind me.

"If you bring a marker anywhere near this, I'll bite off your fingers," I growl, poking Kieran in his chest. "Don't you have shit to do?" I point toward the stage, shooing them again with my hands.

"Be a good girl," Kieran whispers in my ear and kisses my cheek, letting the warmth of his lips linger for longer than necessary.

"Always am," I murmur through a chill spreading down my body, creating goosebumps. I swear, when his lips touch my skin, my resolve drains down the toilet.

"We'll see," he says, swiping his thumb lovingly across my cheek. Affection lights up his eyes, and a soft smile pulls at his lips.

"Let's go, Lover Boy!" Asher barks, waving a hand.

Kieran nods, hopping back onto the stage and grabbing his gear. Together they stand like a wall, taking deep, soothing breaths.

"Whispered Words! Whispered Words!" the crowd chants over and over with excitement, holding their brightly lit phones in the air like lighters.

"You hear that, boys?" I shout over the crowd, leaning my elbows on the tall stage. "They're calling for you!"

I grin when the curtain swings open, and they wave to the crowd with bright smiles—swaggering further on stage, oozing confidence from every inch. They captivate the crowd, drawing them in with their grins and waves.

"Kiss for luck, Pretty Girl?" Rad says, flopping to his belly on stage. Leaning close, he takes my mouth with his, dirtily shoving his tongue in and out. I moan when his hands roam through my hair, pulling me closer.

At this point, he could pull me on stage and fuck me in front of the crowd right now, and I'd say yes, please. It'd definitely show those bitches who they belonged to. The thrill of their eyes on me sends shivers up my spine, and my pussy clenches, ready to take it further. That is, until a certain asshole lightly kicks Rad in the ribs and clears his throat.

"Come on, bro. You're humping the damn stage. Save it for later," Asher grumbles with a shake of his head.

"After this, I'm going to fuck you, and you're going to take it," Rad pants, raising his brow until I nod. "Good girl." I shiver when he says those words and watch in awe when he wanders away, setting himself behind his drums set with a relaxed grin.

Asher watches me from his side of the stage, staring with interest at my heaving chest and flushed face.

"Are you ready for the carnival after this, Little Brat?" he asks, looking off in the distance at the enormous Ferris wheel lighting up the now darkened sky with its red, blues, and yellows.

"The carnival?" I gaze over at the carnival rides in full swing.

Asher smirks, tilting his head at me. "Oh, yes. The carnival. We'll let loose after this. Besides, I have plans for you," he rasps, eyeing me up and down.

"Plans? Wait! What plans?" I blanch, hoping he has time to elaborate or fucking tell me something. Instead, he grins, moving a few feet forward, giving me his back. Strumming a loud tune over the speakers as he tunes his guitar, drowning out my shouts.

The crowd cheers when Kieran smiles at them from the microphone and then, turning, winks at me like a cocky bastard.

"Hello, Central City!" Kieran's raspy voice bellows through the speakers, echoing through what seems like the entire town.

The crowd reacts immediately, jumping in place and cheering as loud as they can. A smile forms on my lips when he grins at the sea of people looking up at him like he's a God. Shit. I'm probably looking at him the same way.

"We love you, Kieran!" Tessa and Sara shout, holding up a poster with all their names and hearts surrounding them.

I roll my eyes as they jump up and down, jiggling their tits in an effort to get Kieran's attention and call his name with a girly shriek. Thank god they're keeping those puppies under wraps. They could poke someone's eyes out.

A weird pinch of jealousy roars through me when he looks at them. Fucking looking at them and grins when he reads the poster, giving them the thumbs up. That's my thumb. Keep it to yourself, assface. Narrowing my eyes, I glue my gaze to his and thankfully; the assface doesn't drop his eyes to their pointy tits, still free-balling in the night air.

"Put away your goddamn titties!" I shout, cupping my hands over my lips to amplify my voice.

Ignoring my demand, they continue to swoon and scream more, inciting weird feelings brewing in the depths of my green monster. I want to rip their hair out and knock their perfect teeth in with one punch and laugh as they scatter on the ground. My fists curl, envisioning tying them to a pole deep in the woods, slathering them in honey, and watching as bears rip them to shreds as they beg for their lives. Try clutching your pearls with no fingers, toes, or body. Fuck.

Jesus. Deep breaths, River. You damn psycho. Stop plotting their deaths and focus on the music, for shit's sake. Music is what you live and breathe. Not violence against two stuck-up Lakeview girls who don't have a chance with the boys rocking out on stage.

My mouth pops open, watching Kieran work the tiny stage with grace and familiarity. Walking back and forth with a goofy grin, he lays down the first note, inciting the crowd more. They yell and scream, the louder the music gets until all the boys join in and open with their first song. I watch them with matched possession. The thought of other girls touching them makes me stabby. I grip my knife, toying with the handle in my shorts pocket, running my thumb over the words printed across it—River Blue. Touch them and die might be my new mantra.

I rub my temple. What the hell am I thinking?

Peeking down at the shirt stretching over my tits, I scoff. Fuck. I'm in this constant war with myself, my mind going to battle with itself repeatedly. Letting go of my reservations is more complicated than I ever thought. Visions of Van and what his stupid ass did to me burn bright. A constant reminder of what could happen if this goes to shit. But taking a deep breath, I shake it off. This is now. I'm having fun. I'm falling hard. And in the end, if I get fucked over. It'll be my fault. For now, I'm along for the ride. I have to keep telling myself that the further they drag me into their wicked web.

The music blares through the speakers again, garnering more attention from the late night crowd enjoying the festival. Person after person loiters with beers in their hands and smiles on their faces, momentarily stopping to catch the free show. Their heads bob, and their swaying bodies move with the tune echoing through the night air. Every hand shoots in the air for what seems like miles, waving around with pure joy. For one singular moment, we live in musical harmony.

Kieran's raspy voice blasts through the microphone again and straight through my damn soul, lifting me to a higher plane. Music always calms the storm brewing in my mind and eases my pain. Music erases everything on my plate and sets me free. It sounds silly. But music has always been my escape from the life I've lived.

"Ahem, bitch," a very unpleasant voice says, knocking me out of my reprieve.

Fuck my life. Is this how Tessa greets everyone, or is this just reserved for me? Probably just for me. Seeing as she looks down her nose at me for the millionth time.

I plaster on a fake smile and shove my tits out. Let's see how much she likes my personalized Whispered Words shirt.

"How can I help you?" My sugary sweet voice gives me cavities. I'd slam her face into this table a few times if it were up to me. Maybe knock some sense into her stupid skull. They don't want you. I am theirs.

She scans my shirt, narrowing her eyes. "We want some shirts," she says, pointing to mine. "Something like that."

I grin more, widening my arms to the shirts folded on the table in front of me. "Sorry, this is an exclusive shirt for their girlfriend." I freeze, dropping my arms. I probably looked as shocked as her pinched face does.

Heat envelopes my neck, creeping onto my face. I wholeheartedly blame my damn jealousy for my decisions. That bitch is going to get me into trouble. But damn, the look on Tessa's face is worth the fallout. Whatever. I'll roll with it. Yeah, their girlfriend. All four of them belong to me. If they're going to put their claim on me, then I'll return the favor. Maybe I can stamp my name on their dicks.

"You're joking, right?" She throws her head back and laughs in my face. "Like they'd ever choose a piece of Central trash like you."

"You've got to be kidding me." She slaps Sara on the shoulder in laughter, and her friend joins in, screeching along and ruining the damn music.

I blow out a breath and cross my arms, deciding not to push it. "These are your only options. Not this. This is mine, and so are they."

Welp. So much for dropping it. It looks like I'm officially about to throw my hat into the ring. Only I'll win, not them. I'm always up for crushing my competition. I'm competitive like that.

"You've got to be joking," Tessa snarls, pounding a fist on the table. "Not you," she scoffs, looking me up and down.

Leaning forward, I get right in her face with a bright, knowing grin. She doesn't know I hang around them every day. Or that they're my stalkers, watching my every move. They join me at work—both places. Play at my bar and drink my drinks while laughing with me. I said Tessa was my competition before, but the reality is, she's nothing. I've already crossed the finish line and won while she's in last place, slowly jogging toward the yellow tape. She doesn't know it yet.

"Does this face look like it's joking?" I grin cockily, tilting my head. Sometimes antagonizing the girl who made high school hell is fun. "Back off, Tessa. Buy a shirt or don't. But you're holding up the line." I gesture to the four people behind her, sending her scathing looks for taking so much damn time.

"Just two shirts, smalls," Sara says in a hurry, placating her fuming friend.

I nod and hand them two black shirts with the Whispered Words printed across the chest.

"That'll be fifty," I say, putting them into a black bag and setting it on the table.

Sara grumbles about the price, digging through her purse. Tessa snatches the bag with a haughty attitude and growls at me, exposing her teeth. Down, girl. I'll put you in the pound.

"Let them have their fun with your diseased ass. But they'll come running back to us, and I can guarantee that," Tessa hisses, stomping away with her friend in tow.

"Sure," I mumble sarcastically, helping the other customers with their purchase and the next after that.

The show continues for another thirty minutes without incidents. When the line for merch lulls, I grab my phone, record their performance, and take several stills for their FlashGram. There's nothing more intoxicating than a sweaty rock star holding their gear on stage, rocking out to the beautiful music they created.

"This last song goes out to a very special girl," Kieran says, side-eyeing me from the side of the stage with a knowing grin. "We have a new song for you all! It's called: The Roaring River."

When the new tune comes through the speakers, I sputter, choking on my spit, and he growls my name into the microphone. Finally, after a solid minute of choking on my tongue, I catch my breath and record the song's chorus. Every word makes my cheeks heat and butterflies blossom in my stomach. When I peer over at Tessa, her lips set into a straight line, and she frowns in my direction.

"I won," I mouth to her and then flip her off for good measure. Take that. You mean girl.

THE ROARING RIVER

RIVER

As the music dies, the boys wave their goodbyes at the edge of the stage. Large, beaming grins adorn their faces when the crowd goes nuts, cheering them on with hoots and hollers. Watching from the sidelines, I smile as they jump up and down with their hands in the air. Their music hums through my veins long after the last note. My fingers tap along my bare leg as the beat pounds in my head, never forgotten. Their lyrics will hide in my mind for years to come, even if they fizzle out—highly doubtful at this point. In my mind, we're already in California, celebrating the win of the Battle of the Bands. Whispered Words isn't meant for the small stage. They're meant for the entire world to hear.

"We want more! We want more! We want more!" the crowd chants, pumping their fists in the air.

Kieran's gaze finds mine immediately. With a nod, he grins more and turns back to the crowd.

"One more!" His voice reverberates through the screaming crowd as they jump for joy.

Standing back, I dig my phone out of my pocket and hold it up for the last time tonight. Kieran gives me the thumbs up, belting out the first line of their encore song. This time when I press record, I test out the live function on ClockTok, hoping to give their other fans a fiery treat of sweaty man meat performing on stage. And boy, their comments don't disappoint.

So fucking hot!

I want to lick the sweat from his nipple!

That one makes me snort and shake my head. No one's licking that man's or any of these men's nipples—but me.

Wow! They sound so good! They aren't signed?

Holy shit, when can I see them in concert? Are you guys coming to Texas?

Come overseas!
Kieran girl for life!
I'd give my left tit for Rad!
Me too, sister. Me too.
Asher looks hot!
Callum's so cute!

Flashes of their future fame fly through my mind in rapid succession. I realize then Whispered Words would be famous enough one day to have gaggles of girls following their every move, hoping for a piece of their pie if I left for California and stayed with them. Is this what it will be like? Will I have to swim through an ocean of horny women begging for a piece of what's mine? Fuck. Why are my thoughts suddenly coming to this futuristic planning of bashing in groupies' faces? *Focus on the present, River! And stay in it.*

"All right, Central City!" Kieran's breathless voice booms through the speakers, quieting down the rambunctious crowd, growing drunker and drunker by the minute. "You guys have been great! Thanks for having us! Check-in with us on FlashGram and ClockTok to stay updated on our performances. We'll see you at Dead End on Halloween. Details are on our sites." He grins, placing the mic back on its stand, waving one last time as I turn off the recording.

Rad doesn't waste a minute rushing off stage, whipping his shirt off with an excited whoop. His bare chest glistens with sweat, reflecting off the dull street lights. It drips down his beautiful abs, forcing my eyes to watch the descent, momentarily stunned by the sight. Shit. They have to stop pulling me in with their bodies, music, and souls. Or I'm a damned goner, for sure. I can keep telling myself over and over that this isn't going anywhere, that this is in the present. But the more I think about it, the more the future calls. Is it so wrong to want to spend years with them instead of months?

"Pretty Girl!" he shouts, charging toward me at full speed with mischief glistening in his eyes.

I grunt when he slams into me, knocking me off my feet. He chuckles when he lifts me into his arms, and his fingertips dig into my ass cheeks until my legs wrap around his waist and my arms around his neck.

"Oh my God, you're so sweaty!" I shriek through laughter, beating a hand into his bare shoulders with fake disgust. I swear every inch of my shirt soaks with his sweat and sticks to my flesh. "Gross!" I shriek when he spins me in circles, roaring with laughter.

Like a child free of worry, he throws his head back, looking up at the sky while clinging to me. These simple moments of pure ecstasy pull me in and keep me in their grasp. When I'm with them—all of them—I'm not River West, the overworked bar manager. I'm just River West—theirs. Carefree from the music infecting my soul, I join him, letting my head fall back and howl at the damn moon.

The full moon shines down on us like a spotlight, aided by the sparkling stars twinkling above in the cloudless sky. A cool breeze blows through my clothes, soothing the nasty sweat from my skin.

"Did we blow your panties off?" Rad rasps, leaning in until his nose touches mine when he stops spinning. "Did we rock that shit hard? Cuz I think we did."

His hardened dick presses into my center to prove his point, swiveling around my already-damp panties. The faint memory of his promise an hour before shines like a neon sign in the forefront of my mind. I grind against him, forcing a gasp from his lips, slowly turning into a soft moan.

I grin, rubbing my nose against his, and let everything go. Our lips graze on a soft kiss, and I hum, gliding my tongue along his sealed lips until he lets me in again. I throw caution to the wind, give in to the nagging feeling slowly taking over, and take what I want. I want him again. Over and over. I want him to lay me down and fuck me behind the curtain where anyone can hear my moans but never get a peek.

"Yes. You rocked it," I whisper against his lips, nibbling them.

"Good. Now we can go to the carnival," he insists, carrying me toward Kieran, Callum, and Asher, crowded backstage.

"The carnival?" I whisper. "Why not behind the stage?" Rad immediately stops, inspecting my eyes. "You could take me against the stage. I could..." Rad growls, shoving his long tongue down my throat again. I moan into his mouth until he pulls away, shaking his head with regret.

"I have an idea for that. You want to ride me? Let's ride some rides first." His eyes sparkle with some knowing look, and he grins, tucking my loose hair behind my ear.

"Don't keep me waiting for too long," I whisper, lust dripping from every word, practically moaning into his ear.

"Oh, I won't," he says, walking forward again with me in his arms. "Pretty Girl says we rocked her panties off!" Rad whoops, throwing a fist in the air.

"Of course we did," Asher says in his usual pompous tone, leaving no room for argument. "We were amazing." His chest puffs out, and his nose raises—cocky shit.

I snort. "Humble much?" Rad drops me to my feet but keeps an arm around my shoulders and me close. Fingers dive into my back pockets, roughly squeezing my ass.

Asher rolls his eyes, drying off his forehead with a white towel. "Always," he says with a tiny smirk, pulling at his lips, which drops the moment his eyes lock on the advancing figure, beelining it toward the boys.

"Oh, my God!" Tessa screeches from nowhere. Seriously, how does she keep finding us? Like, can't she go away?

I mentally groan at her screechy voice as she rounds the backstage area and lunges at Kieran. He grunts, reluctantly catching her when she latches on like the little leech she is. I could have sworn I told her I won. Hell, they even made a song about me and not her. Granted, it was called Roaring River—so not sexy. But still. Get your pink press-ons out of my man's neck and get a move on to someone who wants you.

"What the hell?" he asks, pushing her away and keeping her at arm's length.

"You were so amazing!" she coos again, side-eyeing me with victory. I'm not sure what kind of victory she's feeling, but more power to her.

"Uh, thanks," he says, scratching the back of his neck and looking at me for help.

"I even bought your shirt!" she shrieks again with a grin.

Where the fuck is her handler? Paging annoying Sara, come collect your friend before I pummel her face with my fist. Repeatedly. No one will recognize her when I'm done rearranging her features.

"Pretty Girl," Rad whispers breathily, running his lips up my jawline. "If you beat her ass, I'll pound your ass so hard you'll forget your name. Whattya say?" My breaths quicken when he sucks my earlobe between his teeth, and a soft moan falls from my throat. Well then, in that case. It's time for an ass beating so I can get my ass pounding.

— 282 —

"That's it!" I say, pushing forward and away from his horny ass. "Scoot. You're making the band uncomfortable." I wave a hand, stepping between Kieran and Tessa with force.

"Um, maybe you're the one making them uncomfortable, bitch. They happen to like me," Tessa scoffs at me, crossing her arms with a haughty look.

"Are you sure about that?" Asher asks in a sharp tone. If it were a whip, he'd have left a mark.

Her mouth drops open in defeat, looking at each of the guys for confirmation.

"Tess, you're a nice girl. We had our fun, remember?" My stomach drops when Kieran says that, and my face falls. They fucked before? Why does that make my green-eyed monster growl even more?

"It was fun," she says, batting her eyelashes. "But I was hoping for a little more. I'm throwing a party tonight at my apartment. All the party favors will be available. You know, for old time's sake," she giggles.

I narrow my eyes at Kieran, who scoffs.

"We've got plans, but thanks," Kieran says, pulling me back to his front. "And it doesn't include you."

Hurt glistens in Tessa's eyes, and she gives a pitiful nod. "I'll see you around then. But if you ever get tired of the trash, come to the queen," she snarls, tossing her hair over her shoulder, and giving me one last scathing look.

Who's the trash here? Because it's definitely not me. I'm the mother fucking queen, and it's about damn time someone knocked her off her high horse. I volunteer as the damn tribute because this bitch is two seconds away from meeting the special piece in my pocket.

"No. You won't see them around. Take your stuck-up ass and scoot. I won, remember? And if I ever catch you sniffing around like the desperate poodle you are, I will cut you. They. Are. Mine." I don't know what happens, but something possessive takes over my tongue, and I'm just a passenger on this crazy train ride called: stamping my name on their asses.

By the time her stunned face recovers from my verbal lashing, she's huffing and puffing like she might blow my house away. *Down, big bad bitchy wolf. There's nothing here for you.*

"You heard her," Asher reaffirms with a growl, stepping between us. "Go home." With a flick of his wrist, Tessa stumbles with a crestfallen face and tears in her pitiful eyes.

When Tessa disappears into the shadows, a boohooing mess, Asher turns to me with a grin exploding across his lips. The boys exchange a suspicious look, and with one nod, suddenly the walls close, and four bodies press on either side of me, creating a circle around me. I'm at the center of their attention and panting with need.

"It's about damn time you know your place," Kieran says, moving my hair over my shoulder. "You're the fucking queen of Whispered Words, understand? And next time, knock her teeth loose," he chuckles, kissing the side of my lips.

Callum's face blooms red, and he shyly takes my hand, squeezing our fingers together. "You're-you're the queen, Little Star." His eyes drop to the pavement, fluttering, his long lashes fanning his cheek.

"Now, let's pack up our shit, and then let's go take a ride," Asher smirks knowingly, cocking his head. "You'd like a ride or four, right, Little Brat?"

Heat envelops every inch of my body when he licks his lips and nods in the carnival's direction to our right. Laughs and screams come from the area. The hairs on the back of my neck stand on end when I try to wrap my brain around what he's saying.

"Um, this isn't exactly the kind of ride I expected," I say, looking out through the large cage of the Ferris wheel resting high in the sky above the town.

The cage encompasses the whole cabin, enclosing all of us in the six-seater ride. Usually, I'd enjoy the carnival rides, but the first thing Rad insisted on was this Ferris wheel. It soars above the city, boasting an enormous height, claiming to ride higher than normal carnival Ferris wheels. Lights flicker in the distance from the towns around us when we finally reach the top. The other carnival-goers' distant sounds echo through the metal cage coming from below.

From here, they're tiny ants marching along the darkened ground and barely visible from here.

Abruptly, we stop at the tippy top, leaving us with a breathtaking view of our broken city. I see the darkened outlines of houses, tall businesses, and the tops of trees for miles. The cool October wind whips through the cage, blowing my long strands as I sit nestled between Kieran and Callum on a bench-like seat.

"You're-you're shivering," Callum murmurs, pulling me into him. His fingers run up and down my arms, alleviating the goosebumps spreading across my flesh.

"I have an idea," Asher says with a smirk, taking me in snuggling up to Callum.

I raise a brow. "Oh, yeah? Like maybe getting off this ride?" I quip, and he grins more, shrugging.

"Or you could be a good little brat and strip every piece of clothing off your body and then hand them over." As he delivers the words, the phrase *the woman was too stunned to speak* bounces around inside my head.

As I stare into the hazel-eyed devil's eyes, my entire body locks up, pressed between Callum and Kieran. That familiar tug in my gut heats at the mere look he sends my way. Adding insult to injury, he drags his tongue along his bottom lip, wetting it, so it's glistening under the Ferris Wheel lights. And I melt. I fucking melt under his scrutiny, and that's just bullshit. He gave me a simple demand, and here I am, simping over one little tongue flick.

More vicious shivers run through me, despite not feeling an ounce of cold. Because, yeah—it's not because of that. Every inch of my body heats, and I swear my heartbeat plays a symphony in my ears. Just from Asher's words. Fuck. Me. I'm sick, and the only ailment to relieve my sickness is the four dicks searing me with expectation.

So, I play dumb.

"What?" I barely comprehended the demand he gave me. Blinking, my lips pop open when he does that sexy guy thing and leans his elbows on his widely spread knees. His thumb caresses his pointed chin, and he smirks again, watching my reactions like a hawk. Asher Montgomery knows precisely what he's doing when he leans forward, cocking a brow.

"You heard me, Little Brat. There's a reason we're stopped at the top of the world. Now, strip," he demands again, roaming his hungry eyes all over my body, taking in my heaving chest and trembling fingers.

"Why... Why should I listen to you?" I ask breathlessly, shaking my head.

There's no way in hell I *should* listen to a word he says. Sure, he's calmed his Assface ways down these past three weeks since we started planning. Dare I say he's been cordial? But he's still Asher Montgomery—assface extraordinaire—Evil Ash–the boogeyman in my closet, taunting me with his devilish, warm hazel eyes, lighting me up from the inside out.

Fire ignites everywhere when he looks me up and down, his want desperately showing to the world. My weak heart pounds against my ribs, echoing in my damn ears at that one simple look, begging me to defy his demands.

For him, I am a brat—his little brat, more specifically. Asher has this way about him that draws this need to rebel out of me without even trying. I can't help but fight the feelings brewing inside me, especially when he drives me fucking insane.

This push and pull between us has me on the edge of craving his demands. I want to fall to my knees and bend to his will. With resistance, of course. That's how our relationship has worked so far. He pushes. I pull. Somewhere along the way, we've gotten into this tension-filled relationship, and one of us is about to crack.

Asher cracks his knuckles and shrugs.

Rad grins, getting to his knees in the cramped space. "Fuck Asher. Take off your clothes for me—for them," he says, nodding to Callum and Kieran pressing in on either side of me.

Crawling in my direction on the hard metal floor, Rad finally stops right before me with desire dilating his pupils, making them as dark as shadows. My breath halts in my damn chest when his warm hands spread my legs open. Soft fingers inch up my exposed thighs, drawing circles against my flesh.

"You can't be serious. We're on the Ferris wheel. There are other people," I gasp when the palm of his hand grinds against my teased center, still excited from all the stolen moments before and after the show.

Despite the growing desire flaming to life in my abdomen at the potential eyes watching us, I still have reservations about dropping my pants in public. Anyone could see what we're about to do.

"Did you see other people?" Asher lazily asks, leaning back on the bench opposite us with his legs still spread apart.

I frown, looking below at the empty carts rattling in the wind with no people in sight on the ride. The only voices for miles away are the people walking below, oblivious to what's about to happen. If I let it, that is.

"Um, well—no," I stammer, shaking my head. "There's no way." I throw my head back when Rad's fingers dive into my pussy unexpectedly from the sides of my shorts and pulls my panties to the side, completely exposing me to him.

"I knew you'd be wet for this, Pretty Girl," he whispers, licking up my thigh. His fingers mercilessly dive in and out of my pussy, scissoring when his fingers bottom out.

I cry out, reaching for Kieran's and Callum's hands and squeezing hard. "Holy fuck," I pant, arching my back and begging for more.

Everything ceases to exist at the moment when my eyes roll into the back of my head. Teetering on the edge of an orgasm, Rad pulls back completely, purposely leaving me a wet and needy mess.

"Ashton," I whisper his full name, making him moan.

"Take your damn clothes off, Little Brat," Asher barks in a voice dripping with desire. "There's no one else on this fucking ride. Rad slipped the guy fifty bucks to leave us up here for thirty minutes. So, what are you going to do in that thirty minutes?" he growls, leaning his elbows on his knees.

His hazel eyes eat me alive when I stare him down. Even when I lift my shirts over my head and toss them to him, I keep eye contact.

"Lean forward," Kieran demands, undoing my bra and bringing it down my arms when I do so.

The cool metal of the ride bites into my skin when I lean back, gasping for air. My breasts rise and fall rapidly, begging for their lips to attach around my puckered nipples.

"Good girl," Ash purrs, studying my breasts in the pale moonlight mixed with the beautiful red and blues illuminated by the Ferris wheel, bouncing off my flesh.

"Now take off your shorts and hand your panties over," Asher demands, holding out a hand and curling his fingers. His jaw clenches when I don't immediately bend over and do as he asks.

"Make me," I grit my teeth, snarling in his direction. If he wants my damn panties, he can come take them off with his fucking teeth.

"Asher has officially entered the ring," Rad whispers with a grin, eyeing Asher as he falls to his knees in the confined space and crawls to me with determination.

Raising a brow, he silently questions me again with every slide in my direction. I sit firm. Our cart sways as he inches closer and closer, finally settling in front of me. His lip peels back when he leans closer, a breath away from my lips.

"Be a good little brat and take your panties off for me," he whispers with demand, wrapping his long fingers around my throat. My breath shudders when he takes control, tightening his hold around my throat and squeezing until my heartbeat pounds against his palm.

"Take them off, and I'll let them fuck you," he whispers an inch from my lips, teasing me with the tip of his tongue.

"Make. Me," I hiss in defiance, begging Asher to yank down my shorts and panties and hate fuck me into oblivion.

Having Asher Montgomery on his knees, staring lustful hate vehemently into my eyes, should scare the panties directly off me. Instead, empowerment fills me, and my courage grows. No matter what happens, he will work for this pussy after everything he's ever said to me.

"Oh, Pretty Girl. You're asking for it," Rad chuckles, drawing circles on my inner thigh.

"Take off her damn shorts and then her panties," Asher demands Rad, never taking his eyes off mine. He holds me with his stare, a cocky smirk pulling the edge of his lips.

"As you wish," Rad hums, not waiting for my approval.

When Rad works my shorts and panties down my legs, I don't fight him. Even when I'm bare for the world to see and the chilly breeze puckers my nipples, I don't swat him away as I should because I want this. I want to be at their mercy under Asher's intense stare. I want them to fuck me in this stupid metal cart high above the city with only the wind as our witness.

With a grin, Rad hands Asher my panties without hesitation.

"Look at me," Asher whispers, a breath away from my lips again.

Bringing my thong to his nose, he inhales deeply and shuts his eyes with a groan of approval. The noises he makes go straight to my dripping pussy, convulsing around nothing.

"You are wet for us, aren't you? Do you want them to fuck you, Little Brat? Do you want their cocks so deep inside you that you feel them for the next few days?" Asher whispers, loosening his grip on my throat.

Straightening my thong until the moist material glistens in the lights, Asher runs the length of his tongue along the fabric with a guttural groan, reveling in my arousal.

"Now," he rasps with dilated eyes. Undoing his pants, he settles himself on the bench across from us. "I want you to fuck them," he demands once again, bringing his massive dick out through the fly of his jeans. He moans, wrapping my panties around his aching cock, and slowly strokes himself. Never taking his eyes off me as he does. Up and down my panties go, gliding over his hardened dick.

"Do you do this often?" I rasp, looking between the four of them with wonder.

"What's that?" Kieran groans, sucking on my neck. His fingers roam, squeezing my tit and pinching my nipple.

"Sharing like this," I moan, leaning my head back and falling into the pleasurable sensations taking over my body.

Silence fills the caged car. Nothing but my heavy breaths fill the air. I peek an eye open, greeted by their heat-filled gazes when they look at one another and shake their heads.

"I'm not in the habit of sharing what's mine," Asher says with finality, a growl brewing in the back of his throat as he strokes himself with my panties again, picking up speed. "But for you? For them? It seems to be a packaged deal."

"Only twice before," Rad whispers, sucking my nipple into his mouth. "With you. Kieran and Callum. Those were the only times."

My breaths shudder again, and I loudly cry out. My voice echoes through the cage, and I'm sure if there were other people here, they'd know exactly what we were up to in this isolated cage—raised high in the sky with no soul in sight.

"Turn around," Rad says, twirling his finger. "Put your ass in the air and let me finally fuck my pussy raw." Possession seizes his voice, knocking it into a low growl.

I moan when I lean down, putting my elbows on the bench and my knees on the floor. Rad runs a finger down my spine and spreads my cheeks, blowing his warm breath down my crack. Digging his fingers into my hips, he lines himself up, dragging himself through my arousal dripping out of my cunt.

"You remember what I said before, right, Pretty Girl? There will never be a barrier between us ever again. There hasn't been for three weeks, and now is no exception," he rasps, collecting my hair into his fist, and pulling my back against his chest. "You're the only one I've gone raw with," he breathes into my neck. "The only one I want to feel pulsating around my bare cock."

"Yes," I moan my approval, giving a firm nod.

I cry out when he plows into me and stills, reveling in my clenching cunt. My orgasm sits on the cusp of bursting, aching for him to continue his thrusts and bring me to oblivion.

"Jesus," he rasps, breathing heavily into my neck. "Your pussy feels like a fucking vice around my cock. You're going to milk every damn ounce of my come. You got that? I'm going to spill so hard," he moans, burying his face in my neck, pounding into me harder and harder until he slows again.

"Callum," Kieran calls to his stunned friend, rubbing his fingers along my chin. Drawing my eyes up to his, he gives me a soft smile.

"Yeah-yeah?" Callum rasps, squeezing his dick through his jeans with stiff movements. He stares at me in awe, watching my tits bounce when Rad picks up his pace again.

"Are you ready to take Callum's cock in your mouth, Pretty girl?" Rad whispers in my ear, slowing his thrusts and stills again. He groans when I squeeze around him, giving him my answer.

"Do you want that?" I ask through heavy breaths, licking my lips.

Through my lashes, I gaze up at Callum with want, begging to feel his warmth slide down my throat and coat it. We've kissed, touched, and held hands, but he's never alluded to being ready for more. Hiding away, he usually sits on the sidelines in wait, stroking himself and watching with rapt attention as Rad or Kieran fuck me into oblivion. Only the one time he stepped up to the plate and came on my ass. Tonight, though, feels different from those occasions. I feel it in my bones tonight that Callum's ready to advance to the next base and take what he wants.

Callum's eyes widen, taking a heavy breath. "Only if you want to," he whispers, squeezing his dick again through his jeans and moaning at the simplest sensation.

My pussy flutters at the sound of his deep moan, and I lick my lips, eager for a taste.

"Oh, yeah. I definitely think she wants to," Rad strains, pulling my elbows off the bench.

"Scoot over, Callum," Asher barks out his desperate demand, lending Callum the extra push he needs. "Pull your dick out and get it wet in her mouth." Callum swallows hard, fumbling to get his dick out of his jeans. When he scoots over, he looks down at me with excitement, lust, and a hint of fear. "Good. Now, rub the tip along her lips. Ah," Asher grunts through his directions, breathing heavily and slowing his pace. Leaning back, Ash stops his strokes and stares at the ceiling with glazed-over eyes.

Licking my lips, I look up at Callum. "It's okay," I whisper. "I want to suck you off," I whisper, putting my hands on his knees, gently squeezing.

He shakes his head, a pink tint taking over his cheeks. "I've never..." He closes his eyes in shame and takes a deep breath. "When it happens, I'll remember it forever. I didn't want it to be just anyone," he whispers, trailing a shaky finger down my jaw and tracing over my popped-open lips. "But if I have to relive this moment over and over for the next one hundred years, I want it to be you."

A drum plays in my chest when he grabs his dick and gently strokes his girth. No one says a word when I lean forward and let him use me how he wants. If his memory doesn't let him forget, I'll make this the most incredible experience of his life. There will be no doubt that this will be the moment running through his mind in ten years when he pops a chub randomly in public and curses my name.

"River, fuck," he hisses when I scrape my teeth lightly over his tip and take him all the way in until my cheeks hollow out, and he lets out a deep, drawn-out moan.

Taking a deep breath, I shove him further until he feels the contractions of my throat and moans, grabbing my hair. My pussy clenches, convincing Rad to continue his thrusts with new abandon, slamming our hips together.

Fingers twirl around my clit, calling my orgasm, and bringing me back to the edge of the cliff. I moan around Callum's dick, earning a pleasing groan in return. His hips lift off the bench, shoving himself down my throat even more until he stills, reveling in my contracting throat. Every muscle in his body tightens, and his fingers grab my hair like a handlebar, slamming into my face until he cries out, arching his back, and finally, his salty come splashes down my throat.

Callum's eyes widen when he pulls his semi-hard dick from my mouth with a lazy grin, leaving him in a blissful state. His fingers retrace my lips, gliding over the warmth of his come spread across my glistening lips.

"You missed some," he whispers, gently shoving his thumb in my mouth. My tongue swirls around his thumb, sucking the spilled come from his flesh and swallowing it down without complaint.

"Such a good girl," Asher groans, throwing his head back with several labored breaths falling between his parted lips. White sticky come spills from the tip of his dick, jutting directly into my thong, encasing his length. His heavy breath fills the cart, and another look of contentment passes over his face. "Fuck, River," he mumbles through heavy breaths, staring at the ceiling of the cart with glazed-over eyes.

"My turn," Rad says, ramming into me so hard I double over, coming all over his cock. "Fuck," he shouts, digging his teeth into my shoulder and coming deep inside me with a shout. "You feel that, Pretty Girl?" he whispers in my ear as his fingers roam over my naked body. Squeezing my breast, he groans, slowly pulling out. "That's what marks you as mine. No matter how far you get, I'll always find you." It's a promise, not a threat, weaved in his possessive tone.

I shiver when Rad's come drips down my thighs, sticking to my flesh. As the cool breeze blows through the cart, a shiver works through me. And the moment my eyes connect with the mismatched gaze looking down at me, my pussy clenches again.

Kieran softly moans, stroking his thick length. With one silent demand and finger curl, I crawl toward him on my hands and knees, stopping when I'm directly between his sprawled open legs. Biting into his lip, he moans when I place my hand over his, adding more pressure around his thick cock. Moans spill from his throat when I lean forward, licking his shaft toward his weeping tip. I groan when the taste of his pre-cum lands on my tongue, making my pussy ache even more.

Without wasting a second, Kieran pulls me off the ground and settles me in his lap until I'm straddling him with my knees, biting into the cool metal. His lips savagely attack mine in such a heated kiss my damn toes curl, and I grind against his hard dick.

"I couldn't wait for a second longer, but we're going to have to hurry," he rasps, gripping my hips with bruising force. "Can I fuck you raw?" he whispers, moving his tip over my sensitive clit in heavy circles, sending goosebumps down my flesh. Every part of me shivers as he plays with me how he wants.

"Yes," I gasp out in desperation, sinking onto him until he's nestled deep inside my cunt.

"You feel so damn good," he whispers before plunging his tongue back into my mouth, desperately dancing with mine until we're out of breath.

Working him up and down, I moan when his fingers twirl around my clit, bringing another orgasm slamming right through me, and I clamp down on him.

"Watching you with my friends was torture. I kept thinking that it should be all me. But feeling Rad's cum dripping from you and knowing mine will be there too has me on edge. I'm going to come now," he moans, slamming his hips up into mine until his warmth fills me.

Slumping against his shoulder, I try to regain my breath just as the Ferris Wheel slowly comes back to life, and we're jerked forward from the force.

"Time to get dressed," Rad whispers, helping me dismount Kieran, who tucks himself back into his jeans.

"H-here," Callum says gently, coming before me with my bra in his hands. Working the straps up my arms, he clasps the back of my bra together, only fumbling a little and gently kissing my shoulder. Rad hands me the Property of Whispered Words shirt and helps me put it over my head. He clings tight to my original shirt, clasping it.

"We're almost to the bottom," Ash says in a lazy tone, standing beside me. He grins, holding up my come-filled panties, dripping with his essence onto the floor between us. "Now, for being such a damn brat, you're going to put this back on. You're going to wear it home and remember what happens when you disobey me. Next time, I'll bend you over my knee, spank your ass raw, and then fuck your tight hole." Asher leaves no room for argument, cocking

— 293 —

his brow and watching the delighted twitches erupting across my face.

Jesus. Everything clenches, including my offended asshole. No one has touched it in a long time, especially not this dick. But I bite my tongue for once, reaching for the soaked thong, and put it on. His warm come sticks to my tiny hairs and my lower lips, mixing with his friends' come as it drips from my sopping pussy. It's like they've marked me and ruined me for everyone else. As the ride comes to a halt, I slip my flip-flops back on and turn toward the door, waiting for it to unlock.

The man operating the Ferris wheel turns bright red the moment our eyes meet, letting me know we had an audience of one. Despite being up so high, my loud moans must have traveled down here. Thankfully, no one else was in line after us.

Rad wraps an arm around my shoulders as Callum takes my hand, interlocking our fingers together.

"Thanks for the ride, man," Rad says, digging a wad of cash from his pockets. The man doesn't utter a word when we awkwardly walk away with looks of utter satisfaction lining our faces.

Other carnival goers roam the area with drinks in their hands. Since the sun went down, the children left, and the adults stayed to play. But they don't pay us any mind, not knowing what we did in that unsuspecting Ferris wheel cart.

I groan with the wetness pooling more in my panties. With every miserable step, their combined cum leaks from me, running down my legs.

"You wanna go home, Pretty Girl? Or come over?" Rad asks, kissing my cheek when we get to the SUV still parked near the stage.

I contemplate my life in a matter of three seconds. Ma is probably sleeping and doing okay, and I don't have any other obligations in the morning, making my decision ten times easier.

"Take me back to your place," I squeal when Rad picks me up, throws me in the backseat, and climbs on top of me. Looking up, Callum grins, lifting my head so it's on his thigh. His fingers run through my messy strands as he looks out the window, not once reaching to put his earbuds in.

"I'm still running down your leg, aren't I?" He grins with satisfaction, running his fingers over my soaked thighs, and smearing the leaking come sticking to my flesh. "Lick it," he says, rubbing his wet fingers along my lips until I open wide and suck all their essence off his fingers.

"Jesus," Asher curses, swerving the SUV.

"Eyes on the road, dickbag," Rad grumbles, sucking on my neck.

"Can't you fucking wait? Why does this have to happen in my car? And when do I get my turn?" Asher gripes, choking the steering wheel.

Rad grins, biting my neck and sucking my flesh between his teeth. "The Ferris wheel was just the beginning," he whispers, loudly popping off my neck. "There's more in store for you back at the house. You ready, Pretty Girl? We're going to fuck you all night long."

Staring into his eyes, I see the promise nestled deep; all I can do is nod.

"Rock my world, Ashton," I whisper, earning a groan and an eager tongue down my throat.

RIVER

"I see you're finally putting your managerial skills to good use," Ode says with a grin. Nodding toward the new girl sitting tall at the front door, taking over my old job.

I lean against the bar, watching from behind as the chaos unfolds around us. People pile in, storming the tiny stage in massive waves. New faces. Old faces. People from every walk of life. Just to get a glimpse of Whispered Words. Their excited energy pours through the venue, infecting everyone—including me. Searching the crowd, I furrow my brows, not spotting my stalker, who's been here every night for the past month, watching me. Whatever, so long, Van. I hope never to see your face ever again.

I blow out a breath, focusing on the new girl at the door instead of the fire hazards piling into the already-packed bar.

"Well, Booker gave me the okay to hire someone. He said I couldn't do my job if I sat up front taking tickets. So, he said I should take in Tammy and let her do it." I shrug, watching the new girl with admiration.

"She's good people," Leon remarks, cutting through the bar with a large plate of delicious-smelling nachos.

My mouth waters as the sharp scent of spicy cheese hits my nose, inhaling deeper, wishing the nachos were already resting in my gut. Fuck. When was the last time I ate? Breakfast? Shit. I didn't have time for dinner today after Callum dropped me off at my apartment after work. I knew tonight was going to be big. And if I admitted to working a little harder on my makeup and picking out the perfect pair of shorts, you'd call me desperate. Some days I miss having my car at my fingertips and caring for my own damn self. But having the boys driving me around like a princess? Yeah, I kind of like spending so much time with them in a confined space.

"I think I'm in love with you," I say with a grin when he sets the nachos down in front of me with a wink.

"Oh, you wish, baby girl," he quips, kissing my cheek with a laugh. I'm too desperate to eat to bat him away like I should.

I snort, digging into the delicious melted cheese and chips, moaning into it when it hits my taste buds. "You're too damn good to me," I groan, shoving more food into my mouth.

"Now, that's something we can both agree on," Marcus, the bartender, says from my side, sliding two beers to grabby patrons waiting at the bar.

"Shush," Leon mutters, shoving Marcus as he returns to the kitchen with a laugh.

"Ohh, Pretty Girl. You've got a lil something," Rad says with a smirk, pointing to my chin. With my tongue, I try clearing off the remnants of the cheese but fail. Rad grins more, leaning over to run his tongue up my chin and over my parted lips. "Yummy nachos," he says with a wink, pushing his tongue into my mouth. I groan, holding his face to mine until he pulls back panting and wide-eyed.

"Fucking gross," Asher grumbles, shaking his head at our antics.

"Yo, barkeep!" Rad barks out with a laugh, slamming his hand on the counter.

Marcus sighs, meandering over with a frown. Leaning against the bar, he shakes his head. "Listen, kid. How many times do I have to tell you? I'm not the barkeep," he grumbles, cocking his head to the side.

"Meh," Rad says, waving a hand. "Can you get me..."

"Just four beers," Asher commands through gritted teeth. "You don't need that fruity shit when we're about to perform." He stares daggers at Rad, who puffs out his bottom lip and pouts. "It'll upset your damn stomach. I don't need a barf-fest repeat of last year." I wrinkle my nose at the reference, not wanting to ask what the barf-fest involved.

"You really need to get laid, man. You're getting way too stuck up for your own good. Pretty Girl, why don't you tell him?" Rad wiggles his brows when I shove another cheese-filled chip into my mouth.

"Nope. Not touching that subject," I say through my mouthful of food, tasting the lie on the tip of my tongue instead of the spicy nacho cheese.

Asher raises a brow at me like he's pried my brain open, reading my every thought. If he did, he'd see the images of our night together on the Ferris Wheel running through my mind.

"I got off just fine into your panties," Asher says in a low voice, stopping the cheese-soak chip from entering my mouth. Color me shocked and awed because I swear to hell he's flirting with me, which is confirmed when he moves my hand toward his mouth and eats the chip in my hand, moaning at the taste.

"Yeah, so fucking good. Maybe I'll get some later," he says, wrapping his mouth around my fingers. My body stiffens when the tip of his tongue roams the length of my fingers, sucking it into his mouth. Over and over, he swirls his tongue, sucking all the cheese and salt from my flesh. With a pop, he frees my hand and grins at me, only offering me one small wink in return for my stunned expression.

Fuck. Me.

My cheeks heat when his gaze stares right through my damn soul, and I swear, if they didn't have to go on stage, I'd slather cheese on my lady bits and have him lick his way to the center. How many licks does it take for the Asher to get to the center of the kitty cat? We'll never know because just as I'm about to entertain his panty comment with a quick retort about coming somewhere else besides fabric, we're interrupted by the she-devil I swore I told off.

"Oh my god, Asher Montgomery!" Comes a shrill familiar voice from the depths of the large crowd. My skin immediately crawls, and my stomach sours. Great, there goes my damn nachos. Another meal ruined by some stuck-up jerk. I set my chip down like it offended me and pout.

"Yay! Tiny Tots Tessa," Rad mumbles, running a hand down his face with irritation. "I bet she'd volunteer as tribute." All the air leaves Rad's lungs when Ash's elbow meets his gut, and he huffs. "Not cool, bro. You almost hit the little dangling Rads."

"I'd rather you bite off my dick and feed it to myself after I grill it as sausage than ever dip my dick into that," he grits out, standing rigidly when she approaches with a big smile. "I'd fuck Little Brat for forty-eight hours straight on Viagra, chance chafing and dick pains than ever fuck that," he grunts, sending shivers down my spine.

A sparkle twinkles in his eye when I shiver at the thought of a sexathon with him for hours. Oh, hell. Asher must be growing on me. Or I'm just horny. When I turn to Rad, he's grinning like crazy in my direction with a dreamy look on his face.

"I think we're going to have to put her on the no-fly list," I grumble, earning a smirk from Asher, who snorts.

It's like the night of the celebration never happened, and she's back to looking at Asher like he's her future baby daddy. Fat chance, Blondie. Maybe I'll have to remind her who these boys are dicking down these days. It's definitely not her.

Tessa's long blonde hair is thrown into a pretty bun on the top of her head. And this time, she forgot the pearls at home, replacing them with a small black choker hugging her throat. Well, hey. She's at least trying to fit in with the crowd with attire this time, sporting her new Whispered Words shirt and distressed jeans.

"Asher! I can't wait to see you play tonight!" she says with enthusiasm, bouncing on her toes. "Any new songs yet? My mom said you were going to the Battle of the Bands! You're going to be famous!" With every word Tessa shrieks, the further Asher pulls himself away from her. He visibly cringes when she winds her arm through his, leaning her head against his arm with hearts in her eyes.

My fists curl at his visible discomfort. You know, strange men make my skin crawl with anxiety in situations such as this. Whenever they touch without permission and take, take, take. So what's so different about a woman making a man uncomfortable? The band has repeatedly told her to fuck off and leave them be and that they aren't interested. Yet, Tessa doesn't get the hint and keeps coming around like a desperate hussy looking for dick any way she can.

"We have a rad-diculous new song called, Fuck You," Rad deadpans, taking a long sip of his beer to cover up his disgust. His dark eyes lock on me when I raise a brow, and he shrugs in response.

Tessa beams, looking smugly at me. "Oh my god. We can't wait to hear it! You guys are so good!"

Ugh. Sometimes I wish I had a remote so I could mute people. Like, click—you're muted now, bitch. Then she'd flap her gums, and no one would hear the shit she spews.

"Yeah," Asher says through a tight smile, trying to pry her hand off him. "I can't either. Are you ready?" he begs Rad with furrowed brows, stepping away from the harasser. Tessa swoons, staring at his tall form with hearts in her eyes.

"Fuck off, now," I snarl in Tessa's direction, watching with glee when she rears back with disgust.

For some reason, Tessa doesn't utter a word when the boys wave goodbye, heading for the stage. Instead, she watches them like a fucking predator about to pounce on her prey.

"See ya backstage, Pretty Girl!" Rad hollers as the crowd swallows them whole, and they disappear behind the tall bodies of their fans.

"Are you guys doing anything after? We're having a party!" Tessa screams after them as they walk away, completely ignoring her stupid ass.

She stares after them with such hope. Lust practically pools around her. But I have news for her. They're mine. And the sooner she gets it through her thick, bitchy skull—the better we'll all be. Maybe I should kick her out and never let her come back. Hmm. Manager status does have its perks.

"I'm getting the impression they aren't fond of her," Ode stage-whispers into my ear, loud enough for the perky blonde to hear.

Tessa turns on her toes with a frown, marching up to the bar. Her scathing eyes rake up and down my body, giving me her best stink eye.

"I need four mojitos right now." The venom in her voice makes me want to take her into the alleyway and let my fists have their way with her face. Or maybe I could grab our trusty baseball bat from behind the bar and shove it down her throat...

Nah. She's not worth it. She's a try-hard, trying to get into the good graces of the boys who I have no doubt will be famous in a year. I can't wait to sink my toes into the sands of the beach and wallow in the sun. Ah. Never in a million years did I think I'd be doing something like this. Helping them and potentially meeting some of my family. Not that I'm holding any expectations on that end, but still. I'm allowed to dream of a future that might not be...

"Of course," Marcus replies in a deep, professional voice, turning to mix the drinks even though he's muttering under his breath about her attitude.

"So, what exactly do you do around here?" Tessa asks me haughtily, lifting her nose in the air.

I blow out a breath. Sheesh. People don't have enough respect to read the word Manager on my tit. It's big and bold in red letters, but no one seems to notice. So, I point to the word with a raised brow, laying it all out for her.

"I run the show." Simple but effective.

Her perfectly sculpted eyebrows pop up, and she rolls her eyes with disgust. Lifting her lip, she leans against the bar getting as close to my face as possible. If I were anywhere else, she and I would have major problems.

"By the way, Central Trash. I see how you look at them," she says, pointing to the empty stage. "And I just wanted to warn you; they're mine," she snarls the word mine possessively.

I nod with a smirk. She could piss on them, and they still wouldn't be hers.

"Sure, Tess. Whatever you say," I hum when Marcus slides over her drinks more forcefully than necessary, spilling liquid over the rims of the glasses. "But I swear we had this discussion already. Do my words go in one ear and out the other? Have you choked on too much cock to understand? Has it damaged your hearing? Let me repeat myself. They're mine. You'll find yourself missing fingers if you lay your hands on what's mine again." I raise a brow when her eyes go wide, and she sputters.

"You're...you're threatening me! Did you hear?" No one pays her a lick of attention, and she huffs, turning on her heel.

"Unclench that jaw, bestie," Ode snickers, pinching my cheek and pulling me out of my thoughts.

"Ode," I groan, swatting her away.

"Don't worry, baby girl," Leon says from my side, watching Tessa make her way back through the crowd. She bounces off a few people giving them the stink eye and yells something in their faces. "Guys like that don't want a girl like that. That's who their parents wish they had. Hell, I bet all their parents want some stuck-up rich bitch for a daughter-in-law. But those Lakeview boys always have a weakness for one thing," he says, side-eyeing me with a smirk.

"Yeah? And what's that? Oh, genius," I snark back when he laughs.

"The magical Central pussy." He cackles when I slug him in the arm with a heavy punch.

"You're such a dick," I grumble as the lights dim and the crowd lets out a collective whoop of excitement.

More people pack the place than ever before. Even Sorcha's concert didn't garner this much attention. All my hard work from their social media platforms has finally paid off, and we're about to reap what we've sowed all the way to California.

"I have one!" Leon shouts, grabbing his crotch. Leon ducks his head when I try to swing on him again and cackles when I miss. "Now, Miss manager! I'll go back to the kitchen. No need to resort to violence." A large grin takes over when I narrow my eyes at him.

"Oh, I'll resort to violence, dickhead. Back to work!" I bark out my demand, sending him a wink in return.

Once Leon disappears into the kitchen with a playful grin, I turn back to the men of the hour.

"You have it so damn bad," Ode remarks, leaning against the bar.

"Don't you have work, too?" I grumble when she bursts out laughing, shoving me to the side.

"Nah, bitch. I'm friends with the manager. Didn't you know? She needs my moral support right now," she says with a grin, leaning closer. "How fast are you falling?" Her eyebrows wiggle out of control until I flick them, and she laughs again.

"It's bad, Ode," I groan, rubbing my forehead. "How can this happen again? And not just one...fuck."

"Oh my god, you love all of them? Even the dickhead on guitar?" she says, pointing directly at Asher, who raises a brow at her from the stage like he heard every word. With the chants of the raging crowd and whoops or excitement ringing through the place, there's no way.

"Jesus. Didn't your mama ever tell you it's rude to point?" I gasp, pulling her arm down to her side.

"She did, multiple times. But I'm a rebel." Ode grins more, if that's even possible, and fully faces me. "All four of them, huh? Their dicks that good that they're about to lock down my bestie who swore off love?"

"What can I say? I'm a fucking sucker for musicians. My heart..."

"And pussy," she snickers, interrupting me.

"As I was saying. My heart just can't stay away. I don't know what it is. They're protective, gentle, and they're...fucking hot, and hell, dynamite in the sheets. And fuck. I'm so fucked, Odes. Pull me away from them," I groan, covering my heated face, and the memories of our illicit moments run like a runaway train through my mind.

"Riv. Not everyone is Van. He was a dickless fuck who ran away like a puppy. But these guys? They took you to their neighborhood. Girl, you practically met their families. They're not him and not embarrassed by you. Hell, they stalk you everywhere. If anyone is pathetic, it's them," Ode says, wrapping a supportive arm around my shoulders.

"But what if..."

"No fucking what ifs. Give it a chance and let yourself like them. Fuck them. Do whatever the hell you want to with them. I kinda like 'em, babe. Plus, if they break your heart? I'll hunt them down, and they'll face the wrath of Ode Mills." Her nose wrinkles when she gives a convincing nod.

My heart races in my chest at the prospect of letting all my reservations go. Everything Ode said is precisely what I am afraid of. What if they fucked me over? Shit. My head pounds with an oncoming headache from all my chaotic thoughts. I've given so much to them already.

"Don't stress yourself too much," Ode says into my ear over the sound of the first notes bleeding through the speakers.

"You don't know me very well then," I grumble back, looking at the sweaty boys jumping on stage.

Kieran's sultry voice rasps through the microphone again, belting out a new song. I take out my phone, finding this the perfect moment to showcase their talents. Once Kieran hits the chorus, I jump onto the bar and press record. Kieran smiles at me from the stage, locking his eyes on the camera when the music ends.

"Thank you, Central City. You're fucking great. If you didn't know, we are Whispered Words. You can find us on ClockTok and FlashGram. Join us at whisperedwordsband," he says through a smirk, winking at the camera, capturing them.

I give him the thumbs up when I jump down and immediately lean against the bar watching with admiration.

"They have you doing their bitch work now?" Ode asks, placing drinks on the bar for three patrons.

I snort. "I'm helping them film performances and shit. I told you they're trying to apply to the Battle of the Bands." I give her a pointed look when she raises a skeptical brow.

Speaking of, that's something we'll be doing this week. They only have two more weeks to submit their application before the website won't take them anymore, and they want everything to be perfect—including their social media numbers.

Within a few clicks, I upload their video to ClockTok and watch the notifications from the thousands of followers pour in. I swear, a month ago, no one around the world knew who they were. Now they're getting tens of thousands of likes and comments, begging for more covers and original songs. Oh, and nude photos. Crazy fan girls.

"Yeah, and they promised to take you..." she trails off with a pointed look in my direction.

I shrug. "Maybe they will. Maybe they won't. Gotta film this one, too," I say, quickly jumping on the bar again and away from my nosy BFF.

"You can't avoid me forever, bitch," she cackles, leaning over to take someone's drink order.

"Yes, yes, I can," I murmur, standing high above the crowd. Tonight, they stand shoulder to shoulder, squished together like sardines.

Rad grins at me when he throws this shirt off and tosses it onto the stage. I smirk when he winks at me, wiping away the sweat from his brow. I'm sure if he had it his way, he'd be naked by now instead of in his jeans. Judging by the thirsty shrieks from the front of the stage, I'd say his fangirls wish for it, too. Too bad, suckers, that's mine later. Every girl in the crowd shrieks when Rad flexes his pecs and bangs on the drums with more force than necessary, putting on a show for the crowd.

"Hey there!" a deep voice says from below me, tapping my ankle with his calloused finger.

I frown. "Yeah?" I ask, stepping back and jumping down behind the bar. "Can I help you with something?" I ask, leaning over to hear him over the loud music.

He grins wide, exposing his yellowing teeth. With a nod, he taps the bar, leaning in closer. His crystal blue eyes check every inch of me that he can see. Disgust eats away at my flesh, but I hold my composure. I'm professional and all, even when I want to shrink away.

Alarm bells activate in my mind, blaring a siren to run away, and I'm suddenly very aware of everything around me. But just because the pretty boy with yellow teeth gives me the damn willies doesn't mean he's going to harm me. But my momma always told me to trust my gut, and that's exactly what I'm going to do.

"Give me two beers and your number," he says when another equally intimidating man walks up beside him. They both stare down at me with a grin.

"Beer, sure. My number, hell no," I spit, trying to hold my damn tongue, but she always has a mind of her own.

The man turns up the charm, brightening his smile. "Come on, beautiful. A nice bartender like you could use a little something like me," he says in a gravelly tone, which I'm sure most girls fall to their knees for.

"Sorry, buddy. I'm not interested. But here's your beer. That'll be 12.99," I say, holding my hand after setting down his beers.

"Come on," his buddy says, grabbing my wrist tightly.

"There is no come on about this," I say through clenched teeth, trying to reign in my anger. "But if you don't let my hand go, we'll have some serious problems." I raise a brow when he sneers at my words and tightens his grip on me, attempting to pull me closer.

"Whatcha gonna do?" he teases, trying to pull at me again.

"This," I hiss, whipping out my knife and flicking it open in one move. The man's eyes widen when I hold the tip against his precious fingers, dreaming of cutting them off one by one.

"Get your hands the fuck off her," Kieran's deep, growly voice comes through the microphone, sending chills down my spine.

Every eye in the bar swings in my direction, widening at the sight of my knife digging into grabby-man's fingers. At the sound of Kieran's second growl, every man in the bar takes their hands off whatever woman they showed up with. Screams erupt for the asshole to take his hands off me, and some even attempt to take him away from the bar, but it does nothing but encourage him to cling to me harder. He sneers in my direction, not deterred by Bert screaming from the front door, unable to make it through the crowd standing shoulder to shoulder, watching the entire situation unfold.

"I'm coming!" Bert growls over the roar of the crowd.

"Don't worry!" I shout to Bert, who grunts his disapproval at my nonchalant attitude. Bringing my attention back to the man of the hour, I focus on the digit suffering beneath my blade. "I can cut your fingers off one by one." I'm challenging him. Would I cut off his fingers for funsies? Uh, yeah. Just for the simple fact, he's touching me. Fuck the cops. This is self-defense. He won't let go and keeps leering at me like I'm his favorite Sunday brunch. I'm no biscuit and gravy meal, pal. So, fuck off.

He smirks again until I dig the top further into his finger, drawing blood and watching with glee as it pools on the wooden bar top. Movement catches my attention out of the corner of my eye, and I smirk as two overbearing figures come into view with deep scowls and clenched fists. My heart gallops in my chest as they inch closer and closer, pushing through the crowd of people and shoving them aside with a possessive vibe wafting off every inch of them.

"You bitch," he hisses, but before he gets a chance to do anything else, he's yanked back by the very possessive assholes I've come to enjoy.

"I believe she said no fucking touchy," Asher growls, pulling the scumbags' face into his. "You tell him no, Little Brat?" Holy hotness, Batman. Asher looks at me with a kindling fire sparkling in his eyes, ready to pummel this douche into the ground.

I say, bury him.

"Definitely said don't fucking touch me," I hiss, climbing over the bar and grabbing our beat-up wooden baseball bat for more protection. I can't go around stabbing everyone who touches me, but a friendly knock to the teeth will help.

"Sometimes guys like this just need a little reminder." Before my eyes, my panties melt when Asher connects his forehead to the yellow-toothed offender and knocks him back a step.

Asher grins, rubbing his forehead as his opponent stumbles around. Fuck! As hot as this is, I can't let them fight in my damn bar.

"Back off," I say, putting a hand on Asher's chest, forcing him to stand still.

"This is where you say thank you, Asher," he snaps, staring daggers at me with a heaving chest. His wild eyes glare at the offenders with pure hate, and he's ready to lung at them again to finish the job.

"Asher, Daddy, " I murmur half-jokingly, running my fingers down his jaw and drawing his attention to me. "I appreciate what you did." I swallow hard when his fingers wrap around my wrist, holding my fingers against his jaw. "They scared the shit out of me," I breathe my confession with careful words. "So, thank you." Every ounce of vulnerability leaks from my voice, and he nods. "But I can't let you fight in here." No matter how hot it was. I swear those images will bleed into my dreams forever. The way his forehead smashed into that fucker's face, knocking him back.

"I told you, Little Brat. No one touches what's ours." He gives me a firm nod, squeezing my wrist with reassurance. "Whoever you need me to beat, I'll fucking end them."

Be still my beating heart.

"You good?" Kieran asks through several heaved breaths, peering around the circle that formed around us.

"I'm fine. Let me deal with these idiots," I grumble, nodding at the idiots squaring up for another fight. "All right, boys. Because that's what you are. You're not fucking men. Men don't touch things they're not supposed to. Now, get the fuck out. You're not welcome here ever again." I raise a brow when they square up again, eyeing the bat in my hand with a cocky expression until it falls.

"I got 'em, Riv. We'll take their picture and everything," Bert wheezes out of breath, finally making it to the bar after it's all said and done. Sometimes, I wonder why I still keep him around. Fuckery keeps happening on his watch when he's nowhere to be found. Maybe the bar needs more changes than I initially thought.

"Thank fuck." Once Bert has the two troublemakers kicked to the curb, the boys jump back up on stage but keep their eyes on me, and they continue their set list with more enthusiasm than before.

Leaning on the bar, I eye the boys on stage, rocking the shit out of the crowd. A strange feeling settles over me, thinking back to the two dumb fucks from earlier who were escorted out and thrown on the street. Something about them has anxiety rolling up my arms and prickling my skin. It's like they had a mission marching here to touch and egg me on. There was something dead in their beady eyes, like they never took no for an answer.

As time passes, I make my rounds through the bar, ensuring everything runs smoothly. The rest of the crowd remains respectful, albeit fucking messy, but still. They rock out to the hour-long set, chanting the guys' names and going ballistic when they offer the crowd an encore.

"Thank you, Dead End! It's been fucking great!" Kieran shouts into the microphone breathlessly, trying to catch his breath. Running a hand over his forehead, he swipes the sweat away and smiles at the cheering crowd. "We'll see you next time!" The boys each stand at the edge of the stage, taking their last bow. Reaching down, they shake their fans' hands before waving and disappearing backstage to cool down before they pack everything away.

"Another good show, bossy lady," Ode says over the loud chatter of the crowd, slowly making their way toward the door. Only a few will stay and continue to drink.

"Once everyone's out, I'm going to clean up and take the trash out," I say, squeezing her shoulder.

"Isn't that what we're for?" she shouts back, handing another patron a drink, and then closes their tab.

"Pfft. Bitch," I scoff with a wave. "I may be the manager, but I'll still get dirty." I wink, heading to a supply closet next to my back office and grabbing a trash bag.

As soon as I hit the main floor, I begin cleaning up. Candy wrappers, beer cans and bottles, old receipts, and even old food sticks to the floor. Ugh. Animals! There's a trash can at every friggin corner, and they decide to leave their shit on the ground.

"Ode!" I shout, tying up the heavy trash bag and throwing it over my shoulder with a grunt. Shit. I swear there are a few cement blocks in here. "I'm taking this out!" Ode gives me the thumbs up as I make my way out the backdoor and into the cool air.

I take a deep breath, relieved the staleness of the bar no longer infiltrates my nose. Replaced by the fresh, night air blowing through the abandoned alleyway. An eerie feeling churns in my gut as I approach the dumpster, stopping me in my tracks.

Flipping open the lid, I peer over my shoulders and shake my head. This alleyway at one in the morning had always been a little creepy. Not to mention the attacks that have happened on this side of town. I've always been cautious, hence the knife in my pocket, but tonight it feels like eyes are burning right through me.

Once the heavy bag is deposited into the dumpster, I turn on my heel, ready to get back inside. The guys promised me a ride home after a long day of working, and I can't wait to settle into bed. Lately, Rad and Callum have been stopping by for sleepovers or vice versa. Kieran and Ash hang out but never stay over. They've alluded to family issues but have never gotten specific about why they can't stay over. Often, I find myself squished between their bodies in a warm cocoon of comfort. Something that should cause concern, but doesn't anymore, because I'm free to do what I want with who I wish to and...

Pain erupts in my skull the moment something heavy knocks into me and sends me to my hands and knees, scraping along the pavement. All the air in my lungs blows out into the asphalt, and

I'm left gasping for breath. My fingers dig into the ground, desperate to move and stand, but moving seems impossible. The world around me spins endlessly, and I'm pushed belly first onto the road, scraping every inch of my legs and arms when I skid forward.

"I don't think so," the menacing voice from my nightmares growls, placing his heavy foot between my shoulder blades. "I've got a job to do," he says with a laugh, gripping me by my hair. "I won't find this hard at all. I'm not one to hit it twice, but you were so damn pretty and tight the first time. Why not?" His low chuckle does little to settle my damn nerves.

No. Not again. Not him. What in the ever-living fuck is he talking about? God. My heart races out of my chest, spearing through my damn ribs. I kick my leg out and, by God's grace, land a strike to his knee. He grunts, gripping my hair tighter than before until my eyes burn and tears run down my cheeks. Popping happens in my neck when he yanks it backward, forcing a cry from my lips.

My lips pop open, pleading for help when he turns me over on my back, yanking the strands of my hair between his fingers. Pain encases my entire body like a fire scorching my skin, from the scrapes burning on my exposed legs to my fingers clawing at his arms.

"Scream all you want," he murmurs. "I kind of like it."

The world blurs before me, and I shake my head. Fuck. I must stay coherent or I'll never make it through again. I have to stay the fuck awake and acknowledge the fact my biggest monster holds me captive in the isolated alleyway behind the bar.

"Fuck you, Bradley," I slur, spitting in his face. Or, what I hope is his face. All I see are wiggly lines and weaving colors splashing the world.

By the force of the first blow to my face, my glob of spit must have hit its mark. The next impact reigns down on my face in a fury of fists, crunching my nose and cheekbones. Static takes over my ears when he finally stops his violent assault, leaving me a groaning, pleading mess.

Pain is the only thing radiating through my body, pulsating pain through every inch of my muscles. No matter how hard I try to move my arms and legs, they don't cooperate, leaving me at his mercy. At fucking Bradley's mercy—the last place I want to be. The last time I was, he took my innocence and fucking ran with it.

Time ticks by slowly as I lie there, feeling his hands in places they shouldn't be. He murmurs words in my ear, but I can't fucking hear him over the beating of my broken heart. The entire world fades into the shadows as I fumble for the weapon nestled deep in my pocket, the one I don't leave home without—because of this man. The one time I didn't have it with me, this happened, and I won't let it happen again. I'll die before I let him get what he wants.

"Hey! What the fuck are you doing?!" someone, a familiar resounding voice, shouts, and his footsteps clomp forward loudly as if he is running.

My eyes stay closed, and my body is too spent to move as he remains on top of me, taking his damn time to get what he wants. Thank God my shorts are still on, and he hasn't started doing what I know he wants to do.

"The hell do you want?" Bradley spits, easing off of me, but doesn't fully get up. By the sound of the crunching beside me, he sits his ass on the pavement.

"What the hell?" the voice fills with panic, and a hand touches my warm forehead. "She's bleeding!" he hisses, rubbing a finger down my jaw. "You weren't..."

"Weren't what? You fucking..." I flinch, drowning out the words when the fingers run over my nose, and I cry out from the pain filling every inch of my fucking body.

I'm so fucking tired of everyone thinking they can take whatever the hell they want from me. I've fought too hard for far too long to carve my way into this world. I won't let some pissant fuckboy take what he wants again and again.

I'm fucking done. So, I do the only thing I can.

Flicking open my knife, I wildly stab wherever I can reach, basking in the roar of agony right before my entire world shuts down and I fall deep into the shadows of my mind.

ASHER

Something…is wrong. Something feels out of fucking whack. If you asked me what, though. I have no fucking clue. An urgent alarm desperately claws at the back of my mind, nagging at me.   For some fucking reason, and I can't put my finger on it. Everyone I love sits before me, de-stressing after our third show in a row. River has put us through the fucking ringer, with gigs almost every night this week, exhausting us to the max. But it's so damn worth it. Our rock star dreams rest at the tips of our fingers, finally in grasp.

"That show was badass!" Rad says with a grin, guzzling down a bottle of water twenty minutes after the performance.

Sweat pours from every inch of his glistening body, dripping off the long ends of his mullet. He groans, standing in front of the oscillating fan, opening the fly of his jeans.

"For the love of God, please keep your dick in your pants," I groan with exhaustion, leaning against the wall for support.

"The little Rads are hot as hell! I have swamp dick—Swamp. Dick, Asher. They're basically cooking in my jeans. My chestnuts are roasting! So, unless I want cooked swimmers, I need to cool them off," Rad scoffs at me, pulling his jeans and boxers down, exposing himself for the fucking world to see. "Ah, that's the stuff right there," he mumbles, wiggling around his ass around and allowing the air to flow to his fucking flapping dick blowing in the breeze.

"Your ass is disgusting," Kieran barks, slapping a hand across his butt cheek, rippling the skin, and leaving an angry red welt behind on his pasty skin.

"Oh, baby! Do it again!" Rad howls, locking his hands behind his head. "Ah, this is freedom," he groans with relief, arching his back.

"How the hell did we get to this?" I mumble, closing my eyes, so I don't have to stare at his dimply ass while sliding down the wall. I swear the dude can't keep his pants on to save his life. Every chance he gets, he's dropping trow and letting his dick fly free. Must be nice to have no restraints. But someone has to keep him in line.

We've been dead on our feet since we walked backstage into the darkened space dedicated to the talent. It's small, shabby, and fucking gross. Shifting my weight, my nose wrinkles when my pants stick to the floor. Don't they ever clean this place? Shit. Images of River frantically cleaning every inch of this place, runs through my mind. Hell, she probably hasn't been back here to clean, because she's working her life away and killing herself here.

Taking a deep breath, I revel in the surrounding nothingness—no noises, shouting crowd and, most importantly, no groupies shoving their titties in our faces. This moment of silence gives us time to unwind after such a killer performance. All these gigs are starting to wear us down, but we don't have time to stop. We're persevering and fucking rocking this shit before we hit enter and submit our talent for the most prestigious record company in the US. In the future, this could be our life. Performance after performance. City after fucking city on a tour bus filled with Rad's naked ass. Okay, maybe not that. Shivers of disgust roll through me, envisioning him running naked everywhere. And now I need bleach for my brain.

"If I never have to see your dick again, it'd be a good day," Callum murmurs, tossing his head back and sighing with a grin.

"Agreed," Kieran snaps, running a towel over his face and neck, soaking up the sweat dripping down his skin, grinding his teeth. He closes his eyes, taking several deep breaths, trying to reign in his after-performance anger. I swear it's what got us into this whole debacle, anyway.

If he hadn't banged River, well—we wouldn't be here or on our way to California. Sure, we could have gotten someone else to record our videos or gotten us more gigs. River's been a saint through this whole thing—a dangerous saint, leading us down a path we can't come back from. Doubt seeps into my mind, infecting my runaway thoughts with insidious ideas. Some days I wonder if we're taking the right road with her. Looking around the room, I gaze at the faces of my brothers'. Happiness radiates from every inch of them. But is it from our performance? Or the woman who supplied us with this opportunity? Because of her, we're here. One question repeats in my mind over and over again. Do we actually want to bring her to California? Since River came into the picture, our band dynamic has drastically changed. But for the good? Or bad? How much more damage can she inflict before we implode and throw our dreams away?

Internally, I groan, running a hand down my face. River brings nothing but a whirl of confusion, storming inside me and pulling me in different directions. She's this...annoying gnat, yet beautiful little brat who I want to choke...with my cock so she can't utter another witty remark. She's...getting way too into our heads—especially mine.

The crowd beyond the black curtain's loud chatter slowly fades away into nothing but crickets. Looking at my phone, I note it's almost closing time. Just on cue, the bubbly little bartender's voice rings through the system, telling everyone to get the fuck out, and they comply. Soon, we're left in comfortable silence. But in the quiet, something still nags the back of my mind, and looking around, I notice the missing piece who trails after us like a desperate groupie—River.

"I swear to God, bitch, if you're back here sucking dick," shouts Ode, the bubbly bartender, right before she rips open the curtain and sticks her head in with a frown. "Well, not sucking dick," she says, shaking her head. "But someone certainly has their hairy ass out," she quips, looking the room over. "You four seen your girlfriend?" she asks, raising a brow.

Rad grins, pulling up his boxers and pants and turning around. "I'm glad someone else finally admits that she's my girlfriend!" he says with way too much enthusiasm. "But wait. Where is River?" he asks, making my fucking heart skip a beat.

Something is wrong... Something is off, and it smacks me in the damn face. River isn't here to annoy me.

"That's what I'm fucking asking. Come out, come out wherever you are, bitch!" she yells jokingly, but I see the worry sitting behind her dark eyes as they crinkle when she doesn't get an answer. Her fingers tighten into fists as her eyes flash around the room, and she huffs. "I haven't seen her since she took the trash out. I swore I saw her come back in...." she trails off, looking toward the single window blocked out by a blackout curtain, only letting a sliver of light come through the split down the middle.

"What do you mean she went outside at one in the fucking morning to dump the trash?" Kieran barks, jumping to his fucking feet like a mad dog with his nostrils flaring as he marches toward her. The only thing stopping him is my hand on his heaving chest.

"Cool your shit," I hiss through clenched teeth, side-eyeing him. "You're in—fuck shit up and ask questions later—mode right now."

"I said what I said. River is a big girl despite you treating her like a fucking baby. She did what she always does every night. You'd all probably shit your pants if you knew she's walked home at three in the morning more times than I can count. You all know better than I do. That woman does whatever the fuck she wants to and...." Ode pales when a light flashes between the sliver of the curtain, lighting the room up in reds and blues. "What the fuck!" she shrieks with urgency, marching toward the side door, and slams out of it with a cry.

Kieran doesn't waste a single moment stomping out the door after her. It isn't until I hear the roar of his anger do I pile out the door with Callum and Rad on my tail. Only, we don't make it too far and come to an abrupt stop, freezing on the spot. Every muscle in my body locks tight. My eyes dart around, taking in the scene with a critical eye.

Numerous police offices stalk the alleyway with their heads down and moving up and down with a critical eye. One points to the ground, shaking his head as they follow the trail. On further inspection, my breath leaves my lungs and I'm left gasping for oxygen. Two officers walk along a dark red trail of blood leading out of the alley and onto the street. And that's where I see him, cowering in the shadows with a pale face and vacant expression—fucking Donavan Drake.

"What the fuck?" I murmur with outrage, watching with wide, horrified eyes as the scene gets worse and worse by the second.

"Oh-oh no," Callum cries out through a quivering voice. Covering his mouth, Callum frantically shakes his head and forces his eyes closed—removing himself from the situation mentally.

"It'll be okay, Cal," Rad murmurs through a crack in his voice with the reassurance I'm sure he doesn't feel. Slowly, he rubs circles on Callum's back in a soothing manner, whispering barely audible words, hoping to soothe his grief.

Turning Callum, so his back is to the scene, Rad consoles him through his anguish. With shaky hands, Callum rips his earbuds from his pocket and forces them in his ears, shaking in Rad's embrace. With every fiber of his being, I know he wants to run to her and ensure her safety. He wants to hold her against his chest and heal her wounds. But he also doesn't want to remember the scene. He doesn't want it seared into his memory, where he can recall it for eternity—the blood, the fucking carnage of it all.

My aching heart fucking sinks into my gut, swallowed by the churning acid threatening to obliterate it into pieces. EMTs surround her body. Her fucking body! Frantically checking her pulse and noting the injuries with two police officers who take notes.

Deep red dripping blood catches my eye first, splattered like fucking spaghetti sauce on the white walls. There it is all around her unmoving body laid out on the pavement. And on her face. Her fucking hands gleam in it. Bright red scratches split the skin of her shins and knees, working toward her thighs where her goddamn shorts button was popped open, exposing the front of her panties. My stomach churns more, burning the back of my throat with bile, when the police officers finally notice it too.

If someone touched her, I'll fucking bury them so deep no one will find the evidence.

"You son of a bitch!" Kieran wails before I even think about catching him by the shirt and stopping him from drowning in his emotions and acting without thinking. All the pent-up, after-performance rage rushes through his system and infecting him with violence.

I'm a frozen mass of hysterics when Kieran slams his vicious fist straight into Van's face over and over again, knocking them to the ground in front of two police officers, watching their every move. Great. This is just fucking great. The last thing we need is that idiot getting into trouble or worse, arrested.

"It wasn't me!" Van cries, trying to heave a fist into the side of Kieran's face, but fails. Kieran is way too gone, sinking into the abyss of his blacked-out anger like it's overpowered and taken him over. "It wasn't me! I found her!" Van wails, catching Kieran in the side of the jaw and knocking him on the ground.

"Stand down!" someone shouts in Kieran's direction, but he doesn't pay them any attention.

Kieran grunts, rolling onto the pavement with a snarl and jumping to his feet. He's like a fucking lion with a blood scent stalking toward Van, who jumps to his shaky as fuck feet, staring at Kieran like he's finally gotten the idea of who he's up against. A fucking animal is who. And if I don't jump in and save his stupid ass, he'll be dead before the cops can subdue my foolish brother.

"Kieran!" I bark, running toward him at full speed, slamming into him. My finger curls in his shirt, forcefully turning him until I back him up against the brick wall. "Knock it the fuck off! They're going to take you to fucking jail for suspicion and fucking assault!" I growl through clenched teeth, shaking him.

Too fucking late.

He barks out a humorless laugh, glaring in Van's direction as the cop approaches slowly with his hand on his gun, hanging from his hip.

"Stand down," he barks again, putting a placating hand out, trying to ease the tension between Kieran and Van. "I need you to turn around and face the wall. I'm detaining you." There's no room for arguments in his voice, glaring at us.

Another officer approaches Van and his fucked up and bleeding face with apprehension, checking over his wounds with a careful eye. His hand rests on his hip, shifting away from Van with heavy suspicions. Leaning in, he nods when Van speaks, making me wonder what words he's poisoning the police with. Van points our way, shaking his head and dropping his arm when the officer narrows his eyes at us. More words are exchanged, and the officer begins documenting every word Van says and hands him a card. Most likely, telling him to call if he thinks of anything else.

"Son," the officer barks again. "Turn and face the wall," he growls, stepping even closer to Kieran, ready to pounce on him if he doesn't comply with his words.

"Turn around, you fucking idiot," I hiss, putting my forehead against his. "We'll find out what the fuck happened. But now you've truly outdone yourself. I'll get to the bottom of why the fuck Van's here."

"Go with her," he pleads, slightly slumping against the wall. Tears burn the back of his eyes, glazing them over when River's unmoving body is loaded onto the stretcher and is strapped down for safe travels.

Turmoil takes over my foggy brain, watching as her limp body jostles with their movements as they guide the stretcher toward the open ambulance. People shout, and noise fills the alleyway, but my thumping heart blocks it out. My fingers curl into fists, wanting to march over and ease River's pain. She doesn't have to shout or scream or even be conscious for me to see the bleeding wounds marking up her face.

Kieran's fingers curl again, watching with an intense glare when the ambulance takes off with none of us inside. When she wakes up from the slumber some asshole put her into, she'll be alone in the hospital, wondering what the hell happened and why she's there, of all places. And then to realize someone knocked her around and tried to get into her fucking panties when she wasn't awake. FUCK! Every molecule in my body wants to hitch a ride with the ambulance, hold her hand, and fucking comfort her until she wakes up in my arms.

Huffing several breaths to calm myself down, I eye Van, who's suspect as fuck. Not for a second do I believe that stalking mother fucker had nothing to do with this. He was here. But why? All night I watched the crowd for signs of that slimy snake and came up empty-handed. He's there every fucking night. So, what was that dickhead up to? And why did he show up in the same place River was hurt? Yeah, this place stinks of his doing, and I'm going to find out every fucking thing I can.

"Get on the ground," the same officer repeats with patience, eyeing Kieran with a commanding eye.

From here, I can tell he doesn't want to throw Kieran down to the ground himself, but whatever Van told them has him on edge. His fingers squeeze his gun at his hip again, anxious to pull it out and light my brother up. But he holds back, possibly knowing who we belong to–Nigel Montgomery. Sure, to the naked eye, my stupid brother pounced on Van unprovoked. In their eyes only. To me, my brother pounced on him to get even for fucking with River for so damn long. And he deserved every hit to the face. Plus, so much fucking more. No matter the consequences, I'll sort this out entire fucking situation.

"Do what they fucking say. We don't need Nigel finding out about your fuck up!" I growl, throwing Kieran into the wall and watching helplessly as they cuff his hands behind his back, hauling him between two police officers.

"You see anything?" Another officer approaches with apprehension, staring between me and Callum and Rad, who huddle close with fear crossing their faces.

"No. Where are they taking her?" Rad rasps with tears streaming down his pale cheeks. "She's our girlfriend. We had just walked out here when we saw the lights. Her friend said she had just taken out the trash." He shakes his head, sniffling.

"We didn't see anything. As my friend said, we ran out here when we saw the lights. We were playing in Dead End for over an hour," I say with a sharp nod, refusing to admit anything about my stupid brother and his moronic anger issues.

"And your friend?" the officer asks, pointing to Kieran, who begrudgingly lowers his head and climbs into the back of the cop's car without fanfare.

I scrub a hand down my face. "An overprotective boyfriend with a chip on his damn shoulder," I gripe, trying as best as I can to say my words carefully. The last thing I need to do is implicate that asshole into anything further.

The cop nods, turning and radioing the information we relayed, and begins writing our names and checking out our fists for confirmation we had no part in the attack. After he's done a thorough job of talking to us and gathering information, he finally cracks where they're taking River.

"They're taking her to Central Memorial Hospital," he says as he shoves his notebook into his pocket.

"Any news on her condition?" I ask, but he shakes his head with regret brimming in his eyes.

"Alive and unconscious. That's all I can say," the cop says, waltzing away from us and observing the scene with the three other officers standing in a semi-circle around the blood-soaked pavement, talking in low tones.

"Take me to the hospital with you," Ode says, popping out of nowhere with tears flowing from her eyes. "TAKE ME!" she shouts through her emotions, earning a side hug from Rad. He whispers something in her ear, and her shoulders sag.

"Let's go," I grumble with a sigh, worrying about the girl floating in an ambulance toward the hospital and the man in the back of a cop car for finally beating the tar out of Van—the stupid idiot who can't seem to let go.

"You two go to the damn hospital and monitor River. I have to bail out my stupid brother," I say through gritted teeth. "Take me home first? Gotta grab the damn Tahoe."

"Take some of our saved band money if you have to," Rad says, leading Ode into the backseat of the Tahoe and shutting the door. "It's in the house." I nod, remembering the place we hide all our savings.

"Yeah," I gripe, jumping into the passenger's seat. "I'll do that."

The entire ride home, listening to Ode cry in the backseat, the scene plays over and over in my head. We went from zero to a million in five seconds flat. Now, I have a brother who sits in jail. Another brother who won't listen to our words without music in his ears and tears in his eyes. Another brother who, as we speak, cries hysterically as he steers the car along the road, heading to the hospital. And at the center of it all, a broken girl who they've all fallen head over heels in love with—me included.

Fuck.

ASHER

Today has been a shit show of epic proportions on so many levels. The weight of everything that's happened in the span of twenty-four hours barrels down on me, sitting heavily on my chest and shoulders. Leaning back, I rest my head against the cold, textured wall, drawing in air. It's all I can do to ground myself and stay in the moment. If I don't, her lifeless body, covered in blood spatters, comes back to mind and tortures me all over again.

Seeing River bruised up like that—has me twisted into knots and so goddamn conflicted. Half of me wants to scoop her up, fix her, and soothe her discomfort. The other half of me wants to keep her at arm's length to protect the band in case it all goes sideways like today. One horrific injury has them clawing at the walls like feral animals.

The large waiting room in the emergency department of Central Memorial Hospital is stifling. Rogue coughs from others waiting float through the air, mixed with whimpers and complaints. Jesus. My skin crawls with the onslaught of germs crawling all over the place. I'd rather lick the urinal at Dead End than sit in this germ-infested cesspool.

Fuck. I need fresh air. But I can't leave Kieran. He's on the brink of losing his mind, and I need to catch him when he falls. As cliche as it sounds, I'll always catch my brother when he falls with open arms—any of them. They're my family, and I'd give my life for them and risk it all.

My eyes narrow when police officers waltz into the emergency department with their heads held high, flashing their badges. My eyes follow their every move, wondering what they're doing. If they're here to interrogate River, they have another thing coming.

"We got a call on a stabbing victim," one of them says in a low voice, but it carries through the room.

The nurse behind the desk clicks her nails against the keyboard of her computer and nods.

"Oh, yes. The patient is in room 30B, but be advised, he's very combative. It's superficial, but whoever did it to him accomplished whatever they needed." Her voice trails off when she leads the officers down the long hallway and beeps them into the official emergency department.

I rub my chin, watching through the doors for any sign of River. Secretly, I hope she comes marching through those doors with a grin, telling us it was all a joke, and we can all go home. It's wishful thinking on my part to hope she wasn't injured so badly. So, I'll support the band and make sure my Little Brat pulls through.

By the time Kieran and I show up to the waiting room, Ode has gone back with River, apparently claiming she was her sister. Leaving us out here waiting and waiting with no updates, which is all fine and dandy if Kieran, Rad, and Callum weren't falling apart at the fucking seams.

Kieran leans his elbows on his knees, cradling his face in his hands, constantly fidgeting. He hasn't uttered a word since we left the police station. And I haven't either.

All this consuming rage builds inside me like a fucking storm. Here I am, deathly afraid Kieran's about to burst when I'm the one on edge. Someone put their fucking hands on my Little Brat for no good reason, and someone is going to die with my hands wrapped around their throat.

Van may have been present after the fact, bent over her after the assault, but I have doubts it was him in the back of my mind. Was he involved? Possibly. Maybe? Who the hell knows?

Speaking of... My eyes narrow into slits when I gaze at the suspect sitting as far as humanly possible from Kieran, holding an ice pack on his face with a grimace. Every few seconds, his eyes stray this way with fear tinting them.

Good.

He should be fucking afraid of what Kieran will do if he keeps sniffing around what he's marked as his. Van had his chance, and he blew it. It's pathetic as fuck when grown men can't take no for an answer.

Time and time again, River has blown him off, telling him no. So, why he's here, sitting in the waiting room, still blows my fucking mind. The audacity this asshole has to cling on like a leech dangling from my ass cheek baffles my too-tired brain.

I close my eyes and heave a breath. This has been the longest night and earliest morning yet, but there's still more to come. Kieran and I may be over eighteen and adults, but we didn't check in or make it home last night. Sure, Nigel allows—and I use that word loosely—us to play gigs until three a.m., staying out to fulfill our hobby. But make no mistake, there will be hell to pay when we finally crawl home.

Nigel: We'll have a very long discussion when you two get home.

I roll my lips together, reading the text message again and again. He sent it six hours ago when I walked Kieran from the police station. My stomach rolls and knots all at once. Kieran and I are up shit creek without a paddle the moment we walk through the threshold of our front door.

"I'm here for Kieran Knight," I say with no emotion, grinding my damn teeth at the plated window protecting the front desk.

The woman behind it peers up, doing a once over, and nods. "Ah, yes," she mumbles, typing a few things into the computer. "You're in luck. He should be right out." She nods toward a set of double doors secured by a lock mechanism.

"Out?" I question with skepticism. I didn't expect this fight to be easy. Hell, I half expected Kieran to rot away for a few days until the judge came in and charged him with assault and set his damn bond.

"Yes, Mr. Montgomery," she says with a knowing look. My stomach sinks into my ass at the sound of my name, meaning only one thing. "It seems you have friends in high places." My fucking father. He always gets his way. Wonderful.

I hope Kieran likes the backyard because that's where we'll spend an eternity buried under the dirt with the worms and bugs.

"Mm, thanks," I mutter, curling my fists at my side, waiting on the edge of my seat until my stupid brother smacks through the doors with a growl. He doesn't utter a word when he marches out the front door with me on his tail and still doesn't when we pull into the hospital parking lot.

"Why the fuck is he sitting there?"

Great. After six hours of silent brooding, here comes the bull at a full charge. I take a breath, preparing for the utter shit show that's inevitably about to go down.

"He's just fucking staring at us like he didn't do this." Kieran narrows his eyes again and clenches his fingers into fists around the ice, numbing his pain.

"Maybe he didn't," I remark quietly, earning the full brunt of Kieran's ire.

"You don't think he did? He was right fucking there, Asher!" he hisses so loudly that his voice bounces off the tall ceilings. "He did it! And I'm going to bury him for it." A tick forms in his jaw when he whips his head, holding Van's gaze.

Yup. Shit show.

I shrug, closing my eyes. "Don't jump to so many conclusions," I say through a yawn, sinking further into my chair. Maybe if I fall asleep, this will all be a distant dream.

"You're just...you're just going to let him get away with it?" Kieran growls, I'm sure, throwing spittle everywhere with each word.

I sigh. "You've already been arrested once and released. Do you want to chance it again? It's called silent planning, Kieran," I mutter through the thick fog clouding my mind. If I don't get some sleep soon, my head will explode from the headache working its way up my neck and into the back of my skull. "Maybe you should learn the skill." He huffs at me, throwing himself back into the chair.

"Asher, man." I sigh again, peeking an eye open, revealing Rad's concerned and fallen expression. It twists, contorting his face into an anguish-filled feature. "You gotta do something. He won't take them out. He's losing his shit. I don't know what to do. He hasn't been this bad since-since, Jenny," Rad murmurs the last part, hiccuping at the thought of Callum's little sister and everything he went through concerning the plane crash. "He's in love with her, man. We gotta..."

Holding up a hand, I stop him in his tracks. The sad truth is they're all in love with her. They may not admit it yet, but they're head over heels, stupidly in love, leading us down dangerous roads of sabotage. I won't let my best friend suffer in silence by drowning out the world and ignoring everyone around him.

Climbing to my feet, I make my way to Callum's silent bubble with purpose. His head rests back against the wall with his eyes closed and his hands buried deep in his pockets, slouching in his chair.

Settling beside him, I lightly nudge him with my shoulder until he peeks an eye open. An array of emotions filter through his gray eyes when his broken gaze meets mine. A tiny twitch forms at the edge of his lip, letting me know the man doesn't want to speak about the situation. He'd rather lose himself in the loud music thumping through his earbuds than face reality. I tap my ear until he huffs, yanking out his earbud.

"What's up?" he murmurs in a soft voice, thick with emotions. His eyes drop to the ground, taking in the disgusting tile pattern.

"I should ask you the same. What's going through your mind, Callum?"

He meets my eye at the sound of his name, quickly locking away any emotions he feels. Usually, Callum is an easy book to read. For me, anyway. Every emotion inside him slides across his face like an open book. Today he's a blank canvas, not giving any hints as to why he's isolated himself. Given the circumstances, I understand why.

"It's all I see," he mutters, fidgeting with his earbuds between his fingers.

"What is?"

Even though I know the answer, I still ask. It's the only way to break Callum out of his rut, by forcing him to utter the dreaded words. He's not alone, though. The second my eyes fall shut, she's all I see. All broken, bruised, bloodied, lying on the cold, dark pavement forever haunts my nightmares. But for him, he'll literally never forget.

He shakes his head, and his face contorts into deep hurt. "Her just lying there," he whispers as tears fall down his cheeks. "I can't get that image out of here," he cries out, thumping his fist into his head several times. "I can't make it stop, Asher." My heart fucking breaks for my friend, shattering into pieces at the emotions rolling through him.

"Think of happier times, man," I murmur, rubbing a hand down his back and soothing his pain. "Think of the time we had on the Ferris wheel. Or the amazing show she helped us put on last night. Think of anything else." Images of River's broad smile and snarky attitude come to mind, and my shoulders sag at the memories in tune with his.

"Those were good times," he whispers with a nod. The more I rub his back, the calmer he becomes, and soon, all his anxiety leaves. Sure, the image will live inside him forever. There's nothing I can do about that. But for now, I can ease his worries.

"Yeah, because you finally got your dick sucked by a gorgeous chick," Rad quips, coming to rest beside him. "Let those be the images you think about forever. You gotta block that depressing shit out."

"I'm going to fucking kill him," Kieran growls, jumping to his feet.

Under normal circumstances, I'd tell his ass to sit down and take a chill pill. But Kieran's emotions are in the driver's seat, controlling his actions. There's no stopping him from doing stupid shit like marching toward Van like he's about to chew him up and spit him out. Only this time, Kieran won't leave any bones behind.

"Fuck sake," I grumble, jumping up to catch him by the scruff of his shirt and haul him back. "We're in public. Unless you want Nigel to beat your ass even worse," I mumble the last part, earning a scowl. "I'll make him leave," I say, silently pleading with the idiot to sit down.

"Fine. I can't look at his stupid face anymore," he grumbles, turning on his toes and plopping back down in the chair with a grunt. Running a hand over his face, he closes his eyes and hopefully counts to ten.

I shove my hands in my pockets and walk toward Van, sitting a good thirty feet away with an ice pack resting against his swollen face. If one good thing came out of this situation, it's the bruising on Van's pathetic face.

"My suggestion would be to leave," I say, sitting beside him. "Unless you want my idiot brother to rip your face off. Again," I huff, rolling my eyes. "Look at him; he wants to march over and put his fist through your teeth." A chuckle works its way up my throat when Van stiffens, clearly threatened by the big dummy death-glaring in his direction.

That's right, Van. Be deeply afraid of him. He's had years and years of pent-up aggression. And he'd be excited to use it on you.

"I'm waiting to hear how she's doing," Van stubbornly grumbles, crossing his arms over his chest.

"I'm curious," I say, slumping down into the seat. Running my fingertips along my chin, I pop my eyebrow when I pique his interest. "How would Whitley feel about you being here, waiting for River to get released?"

"What the hell does it matter to you, man?" he asks through gritted teeth. "Why're you so damn hellbent on telling her anything? She has nothing to do with any of this. River is my...."

"I'm just saying," I say, waving a hand lazily. "One of these days, your fiance will catch on." I shrug, climbing to my feet and letting my implication hit its mark. "Besides, I can text you when she gets out and is healthy."

"You would, wouldn't you?" he growls, shifting the ice on his face to scowl at me. "You'd really send that email and let her know..." He swallows hard, shaking his head.

"What? That you used to fuck River behind her back at the record store? Or that you're stalking her now? Or that you really had something to do with all this?" I wave a finger, smirking when he gets paler and paler with every word I speak, eventually turning green.

There's plenty I can do. Now or later, that's your choice," I say with a shrug, waltzing back toward Kieran and plopping down next to him. He raises a brow at me, practically begging with his eyes about what I said.

Satisfaction spears through me when Van grabs his shit and stomps out of the emergency department. Seconds later, his engine roars to life, reverberating through the lofty room. Finally, I settle back in my chair, letting my eyes fall shut. Maybe now I can get some rest. All the children are snug in their chairs without worry.

"Finally," Kieran shouts, jumping to his feet.

My damn body bounces out of the chair on instinct with a pounding heart. Swallowing hard, I blow out a breath as Ode emerges from behind the locked ER doors.

"Nice to see you, too," Ode quips with a tired groan. Bags sit under her red, puffy eyes, letting me know she hasn't slept a wink.

"How is she?" Rad asks, out of breath, rushing Ode with urgency, furrowing his brows.

Ode sighs, running her fingers over her forehead. "She's finally awake and talking to the doctors and cops. It's fuzzy for her, but she's doing okay. They're going to run tests and shit. Doc thinks she has a concussion and abrasions from the attack. So, she's fortunate it wasn't worse. But we'll see after the MRI."

"Jesus-Jesus," Callum mutters with a quivering chin, pulling his fist to his mouth.

"She's a tough cookie," Ode says, clapping him on the shoulder and gently squeezing. "Believe me, and she's already bossing around the doctors and demanding to leave. Don't worry too much about her, okay? I'd say you should probably go, but then I'd probably be talking to brick walls," she huffs.

"Yeah, we're not going anywhere until I know my pretty girl is feeling okay."

"Can we see her?" Kieran asks with hope.

Ode wrinkles her nose. "I think like one at a friggin time. Whoa, dude!" she hisses, turning on her toes when Kieran pushes past without care and marches back into the ER, disappearing behind the doors.

I roll my eyes. "Friggin idiot," I mumble through a tired sigh.

"I'm next," Rad says, rubbing his hands together. "My pretty girl needs a nice massage and a dose of penis-cyclin."

"You'll only hurt her," Callum grumbles, slapping him on the back of his head. "By the way," Ode says with furrowed brows. "Did you guys know that Bradley from high school came in with a stab wound?"

"He what?" Rad yelps, and his body stiffens, fury taking over his face.

Yeah, there's something up with him and Bradley. Every time that fucker enters a room, he tenses. And those cops before, they were here for him. Who the hell finally stabbed that dick? My entire body locks up, drowning out the noises around me.

Bradley Bradford is officially on my shit list. A stab wound? That's awfully fucking coincidental. Images of River's fingers dripping with blood run through my mind, and before I know what I'm doing, I'm marching down the hallway without a clue as to where I'm going. Kieran grumbles something behind a curtain before I throw it open, revealing River nestled against his chest. His arms lock around her protectively, gently running his fingers through her long, ratted strands.

Looking around, I pull the curtain back behind me, huffing when the rest of the idiots pile into the room and hover around a broken-looking River. Tears threaten to burn the back of my eyes as I take her in, noting the black and blue bruises lining her face. The three of us stand there with gaping mouths as she untucks herself from Kieran's grasp and refuses to look in our direction. Keeping her eye downcast, she summons Ode to the edge of the bed.

"Leave," River rasps, taking Ode's shaking hand. "Get some sleep, please." Exhaustion pulls at her tiny voice, tugging at my fucking black heartstrings. She sounds like she's fighting a battle she won't win—like she's already given in to the pain, and defeat has taken over. But that's not the River I know. The girl I know fights tooth and nail through anything and with anybody. Fuck.

Ode's face falls, but she squeezes River's hand. "Fine, I'll leave y'all to it. Bitch, I love you. But don't you ever pull that shit again." Leaning down, she plants a soft kiss on River's cheek, lingering long enough to whisper something, and pulls back with a stern look. "I'll check in with your momma, too. And you four," she says with a demanding tone, putting a hand on her hip. "You fuck with River. You fuck with me. Got it?"

We all nod in unison. Not daring to toe an inch out of line while she death glares at us with mama bear vibes emanating from her. The fierce expression doesn't leave until we're protectively cupping our balls and shivering from her threat, and with one last look, she waves, walking out the door with apprehension.

Once Ode clears the room, Rad wraps his arms around River, smothering her with light kisses.

"I'm fine," she groans, trying to weakly shove him off.

"No, Pretty Girl. You're not," he murmurs lovingly, moving a piece of her hair out of her face. "Bradley did this, didn't he? Did he...?"

River visibly cringes at his words, recoiling into Kieran's chest and hiding her face from us. The world blurs around me, mixing into a multitude of colors, and my heart fucking drops out of my fucking body. Ice runs through my veins, raising the tiny hairs on the back of my neck. Grabbing my skull with force, I massage my temples until the pain subsides into a dull ache. It all makes fucking sense now. Every goddamn piece of the puzzle clicks into place, and murder vibrates through me.

"You stabbed him?" I blurt breathlessly as piles of information storm through my mind like wildfire blowing through. "He did it?" I accuse now, narrowing my eyes and taking in her reaction.

"You what?" Kieran asks in a deadly voice, looking down at her with fear twisting his expression. His eyes widen, and he tugs her impossibly closer, with emotions pulling him in every direction. By the time we make it home, he will be so rung out. "He what?" he murmurs in disbelief.

River hides her face in his chest, taking several deep breaths before she collects herself and speaks.

"Please, let it go," she murmurs in a broken voice. "Please, just let go. I don't want to talk about it right now." No. It seems she doesn't want to talk about it ever again. So, it's time to force the words from her tongue so we can cut Bradley open and feed him to the vultures.

"River," I bark, marching to her side. Leaning over Kieran, I gently grab her chin and force her to stare at me. So many emotions rest in her moss-green eyes. It's hard to tell how she's feeling. Fear. Anguish. Pain. Resentment. It's all those wrapped into one. "He'll get what's coming to him, Little Brat. Don't even worry about it," I promise through a growl, envisioning his death by my hands.

"Don't worry about it?" she whispers as fat tears drop onto her cheeks, sending searing pain through my chest at the sight of her pain. "I have to worry about it. I have to make sure he gets punished for his crimes! He got away with it once, and I won't stand back and let him harm any more women." Her body trembles in Kieran's embrace, and the room falls silent.

I don't miss her words. Or how she said them. All the answers reside there, and understanding pushes through me. River was the girl Bradley bragged about for months on end. Only, she wasn't a willing participant like he eluded her to be.

"Got away with it once?" Kieran asks, furrowing his brow. "What?" River's face pales when the realization hits Kieran hard, and a gasp forces its way through his parted lips. "No," he murmurs, running a thumb gently across her cheeks and jolts, eyes bulging. I swear he stops breathing, and his head shakes in denial. "The fucking beating we gave him over the girl you found? No!" His fingers flex, engorging the veins lining his forearms.

Grabbing his arm, River shakes her head with a pained expression. "It was a long time ago. I don't want to talk about it. I just want to move forward. I want Bradley to get what's coming to him."

She rolls her lips together, sadness glazing over her eyes. Something about the situation sends shame through her; it's even more apparent when she closes her eyes. Kieran swallows hard, rubbing the back of his neck. Anguish takes over his expression when he kisses her cheek, murmuring words I can't hear.

"More than a stabbing, Little Brat?" I quip, finally earning a soft smile that doesn't quite reach her eyes.

"Jail time. Anything to make sure he doesn't hurt anyone else," she whispers in complete and utter defeat—something I've never seen from her.

Sitting back, River stays snuggled in Kieran's arms, soaking up his support. "We'll get you a wonderful lawyer. We'll help with whatever you need," Kieran promises, kissing her forehead with a feather-light kiss.

"Everything we have, we'll give you," Callum promises, leaning over to kiss her head.

"I'll bury him in acid and laugh as his bones disintegrate," Rad mumbles, kissing her temple.

A million thoughts rush through me when we leave River lying in the hospital. After sitting there all day and through nine p.m., they kicked us out, stating they admitted her until they got her results back. Our visit was over, but our night had only just begun.

Tension rises in my chest when we pull into the house's driveway, looming in front of us.

"It was nice knowing you," Kieran mumbles, hanging his head with a heavy sigh.

"I can't believe you got arrested," I say, sitting back in my seat and huffing a breath.

Over her—the girl we need in our corner. Over the entire situation—is what I want to say. Every inch of Kieran vibrates with a restless rage begging to come back out. So, I zip my lips and inspect the situation one more time. Another time and place, I'd let him pummel Van into oblivion. Not now. Not on the heels of his arrest.

Getting arrested is the least of our worries at the moment. Kieran didn't just get himself thrown into jail; he got the both of us thrown into the lion's den, covered in blood and defenseless. Now it's time to face the devil himself.

Raising a brow, I stare at the dark, empty office window my father always peers out of and note the darkened room and closed blinds. In fact, the entire house swims in darkness, ready to swallow us whole. Somewhere in the depths of hell, our demon waits to attack us when we least expect it.

"Where is he?" I murmur, peering at every window, half expecting the damn boogeyman to pop out and attack.

My skin tingles in anticipation of the night ahead. We've been out for twenty-four hours and haven't reached out. We may be twenty-one and old enough to hold our own, but in his eyes, we are children he's successfully controlled.

"I don't care as long as he's not lying in wait, ready to attack us," Kieran says, frowning up at the window when we exit the car. "Again," he murmurs, shivering at the memory of Nigel popping out and taking us by surprise. He lives to make our lives miserable.

Looking around, I take stock of everything around us. Empty driveway. Empty street. The only logical explanation is his vehicle is in the garage, or he's not here. I peek in the garage window, only to find Gloria's BMW. Relief slams into me, and for the first time today, I feel like I can breathe, and the heavy pressure lifts. Not that my father won't punish us when he returns, but we have a reprieve from his cruelty. For now, at least. That's all I can ask for after a long day of waiting.

"He's not here," I rejoice confidently, leading the way and quietly entering through the front door. Silence clings to every inch of the space, and peace washes over me for once in my damn life.

"Maybe we got away with it," Kieran says with false hope.

"Don't hold your breath. Now, I'm going to bed," I say, not waiting for his response, and quietly enter my bedroom at the top of the stairs.

Darkness greets me like an old friend, enveloping me in a warm hug. Once again, something eerie crashes over me, and my hairs stand on end. A lone figure hovers in the shadows, looking out my window.

"It's that girl, isn't it?" Gloria asks in a haughty tone, turning toward me. No expression breaks through the darkness concealing her face. "That bitch from Central City? The same one Kieran obsessed over as a kid." She scoffs at that, coming toward me. "My advice?"

"Sure," I say, committing to a non-answer with a shrug.

"Leave her as far behind as possible. Those Central girls will only bring you one of two things: disease or pregnancy," she hisses in disgust. "She'll only bring you boys down. You're destined for greatness."

"Greatness, huh?" I rub my chin, milling over her words.

A normal child would preen under her confidence and praise with a grin. But I refuse. Gloria may seem like she's looking out for our best interest, but by the devious gleam in her eyes, she's up to something. I'm not sure what. What could she gain from this conversation?

"You boys have talent, and the word on the street is you are applying to a big competition?" She raises a brow, stepping more into the light of the moon beaming through the window panes. "Something in, say... California?"

I raise a brow, my heart secretly thumping against my ribs. If it's out in the open that we may go to California, my father might screw it all up by lifting his finger. It's bad enough we're financially strapped to him with our cars and phones, but he could take them away with the snap of his fingers. There's nothing more heart-stopping than realizing we're dangling a treat in front of his face to hurt us with more.

"I can make sure he doesn't have a clue," she sniffs, sticking her nose in the air.

"And what do you want in return, Gloria? You can't be doing this out of the kindness of your heart. So, tell me what you're willing to do and what you want in return." I lift a brow when her shoulders push back, and she turns on the lamp next to my bed, revealing the black and blue bruises lining her face. I'd gasp if I were surprised by the marks on her body, but I'm not. Figures Nigel would work out his frustrations on her.

"I'm your reminder, Asher," she says, cringing when she runs a finger down her bruised cheek. "When you're not here, he does this. And I'm tired of being a punching bag." She waves a hand, showing the damage on her face and further down her body.

"Fair enough," I say, looking her up and down as she clings to the silk robe encasing her body.

"You want the money to go? You want the car to get you there without issues? Do you want your father not to know anything about it? I can help, but I have stipulations," she says, straightening more with a cringe.

"Enlighten me, Gloria. How would my father not know about the missing money or the Tahoe? How do you intend to get away with any of that when you're just as stuck? Hmm?" I raise a brow, trying to keep the condescending tone from leaking through. If I remain pessimistic about the situation, I can't get my hopes up on making our great escape. Nothing will stop us. Not even Nigel Montgomery.

You know, all I wanted was my bed and a nice long sleep without this bullshit floating around in my mind. A clean cut from my father's grasp is all I've begged for, for years now. But every day gets worse and worse, and his control tightens on our reigns. Some would scoff at our age and tell us to leave without notice, but they don't have a fucking clue what this life is like. Having someone hovering above you and micromanaging your every financial move is more complex than they could imagine. Add in fists and shouting matches—yeah, it's heaven. Nigel controls every aspect of our life. So, even at twenty-one, we're stuck in his grasp until we can slowly ease our way out.

For once in Gloria's pathetic life, she looks stricken when she scrunches her bruised nose. "It's my money," she says in a soft voice. "It's all I have, but I could help you get there and set up. Any extras will help."

My brows fly into my hairline, and my lips pop open. Hers? My father doesn't allow us to have our means, keeping us tightly wound around his grubby finger.

"Why?" I ask, crossing my arms. "What's stopping you from taking Camilla and running with what you have?" Leaning against the wooden door frame, I sigh, watching the indecisive cross her face. If she had money, then she could flee without a glance back.

"It has to be you. Once you're out, I can get out," she whispers with glossy eyes. "I have something to take care of before I can leave. Besides, he'd hunt me down and drag me back, kicking and screaming. Think of Camilla. What would he do to her? He'd take custody and bury me so deep in court fees I'd never come up for air. I'd end up like your mother." A cold slap in the face would have been better than hearing my past on her lips. For once, Gloria is right. She'd end up at the wrong end of a needle and buried so deep her secrets would never resurface—like my mother. Longing hits me out of nowhere, but I swallow it down. I don't have the time or energy to relive my tragic past with the cravings for my mother.

"And what's that?" I ask, clearing my throat and shaking away the thoughts in my head.

"Do you want the deal or not?" she huffs with obvious annoyance.

"Maybe," I say with a nonchalant shrug. "If you keep your mouth shut about it."

Gloria's lips thin, and she nods. "I have two stipulations."

Of course, she does; Gloria can't do anything as simple as turning the other cheek when we need her to. Keeping my father's nose out of my business is priority number one. Especially when it concerns the Battle of the Bands—the one thing we need. He gave us one year to sow our wild oats with the damn band, and I'm making the best of it without his interference. There's no stopping us now.

"What are they?" I ask, holding back a yawn.

"When you win the Battle of the Bands, help me leave," she says, looking directly into my eyes.

"If we win. There's a whole competition. It's us against fifteen bands, and it's not a guarantee." I shake my head, running a hand through my hair. "And where'd you like to go, Gloria?" I ask, seriously wondering where this woman would want to go.

"Anywhere but here," she says with a shaky nod. "Far away from him..." She swallows hard at that admission, but good for her. "You'll win. You guys have to win. Second stipulation..."

"Go on," I say, waving a hand.

"The Central Girl stays here," she says, firmly pointing a finger down. "I know you've offered to take her with you, but she belongs where she is. Not out there."

I snort. "Right. Try prying her out of your son's hands." Or mine. She's valuable to us, especially in East Point, California. If she doesn't go, then we might not have a chance at winning. There's no way.... I shake my head, rubbing my chin.

"Think it over, Asher. Watch the way she's wearing each of you down. Soon, she'll split you all up, and Whispered Words won't be a thing anymore. In less than a year, you'll be suited up under your father's thumb. All because you couldn't leave one girl where she belongs. You're going to be famous. Do you want some lost, stray skank following you around?"

Fuck! My eye twitches. Hook. Line. And sinker. An ache forms in my chest as she hits every point of my worries in the head. She raises a brow, reaching for the handle until I grab her wrist.

"How much money are you offering to get us away from here?" I growl through gritted teeth.

She smiles at me like the snake she is, winding her tail around me and squeezing me until I give in to her every whim. "I have five thousand. It's good enough to get you there, help you get established, and then once you win, you'll have so much more than that. Plus, whatever you've been saving over the years."

"Are you spying on us, Gloria? And how do you know what the prize is?" I ask, raising a brow.

"You should be more careful with your internet searches," she says with a cluck of her tongue. "Just think it over. Watch the girl. See how easily she gets what she wants. Central girls are all the same," she says with a shake of her head.

"Like you?" I mutter when she walks out and shuts the door behind her.

RIVER

Every piece of fucking skin attached to my bones pulsates with my heartbeat, burning from the dark bruises dotting my body and face. Flashbacks from my night of terror overwhelm me as I lie awake in the early morning. Bright sunlight beams in from the fucked up curtains I told Rad to secure the night before.

Clamping my aching eyes shut, I try to block out the horrors following my every step. The phantom feel of Bradley's fists driving into my face over and over again sends my heart pounding against my ribs. Oxygen seems to thin, evading my lungs. Warmth presses into each side of me, like most days and nights now, bringing me back from the brink of my waking nightmare.

Squished between Rad and Callum in my bed, their presence doesn't drive the memories of my attack any further away, but they help to keep me grounded here on earth. I would have sent them home the first night and suffered in silence if it wasn't for their insistence. And I'd rather suffer between their bodies than between my cold sheets. Their presence keeps the monster in my mind at bay, but the memory of my attack will live forever.

Groaning, I try flipping to my other side. A giant hand wraps around my waist, holding me down. Even when he's snoring, Rad's handsy as hell and pulling me into him like I'm his precious possession. Next thing I know, he'll have his tongue down my throat while experiencing some sort of sex dream, and then... A flush of warmth spreads straight to my pussy at the thought. Shit. I need to get laid soon. They've each treated me like a little porcelain doll since I came home, and it's driving me bonkers. I may be broken, but I'm damn horny.

The tip of his nose drags across my neck, murmuring sleepy gibberish. The tone of his deep voice sounds so damn happy and raspy. His hands wander across my stomach, peeling up my sleep shirt and rubbing circles across my belly. *Lower. Go lower,* I mentally chant, feeling empty when his hand stills and a snore escapes him. From the moment I got home from the hospital, Rad's been clingier than ever, following my every move and watching me every chance he gets.

"I'll be okay," I murmur, grimacing when I lay in my cold sheets *for the first time since getting home. A headache forms in the back of my skull, pounding until I squeeze my eyes shut.*

"It almost happened again. On my watch, Pretty Girl." Deep anguish leaks into his low voice, and his eyes fill with tears. *"I can't ever let that happen again,"* he mumbles, kissing my cheek and silently promising protection.

With major reluctance, I peel myself away from Rad and climb over Callum, missing their warmth. Silently, I giggle, forcing my hand over my mouth when they scoot together, filling the space. Rad's hand lands on Callum's hip, squeezing until Callum groans, wrinkling his nose. Rad's hand turns circles over Callum's hip until it freezes, and another snore fills the room.

I shake my head, running a hand over my forehead, and wince when the blinding pain hits me again, whitening my vision. It's been a whole week since the attack and five days since they let me out of the hospital. There, they determined my injuries weren't life-threatening, but they wanted to keep me on stronger pain meds through the IV. So, I sat with four vigilant guys, watching my every move.

"Go. Home," I groan when Kieran lays in the hospital bed next to me. *"I'm getting out tomorrow."*

Please let me breathe, you overbearing oaf.

"I'll stay the night, Pretty Girl. Your momma wanted hourly updates!" Rad chirps, sitting on the small couch next to Callum in my *assigned hospital room, staring down at their phones. "Besides, Angel Warrior has a mobile app now. We have plenty to do. Die demon!"* he *hisses, smacking his phone screen with his thumb several times.*

"I got 'em," Callum murmurs, poking his tongue out in *concentration. "Onto the pearly gates."*

"Hells yes, die, you dirty demons! We're headed to Heaven's light. Shit, look. Someone else is here, too." Rad leans in further, *squinting his eyes. "Looks like it's just you, me, and this SGW2100.*

Fighting the good fight. Yessss!" Rad cries out in victory, high-fiving Callum. *"And high five to you, too, internet dude."*

I blow out a breath, blocking out their overjoyous celebration. "Didn't you hear what I said?" I groan, snuggling into Kieran more despite my protests of wanting to be left alone.

I need peace and quiet, something I don't get when they're around. But yet, they're a comfort I can't explain. It's a weird twist of fate to want peace, but they're the peace I need.

Leaning into Kieran, I sigh with exhaustion. *It's only three p.m., but the urge to close my eyes and sleep the day away settles in. Probably thanks to my pain meds.*

"Close your eyes, River Blue. We've got you, baby," Kieran murmurs, kissing my hair with a sigh. "They've taken Bradley to the station. That asshole isn't getting out any time soon." *Finally, that prick is going to pay for his crimes. Knowing my luck, though, they'll come after me for injuring him. Worth it.*

"They kept my knife," I grumble, closing my eyes and relaxing into him more.

"I'll get it back for you, Little Brat. It seems you need to protect yourself more these days. Always looking for trouble." *I don't bother giving him an appropriate answer. I lift my middle finger in the air, earning a scoffed "rude" remark and then a deep, rumbling chuckle.*

Looking at Callum and Rad snuggled together in my bed makes a smile cross my lips. They're so damn cute together, and I can't help but snap a picture for blackmail later. But right now? I need pain meds like my life depends on them. Every step toward the living room jostles my face, and my nerves light up with pain like a damn Christmas tree.

"Hey, Ma," I murmur, heading to the kitchen for a glass of water.

I need pain meds, food, sex, and sleep, in that order.

"Baby," she says softly, slowly climbing to her feet with a grunt, grabbing her walker beside her, and balancing herself. Standing straight, she puts weight on her booted foot, only wincing once.

"You're getting around better," I say with a small smile, gulping water. "But wait. Why're you dressed?" I ask, taking in the loose jeans and white blouse, even her shoe that is slipped on.

She flashes me a beaming smile, slowly sliding forward. "It's a good day. Korrine and I are going out for lunch after she takes me to my doctor's appointment. They're going to see how my ankle is healing, and I think I'm getting a bladder infection," she says, making her way toward me. "How are you feeling? My poor baby," she mumbles, running a trembling finger along my jawline. "I can't believe someone did this to you." She shakes her head. "I always knew Booker's place was dangerous."

I take a deep breath, ignoring her last comment. As a whole, Central City is rough, but we've always made it. Booker's place is definitely not in the best area, but it's what I've had to do to contribute to our financial situation. If it weren't for me, we would have frozen over many winters and not had the extra cash for food.

"I'm okay. It hurts, but I'll survive," I say, blowing her off with a shrug, causing her to drop a hand with a frown.

"You're not working, right?" she asks, raising a brow as a knock sounds on the door, followed by Korrine's voice.

"I'm here for ya, Stella. Car is warming up," she shouts through the door.

"Gimme just a sec!" Ma shouts with a head shake.

I snort into my glass of water, swallowing more and soothing the constant burning in my throat. "No. Booker informed me I'm off for a month until my face heals."

Internally, I groan at the sedentary life I'll be living. Sure, I'll still have schoolwork and online classes to attend, but I'm sitting still without my work. And that's not me. I've held a job since I was fifteen, and to do nothing is messing me up. Fuck. At least I'll have Whispered Words to keep me company and busy with their schedule coming up. They'll press submit on their application tonight, and then we'll cross our fingers.

"Good," she says, kissing my cheek. "Those boys still here?" My face heats when a knowing grin plasters on her face." They're sweet. I like them. But now, I have to go, baby. Be good today, okay?" she mumbles, kissing my cheek.

Opening the door for her, I put my hand on her forearm and help her get over the lip of the door frame.

"Bye! Be good," I say, waving them off as they head to Korrine's bright red Lincoln and take off down the road.

Blowing out a breath, I head back into the bedroom, stopping short.

"What the hell are you doing?" I ask, wrinkling my nose.

I half expected the idiots to be asleep still, not rifling through my panty drawer.

"Listen, Pretty Girl! I woke up stroking Callum's..."

"Rad," Callum hisses, shaking his head with red tinting his cheeks and over the bridge of his nose. He quickly covers his face with his hands and groans.

"His leg! His damn leg! But it should have been you, Pretty Girl. Then I felt hair where hair shouldn't have been, and I freaked. I might have smacked him...."

"In my-my dick." Callum frowns, holding a hand over his boxers. "You punched my dick."

"But it was a sexy dick punch, right?" Rad beams, looking between the two of our fallen faces. "Right. There's no such thing as a sexy dick punch." He shrugs, continuing to paw through my damn panty drawer like it's normal.

"What exactly are you doing?" I ask again, earning a wave in my direction. "The fuck?" I sigh, pinching the bridge of my nose despite the pain.

Humming a wild tune under his breath, he finally finds a tiny pink thong and holds it up in the air in victory.

"Ah, look! Your panties are Simba, Pretty Girl. Welcome to the winning circle of life! You're going to win me a race." He bobs his head, shoving the tiny panties into his pocket, and shuts the drawer with a thud.

Standing before me, Rad buttons the top of his distressed jeans and grins more, taking me in with lustful eyes. I groan, shaking my head, too damn tired to deal with his crazy ass. By the gleaming look on his face and his delicious shirtless chest, I know exactly where he's headed.

"You've got a race?" I surmise, stepping up to Callum, who rests on the edge of my bed in his cute Batman boxers. His golden skin glows in the late morning sun beaming through the opened curtains.

"Your-your pills," he says, opening his hand and revealing two tiny pills. One from pain and one a preventative antibiotic in case of infection.

"Thank you." Throwing my head back, I wash the pills with the rest of the cold water and hum as they go down my throat. In thirty minutes or less, the pain will evaporate, and I'll be free for another four hours.

"Yes, Pretty Girl! It's a huge race. Some fools from up north are coming down and entering the race. Can you believe it? Someone thinks they can beat the speedy Rad," he scoffs, rolling his eyes and thumping his chest. "But I'm the best, baby! No losing for me. And now that I have your pretty girl panties in my pocket, I'm sure going to cross that finish line a thousand dollars richer." He nods a few times, so damn sure of himself.

"The horror," I mumble, groaning when I climb back into bed and cover my face with my hands. I don't want to see the sun or the outside for another five days.

Rad huffs and heavy footsteps march toward the bed with intent.

"Pretty Girl, you can't just lay in bed for the next month. You have to get up and do things," Rad mumbles, kneeling at the side of the bed. "Don't waste away," he mumbles, kissing my cheek when I sigh. "Come play with me?" he asks with a hopeful expression, giving me his best puppy dog eyes and puffing out his lip.

"Not today," I whisper, leaning into his fingers as they stroke through my hair and disappointment pulls at his face.

The fact is, I'd rather hide away in my damn apartment than show my broken face to the world. Not until it heals. The moment they showed up and barged into my hospital room, I wanted to hide and not let them see me. Somehow, they've peeled back every layer protecting me, getting right down to my vulnerabilities. They see the real me hiding behind my snark and knife—the real River. A cold sweat covers my skin at the realization, and I blow out a breath.

"I-I know," Callum says, scooping me into the side of his body, infecting me with his warmth. Snuggling deeper into him, I sigh, basking in his comfort and letting everything else disappear.

"Kieran and Asher will be off house arrest soon," Rad says with a determined look, clenching his fist.

"Why haven't they ever moved in with you?" I ask, peeking an eye open, feeling something open up in the pit of my stomach.

They both avoid my eyes, staring at the comforter, the floor, and each other's eyes with an intense stare. Shaking their heads in unison, they blow it off. But I know something is up with Asher's dad. I remember him from years ago. The man who marched through the complex in a tight suit, sticking his nose in the air. Once he made it to Gloria's apartment, he'd promptly kicked Kieran out, sometimes without shoes. Then, we'd meet on the hill and bask in each other's company.

"Their-their father's the biggest dick around," Callum mutters, burying his nose in my neck and hiding the guilt crossing his face.

"They'll be out tomorrow. Thank God. One bark from Asher, and you'll be out of bed before he can slap you with his dick."

I wrinkle my nose. "They're twenty-one...why're they still listening to him? Like they're grounded? That's stupid." Swallowing hard, I wonder how hard life is for them. If they can't leave, he has some sort of hold on the boys, keeping them there. But how? And why?

Rad's lips turn down, and his face softens. "I know, Pretty Girl. It's hard to understand. Believe me. We've tried to get them to move in and say screw school and go all in for the band...." He shakes his head, running a hand through his unruly mullet. "They just can't, babe. They...he's...."

"He's holding something over them and-and, I don't know what he does to them, but I don't think it's good. Not with Nigel Montgomery hanging around," Callum mumbles with sadness, tinting his tone.

"Does he?" I ask, swallowing my words before they can even leave my tongue.

"They don't say," Rad says, picking at the comforter and scrunching his face. "But we do what we can. However we know how," he mumbles, swallowing thickly.

"Okay," I whisper, unconvinced of their words. Someone has to be able to get them out if they're in a bad situation.

Clearing his throat, Rad straightens up and takes my hands. "Well, Pretty Girl. You're staying here with Callum today. Make sure you corrupt him a little," Rad says with a wink, kissing my cheek one last time before jumping to his feet.

"No shirt?" I ask when he pulls his sneakers on and shrugs off my comment.

"No shirt, panties in my pocket. This is all I need for good luck," Rad says, jumping to his feet. "I'll see you later!"

And with that, Rad marches out the sliding glass door toward the parking lot. A loud rumble sounds as his dirt bike sparks to life and reverberates through the walls, making my brows dip. Did he seriously bring that here and leave it outside? He's lucky the thing is still there.

"Looks like it's just me and you, hot stuff," I mumble, turning in his arms to look up at his beautiful face.

His gray eyes cloud over with some emotion when his hand brushes back the hair from my face and tucks it behind my ears.

"Looks-looks like it," he breathes, roaming his eyes down the dark bruises on my cheeks. "How's it feeling now, Little Star?"

The first night after my attack, Callum pulled into himself more, relying on his earbuds to guide him through the trauma. My heart broke for him when he broke down with tears in his eyes, telling me he could barely look at me.

"It's not-not because of your looks," he sniffles, wiping away the tears on his cheeks. "I just... I can't look at you and see the mess he left-left after hurting you so badly. If I have to remember those bruises for the rest of my life, I'll hunt him down and kill-kill him," he breathlessly proclaims, growing increasingly agitated by the second.

Gripping his hand tightly, I lean my head on his shoulder, keeping my eyes down. "I know," I mutter, emotions digging their dirty claws into my throat. "I'm sor-"

"Don't you dare," he hisses, pushing his fingers through my hair and bringing his face to mine. Stormy gray eyes blaze into mine, and he shakes his head, lightly pressing his lips into mine. "Don't ever be sorry, Little Star. Not now. Not ever."

As the bruises darkened and then moved into the healing stage, he managed to look at me for more than a split second. I don't blame him for his caution. Callum has to take care of his needs in any way he knows, and I respect that.

Placing my hand on his, I intertwine our fingers together. "So much better now. I think the medicine is finally kicking in," I hum, finally feeling the relief run through my veins and take away the bits of pain left over. Thank God for pain meds, or I'd have rolled over and died from the pounding taking over my nerves.

"Good," he whispers, examining me again until his eyes fall to my lips. "Can I kiss you, Little Star? I've been aching to put my lips on yours," he whispers an inch from my lips.

I nod, sighing into the soft kiss. Whenever his lips touch mine, it's like coming home, and the sun shines through, warming my entire being. Bravely, his tongue brushes along the seam of my lips, begging for entry with a small, desperate moan.

Our tongues twist together in a slow dance, tasting each other and taking our time. Callum molds his body to mine, becoming more frantic when his fingers clasp my hair, forcing my lips harder against his with urgency.

Pain spreads through my face from my injuries, but I don't dare stop him when he's gracefully taking what he wants for the first time in his life. It feels too damn good to stop, and I want this. I want to give Callum the damn world.

A deep groan vibrates through his chest when his trembling fingers clasp around my breast and squeezes tight through my long shirt.

"Do what you want to," I murmur against his lips when he kisses down my neck, softly avoiding the bruises and wounds.

Sucking my skin between his teeth, he leaves his marks behind, stoking the fire brewing under my skin. My back arches, pressing my breasts into his hand, and I moan when he tweaks my nipple between his fingers. My pussy suddenly flutters, begging for him—all of him.

"Finger me, Callum," I breathe with desperation, arching my back and begging him to do me in when his hand slowly moves south. "I need you," I gasp out when he rolls his hardness into me, pushing it right into my aching center.

"I-I—" His breath shudders when I take his wrist and force his fingers on my upper thigh, letting him rest until he's ready to go up to my weeping pussy, begging for his long fingers to plunge in and make me cum.

His warm breaths blow across my hair, picking up speed. His hardness presses through his boxers, poking me in the belly and twitching against me.

"Just like that," I gasp, guiding his fingers in tiny circles over my aching clit. "Tiny-tiny circles," I moan, bringing his lips back down to mine with desperation, thrusting his tongue into my mouth and confidently overtaking every inch of me.

"And-and this?" he whispers with uncertainty, furrowing his brows.

"God, yes!" I shout when his fingers tentatively slip inside me.

Callum's gaze spears through me, taking in every facial twitch and moan. Slowly, he glides them in and out, taking his time and savoring every moment.

I nod with encouragement, biting my bottom lip, trying to keep my moans at bay. Silent screams force my mouth wide open, and my back bows when he scissors his fingers, hitting all the right spots inside me. Bright lights blossom behind my eyelids, with my orgasm on the brink of exploding through.

"Fuck yes, Callum," I cry when stars burst behind my eyes, and my pussy clamps down on his fingers, holding him there. My hips roll with tiny thrusts, begging for more as my orgasm slowly ebbs away, leaving every inch of my flesh tingling with pleasure.

My eyes pop open when Callum shifts beside me. His dilated eyes, thick with lust, meet mine. Heavy pants heave his glistening chest, vibrating with moans when he pulls his fingers out. I cannot look away when he brings them to his mouth and thoroughly licks them clean with a loud, pussy-fluttering groan, satisfied with the taste.

With trepidation and shaking limbs, Callum cradles the back of my head, turning me to my back with such devotion I nearly burst into tears. The moment the weight of his body presses down on me, hazy memories resurface from the brutal attack I endured at the hands of some grabby asshole. Clamping my eyes shut, I take a deep breath as he settles his chest against mine.

"Little Star," he whispers with urgency, nudging his nose against mine. "Tell me you're okay. I can..." he trails off when my fingers dig into his shoulders, holding him there and not letting him go.

The warmth of his skin grounds me back to the moment, zapping me from the alleyway my mind drifted to. It's bad enough that the monster had restarted the nightmares from when I was fifteen, but now when Callum trusts me the most with intimacy, that bastard is interfering too much.

"I'm fine," I say, peeling my eyes open, getting lost in the vastness of his irises, staring back at me with concern.

"I don't...."

"I'm fine, Callum. This is the first time we've... And the first time someone has touched me since the attack. I'm just tamping down the bullshit panic rising, okay? But I want this... Whatever we're going to do," I whisper, running my fingers through his shaggy blonde locks.

His breaths pick up, leaning into my touch, and his tense muscles relax. For a solid minute, we lie together—skin to skin, soaking in each other's presence.

"I-I want inside of you," he whispers with a crack in his voice.

Redness blooms over his cheeks, and his eyes shut tight when he rests his forehead against mine.

"Is that what you want?" I whisper, pressing my lips against his until he nods. "You're ready?" I ask, searching the lust-filled storm brewing in his gray eyes.

"I want to fuck you, Little Star. I want this memory to live with me for the rest of my life. I want to see this...your face when you come...and remember the feel of your pussy wrapped around my dick. It's you, River. I've been waiting for you," he says with such conviction I can't turn him away.

All the panic I felt before vanishes when I look into his hungry eyes, begging for a taste of me. It's him and me. River and Callum. Our time to show what we mean to each other.

"Then fuck me, Callum," I practically beg, staring into his eyes and pleading with him to take the ache from between my legs. His entire body shivers, and he closes his eyes. "It's just you and me, Callum," I whisper with encouragement. "Just us. This is our moment. If you want...."

"You and me, Little Star. I don't know....know how long I'll last," he whispers, swallowing hard.

"That's okay. We have plenty more opportunities, okay?"

He nods, and a small smile breaks out. Kissing my lips one last time, he pulls back, dragging his fingers down my bare legs. He hooks the edge of my panties and brings them down my legs and over my feet. In stunned awe, he stares at my glistening pussy with rapt attention. Spreading my legs further, he licks his lips like he's hypnotized by the heat blossoming between my legs.

Swallowing hard, I see the nerves roaring through him when he carefully removes his boxers and tosses them aside, leaving him bare to me. And what a beautiful sight it is. His long and thick dick stands at attention, red and purple, with desperation for me. Pre-cum glistens in the sunlight when it twitches and leaks down his reddened tip and twitching length.

"Why don't you lay down?" I ask, patting the spot beside me on the bed.

"O-okay," he gasps, settling down on the bed.

His fingers fidget in the sheet, twisting it until he's gripping it hard with white knuckles. He blinks rapidly up at me when I step back, lifting my sleep shirt over my head and tossing it aside, standing naked before him at the end of the bed.

Goosebumps erupt, puckering my skin when he gazes at me in wonder, like I'm the most perfect woman in the world, taking every inch of my body. His lips pop open in awe, and his irises disappear beneath the blackness of his dilated eyes. My heart beats double time when I step forward, running my fingers through the blonde hairs lining his muscular thighs. Every inch my fingers move up his leg and over his abdomen, he groans softly, arching his back to receive my touch.

Callum may have seen me naked before, but this time is entirely different. I'm all his—all he can focus on. There's no one else in the room to eat up his time but me. The way his eyes eat me alive as I hover above him has my breath catching in my throat. Anticipation trembles his fingers when he curls them in the sheets, desperate to reach for me but not daring to make a move. Not yet, at least.

This moment is for him and only him. Our time together. A special occasion we'll covet for the rest of our lives—him more than me. The trust he's putting in me to give him that memorable first time brings butterflies to my belly. Almost as if it were my first time, too.

Heavy breaths heave his chest, and he nibbles into his bottom lip, locking his gaze on my puckered nipples, begging for his warm mouth.

"You're okay with this, right? You're really ready?" I ask with furrowed brows, climbing onto the bottom of the bed and resting on my knees.

Hesitation slams into me, and I can't help but wonder if I'm the one to do this for him. But all that soon disappears with his following words, knocking me into action.

"River, please," he begs, moving his shaky fingers up and down his hardened and angry shaft, rubbing his thumb over his weeping slit, spreading around his precum.

Moving up his body slowly, I trail my finger up his thigh, lightly coated in blonde hairs, and swirl them around. I smirk when his hips jump, begging for friction, and he groans. Gently, I move his hand away from his twitching cock and place it at his side. Immediately, he twists the sheet again for leverage.

"Please, River," he pleads as I blow a breath over his length, loving the groaned response he gives me.

Wetness explodes in my pussy as I blow again, and his head turns from side to side.

"How bad do you want it, Callum?" I ask huskily, running the flat part of my tongue up his length and circling his tip.

"Please-please, River!" he cries out, thrusting his fingers into my hair and pulling me up to his mouth until his lips attack mine. He groans when I straddle his lap, grinding myself against his hardening dick. "I need you. I'm ready, Little Star. Please! Please fuck me. I've dreamed-dreamed of this moment for months. Since the moment I saw you...I knew. I want to remember this until the day I die. I'm yours, Little Star," he breathes his confession against my lips, grunting when I take him in my hands and line him up. "I'm yours," he breathes again, barely above a whisper, staring deep into my eyes.

"You're good with no condoms?" I ask with hesitation, eyeing him as he nods without hesitation.

"Yes, Little Star. I want you raw. I want to feel the flutters of your pussy when I finally settle inside you. Please, do it now. I'm so desperate—" His entire body locks up, and his fingers dig into my hip when I push him inside, and he gasps. "Oh, fuck," he moans wide-eyed, staying rigid until I sink down on him, taking him in all the way.

With approval, my pussy rejoices and flutters around him, basking in the thickness of his cock, stretching me.

"How does it feel?" I rasp through a moan when I lift my hips slowly and slam back down onto him, grinding my pelvis against his until he's crying out.

"Like I'm meant to be here. Like I'm finally home," he moans, and his eyes roll into the back of his head. "You're going to be my most cherished memory, Little Star. This moment...will—ah!" He moans as his entire body locks up, and his dick pulsates inside me repeatedly, spilling himself into me and coating my walls.

"That good, Big Guy?" I murmur breathlessly, resting my chin on his heaving chest. His fingers work through my crazy hair, and his cheeks turn red again.

Closing his eyes, his breaths shudder. "I-I thought...I could hold off-off. I thought-thought I could last. But-but." I follow the movement of his tongue when it darts out, and he licks his lips.

Redness tints his cheeks, and he clamps his eyes shut, huffing an annoyed breath at himself.

"It's okay. We have plenty of time to do that again...."

"And again and again?" he asks with a slight grin, opening his eyes to take me in again.

"However many times you want," I say with a snort, kissing his chest. "Was it good?" I murmur, kissing my way up his flesh and pressing a kiss to the edge of his lips and down his neck, sucking his skin between my teeth.

"More than good. I don't-don't want to move. Stay here," he whispers, burying his face in my neck and forcing my hips to sink on his hardened cock again, grinding my hips back and forth.

"Again?" I ask with amusement, and he nods, thrusting up with a deep groan.

My lips pop open as the pleasure soars through my veins, and a fire erupts in my belly.

"I want—" Callum's breaths shudder, falling into moans.

"Tell me what you want, Callum. Don't be afraid now," I murmur, kissing his lips again, growing more frantic until our tongues dance, and he cradles the back of my head.

"I want on top. Turn over?" he hesitantly asks, searching my eyes, and I nod, placing myself flat against him.

"Turn us over, Big Guy," I murmur, almost giggling when he turns us over clumsily and his elbow rams into my boob. I yelp, laughing when a look of horror crosses his beautiful face. His eyes frantically check me over, looking for spilled blood or instant bruises.

"Sorry-sorry," he whispers, peppering kisses all over my face and chin and down to my breasts. "I didn't mean to hurt you."

"It's okay," I whisper, moving his blonde locks from his eyes. "Now, fuck me again, Callum. Fuck me until you can't anymore," I moan when he thrusts himself into me with a loud groan, knocking the headboard against the wall.

Sorry, Ode. Now's a bad time to be my neighbor, I think when he does it again and again, plowing into me at a rapid pace. I move my legs, wrapping them entirely around his waist until my heels dig into his flexing ass muscles, begging him to go deeper.

"God, you're doing amazing, Callum. Just like that!" I moan, arching my back when a searing fire brews in my lower abdomen, flaring heat through my limbs and down to my curling toes.

"Come," he grunts with force, demanding me. "Come around my dick, River. Please. I want to feel you flutter around me, Little Star."

As soon as the words leave his mouth, my fingers twist around my clit, and I come with an explosion around Callum's cock, screaming my pleasures for the world to hear.

Callum's body stills again, and his muscles lock up, spilling into me a second time with a loud, drawn-out, satisfied moan. Staying nestled deep inside me, Callum leans down and presses his lips into mine, hovering there.

"I never want to leave," he admits, kissing my cheek. "Should-should I get a washcloth?" Looking down, he groans when he pulls out, spilling our mess onto the sheets. His eyes lock on the come dripping out of me, and his teeth sink into his bottom lip, mentally absorbing the scene and taking it all in.

I snort. "I don't think it matters now. Let's rest?" I ask when he falls to my side and pulls my naked body into his again.

"Of course, Little Star." He gently runs his fingers up and down my lower back when I pull my comforter up to our chins, heaving a sigh. "Thank you," he whispers when my eyes flutter shut. "For making this-this so special."

"Don't thank me," I mumble sleepily through a yawn. "You were amazing. But I need to pee," I grumble, not wanting to move from the cocoon of warmth. Exhaustion sweeps in, threatening to take me under.

"Your wish-wish is my demand," he says, pulling the blanket back from our naked bodies, scooping me into his arms, and taking us to the bathroom.

Gently, he lowers me to my feet and gets a washrag from the edge of the sink. Without a thought, I do my business and flush.

"Spread," Callum demands, gesturing to my legs until I spread them out. I shiver when the warm water hits my sore pussy, and he cleans me up before taking me back to bed.

As the clock strikes noon, we snuggle together and fall asleep in each other's arms under the warmth of my comforter and our combined mess beneath us.

"What the hell! I leave for three hours, and you two bump uglies without me? Without. Me?" Rad shouts, jolting my body from a glorious deep sleep.

"Dude," Callum curses, throwing a pillow in Rad's direction.

"It smells like *budussy* in here," he says, waving a hand in front of his nose and taking a deep breath. "You finally corrupted my boy, didn't you? How was it, Cal? Her pussy is the chef's kiss of all pussy." Rad obnoxiously brings his fingers to his mouth and kisses them.

"Dude," Callum whines, pinching the bridge of his nose.

"Tell me! Tell me!" Rad chants, charging forward until he's at the end of the bed and crawling over our bodies. He grins, lifting the blanket. "You two are naked under here. Oh man, my boy finally lost his V-card!" He whoops, shaking the entire bed. "This is the best day ever!" he proclaims. "We should celebrate." He grins more, with dirt gleaming between his teeth.

"Celebrate?" I question, rearing back when he leans in and presses his lips into mine.

"We're going to hit submit tonight and finally enter the Battle of the Bands on the damn wire, too. Shit, we only got twelve more hours until it's closed! Also, I won my race, Kieran and Asher are free from jail, and Callum jammed his dick in the best cock socket in town. I'd say today is a damn victory! Besides, my pretty, Pretty girl. Your face is more beautiful than ever," he says with a grin, hovering above me.

I blow out a breath at his long-winded answer. "Your point?" I ask, raising a brow. "And seriously? Cock socket? What the hell? It's a vagina. Say it with me now...." I grumble when he covers my mouth and shakes his head.

"Listen, Pretty Girl... Pack your panties, pills, and nothing else, because we're going to the Ozarks!" he shouts, pulling out a set of keys from his pocket.

"The Ozarks?" Callum asks, raising his brow. "The lake my parents used to drag me to in Missouri?"

"That's the one," Rad says, wiggling his brows. "Not only did I win the race, but I convinced Reese to give me his vacation house for seven days. Imagine the possibilities! Far from town, in a secluded cabin by the lake. It's prime, pound town territory. Now, let's go!" he shouts, jumping off the bed.

I look over at Callum and smirk when he shrugs. "Looks like we're going to the Ozarks, Little Star," he says with a grin.

"To the Ozarks, we go," I murmur, leaning in to kiss his lips.

"All right, clothes on! We've got shit to do. Up! Up!" Rad shouts, pulling back the blanket from our bodies. "Ohhh, on second thought. I've gotta eat dinner first," he says with a grin, shoving my legs apart and burying his face in my pussy until I'm a moaning mess, writhing beneath his wicked tongue.

RIVER

"Uhhhhh," I stammer, pulling my poor excuse for a coat closer to my body as the crisp November wind whips through the thin material. "You said cabin." My teeth chatter when the wind picks up, and I curse my lack of good winter wear. Frowning, I look down at my phone and sigh. "And I have no phone signal."

"Nope!" Rad says with a satisfied grin, rocking on his toes in his T-shirt and shorts. "We're out in the middle of nowhere! There's not a single neighbor for ten miles. Isn't it glorious?" Rad grins more, tossing his phone into the Tahoe and shutting it inside.

I swear, I don't know what it is about these Midwestern boys and their shorts in the middle of November, but they're all the damn same. I had a thirty-minute conversation with him about why he shouldn't wear his socks and sandals. He argued with me every step of the way until he huffed, shoving his feet into sneakers.

"You-you definitely said cabin," Callum mutters, putting an arm over my shoulders, and rubbing a hand up and down my arm.

"This is a fucking castle, Rad," Asher says, staring up at the curious-looking structure with furrowed brows. Skepticism lines his face, and he shakes his head. "Not a cabin. We're at the right place, right? You didn't Rad this up and write down the wrong house numbers?"

Kieran snorts. "We're about to walk into someone's family home as they get busy on a Sunday night." Shaking his head, he runs a hand down his face and steps toward me until he's at my back and invading my space.

"Yes! You guys are such buzzkills. We're at the right place, damn it!" Rad grumbles, cursing under his breath. "My track manager loaned me this place for a week. Here...." Poking out his tongue, he digs through his pocket and pulls out a sheet of paper.

"Right here! Here's the address, and right there," he says, pointing to the fucking castle with large numbers printed on the front. "It matches. So, we're staying at a castle. And boy, do I have plans to defile every inch of it." Wiggling his brows, he cockily smirks at me.

"Who builds a castle on the lake in the middle of Missouri?" Kieran murmurs, laying his chin on my head from behind me with a sigh, staring up at the massive fortress with the beautiful lake as the backdrop.

The autumn sun beams down on the crystal lake, reflecting off the turbulent white waves rolling along the surface. A boat in the dock near the water sways on its lift, far above the waters. My nose wrinkles. It's too damn cold to be at a lake house, let alone loitering outside for an obscene amount of time.

"Who cares. It's cold as hell," I grumble through a sharp shiver. "Let's go. I'm freezing my nonexistent dick off."

Asher snorts at my comment and shakes his head. "She has a point," he grunts, tightening his sweatshirt around him.

Rad snorts. "What're you guys complaining for? It's beautiful out!"

"Says the idiot in shorts." Callum scowls, pulling me further into him, letting me eat up his warmth like a greedy girl.

The large castle-like structure looms above us in white brick, and millions—okay, that's an exaggeration—of windows line the structure. A round turret hangs off the front of the house with large, reddish-colored vines creeping up the side.

In unison, we finally head to the front door, fighting against the wind as it whips around me, knocking my long strands in front of my face. I huff a breath, scowling at Rad when he looks at his keys with furrowed brows. With so much damn relief that we'll be in heat soon, Rad turns the key, and we walk inside, greeted by the warmth of the house.

"Ah," I grunt, shaking my hands out and basking in the glorious warmth of the gigantic lake-side castle. "Glorious heat!" I moan, wanting to hug the damn furnace and never leave.

"Fuck. Next time, let's make this a summer trip," Asher gripes, waltzing toward the thermostat and turning it up even more.

He rubs his arms as he looks around, gazing up at the tall ceiling and skylights blasting sunlight into the large living room with an enormous chandelier glistening in the sun, creating small diamonds on the wall.

"So, this is how the over-privileged live," I murmur, running a finger over the marble countertops of the oversized kitchen, inspecting the beautiful brand-new appliances.

Peering around, I see no dust on any countertops or cabinets. The fridge is smudge-free, and even the sink is perfectly polished. It's like a damn show house you see on TV where the wealthy live, and I've only dreamed of staying in. Today, though, it seems my dreams are finally coming true. The kitchen is as big as my apartment and fit for a chef.

"So many places to fuck you against," Rad quips, kissing my temple affectionately. "But first, we need lots of grub and lube to get through this beautiful week of fornication."

I roll my eyes at his stupid words and wander around the large living room, running my fingers over the turquoise leather couches and oversized chair.

"We're off for the food and sex toys. Be naked when we get back, and we'll get the orgy started ASAP. Ouch!" Rad grunts when Callum knocks him in the back of the head with a smirk.

"Shut up," Callum says through a small laugh.

"I'm serious," Rad says, pointing a finger right at me. "This," he says, waving his finger now, "is a group dynamic. We're all boning. Asher needs to let loose and discover how beautiful your...." Rad's brows furrow when Asher covers his mouth with a grunt.

"Food. Now," Asher demands, sending the two on their way.

As soon as they leave, I meander to the back wall, wholly made up of windows overlooking the lake. If it were warmer, I'd demand we strip down naked and jump into the water for hours of swimming.

"There's a hot tub," I say, pushing my nose against the glass door, eyeing the massive hot tub sitting on the deck outside.

"Getting naked outside in the freezing cold sounds like a dream," Asher grunts sarcastically. Walking forward, he side-eyes me until stopping in front of the glass.

For several minutes we stand in silence, taking in the beauty of our new home for the week. Asher nibbles his lip, shoving his hands into his jeans pockets. Clearing his throat, he scoots closer until we're shoulder to shoulder. Something sparks between our connection and heat encompasses my face.

Looking up into his gorgeous hazel eyes, something about him strikes me as different. His shoulders sag lower—almost in relief.

His hard-as-stone face softens, letting his genuine emotions peek through the dark veil.

"How're you feeling, Little Brat?" he asks with a hint of concern, searching the yellowing bruises on my face with twisting anguish.

"Concerned about me, Evil Ash?" I jokingly say, shoving my shoulder lightly into his until he smiles. "But I'm fine," I say, shrugging it off.

I'm still on my pain meds and only have one day left of the antibiotics, so I'm looking forward to finishing it all. The tiny pills are a constant reminder of my attack. Each and every time I swallow them down, the memories replay on repeat. Once the bruises fade and the pain meds are gone, it'll be like it never happened. Only it did happen. But from my experience, I've learned how to heal and slowly move on. Not entirely, but I'll get there knowing this won't break me.

"Fuck it. I got you something," he says quickly, shaking his head.

My heart pounds against my ribs when he removes his hand from his pocket and holds it out. The room spins, and my heart leaps from my chest. Sitting in the middle of his palm is my most prized possession that the cops refused to give back to me. I fought and fought with them, telling them I needed it to protect myself, but it was evidence of a crime, and they could not hand it over until all the proceedings were finished.

And now, here it sits right before my eyes, shiny and looking brand new. Last I saw, dark, red blood stained every inch from stabbing stupid Bradley.

Tears prickle at the backs of my eyes. "Asher." My voice comes out rough, clogged with so many emotions.

The tip of my nose burns, and my eyes cloud over as I stroke the name carved into the knife I've held dear for more than ten years. It's my lifesaver, the one thing that saved me when a maniac thought he could take what he wanted, sending him right into the arms of the cops. There was no denying what he had done to me this time. They couldn't push it under the rug and laugh me away. This time, they listened to every word I had to say, wrote it down, and took me seriously. So seriously, Bradley sits behind bars with no bail available to get him out. After he recovered from his stab wound, that is.

"Don't even mention it, Little Brat," he says, clearing his throat and keeping his eyes on the turbulent waters in front of us.

"Thank you," I murmur, leaning up to kiss his cheek and linger, basking in the feel of his skin beneath my lips. He stiffens, taking a deep breath. "This is the nicest thing anyone has done for me in a long time. How?"

Taking my chin between his thumb and index finger, he backs me against the windows, pressing his entire body into mine, letting me feel the planes on every inch of him. Standing tall above me, he pauses and takes in the length of my body in with one swoop. I swallow hard, staring into the abyss of his turbulent eyes filled with deep longing.

My breath shudders when his hip presses into mine. Chest to chest, we breathe each other's air, practically gasping for it. For one split second, thoughts of Asher giving in to the desperate craving surrounding us for months. It chokes me when I breathe. And he's the oxygen I ache for. Dangling like a sweet treat in front of my face, it rests there like a temptation out of grasp and forbidden from touching. The closest we've dared was the night on the Ferris Wheel. That dark scene plays on a shrine in the back of my mind. Whenever my fingers slip beneath my panties, it's their faces watching me work my clit in circles.

"I have my ways," he murmurs in a low, raspy voice, keeping the details locked tight behind his luscious lips. Leaning in a little, he's a breath away from me—a millimeter from pressing his lips into mine. "Make it up to me later, Little Brat. You can even call me daddy." The last words leave his wicked tongue on nothing but a murmur, barely audible against my flesh. It's a promise, sealed with a tiny peck on my cheek.

Fuck. I swallow my moan lodged in the back of my throat. Every inch of me throbs, aching for this man who's mercilessly flirted with me the more time has passed. Shivers roll through me when the faintest kiss presses to the edge of my mouth, and my eyes flutter shut on instinct, leaning into the feel of him. As quickly as the warmth of his kiss presses against me, his body vanishes, replaced by the frigid planes of the window pressing into my back.

"What the hell?" I groan out of frustration, curling my fingers into a fist.

Kieran's chuckle comes from somewhere beside me, and my body sags, letting all the frustrations go. "Oh, River Blue. We've got plans for you this week."

Promises. Promises. The whole way down here, Rad went on and on about his plans for me this week.

"Oh, Pretty Girl," Rad whispers directly in my ear, wrapping his fingers around my throat. "I'm going to fuck you within an inch of your life. I'm going to flood your pussy with so much come, and you'll feel me leaking out of you for a week." My breath hitches when he grins, kissing my cheek and tightening his grip. "Yeah, I thought you might like that. We're going to have so much fun this weekend," he murmurs in a deep, husky voice thick with lust.

Rad wasn't the only one to whisper sweet nothings into my ear, working me up and letting me flatline in the land of almost orgasming. Over and over, they teased and primed me for this exact moment to finally let me detonate. I knew every whispered word they promised would eventually come true—well, later. Asher had zero plans to help the ache between my legs right now.

"What the hell was that?" I whisper through my frustrations, searching for Asher amongst the shadows of the house.

If his touch hadn't seared into my skin five seconds ago, branding me with his fingertips, I would have sworn he was a ghost passing by.

"Don't mind him. He's fighting a lot of feelings right now," Kieran whispers, taking me into the warmth of his arms, and rests his cheek on my head with a satisfied sigh.

"Fighting what?" I murmur, placing my ear against his heartbeat and basking in the familiarity of it.

"Everything about you. You scare him. This band is the only thing he has, and here you are, bringing us happily to our knees. He's afraid to fall. He's afraid you'll tear us apart," Kieran murmurs, leaning into me more. "But don't worry, River Blue. Asher's coming around, and once he does, you'll be all he thinks about and obsesses over. I can see it now." A grin tips up the edges of his lips, and he nods with certainty that it will all play out how he says.

But half of me disagrees as a lump forms in my throat at Kieran's nonchalant confession. *He's afraid you'll tear us apart.* Tear them apart? Whispered Words? They're tighter than any family I've ever witnessed. There's no way little old me would come close to being a threat. The boys are more than a band; they're a damn family unit. Has my presence disrupted that in any way? Am I doing more harm than good by being so close to each of them?

"That's stupid," I murmur, shaking my head. "I don't plan on breaking anyone up."

"I know, River Blue. But he's always cautious and calculating our next moves. You're a move he didn't anticipate," he says, kissing my temple.

"But you actively set out to meet me, right?" Kieran blanches at my question and stiffens with me in his arms, giving away his true intentions.

Blowing out a breath. "Truth?" he questions, and I nod. "We wanted to meet you because of who your dad was, but I didn't expect it to be you. You were a surprise, River Blue. The truth is, I'd track you down, again and again, to be with you. No matter what."

Kieran's confession doesn't surprise me in the least. But my heart does sting. What would have happened if I hadn't been his River Blue and was just some rando they intended on using? Would they have taken it this far and brought me here for a weekend of fun? Doubt creeps in where it shouldn't, filtering through the sliced-open cracks of my heart. In the back of my mind, I've always had my guard up around them and lived in the present. But sometimes, it does nag and tugs at me, making me re-examine every interaction.

The number of times people have come into the record shop claiming to be my brothers and wanting to talk to me is astronomical. They waltz in with a chip on their shoulder and a smarmy smile and run out like their asses are on fire, with fear lining their faces.

Let's say these persistent ass people don't like meeting the end of my knife when I whip it out and tell them to kick rocks. They'll hesitate. They'll beg, flashing me megawatt grins. Pfft. Like that shit will convince me. In the end, I shoo them out with a knife shake and a cackle. Never seeing their scammy faces ever again. Seriously, who is afraid of a five-foot-five girl holding a knife? Apparently, those jokers. But good thing.

People hear the West name and go bonkers with greed, wanting to meet with my sperm donor in person. For some reason, they always think I'm that person. Sure, I am a West, but I'm not connected to shit. My brothers, possibly sisters, and father—are strangers to me. One day though, I'll waltz into their operations and introduce myself after I've lifted myself out of poverty and have made it as some big-wig manager. Then they'll see and regret the day they blew off River West.

I always wanted to distance myself from my family and run from the West name-sake. But family is everything. I couldn't have gotten through the last few days or weeks without my mom, Ode, and her family—hell, even the boys. Helping the guys has shown me that music lives and runs in my veins. I've nailed many of the challenges a business career could throw at me.

Managing a music venue—check. Building a band's social profiles—check. Managing a band—check.

"Well, now we're hopefully going to California," I say, leaning back to look at him, dreaming of our future at the tips of our fingers, ready for grasping.

Well, maybe. They may have submitted their application to the Battle of the Bands, but it still has to be reviewed and announced, which should be coming up in the next week or two. For now, we sit on the edges of our seats in anticipation of what will come.

"We're definitely going. There's no question about it," Kieran proclaims. "They're going to beat down our doors to get a piece of us." I snort at his confidence but revel in it, too. Whispered Words is good—well—more than fucking good. They're unique and saturated in raw talent that the world will eat up and take hostage. I can only imagine what people across the globe will think when their ears feast on Whisper Words' tunes.

"Will you go anyway?" I ask, biting my bottom lip. The question has been on the tip of my tongue for weeks. And why wouldn't they? They're free to live their dreams and leave this hellhole, even if I'm not a part of the equation.

His palms lightly encase my cheeks, holding me still as his mismatched eyes examine the sadness taking over my face. The thought of separating from them sends pain across my chest. Rubber bands constrict around my lungs, and panic soon settles into my soul. Never in my life did I think I'd want to depend on anyone again; yet, I am right back down the love...rabbit hole. The same damn place I refused to return to after Van obliterated my trust and crushed my cracked heart into pieces. It took me months to get over the sudden breakup. I mean, obviously. I still let that bastard slither between my legs when I was supposed to be working.

The front door bursts open with a loud bang reverberating off the tall, vaulted ceilings, and Rad and Callum's loud laughter and chatter fill the space. Noisy plastic bags rustle in their hands, but I can't drag my eyes away from Kieran as he stands tall. Those mismatched eyes take all of me in. From the tips of my toes to my heaving chest and finally gaze longingly into my eyes.

"We'll wait for you, River Blue, to finish whatever you have to do at home. You're in school and..."

"Fuck no," I say, swallowing the pain of my words. "You guys have to take the opportunity now. You can't wait." I shake my head in his grip, refusing to believe they'd wait around for me when something so spectacular has been laid before them. As much as I want them by my side, I can't destroy their dreams.

"That's right, we will, Pretty Girl! You're our girlfriend." My lips pop open to refute his proclamation, but I hold my tongue. That fact is, I am their damn girlfriend by now—all of them—even the evil one who refuses to show me how he feels. Wrinkling my nose, I glare at a grinning Rad, who zeros in on my unsaid realization with a knowing look.

"Fuck yes! You finally get it, don't you? We'll wait for you if you can't make it to California. Maybe we'll try the Chicago circuit. They're always looking for new talent, and it's only two hours away," Rad says with a grin, grunting when he sets the groceries down on the kitchen counters.

"We'll-we'll wait for you," Callum says with conviction, setting more bags down and rifles through them.

Finally, Asher comes into view, frowning at the island in front of the groceries, lost in thought. A crinkle takes over his forehead, and the color slowly drains from his face. His eyes shift between the boys and finally land on me, where something odd sparks but extinguishes just as quickly.

"You guys can't give up your dreams because of me. I can finish school anywhere," I say with a shrug. "It's basically all online, anyways." At least, that's what I planned to do on our trip. All my professors agreed to send me online material to complete while I was gone.

"But your mom," Rad says with a frown, running a hand across his neck. "You'd leave her?"

The realization smacks me square in the face, and my stomach sinks into the depths of my churning stomach. Could I leave my mother, who is so ill amid a flare-up that she's barely functioning? Could I leave her while she's hobbling around on her broken ankle with no income? Shit. Sweat breaks out on my brow as the worry slams into me and knocks the breaths from my lungs.

"I don't know," I say, swallowing the cold, hard truth.

"Don't you dare worry about me, River. My health is on the rise. My medicine is getting squared away, and I can move more. Enjoy this tiny vacation, okay? You're nineteen. You shouldn't have to worry about your mother," she says, cradling my face with a sad smile.

"But, Ma. I'll be away in another state for like a week. I can't just...."

"You can and you will. This is my illness to carry. Besides, the nurse is coming over again to help me get around and help with showers and meds. Even she says I'm on my way to coming out of this flare-up." She cringes when she holds a hand to her side and shakes her head. "It's just a pesky bladder infection. I've got antibiotics to help and all the pain meds I need. I have a neighbor and a nurse on speed dial. Please, be a kid for once," she pleads with me, and my eyes well up, burning with unshed tears.

"Okay," I say as a tear slips down my cheek.

The responsibility I hold for my mother sits heavily on my chest. Her well-being is something that goes through my mind on several occasions. All I can think about when I'm away is, is she okay? Did she fall? Can she walk without feeling dizzy and make it to the bathroom okay? Can she get to the store? So many damn worries rest on my shoulders when I'm running around working two jobs and trying to balance it with some fun with Whispered Words.

"Go have fun. Don't worry about me. Come back refreshed and renewed." Her smile lights up the room, and she looks healthier than ever when she kisses my cheek and returns to her recliner. That night we have dinner together in front of the television, watching some murder mystery she loves. We laugh for the first time in a long time together and enjoy each other's company.

"Enough of that," Asher barks, raising a brow when he pulls out an entire bottle of fancy tequila, staring at it. A wrinkle forms on his brow, and he scoffs. "Seriously? We send you for food, and you come back with seven bottles of tequila?" he asks with a grunt, pulling out multiple bottles of booze and setting them down on the countertop.

"Tequila makes her panties drop," Rad says with a scoff, taking the bottle from him and cradling it in his arms like a baby.

"And the lube makes the booty pop," he says, nodding to the large bottle of lube Asher places on the counter with twisted lips.

"Pretty sure you don't need tequila to make Little Brat's panties drop. She does that all on her own," he quips with a cocky smirk. "But the booty pop? Well, we can make that happen tonight." He shrugs when I blanch, and my butt cheeks instinctively clench together at his unsaid promise.

"I think I need to sleep with a salt circle around me tonight," I grumble, flipping him off. A glorious smile spreads across Asher's lips when he barks out a laugh, grabs the bottle of booze, uncaps it, and gulps down a few swings.

"Ah, the return of Evil Ash!" Rad proclaims, thumping Asher on the back several times until he chokes and rights himself, swiping a hand across his wet lips. Asher promptly shoves him away with a grunt, cursing him under his breath.

"All right," Callum says, stepping up to the bags. "Let's grill some steaks, drink some tequila, and maybe utilize the hot tub?" At that, his eyes turn to me, and I grin.

"Sounds like a good plan," I say as we get to work seasoning the steaks.

We drink mixed drinks and watch a few movies for the rest of the night. Once we're good and sloshed, we head out to the hot tub and take advantage of the warm bubbles and jetted sides.

The same happens every night we're locked away in this glorious house. We even convince Rad to skinny-dip in the freezing lake on a dare. Let's say little Rad didn't fare well when he jumped out of the water and ran for the house, screaming bloody murder. We laughed our asses off that night, getting sloppy drunk, and fucking on almost every surface of the house.

RIVER

When Rad said he wanted to defile it, he meant it. The couch. The kitchen. Every bed in the house. Against the railing and on the stairs. Up against the fridge and in the shower. No surface went untouched as we went rounds and rounds every night since we'd stepped foot into the castle house of fucking.

The only person who didn't take the bait was Asher. It's been six nights of him on the sidelines with those hazel eyes flaring with lust as the guys take turns railing me over and over again. I was the fruit for the taking right in reach, but he never caved. He sat in the corner of the room, stroking himself to oblivion, coming hard with my silent name on his lips. But there's always something holding him back from taking what he wants—me.

So tonight is our last night at the house, and I promised myself I'd seduce the ever-living fuck out of the man standing on the sidelines. Operation get Asher to fuck me is in full effect, and boy, is he taking the bait at every turn. The more alcohol he drinks, the fierier the looks he tosses in my direction, heating my entire being. Asher rests on the edge with his toes testing the waters. But what will it take for him to dive head first and take the leap? Only time will tell, but I'll try my hardest to convince him.

"Who's ready for the hot tub? One last time?" Rad asks, looking around the eight-seater, oak dining room table with massive, hopeful eyes. Without answers, he throws his shirt off and tosses it aside, revealing his gorgeous tattooed chest and slim waist. "We'll all go naked this time. No more boxers or hiding your hiney! Time to let it all hang out." He emphasizes his words by wiggling his hips and brows simultaneously, giving me a slow, seductive smirk.

Asher drunkenly frowns, takes a swig of the last bottle of straight tequila, and shakes his head. "I'm not getting naked with you," he scoffs, wrinkling his nose.

"Aw! Come on, man! Live a little. Those who get naked together get pussy together! You need to loosen up and get some," Rad whines, leaning his elbows on the table and puffing out his bottom lip.

I snort into my now empty glass and set it down. "Maybe I don't want to get naked with you either," I quip, raising a brow when Asher's gaze sears through me, and I fucking melt under his stare, heating me from one to a boiling one hundred. My face flushes when I reach for the bottle of tequila and take a large gulp, hating the burn running down my throat.

"Why wouldn't you, Little Brat?" Asher asks, furrowing his brows. "Stand up," he gestures calmly, waving his wrist.

I cross my arms over my chest, running my tongue along my bottom lip. "Why?" I ask in defiance, earning a chuckle from Kieran.

"I'll get the hot tub going. Then, we're getting naked," Kieran says, giving Asher a pointed stare before walking out of the room toward the hot tub resting on the deck outside in the frigid air.

"Stand up," Asher directs, leisurely taking a drink and gulping it down. His red-glazed eyes stare holes through me, lighting me on fire without saying more words. "And come here," he demands with a feral growl, pointing to the table in front of him.

Every part of me throbs and rejoices all at once. We've walked on thin ice around each other, suffocating in the tension growing thick in the air for days. And now, my brain chants a tune of "fucking finally!" No matter how often I told myself I'd never touch Asher's psycho ass with a ten-foot pole. Well, call me a liar all you want, but I'm about to get dicked down and hate fucked within an inch of my life. It's all that rests in the back of his dilated hazel eyes, promising me a multitude of things with one glance.

Rad chuckles, rubbing his hands together. "Oh, finally! Asher, my man!" Rad whoops, sitting back in his seat with wide eyes like he's about to watch the best movie of his life.

"Not another word," Asher demands, pointing in Rad and Callum's direction, and they nod, zipping their lips like good little boys. "Little Brat. You have three seconds to crawl to me. I won't tell you again."

"And if I don't?" I ask, getting to my feet on the other side of the table and placing my palms against the cold wood. My palms are slick with sweat, and my heart pounds a crazy beat inside my chest when his eyes narrow at my reaction.

"Then you won't sit right for a week." He stares with no emotion, drumming his long fingers against the tabletop. "Come here," he rasps, desperation leaking into his tone. "I want my fucking dessert."

Shivers roll through me at the slightly drunken state he's in. I've never seen any sort of desperation come through, but now he acts like he wants me badly and can't stand to stay away. Maybe it's the booze. Perhaps it's the distance from Central City, but I'm giving in—all in. We're doing this no matter the consequences. No matter how hard he'll hate himself and me tomorrow morning when he rolls out of bed, realizing what he's done. The moment we get home, he can return to the same dickbag I've come to love and hate and keep his distance. He can return to the jerk bag, who watches from the shadows while stroking himself until he's exploding all over his fist. But tonight? Tonight is our time to explore each other's bodies and say fuck the consequences of our tryst.

Without a second thought and fanfare from the silent audience of two, Callum and Rad, who watch with rapt attention, I climb onto the large wooden table. It squeaks beneath my pressure as I hesitantly crawl across the hard surface, digging into my knees. Inch by inch, I come closer and closer to Asher, who stares at me with hooded eyes, zoning in on my low-cut shirt, exposing my black, lacy bra and swaying tits. Heavy breaths heave his sculpted chest, and with every slide of my knees, my heart works double time, pumping against my ribs. The tip of his tongue darts out, running the length of his bottom lip. His heavy eyes drag from my fingers, curling into the table, slowly dragging up my bare arms to my wide eyes staring down at him.

"Now what?" I ask breathlessly, an inch in front of his blank face, begging for the direction to fall from his lips. Leaning in, I test the waters, running the tip of my nose against his.

His eyes darken when my nose brushes against his, and his breath shudders, affected by me. Little by little, Asher is losing the tight grip of control he's held tightly to for the past few months. For some reason, I'm here for it. Eager to see his breaking point. How far can I push Asher until he's choking me with his cock as punishment? Fuck. The imagery alone makes my pussy flutter around air, begging for him to fill me.

I'm living for today and today only. No regrets. No holding back. I'm taking what I want by the balls and seizing the day.

His eyes fall to my lips, and he licks his without thinking, forcing me to back up an inch. "Take your fucking clothes off," he demands, resting his elbows on the table with anticipation sparking in his eyes. Nervously, he shifts, adjusting himself in the chair, but keeps those steely eyes locked on me.

His voice brooks no arguments, snapping like a whip at my resolve. I don't argue this time—well, maybe just a little. Something about Asher brings out my inner brat, desperate to poke and prod the beast until he snaps and takes what he wants. Mischief dances in my eyes, and a smirk plays on my lips when his gaze heats me to the core. The look he gives me lets me know I am the main course, and he's hungry to devour me.

I cock my head and lean back, resting on my knees. My arms float above me in a warm sensual dance of seduction. Digging my knees into the smooth, wooden table and creasing my flesh, I raise and slowly rake my fingertips up and down my arms keeping it teasingly slow. Asher's eyes darken, taking in every movement I make as I sway him with a slow strip tease.

My skin puckers with goosebumps when I lift my shirt over my head, twirling it a few times, throwing it in Asher's unamused face. Tossing it aside with a flick of his wrist, he sits back and watches me without speaking. Everything heats under the intensity of his stare, bursting every inch of me into heated flames. Without warning, I'm aching for his touch to soothe the pressure building under my flesh.

"Everything," he rasps with urgency, grabbing the bottle of tequila. Mesmerized, I watch in fascination as his Adam's apple bobs with every gulp he takes, hypnotizing me until, piece by piece, my clothes are gone and thrown in Rad's direction.

"I'll keep these for luck," Rad murmurs, burying his nose into the fabric of my panties and groaning. "She's so fucking wet already," he rasps in a low, gravelly voice, unbuckling his pants with no shame and strips until he's completely naked. His moans rumble through the room as his hand works up and down his shaft, using my panties for friction. "You do what you want; I'm going to stroke one out to her bouncing tits."

"Eyes on me, Little Brat," Asher says, beckoning me with a finger until he's sitting back in the chair with a bottle of tequila in his hand, commanding the scene like a king. "Callum," he says with authority. "I need salt and a lime," he demands again, climbing to his feet and towering above me. His calloused fingers run the length of my jaw, standing silently before me without muttering a word or new demand. It's there, resting in the back of his dark hazel eyes— the promise of what's to come.

My head spins when he barks those orders, and Callum pushes from the chair, stumbling over his feet a few times before disappearing into the kitchen. Drawers slam, and cabinets open and close before he reappears with a flushed face. He nibbles his lips, nervously looking anywhere but me, when he sets the chunky, wooden chopping board on the table beside us, along with a sharp knife and the glass salt shaker.

"Mmm," Asher hums, picking up the salt and shaking it. "Hold out your wrist," he mumbles, grabbing my wrist when I don't do it fast enough and yanks it forward with force. "Look at me, Little Brat," he says, closing in on me with a deadly expression. "I'm holding on by a fragile string. Please don't test me right now. Okay?" When I nod, he swallows heavily, squeezing my wrist between his large fingers. "Now, hold it here, and don't move."

Through several shaky breaths, I confirm his demand with one nod. Practically trembling under his stern fingers latched around my hand, restraining me from moving. My mind conjures ropes and chains securing me to the bedposts as he takes what he wants and laps away at me with vigor. But I shake those away, returning to the present when he methodically touches my wrist with soft, feather-like strokes, gaining my attention. Turning my arm over slowly, he exposes the inside of my wrist and deposits several shakes of salt on my flesh, falling like snow, and covering my skin in tiny white specks.

His darkened hazel eyes snap to mine, holding me captive in his desire-filled gaze. Tingling sensations of pleasure flood my body like a fire igniting under my skin.

"Hold it," Asher orders me, taking his hand from my wrist. "And don't lose a single grain of salt. If you do, you'll regret ever defying me. I'll bend you over my knee and paddle your ass until it's red and blistered." He quirks a brow, eyeing the multitude of white specks on my wrist, and steps beside me, beginning the process of cutting limes into several bite-sized pieces—perfect for sucking.

"Okay," I say through a shaky breath, counting down the seconds until his tongue brushes over my flesh.

Heat overtakes me like a damn fever as I strain to keep my arm straight out in front of me. Too damn scared to lose a single grain to the floor. A thrill shoots through me at the thought of his punishment if I did happen to lose one, but my ass wants to be pounded into next week. Sooner rather than later. So, I stay as still as possible, closing my eyes and counting down each shink of the knife severing through the limes.

One. Steady your fucking arm. Two. Shit! Don't fucking move. I breathe, counting the knife's third, fourth, and fifth clink against the wooden cutter until a deafening silence fills the room. My eyes flutter open, focusing on the man in front of me, looking as wild and dangerous as ever.

"Open," Asher murmurs, holding the lime to my lips and placing it peel first between my teeth so the juicy fruit sits on the outside. "Good little brats get rewards," he whispers against my cheek, and I whimper around the lime, begging for more contact. "Now, I'm going to lick, drink, and suck—in that order. Don't move a muscle, baby."

I swear his eyes dilate to blackness when the warmth of his tongue glides across my wrist, licking up every speck of salt. Scooping up the bottle of tequila, he gulps down a few drinks until he's swiping the extra droplets from his lips. Lurching forward, he desperately crashes his lips down on mine, sucking the lime between my teeth and holding me still between his palms on my cheeks. Stepping back, his chest heaves up and down quickly when he spits the lime out onto the ground with a feral growl.

"Lay down," he demands in a gravelly voice, pointing to the table. "And spread your legs like a good girl." My lips pop open in retort, but before I can speak, his fingers wrap around my throat, and he drags me closer until we're nose to nose as he lightly squeezes, knocking the air from my lungs. Silently, I beg for oxygen beneath his cruel fingers, but none comes, heating my face. "Don't fight this," he pleads in a breathless whisper, brushing a stray strand of hair from my moistened face. "I've held back for so long. And now I want what I want, liquid courage and all."

I swallow his moan when his lips attack mine, swirling his tequila-soaked tongue with mine in a dance of domination. He takes me completely. Body. Mind. Soul. With one kiss and I'm a goner, bending to his demented will and happily doing it without a fuss.

"Holy shit," Rad whispers in a throaty tone somewhere in the dining room.

"Down," Asher demands, loosening his grip on my throat, but he doesn't completely let go until I'm laid on my back. Shivers break out when my heated back comes into contact with the cold surface, and a gasp escapes me as the overwhelming sensations expand through my body.

Asher spreads my legs wide, placing my feet on the edge, showing off my glistening pussy, as he drags my ass off the edge table. Now, I am open and exposed to the last man I ever thought I'd let touch me. But this has been building and building for months.

"We're doing this again. All of us," he says, adjusting the growing want bulging from his pants with a low groan.

"Lick, drink, suck?" Rad asks with a grin, climbing on the table and hovering above my face. His dick throbs right above my line of vision, thick with precum, red and angry, almost poking me in the damn ear. "Come on, bro! You're missing out on the best tequila shots!" he shouts, looking in the direction of the living room.

Kieran stops short, wiping his hands down his jeans when he waltzes back into the house. Bewilderment widens those beautiful mismatched eyes as he takes in the scene before him: me, laid out on the table with my feet propped up on the table edge and my pussy dangling, ready for the taking. Swallowing hard, he takes a side, staring at Asher with a twisted expression.

"The game?" Kieran asks, tilting his head to the side as Asher takes another few gulps of tequila straight from the bottle.

"Tequila shots. Drop the salt anywhere you want to lick. Take a shot, and then get the lime from her mouth, pussy, or wherever you want. But right now, this pussy is mine," Asher says with determination as a cold-like sensation enters my aching and swollen pussy, doing little to alleviate the pulsating between my legs.

I swallow down the gasp stuck in my throat. Anticipation fries my damn nerves, and my fingers tremble against the wooden table top, waiting for the first stroke of someone's tongue. Or fuck, anything! They all hover above me, standing motionless, forming a circle around my naked body like I'm some sort of sacrifice.

Moving as one, they pass the salt shaker around the circle, depositing heavy amounts all over certain parts of my body. From my stiff and aching nipples to my belly button and the spot right above my pussy, they all pick a place, admiring it from above with heated eyes. Cocking his head to the side, Asher grins, rubbing his fingers up and down my thigh.

"Who is in the salt circle now, Little Brat?" He quirks a brow and then nods, beginning their synchronized torture with the flick of their tongues in unison.

I moan when they lick the salt simultaneously, and the warmth of their tongues overtakes me. Uncontrollable gasps spill from my throat when Asher pours his tequila shot over my clit, and through my pussy, letting it flow straight into his mouth and drenching me completely.

My eyes roll back into my head when his manic tongue darts into my pussy over and over, vibrating his moans against me as he sucks the lime into his mouth and spits it out onto the floor before diving back in for more. His tongue thrashes against my clit as his long fingers enter my pussy, wildly thrusting in and out, moving my body against the table. Fire spreads through every limb deep in my gut until I'm on the brink of exploding. A mouth comes down on mine, moaning into me as my back arches off the damn table in preparation for the best orgasm I'm ever going to experience in my damn life.

My fingers urgently dig into someone's hair until I'm exploding around Asher's fingers, eagerly thrusting in and out of my pussy. On a loud cry, filling the space with my raspy moans and begging for more, I come. And I come hard. Harder than fucking hard. Shit. I think I meet Jesus behind the stars dancing in my eyesight.

"Jesus!" Rad whimpers.

Yeah. Met him. I groan and babble through my thick tongue when Rad leans down, gently kissing my cheek with a grin widening his face until he steps back. In fact, they all step back, giving me and the man of the hour the space we need to consummate our union.

Locking eyes with Asher, I see my life flash before my eyes. There's a promise hiding in the depth of his glazed-over hazel eyes, and I don't know if I'll survive to tell the tale of our adventures. Death by dick—is what the headlines will say when they tell the story of how Asher Montgomery royally dicked me down and fucked me to death. Dig my grave now because there's no coming back from this moment.

"Turn over, Little Brat," Asher says, heaving a breath.

Keeping those perceptive eyes searing into mine, he takes every ich of clothing off and tosses them aside. I see him in all his naked glory for the first time since getting to know him. Lean muscle lines his arms, accented by the thick blue veins protruding from his flesh—has me panting like a pathetic bitch in heat. All I can imagine is running the length of my tongue over his skin and tasting him for the first time. My eyes fall toward his thick and hairy legs, working up over his dick, standing at attention and leading to a fit stomach without defined abs. Darting my tongue out, I lick my lips, imagining how he'll taste in my mouth when he coats my throat.

"Please," he rasps until I comply and turn over with my ass in the air, presenting my aching pussy to him.

I yelp when he grabs my ankles and shoves my feet flat onto the ground. With force, he places my palms on the table, and I give into him, letting him take what he wants and how he wants. I'm all fucking his right now. No interference from me or the other three, who look on in fascination. My pussy flutters with excitement at his take-charge attitude, and my mind goes blank, leaning into him to make the decisions.

"Don't move your hands," he whispers against my neck, carefully wrapping his fingers around my throat. "I'm going to fuck you now, okay?"

For a moment, it's just us in the room; the others slink into the shadows and cease to exist.

"Yes, please, Asher," I moan, crying out when his thick dick roars into my pussy without warning.

Asher grunts as he pounds into me, mercilessly pushing the table with our force and digging my hips into the edge with every frantic thrust of his hips.

"This has been building for days. I won't last long, so come for me, Little Brat. Come all over my cock and show me how much you love it when I fuck you hard enough to leave bruises," he groans, gripping my throat harder until my lips pop open in a silent, breathless scream.

My head swims in a mess of emotions as my orgasm plows through me with such force everything turns white behind my eyes, and I leave this earth once again. At this rate, I'll have to fuck Asher's evil ass to get these fantastic orgasms I'm sure I'll be hooked on for the rest of my damn life. His body stills, and he spills everything inside me in one long, drawn-out groan resembling my name in hushed whispers.

Breathlessly, Asher pulls out, briefly kissing my cheek. "Good girl," he praises between breaths. "Now, let the others enjoy our pussy." I shiver when he pulls away, moving to the chair across from my face, and sits back with his hands behind his head. "I'll give you one hour, and then, I'm taking you again," he commands me again with a cocky smirk, looking lighter than before. Reaching down, he takes his dick, stroking himself as he lazily watches from the sidelines.

Rad leans forward without hesitation and takes my mouth with his, pulling back. "We've done some group stuff, Pretty Girl. But have you ever been fucked in the ass?"

I swallow thickly and blanch at his crass words. It's the one sexual experience I've only been brave enough to do a handful of times with reluctance. It didn't hurt, but it wasn't with people I felt I could trust. But with my boys, I have faith in every molecule in their bodies, and I know they'd never hurt me on purpose or make it too painful. So, with those words running through my mind like a warning, I give in to them.

"I haven't done it in a while. It's only been a few times," I whisper, licking my lips.

"First time with us. We'll make it hot as fuck, Pretty Girl," Rad says with a smirk, looking deep into my eyes when I nod in confirmation, and my heart skips a fucking beat. Holy hell, I'm going to let one of them stick their big fat cocks into my asshole while the other fucks my pussy. Shivers roll through me at the thought, and excitement thrums through my veins with anticipation.

"It'll burn a little at first, Little Brat. But once you're nice and stretched out, taking two at a time will be easier. Kieran, stretch her asshole out." My eyebrows raise into my hairline when Kieran nods without putting up a fight and marches toward me with determination.

Fingertips run down my spine, sending goosebumps everywhere as I lean on the table where Asher left me, not daring to move an inch. I swallow hard, focusing on the compassion in Rad's eyes when Kieran runs his fingers over my ass and dives them deep into my come-filled pussy.

"I'll make it feel so good, River Blue, okay?" he murmurs, and I nod in confirmation, desperately aching for them both.

"Scoot her back," Rad says, waving a hand.

Kieran steps back with me in his arms several steps until Rad can fit in between us and the table. A devilish smirk crosses his face when he drops to his knees, still stroking himself with my panties.

Looking up at me, he grins more, with purpose settling across his face.

"I'm going to eat you until you come at least two times on my tongue. I don't even care about Asher's come dripping out of you." Rad runs a finger up my calf, catching it in his hand and heaving it over his shoulder, moaning when he runs his nose through my folds, bumping into Kieran's fingers as he stills. "God, Pretty Girl. You smell like sex on a stick." The tip of his tongue barely brushes my bundle of nerves, and I cry out through the overstimulation. My skin crawls with the need to run away, but they both hold me captive in their arms, tightening their grips.

Kieran curls his fingers inside me, slowly working them in and out at a torturous pace. My head falls back onto his shoulder, moaning loudly at the onslaught of sensations pounding through my entire body. My nerves are on fire again, ready to combust, and the moment Rad's tongue turns circles around my clit, I'm prepared to detonate.

"That's my River Blue," he whispers huskily against my neck. "Come for us again, baby. Come on my fingers and Rad's tongue."

Crying out, my head moves back and forth as another orgasm presses through, squeezing the life out of Kieran's fingers. My body sags in Kieran's arms, utterly fucking spent. Can I go on? I hope fucking so. I have three more boyfriends to fuck before the night is through. And then again in a few hours. I'm living life to the fullest at this moment before we have to go back to reality—something I almost don't want to do. If I could stay in a fairytale land with endless orgasms and four men at my beck and call, I would.

"Now, River Blue. You'll feel a lot of pressure, and I want you to relax. Focus on Callum." My eyes flutter open as Rad backs away, stroking himself with no restraint. Callum comes into view with his shirt off and his boxers hiding the massive stiffy tenting them.

"Cal," I murmur, trying to relax as much as possible when Kieran removes his fingers from my soaking pussy and glides them through my crack.

"That's a good girl," Asher reaffirms from across the table, watching them work me over. Standing, he marches around the table, grabs the large bottle of lube, and pumps a few streams in my crack. "Now let my brother fuck your ass," he murmurs, kissing my cheek. His eyes never stray from Kieran's finger, working into me, slowly opening me up.

Callum's fingers brush against my jaw, leaning in slowly and kissing me. His tongue mixes with mine, engulfing me in him as Kieran slowly parts my ass and pushes in one finger, knuckle deep.

"So fucking beautifully done," Kieran rasps in my ear, working his second finger through the burning ring of muscles. "Relax, River Blue. That's it," he breathes heavily, working on a third and fourth finger until I'm completely open and relaxed.

"Not-not too bad?" Callum asks, furrowing his brows when my eyes roll into the back of my head, and I gasp for air, clinging to Callum. He groans when my fingernails dig into his arm, and I swear to fuck, another orgasm sits at the brink of it all, and I don't know if I can fucking come again without becoming a noodle in their arms.

"More," I moan, earning a chuckle from Asher.

"I'd say it's time to lube up your prick and fuck her with it. Callum," Asher says, gaining the trembling man's attention away from me. "What do you want to do? Take her pussy while Kieran takes the back?"

Callum swallows nervously, looking between the two of us. Eventually, his eyes drop toward my pussy as Kieran pushes his lubed-up dick into my ass an inch at a time, slightly bending me over.

"Doing good," he gasps, sinking all the way in. "We'll take our time, baby. I don't want to hurt you, okay?" I nod several times, catching my breath as he remains still.

"Kieran, how about you sit on the edge of the table? Callum wants to tag in," Asher says with a vicious grin across his lips.

Kieran doesn't waste a moment, wrapping an arm around my waist. With ease and precision, Kieran rests his ass on the table, carefully rearranging us, so I'm spread wide, ready for Callum.

"Jesus," I shout, throwing my head back onto his shoulder.

"Pretty Girl. Are you okay?" Rad asks with concern, brushing a finger down my tightened face.

When I peek an eye open, I'm greeted by his dark eyes and him resting on the table beside us.

"Too full," I say, blowing out a breath.

Asher scoffs, walking around the table and into my eyesight. Leaning against the wall, he crosses his arms over his chest and smirks. "You can take it, Little Brat. Spread your legs and let Callum in," Asher demands with the cock of his head. He watches for several minutes until my pinched face relaxes, and I nod, permitting Asher to spread my legs slowly like before. "You're being such a good Little

Brat," he murmurs, fixing my legs, so they're spread wide open. "You know... You know we would never hurt you, right?" His brows furrow, and he squeezes my knee.

"Thanks, Evil Ash," I whisper, snorting when he kisses my cheek affectionately.

"Good girl. Now, Callum, it's your time to shine," he says, stepping back so Callum can take his place.

Callum steps between my spread legs with trepidation and takes it all in with a heated gaze. No doubt, memorizing this moment as a shrine in his head for years to come.

"You're good?" he asks, slowly pulling his boxers down and kicking them to the side. I nod, breathlessly unable to answer as the tip of his dick slowly works into my pussy, and he grunts. "Oh, f-f-f-uck," he mutters, leaning his forehead against mine. "You feel exceptional, Little Star."

"Aw, my little Callum is all grown up. But now, you gotta get a move on, man. My dick has an appointment with her mouth in five seconds," Rad grumbles, standing tall on the table, stroking himself while patiently waiting for Callum to pull away from my face.

Callum grumbles under his breath, pressing one last kiss to my lips. Pulling back, he snaps his hips forward, sending lightning bolts throughout my body. I silently scream through the sensation, but as soon as my mouth pops open, Rad seizes the opportunity and acts as my gag before any noise can push through my lips.

"Jesus fucking hell," Kieran curses, barely moving beneath me. "This...this is something that...fuck," he grunts, holding my hips with bruising force until he's burying his face in my neck, thrusting up into me.

"Jesus. I don't know how long I can last," Callum mutters, moving in unison with Kieran and Rad.

"Don't hold back, boys. We have all night to tie her up and come in her, on her, and everywhere," Asher rasps from somewhere in front of us, sounding like a ghost in the shadows, enjoying his view.

Callum's the first to go, frozen in time as his mouth hangs open and his thrusts stop, depositing his come deep inside me and mixing with Asher's, painting my fluttering pussy walls.

"Shit," he murmurs, kissing my cheek and pulling out. Slowly, he stumbles back, plopping into a chair with a dazed look on his face.

"And just like that, one down, two to go," Rad grunts, working his dick in and out of my lips at a steady pace.

"Fuck this. I gotta move better than this, man," Kieran grunts, wrapping his arms around my body. Rad's dick is forced from my mouth as Kieran leans my front side over the edge of the table again and pounds into me repeatedly. "Fuck yes," he grunts one last time, pulling out until the heat of his cum spreads all over my ass cheeks.

"Move, dickhead. It's my turn now," Rad proclaims, practically jumping down from the table and pushing Kieran out of the way.

"You're mine now, Pretty Girl," he whispers, swiping my hair over my shoulder and kissing my flesh. "You're still good?" he murmurs, teasing his tip through my folds until I nod. "Good girl," he says, groaning when he entirely pushes inside and gently thrusts in and out, savoring the feel of me around him.

"I can't," I whine in a tired voice when his fingers circle my clit, eliciting more moans from my throat. "I can't, Ashton," I groan a protest when he presses harder, quickening his thrusts.

"One last time, Pretty Girl. Come on my cock, and then I won't make you come anymore," he grunts, pounding his hips into mine and filling the house with the sound of smacking flesh.

Without warning, another orgasm barrels through me, tightening around Rad's dick until he comes on a grunt and stills behind me.

"You did so damn good, Pretty Girl. I think I might live in your pussy forever," he murmurs in a tired voice, kissing my shoulder one last time before pulling out and stumbling over his feet. Groaning, he dramatically lies on the ground, putting his arm over his eyes. "Wake me when we fuck again," he quips through a heavy breath.

"All right," Asher says.

"Who is ready for round two?" His deep voice sounds from right behind me, his fingers moving through the come dripping out of my pussy and running down my leg. "You're leaving some behind," he tsks while clucking his tongue, gathering it all up on his finger, and shoving it back inside.

"Looks like someone needs to be the plug." And with that, Asher enters my pussy once again with a groan, not giving me time to recuperate.

But there are no complaints from me when we start another round of—Fuck River silly until she can't walk anymore—my favorite type of game.

After another round, I'm lying dead on the table, looking up at the tall ceilings and examining the peculiar-looking chandelier. My heartbeat pounds in my ears as a body crawls over mine and settles against me.

"Good, Pretty Girl?" Rad asks, moving some of my sweaty hair from my forehead.

"Dead," I mumble, closing my eyes.

"Aw, Pretty Girl. We killed you, didn't we? Next time we'll...."

"Next time?" I grumble, swatting him away from me as he laughs.

"Uh, duh. You don't just live through one fiveway and think that's the end. This is just the beginning of our gang bangs, baby," he quips, kissing my cheek with a chuckle.

Footsteps sound beside us as Rad's ripped away, and a familiar face hovers above mine with flushed cheeks and a grin.

"How about we get cleaned up in the hot tub? It should be nice and ready by now. Shit, it's been three hours," Kieran says, scooping me up from the table and holding me in his arms.

"Don't let me drown," I say through a yawn, leaning my head on his sweaty chest, completely relaxing into him.

I hum when the five of us sink into the heated water of the hot tub and look up at the stars shining down, accompanied by the bright moonlight. No streetlights or other neighbors interrupt our serenity as we relax together until it is time to crawl into the large king-sized bed we all manage to squeeze into—one last time.

The following day we eat a quick breakfast, hit the showers, and make sure the house is spotless for the owners when they return next. The last thing I wanted them to see was the ass impressions we left on the dining room table they eat meals on. What a shock that would be.

"So," I say as we pack up the Tahoe and stare back at the castle we're about to leave behind forever. "Thanks for this week."

Rad smirks, swooping in to cover me in kisses. "You needed it, Pretty Girl. And so did we."

"It was nice-nice to get away," Callum murmurs, kissing my cheek. "Nice to spend time with you."

"And in you!" Rad whoops with a grin, pulling me by the front of my shirt. I swat him away with a roll of my eyes. "So, do you understand now?" Rad asks, twisting me until my back hits the cold metal of the vehicle.

"Understand what?" I ask, raising a brow.

"That you're ours. Forever. There's no getting away from us now." He grins, not giving me a moment to argue when his lips descend on mine, and his tongue eats my answer.

"Exclusively ours," Kieran reiterates, shutting the back hutch after putting our bags inside.

"Exclusive, huh? When did that happen?" I quip as Kieran rounds on me, shoving Rad out of the way.

"Dude!" Rad gripes, stumbling sideways.

Grasping my chin, he growls, baring his teeth. "Don't play with me, River Blue," he says in a low, no-nonsense voice like a possessive idiot.

I snort. "I guess I'll have to let my other boyfriends down easy." I roll my eyes when they all tense and grunt, ready to shout their outrages.

Asher rolls his eyes, forcefully removing the big lug's body from draping over mine. "She gets it. You pissed on her enough. Let's go." Asher drags me around the car by my arm and throws open the passenger's side door. Without a word, he grabs me by the hips and puts me in the seat, only pausing to put my seatbelt on.

"Let's go home," Asher grumbles, jumping into the third-row seats and lounging with his eyes closed. "Don't kill us with your driving," he quips with an easygoing grin.

Rad snorts. "You're the asshole who gets us stuck in ditches and mud puddles. K at least drives like an adult."

Asher frowns as Kieran pulls out of the drive and heads down the miles-long curvy road with one destination in mind—home.

"I'm not that bad," Asher grumbles, throwing an arm over his eyes.

"Worse than bad," Callum quips with a twinkle in his eye, ducking as Asher's hand wildly swings for him and misses. "You always stop in the middle of the road! Remember that squirrel you hit? Or the mailbox? Or the... Ah!"

"Shut it," Asher playfully barks, leaning over the bench and taking Callum's head hostage with an evil grin. "What should I do to your lover boy, Little Brat?" he asks with a big wolfy grin, squeezing his arm around Callum's throat with a laugh.

"Asshole!" Callum grunts, trying to shove him off.

My heart squeezes in my chest at the lightness surrounding Asher like a halo draping over him. This whole vacation, he's held back, and then yesterday, something burst through, and he allowed himself to let go of whatever was holding him on the sidelines, introducing the real Asher. The one who had been shoved down into the pit of his misery. The man who brightly smiles at me now as if the sun reflects off him, producing a halo hanging over his head.

"Nothing," I say, turning to watch as he knocks Callum's head to the side with a slight shove and snorts at me.

For the rest of the six-hour trip, we joke, nap, and stop for snacks until we're back in Central City as dinner hits residents' tables.

"Home sweet misery," Asher grumbles, sitting up with the same frown he's always worn, scowling at the world as it passes. "Take us home. I'm sure the devil will want us there ASAP," he grumbles, swiping a hand down his sleepy face.

"We'll take you home, Pretty Girl!" Rad says as we pull into Callum and Rad's driveway.

"Thanks for this," I say, leaning over and kissing Kieran on the cheek. "I'll see you later?"

His lips roll together, and he nods, bringing his lips to mine.

"Definitely," he murmurs, kissing me again before letting me go on my way, and I step out into the fading sunshine with a groan.

Asher hops out of the back, stretching his arms above his head and exposing his stomach. I bite my lip, imagining the delicious things he did to me yesterday against the table, getting lost in my thoughts. Before I climb into Callum's car, Asher grabs me by the arm, pulling me into him.

Wrapping his arms around me, Asher secures my head against his chest without saying a word. My heart squeezes when he hugs me tighter. It's like something sits on his tongue, ready to be said, but he kisses my head and lets me get in the vehicle. Even as we pull away from Callum's house and they get into the Tahoe, I feel him. His stare. His hug. Something shifts, turning sideways inside me. What was that all about?

Rad rambles away from the front seat on our way back to the center of Central City, pulling into the parking lot of my apartment building. I stiffen when chaos unfolds in front of me. People sit outside on their porches, and some wander around the crowded parking lot, watching the spectacle playing out.

My eyes widen when an ambulance, a fire truck, and police vehicles surround the parking spot located in front of my apartment. My. Apartment.

With shaky hands, I get my phone from my pocket, scrolling through the multitude of missed messages and calls I received in the last thirty minutes. Bile burns in the back of my throat.

"What the hell?" Rad asks, throwing the passenger's door open and opening mine. "Is that?"

My heart sinks into my ass when Ma's body is wheeled out of the apartment on a stretcher. A paramedic straddles her, pushing into her chest repeatedly as someone holds a bag to her mouth, pumping air into her lungs.

"River!" I turn toward a teary-eyed Ode, covering her mouth with her hand.

"What the hell happened?" I ask in a raspy voice, not processing the scene before my eyes.

"We don't know yet, baby," Korrine says, swallowing hard as I lean into her open arms. Her hug settles the anguish beating down on me and the guilt crushing my heart. "We checked on her last night, and she said she had the flu and wanted to be left alone. I went over about an hour ago, and she was barely responsive." Tears stream down Korrine's face when she pulls away, patting my cheeks with affection. "Follow the ambulance to Central Memorial," she says, nodding as they close the doors and take off out of the apartment complex parking lot at a high rate of speed.

Rad immediately jumps into action, holding me in his arms, and guides me back to the car.

"Let's go to the hospital, Pretty Girl. We'll see what's going on," he says in a small voice.

"Okay," I say, climbing back into the car, and we head to the hospital, following behind the ambulance.

ASHER

Kieran slams the Tahoe door, running a hand down his face. Glaring up at my father's office window, he shakes his head and shrugs at me. Maybe that's a good sign that the old bastard is finally loosening the leash of our collars. Pfft. Fat fucking chance. Nigel Montgomery has a knack for being in control. If it isn't his idea, then it's not possible.

Kieran doesn't wait for me, opting to head into the house with his head hung low and his hands in his jeans.

The weekend plays on repeat in my mind. I promised myself the moment we left Central City that I would let whatever happens—happen. It didn't take a genius to know what we would do to pass the time the moment we stepped into a secluded lake house.

My time with River was highly eye-opening and fucking hot. Being deep inside her pussy and feeling the effect I had on her—twice over was invigorating. Swallowing hard, I squeeze my eyes shut, willing my damn dick to go back down before I step out and deal with my father. Oh, yeah. That did it.

Just as my hand attempts to open the door, my phone vibrates in my pocket repeatedly. Scrunching my brows, I dig it out of my pocket. Who the hell calls people these days? Especially so late in the evening? Scammers, that's who. Shit. Looking at the number on the screen, it screams scam call. Out of the area, area code. Long number. I roll my eyes, expecting a robot when I answer the phone.

"Yeah?" I ask, blowing out a breath. "Listen, if this is a robot scammer.."

A chuckle greets my ears. "Uh, nah, Man. Not a scammer, I promise. You'll want to hear this. Is this, by chance, Asher Montgomery, Ashton Radcliffe, Kieran Knight, or Callum Rose? This was the phone number we had on the application for the submission."

Number on the submission? Jesus. Fuck. My fingers tighten around the phone in fear of dropping it as my palms dampen. My heart beats out of my damn chest and falls onto the dash. All the blood in my body swishes in my ears, almost drowning out the voice on the other end.

"Uh, yeah. This is Asher," I say, swallowing hard.

My back stiffens at attention when I bring the phone off my ear and stare at the number again. Only this time, the location of the call sits under the number—East Point Bluff, California. California. Fucking, California. Gasping for breath, I bring the phone back to my ear just in time.

"Fucking awesome, man. I was looking at your submission again for the thousandth time, and I'm blown away. Do you know how many applications we've gone through trying to find such a unique sound? Thousands. And you guys are fucking it," he says with so much excitement that goosebumps break out my arms.

My entire body locks up. Butterflies blossom in my churning gut, threatening to send my dinner up. Is this happening? Is this a fucking joke at my expense? Deep breaths, Asher. Deep fucking breaths.

"You...you what? Wait? Is this..."

"Hey, man, I'm Seger West. I'm calling on behalf of West Records. We are pouring through the submissions this week, and I gotta say, Whispered Words has the shit we're looking for. Fuck. You guys were..."

"Not professional, dude. You can't say fuck to potential winners. You'll scare them away with your Seger attitude," another voice says in the background with a scoff.

"Fuck off, Elf Ears," Seger grumbles, returning to the phone. "Sorry, man. My brother is..."

"Husband-in-law! I swear you're ashamed of me. It's been how many years now?"

"Shut the fuck up, Elf Ears!" another person growls in the background. "He's in the middle of a phone call. You're worse than Dash when he wants a fucking cookie. Jesus. I have enough kids to wrangle. I don't need you, too."

Seger sighs heavily, muttering a few colorful words into the phone, and everything dies down behind him.

"Jesus. Sorry. My brothers are helping me with this whole event," Seger says through a tired breath. "Anyway, you'll get something in the mail with a formal invitation today. We've overnighted everything. But we just wanted to talk to the guys behind the music. Your fans are incredible, too, and your sound... I can't wait to hear you live," he gushes in a low voice.

"Holy...fuck," I gasp out. "You're serious? You're fucking serious! We got...we got in? We fucking made it?" I ramble into the phone as my thoughts catch up to the situation.

"Yeah, man. You guys are the shit! Once you read the letter, it'll have all the information you need. We'll see you guys in a few weeks!"

"Holy shit. Thanks, man! Thanks for taking a chance on us! Wait till I tell the guys they'll be..." I trail off as haunting words play on repeat in my mind.

"We'll wait for you, River!"

"We can play in Chicago! No problem!"

"There will be a next time."

After exchanging goodbyes, I hang up the phone, slowly dropping it into my lap. Slumping in the seat, I lick my lips. How the fuck am I going to get them to California if they're more concerned with staying with River than playing in the band. This is our fucking band—our only chance to make it in the big leagues. Tours. Buses. Recording studios. Screaming fans. They're all within grasp, handed to us on a silver platter for the taking. And here they are, convinced they'd wait for her.

Like fuck.

I will not let my brothers wake up regretting their life choices one day. No matter the consequences. No matter how much I'll hate myself and drown in my guilt, we're going to California. No. Matter. What. With or without River West.

Callum: River's mom is in the hospital. Something happened last night.

Rad: She's super sick, man, and River...she's...

Callum: She's not okay. I can't get her to...move or speak. She's just....

Rad: Catatonic.

I take a few breaths, swallowing down the panic rising inside me. Despite the win we just achieved, nothing but desperation claws through me, threatening to pull me under the waves of anxiety. If River's mom is sick, how the hell am I going to convince them to go to California with me? They'll insist on staying behind and caring for her even more than they already do. Fuck. Listen, I'm not a cold-hearted bastard, but we've had our sights set on this goal for years now. I can't idly sit back and let our plans derail off the tracks. If there's one person who can keep these fuckers' eyes on the prize, it's me.

Whatever it takes.

Asher: Fuck, man. Tell Little Brat I'm sorry. We'll be there soon.

Kieran frantically knocks on my window with concern etched on his face. Rolling it down, all the energy rushes from me, and my head swims in a fog of confusion. It's on the tip of my tongue to sing our win and confess everything. Something holds me back, though, keeping my lips sealed. For some reason, I need time to think about everything. River. The competition. And our promise to her.

"I'm going to meet them at the hospital. Wanna go?" he asks with his brows furrowed. His fingers fidget in the open window, drumming against the car's interior.

I shake my head. "I'll meet up with you in a bit. I'll grab whatever River needs. Just text me, okay?"

"You good?" Kieran asks, looking me up and down. "You look like you're up to something." His nose scrunches. "Or about to shit your pants." I blanch at his words, shoving my hand into his chest and pushing him away. He smirks, swatting at me when he rights himself.

"I'm fine, asshole. Just go away. I'll be by in a bit. I'll unpack and shit." I pinch the bridge of my nose.

"Fine, shitbag," he grunts, shoving off my Tahoe and climbing into his own. He glares at me with suspicion when he pulls out of the driveway and peels out of the neighborhood.

My eyes gaze up at the large, intimidating house full of an array of monsters ready to attack. Whether they're manipulative gold diggers or the devil himself, they reside here in a seemingly ordinary neighborhood. With trepidation, I climb out of the car and head into the pits of Hell with my head held high. Finally, hope shines somewhere in the back of my darkened mind, slowly coming out of the box I shoved it into years ago. It fills me to the brim with anticipation and so much goddamn hope I could vomit. This is fucking it. We're achieving what we set out to do. We fucking got in! We did it! Now, all we have to do is blow the rest of the competition away and leave no doubt in the West brothers' minds that we're the best.

When the front door closes behind me, I'm greeted by a smug-looking Gloria bustling around the kitchen. With practiced grace, she sets a few sets of papers on the countertop, grinning as she reads the words. Eyeing her face, I note the lack of bruising and swelling, meaning my father must be far away on his so-called business trips.

"It seems we have a score to settle," she says, sitting on the edge of the stool in front of the paper, tapping them with her nail.

"How so?" I raise a brow, strolling through the living room with my hands in my pockets.

A million thoughts race through my mind as I settle across from her, crossing my legs. A bored look crosses my face when she grins more, tapping her nails against the papers on the counter. Thick silence encases the room, doing little to rile me up. Her beady blue eyes glare at me when I huff, rolling my eyes.

"Speak, for God's sake, Gloria. Spit it out already," I growl, reaching the thin end of my patience.

My fingers curl and uncurl on the countertop, waiting on her to finally open her mouth and reveal whatever bullshit she has up her sleeve. But my patience wears thin when her eyes widen, and her lips flap like a fucking fish out of water.

The stool squeaks against the linoleum floor when I abruptly stand, digging my phone from my pocket. I don't have time for her shit, especially not today. Not after this weekend. And not after that phone call I received. I need to plot this entire thing and expertly move the pieces on my board before I make any moves.

"This is yours," she says, gesturing to the paperwork on the counter.

I grunt, walking back and sitting down. She swallows hard when I scowl in her direction, making the poor woman flinch. If I were nicer, I would hold back the anger brewing slowly inside me, but I can't seem to help it around her.

"What is it?" I ask, putting a hand out, and thankfully, she gives it to me.

"It's everything you need for the competition," she says, sitting back and folding her arms across her chest in victory. "Remember our deal?"

I raise a brow, flipping through the pages.

Congratulations on your win! The West brothers have officially chosen you and hand-picked you to participate. Please read the rules below...

The contest will be held at the KC Club in East Point Bluff, California, on December 15th of this year. All chosen participants will receive a call directly from the showrunners, confirming their win. All selected participants must RSVP within seventy-two hours by texting 555-425-1933 with their answers. All chosen participants must arrive on December 14th for registration.

"Seems you only have two weeks to make it out there," Gloria says, staring down at her manicured nails with a smirk.

"Seems that way," I huff, continuing to read the stipulations and rules. Fuck. I need Callum to read these over, so we don't miss a damn thing. The last thing we need is to forget a damn rule.

"Which means," she says in her snobby voice. "You only have a week to get everything in order."

My heart pumps double time at all the shit we have to do to get to the damn contest before it starts. Packing. Getting money. The car. Fuck. Getting the guys on board and...

"Here's the five grand," she says, waving around an envelope full of cash. "And my word that your father hasn't found out. In fact, he'll be on a business trip for the next week or so." She lifts her chin, looking smug as hell. But I'm too concerned with the amount of shit I have to do to pay her any mind. She can jump off a cliff for all I care.

"Great," I say, collecting the paper and shoveling it back into the envelope they came in. "You know it's a crime to rifle through other people's mail." Looking over my shoulder, I look at her, and she shrugs, holding onto the cash with a firm grip.

"Callum asked me to look for the mail," she sniffs. "You have been away for a week."

Every possible outcome runs through my mind.

"Remember, though," Gloria says, climbing to her feet and brushing her hands down her pants. "The other part of our deal. I'll give you the extra funds if you...."

"Yeah. Don't worry. I won't forget about you and Camilla." I shake my head. I can only imagine how insufferable my father will be when his two main punching bags disappear from the situation.

"And?" She raises a brow, coming to stand in front of me.

"Would you spit it out? I don't have time for this."

"The girl stays here. No matter what. She'll ruin everything we've set out to do."

"We've? You mean the band?" She swallows hard and waves a hand.

"Of course, your band," she scoffs.

I wipe every emotion from my face and nod. No matter how much I want to fight it, Gloria's right. The guys are ready to hand over the keys and fucking stay here in Central City, where we'll never go anywhere. We'll never get our band off the ground if we stay for River.

Gloria's grin grows a mile, and she bounces on her toes. "If you want my advice," she says, leaning in as I scowl. I don't want anything from her. I want to lie down and collect myself. Maybe take a hot shower and leave the memory of River down the drain, which is impossible to do. "A little birdy told me you'll want to speak with Donavan Drake. He might have a few ideas on how to rid yourselves of the trash. Pictures included." She taps my cheek condescendingly and waltzes away with a victorious pep in her step.

God. Burn my eyes out now. Please take me away from this miserable place.

Although, I don't blame her for wanting to take my sister and run for the hills. My father is less than desirable. She has an ass-backward way of doing things. I sigh, rub the headache away from my forehead and pull out my phone. My plate fills higher and higher with bullshit, but I know the remedy to alleviate it.

As I step into my bathroom and set my phone on the counter, I take a long look in the mirror. My tired, hazel eyes stare back at me, bloodshot and guilt-ridden. My messy blonde hair sticks on end as the room fills with steam, slowly erasing the face in front of me.

Every choice I've made has been for the band—my family. The boys who have grown to be my brothers in the shit storm called life. Whatever I do with this information will affect us, even River. She won't go unscathed. It may break her heart for a week or two, but she's resilient and one tough chick. She'll move on to some other poor schmuck, and then, we'll be a distant, painful memory. That's all the motivation I need to contact the last person I ever thought I'd want to speak with.

Asher: We need to talk.

Staring at the blank screen, I shake my head and jump into the shower. Memories of our weekend flash through my mind as my fingers work through my hair, massaging my roots. My eyes squeeze shut, and I groan at the images sitting behind my eyes. River's naked form sprawled out and ready for the taking. River panting and moaning as we fuck her against the dining room table. The taste of her flesh as I licked the salt off and forced my tongue down her throat. My fingers tightly wrapped around her throat, squeezing until she silently begged for breath. My dick impaling her over and over until she screamed my name. Fuck. My dick gets hard as the heat pounds against my back and neck, washing away the world pressing down on me. I stare at my traitorous dick. It was one weekend of fun, and that's it. I made myself a promise and let go, embracing what I had wanted since the Ferris wheel. Her. The whole package. And now that I had her, I had to let go and let her essence wash down the drain with every ounce of guilt pressing down on me.

Once I'm out of the shower and running the soft towel across my skin, clarity hits me smack in the head. I know exactly what I have to do to get us through this and onto California without the distraction. Now, all I have to do is set it all up.

Asher: How's Little Brat?

Walking into my room, I get dressed in jeans, a shirt, and a sweatshirt.

Kieran: .... Meet us in the ER.

Rad: Can't say it through text, bro. But it isn't good and...

My heart sinks. They said her mom was taken by ambulance and sick but did she succumb to whatever was ailing her? Jesus. That would complicate everything times ten. But whatever the issue, I'll push forward with all my might and get what we need. It's for the better of the band...my family.

The smell of cheap, burned coffee fills my nose when I round the corner, greeting the solemn faces of Callum and Rad, resting in the uncomfortable-looking ER waiting room. Tears stain their cheeks, and a deep-red tint fills their glazed eyes.

The whole drive to the hospital had my thoughts in a tailspin of worry, guilt, and trying to convince myself I was doing the right thing. I am, right? Am I doing the best thing I can for the guys? For the fucking band? I'm the one looking out for them. They don't know what the fuck they want right now. Well, except for a win at the Battle of the Bands. One day, I'll be able to reflect on this and not drown in the misery I've created for myself.

"What's going on?" I ask, coming to a halt right in front of them.

My brows furrow when Rad shakes his head with tears streaming down his cheeks, and his bottom lip quivers with anguish resting in the depths of his dark eyes. Instantly my heart drops, and the worst possible outcome runs through my mind. What the fuck happened? My gaze drifts to Callum, burrowing into the stiff seat with white earbuds resting in his ears as he drowns out the rest of the world, covering his eyes with his hands. The old Callum, the one so stuck inside his head with the awful memories of his past, slowly emerges, taking away the blossoming butterfly Callum had become. My jaw clenches. She may have brought him out of his shell, breathing life into his lungs with her wild ways, but she's the cause of all the heartache on his fallen face. If it weren't for her, then we'd all be peachy. But she's come in and fucked us all up. This is just the cherry on fucking top.

"It's bad, bro," Rad whispers through an array of emotions clogging his throat.

"What is it?" I ask through the tension rising in my chest, beating down on me.

"They tried so fucking hard," Rad says, wiping away the tears. "Her mom is gone," he mumbles, gripping his hair tightly. "She fucking...she fucking died because we took River away from here. They said something about an infection in her blood."

"No," I bark, plopping down next to him and gripping his shoulder. "This is no one's fault. If she was sick, this was meant to happen." I give him a sharp nod when he slumps in the seat with a twisting expression. More tears escape down his cheeks, and he sniffles.

"Where is River?"

Rad's lips roll together, and his brows furrow. "Talking to the funeral home people. Some pastor came by and prayed with us, but uh, they needed to know where to take the body in the morning." He shakes his head in disbelief. "How did this happen, man? I don't understand. Stella was a good woman she..." he chokes on his words, bringing a fist to his mouth, stopping his words.

Knots form in my gut, memories of death smothering me. Stella, River's mom, is no longer with us. Unlike my mother, it wasn't by her own hands. It was something her body did to her and let her suffer. My heart mourns with River, who's probably so distraught she doesn't know what to do with herself. And I feel for her. I've been through it before at a younger age. No one prepares you for life without the woman who brought you into this world. She's supposed to live for an eternity by your side, helping you as all mothers should. But now, River won't have that opportunity.

"It happens to the best of people," I murmur, eyeing Callum as he heaves a shuddering breath. The storm hiding in the back of his blank eyes startles me into putting my hand on his shoulder and gently squeezing. Looking at me, he shakes his head, breaking our eye contact. Slowly, the old closed-off Callum takes the reigns and refuses to meet my eye, staring at the floor instead.

"Where was her nurse?" Rad sniffles. "Where was anyone?"

"Her symptoms were like the flu," Kieran says, stumbling into the seat beside me. "They said she would have been feverish, puking, and feeling sick. The neighbor checked in on her and gave her Tylenol but didn't recognize the symptoms for what they were." Grabbing his long, dark locks, misery takes over his twisted expression.

"How's Pretty Girl?" Rad asks, jumping to his feet. "We need to be with her."

"She asked me to leave," Kieran grumbles, lips twisting into furry. "She's hiding in her fucking grief and pushing me away."

"Maybe we should give her some space," I say, folding my hands in my lap. "She doesn't...."

"Like fuck, bro. Respectfully, of course. River pushes us away when she doesn't want us to see her vulnerabilities," Rad snaps, getting in my face. "I won't be dragged away when she needs us."

I sigh, nodding. I knew it would not be easy to convince them that we needed to give her some space and talk sense into them.

"She wants to be alone." We all jump when her best friend Ode marches out of the emergency room doors with a grim expression, shaking her head. Her heated, dark eyes lock on us, and she sighs, hurt, making her face fall. "She even kicked me out," she mutters, putting a hand on her forehead. "My mom is going to take her home. We need to give her a day or two to process, alone. That's how she handles shit. It's stupid, but that's the River West way."

"Let's regroup at Callum's," I suggest, getting to my feet. "Make her think we've given her her space."

Looking around, I see the war brewing in their minds. They don't want to, but they know we need to. River will push and push until we're so far away we'll never get back. And somehow, this works into my plan to pull them as far apart from her as I can. Pain tightens my chest at the thought of abandoning her like my father did to me the moment my mother took things into her own hands and ended her existence. Unlike me at the time of my mother's death, River has a family with Ode and Korrine. They'll guide her through this rough time with love and compassion.

River doesn't need us. Not now.

"Fine," Kieran barks with a frown, pushing past me with a rough shoulder check. "Let's go to Callum's and work out a plan. But after tomorrow, I'm not leaving her alone. Do you fucking understand? I'm here for her. No matter what."

Fury blazes to life, lighting up his haunting mismatched eyes, giving me all the confirmation I need. He's too deep, and it's time to pull the plug.

"Men," Ode mutters under her breath, rolling her eyes. "Could one of you run me home, please?" she asks, eyeing each of us with raised brows.

"I will," I say with a sharp nod, gesturing for her to follow. The more distance I can put between the guys and River's apartment, the better. "I'll meet you back at the house," I confirm before they do something stupid like camp out at the hospital all night or try to break into her apartment again.

"I'm going to bake her a pie," Rad murmurs, putting his love into his food. "And fried chicken, potatoes, and corn." Listing off more food, he rambles on until he's settled into his car and starts it, cutting him off. I wave each of them off and take Ode home without a word.

"Thanks," she says, climbing out. "And uh, you know. I don't usually say this shit, but you guys have turned River around. She's been in this funk for years, working her ass off. And then you guys come into her life, and I've never seen her smile more. You guys don't know what a gift you've been to her. She's my best friend; all I want for her is the best. So, uh, thanks," she says with a grimace, shutting the door before I can speak.

She won't be as accommodating when I have the courage to answer the text message awaiting me. It came through at the hospital, discreetly vibrating in my pocket, but I refused to answer when so many people were around. Indecision pushes at my mind, and guilt pushes down on me like a heavy weight on my shoulders. Now is the time to embrace River and take her with us; let her grieve in our arms as we make our dreams come true. Not run away and do it all ourselves. But what other choice do I have? They're eating out of the palm of her hand, bending over backward to make her happy. What about us? Me? Our dreams? That's what it all boils down to—our future. We can't sit around here forever waiting for River to decide what she wants to do with her life. We need to act now while the iron is hot and our talent is what they're looking for—not three years from now when she graduates.

Leaning over, I catch my reflection in the mirror and quickly look away. I do what I have to do to ensure our future stays on track.

Their words from our trip play in my mind, making the decisions all the more easier.

"We'll wait for you."

"We'll wait for you..."

"We'll stay if you can't go..."

Instead of going to California, they'd rather risk our careers and stay with River. Sweet, sweet fucking River. The girl we sought out to help us get to this point. And now, everything is one big fucking mess. They're damn near in love with her and ready to propose a fucking five-way marriage.

I heave a breath, glaring at the ceiling. Without overthinking my actions anymore, I grab my phone and look at the screen, swallowing the heavy lump in my throat. One message rests unread from an hour ago that I haven't bothered to answer. Or fucking look. If the guys knew what I was up to, they'd fucking murder me on the spot.

Asher: I need to talk to you.

Van: Why?

Asher: You want your girl back, right?

Asher: Don't get shy about it now.

Asher: We all know who you want.

Silence rests in the night air around me when I pull the Tahoe out of the parking lot of River's apartment complex and drive toward home. Looking down, I spy his response and risk texting and driving.

Van: We can talk. When?

Asher: Now. I'll be there in twenty.

Nerves eat away at me the closer I get to my damnation. There's no going back. The moment I open my mouth, I can't take it back.

As I get closer to my destination, the world passes by in a blur. I'm so lost in my guilt that I don't register when I pull up in front of Van's house, or he gets into the passenger's side, slamming the door hard.

"What do you mean to get your girl back?" he asks with slight desperation ringing in his voice.

Fuck. This might be easier than I initially thought. From what I have planned, Van will be an intricate part I can't afford to lose.

"Exactly what I said," I grumble, throwing the car into park and keeping in the shadows. Callum's house may be a block away, but there's no way they'll see me from here. "So, do you want her eating out of the palm of your hand again? Or what?" Disgust burrows in my gut at my own damn words. What in the fuck am I doing? I close my eyes. It's what I have to do. But fuck. River's mom just died. She's in goddamn grieving, and here I am, plotting behind her back.

Images of River float through my mind. Me behind her, pounding her hips against the table. Her moans will forever live on a shrine in the back of my mind. Nothing will erase them. Not even the hate she'll feel for me, in the end, could erase our intricate past. But as far as I'm concerned, in another week, we'll never hear from her again. We'll be too far away in California, living our dream. And she'll be here, living hers.

"What's in it for you?" Van rightfully asks with suspicion.

"Her away from them. Us in California. Take your pick." I shrug, watching the shadows dance along his face as he processes my words.

"You got in?" he asks in disbelief, with his jaw hanging open. "Holy hell."

"Now, imagine once we leave. Her mom just died. Who do you think River will come running back to?" I lift a brow when something dark sparkles in his eyes, and he nods.

"Oh shit," he breathes, eyes widening at my words. "She's dead? Now she's more vulnerable. Perfect," he mumbles more to himself than me, rubbing his palms together. "She's always been mine." A certain amount of possession rests in his tone, enough to raise the tiny hairs on my arm in alert.

Right. Always been his? Isn't that a load of shit? My heart squeezes. Fuck. What am I doing? I'm handing River over to a fucking psychopath. Not that she'd ever waltz back into his life, anyway. But that's the grand illusion of it all. River will never want Van. Not again. Ever. She'll always pine for the boys who walked away if I can get this plan to work. If I.... I take a deep breath, already regretting this conversation. What the fuck am I doing?

How's that saying go? If you love something enough, you should let it go, and if it genuinely loves you, it'll come back. That's laughable at best. Once we escape and the boys forget about her, we'll never see her face again. And that's what I'm forcefully doing. I'm peeling their fingers from around the butterfly, setting us free and letting our band escape.

My heart pounds as I stare out the front windshield, noting the cold wind knocking against the windows. Little white flakes float down from the sky, melting on my windshield when they hit, leaving tiny wet droplets behind.

"So, you didn't come talk to me without reason. What is it?" he finally asks, focusing entirely on me.

"You have something I need." Something crucial to pry their fingers away from River and something that will knock them back and down a peg or two and reevaluate their relationship with her. They wanted her exclusively, with no extra boyfriends in the background. With a sigh, I feel the enormity of my words.

He snorts. "Something you need? And what could that be? You've been pricks to me since you all started seeing her and stealing her away from me." He shakes his head. "So, why should I even help you?"

"Because I know what you did," I say, side-eyeing him when he stiffens and his expression hardens.

"You don't know shit about me," he growls through clenched teeth. "Are we done?"

— 400 —

"I find it funny the one night you're not stalking River through the bar is the same night she gets laid out and almost taken advantage of. Or is that just a coincidence?" I raise a brow when he pales, unable to keep his shame off his face, but quickly hides it behind his rolling eyes and twisting lips. "I'm sure the cops would love to hear the tidbit about you organizing the entire thing so you could feel like some sort of disgusting hero," I huff, feeling revulsion slither through my veins like a thick sludge weighing me down, hoping what I'm saying isn't true. But the fact is Van's a slimy piece of shit who is desperate enough to pull something as disgusting as this off.

"You... What the hell do you want?" he asks, swallowing his nerves without refuting my claims against him. My damn heart sinks at the realization of what he's done, but I shake it off and push forward with my stupid plan, even when my stomach rolls and vomit creeps up my throat.

"A little birdy told me you have some videos. Videos, I don't want to know how you obtained pictures. You. River. I need them." My eyes burn into him as he wilts under the pressure and slumps.

"Why?"

"I should ask the same. Does River know you filmed your sex life with her?" I seal my lips shut, holding back the vomit threatening to break through. If there's one thing in my life I'll regret forever, it's this. I am stooping so damn low to obtain the ultimate dream that I'm disgusted at my actions. "Send them to me, and all will be forgotten. By next week, we'll be forgotten. River will run to you, and all will be normal."

We sit silently for another moment, and Van nods, getting his phone out. "Sure," he says, scanning through his phone, clicking a few pictures, and then hitting send. "What're you using them for?" he asks when my phone vibrates, but I refuse to look at the multiple videos and photos he sent.

"Be available tomorrow," I say, narrowing my eyes at him. "Your girl might need some dinner at her place to make her feel better." Every word I speak feels like ash on my tongue, turning bitter and chalky.

I fucking hate myself.

"Sure," he mumbles, getting out of the car with crinkled brows. He doesn't look back at me when he goes inside, and I don't look at him.

This is a means to an end. A way to live our dream, and that's it.

A plan formulates in my mind as I drive back to Callum's, and we regroup, coming up with a solid idea on how to get us the fuck out of here and keep River here. Now all I have to do is break my best friends' hearts.

RIVER

Numbness fills every molecule in my body. The past day's events play like a movie that happened to someone else. Not me. Never me. There's no way I went from the best fucking vacation to this dismal existence bathed in loneliness.

Emptiness surrounds me—a nothingness sinking deep into my bones. The world around me keeps moving and has been for the past two days, leaving me here, in the home I once shared with my mother. She's the same woman who suffered while I was away, having the time of my life and insisting to the neighbor that she was okay—insisting to her nurse that she didn't need her on those days and let her have a few days off. Why did my mom do this? Why would she leave me when I needed her in my life? Things were going to look up for us in the future. So, why did she leave me now?

Sitting on the edge of my bed, I stare out into the dark abyss. Shadows dance along the sliding glass door, but no one enters through hellbent on getting me out of bed. Their voices play in the back of my mind like ghosts whispering in my ear, trying to pry me out of bed. But I'm a frozen mass, unable to motivate myself. It's been like this for days. Me, myself, and I—planning a funeral. Something I never thought I'd have to do. I mean, who the fuck does that? Who plans a funeral for their mother at nineteen? Fuck. Why? Why did this happen?

Why did she leave me?

Of course, my neighbors, Odette, Leon, and Korrine, stopped by and ensured I was okay by feeding me dinner and keeping me company—until I shooed them away. But the boys? It's like the moment I told them to leave me alone in the ER, they listened. Half of me is pissed off and conflicted because I wanted the solitude to process the immeasurable amount of grief pressing down on me. The other half wants them by my side, hugging me and telling me everything will be okay. I'll be okay, right? Everything will work out, right? But fuck. Why aren't they here? Where the fuck have they been while I've been drowning in grief and unable to find a liferaft to pull me ashore? Don't they understand I didn't *really* want them to leave me alone? They were supposed to fight me tooth and nail, hovering above me until I gave in. But they... They left me when I needed them, and I only have myself to blame.

My body desperately craves Callum in my bed, snuggling with me until I fall asleep with peaceful dreams. Or Rad taking me on his dirt bike through the light snow dusting the ground, erasing the depression darkening my mind. I want Kieran to hold me and tell me I'll be okay with his possessive nature and nurturing me until I'm well again. And Asher, I'd let him fuck me out of my grief, bringing me to so many damn orgasms I forget why my world is unraveling.

I sigh, massaging my temples. I never thought loneliness would settle so deep inside me, overshadowing my damn life. With a sigh, I head to the kitchen and grab a glass of water. No matter what happens in my life, I must press forward and continue with my goals. And the first step is getting out of bed.

River: Hey, uh...you guys want to hang out?

I tap my nails on the counter, watching the screen with a sharp eye. I scroll up, looking at the two other unanswered messages I'd sent last night, asking if they'd want to come to see me and maybe watch a damn movie. Yet, I was ghosted.

A deep ache forms in my gut, turning it into knots as I over-analyze their shifty ways. Maybe they're playing a gig somewhere, leaving me alone to pick up the pieces, which I'm barely doing. One false move and my reality will shatter, and I'll be no more than a pile of broken edges on the floor.

Tomorrow my mother's funeral will kick off at noon at the Central Funeral Home. A part of me is ready to continue with this life and move on as quickly as possible. I'll miss the hell out of my mom, but everything happened so fast. It hasn't set in yet that she's truly gone. It's only been a day, but it feels like she's at the grocery store and will march through the front door with a grin at any time. Nothing feels real right now.

When I walk past her recliner, my stomach churns at the misery she must have felt lying there and slowly dying all by herself. I stop beside it, running a finger over the worn material, reveling in the feel of the rough fabric against my fingertips. Why didn't she call for help? Why didn't she ask someone to take her to the hospital before it was too late? Or had she just given up on life?

So many questions run through my mind with little indication of the answers. The only person who could give me clues has been shoved into a large box destined for the ground tomorrow.

My heart jumps through my chest when a knock sounds at the front door, alerting me to unexpected company. For the most part, everyone has respected the space I requested—almost too much. Ugh. My head swims in confusion. I want people here, but I don't want people here. I want to wallow in my own misery, yet I want people here to guide me through it. I'm so damn conflicted with what I want; it makes my fingers curl into fists, ready to punch my frustrations away.

"Van?" I blanch when I open my front door, greeted by a sheepish-looking Van holding out a food container.

"I-I heard about your mom, Rivy," he mutters, rubbing the back of his neck. "I know you've always lived alone with her, so I wanted to stop by and see if you were okay. Also, I wanted to drop off some food." Licking his lips, he hands it over, and the most delicious smell wafts from the lid, making my stomach grumble loud enough for him to pop a smile. "You always did have a hard time taking care of yourself," he rumbles, pushing past me and waltzing into my apartment like he's been here before.

I frown at his chastising words, momentarily stunned at his actions. How dare he march into my home and scold me on how I take care of myself. I mean, sure. I haven't technically eaten all day. Eating when you're stuck at home with nowhere to go and numbing pain gnawing at your insides makes it challenging to crave food. It's the last thing on your mind.

"Um, thanks for the food," I say, shutting the front door and locking it before facing him. "I appreciate the concern. But, uh— what're you doing here? You've never come here before." Placing the food on the kitchen counter, I peel open the lid. My mouth waters at the sight of the freshly baked meatloaf, mashed potatoes, and a side of corn, and a small biscuit with melted butter rests on top of it all, and my brows furrow. "Did you...?"

Van grins with pride, leaning against the counter next to me, and nods. "Yeah. I made it just for you, Rivy. I thought you would need comfort food." He shrugs, looking smugly satisfied with himself, and my hackles rise.

I've pushed this asshole away for months now, and suddenly, he's standing in my kitchen like I'm his number one concern. He's the one who dumped me and pushed me away. Usually, he's watching from the shadows, stalking my every move. Now, he's in the home he swore he wouldn't be caught dead in. This is the same douchecanoe who used to fuck me in his car and then drop me off a block from home because he was too scared to be here.

"Thanks," I say with apprehension, grabbing a fork and tentatively taking a bite of the delicious mashed potatoes smothered in gravy. I'm so fucked if this is laced with poison, and Van's sole purpose is to kidnap me because it's so damn good, it melts on my tongue—poison be damned, I grab more. "This is delicious. Exactly what I needed," I mumble through my bite, shoveling more food into my mouth with a hum of satisfaction. Maybe this is one more step in the right direction to getting myself out of this dark, miserable state I've put myself in for the last two days.

Van's eyes track around the apartment, taking every dismal detail in with the scrunch of his judgemental nose. "So, this is where you live?" he asks, coming to stand beside me, knocking his shoulder into mine. "It's not too scary here," he says with another unsettling, cocky grin.

"Um, thanks," I say, pushing the half-eaten food away. "Is this all you came by for?" I ask, gesturing to the food as I put the lid back on and hand it back to him. "I mean, I appreciate it. But I'm kind of busy..."

Busy getting the fuck away from this intruding asshole. Where's Odette when I need her to barge in with a bat and whack this chucklehead all the way back to his car and send him back to Lakeview?

My hairs stand on end when he pushes the Tupperware back into my hands, shaking his head. "Just keep it. You can wash it and give it back to me." Give it back to him? That means he wants me to see him again or bring it by.

"I don't have a car, remember? I can't bring it back. So here, take it back now, and I appreciate it, Van. Seriously, this was so nice of you, but I need to get back to funeral planning," I mumble, shoving the plastic back into his stomach until he grips it.

"Shit!" he yelps when the lid blows open, spilling the contents of the container onto his white shirt, staining it brown.

"I'm so sorry," I say, grabbing a paper towel, wiping it off the floor, and handing him one for his shirt.

Shaking his head, he cringes. "It's okay," he says with a pained expression; grabbing the back of his shirt, he takes it off and shrugs. "It's no biggie. Do you have a washer here? Can you put it in there?" Van slowly leans down, pinning my back against the kitchen cabinet like a predator swooping in for its kill.

I jerk back, trying to keep him as far away from me as possible. My skin crawls at the sadistic look crossing his face that he's hiding behind a sympathetic expression. Van has always had his claws in me by following me around and luring me out of my pants. But not this time.

"Maybe you should leave," I say through a heavy breath, keeping my eyes on the predator in front of me. I swear if I blink, he'll keep getting closer until he swallows me whole.

"Rivy, I can't leave now," he says, furrowing his brows. "You're hurting," he murmurs, running a finger down my cheek, and I flinch away. Hurt sears into his face, but he shakes it off, looking at me with pity. "Your mom just died. You can't stay here all by yourself."

"I can. I'm fine." I put my hands up, resting them on his chest and attempting to push him away.

I'd be much better if he stopped looking at me like I was a broken doll needing healing. He's not the one I want. I want the boys who hold my heart in their hands, the ones I didn't even mean to fall in love with. That's how it happens, though, right? We fall for those bad boys we swear off, knowing they're tinged in poison, ready to infect us with their wicked ways.

"No. You can't! You need someone, and obviously, those idiots who've been following you around like puppies aren't around. Where are they, Rivy?" he asks, leaning in closer to look me in the eyes. "Where are they now?"

"I...I..." I roll my lips together because I have no idea. It's like they're avoiding me for some reason, but I can't think of why. Did I do something to piss them off? I mean, I told them to leave me be, but I didn't actually think they would for this long.

"I tried to tell you," Van murmurs, pinching my chin. "They're users, Riv. You know they made it into Battle of the Bands, right?"

"Wait, what?" I ask, sucking in a breath. "No, they would have...they would have told me..."

Wouldn't they have? Wouldn't I have been the first person they told? They promised they'd take me. They promised me a lot of shit. And now they've gotten what they wanted from me. Closing my eyes, I take a deep breath. I'm a fucking adult, and I'll talk to them about it after everything settles down.

My heart skips a beat when Van's brown eyes lock on something behind us, and he growls. Before I have time to analyze what's happening, he leans in, putting his lips on mine with vigor. From the moment our lips touch, my stomach turns, wanting to vomit right into his mouth. Maybe that'd get him to back off and stop touching me like he owns me.

Letting out a shriek into his probing mouth, I jam my fist into his side several times without results. Jamming his tongue onto my mouth, he plasters himself against me, holding me hostage with his unwanted kiss. A sharp pain pierces my lip when he bites down, splitting my flesh. An angry moan bubbles up from my throat when he licks at the spot and returns to forcing his tongue into my mouth. I couldn't fucking move if I wanted to. Shit. With his hands in my hair and body pressed into mine, I'm at his mercy until he pulls away, panting for air with a flushed look.

"I've missed you so damn much," he says louder than necessary. "You're so damn perfect for me, Riv. I knew you'd finally choose me over them."

I grunt, trying to squirm out of his grip, but he holds me tighter. A devious grin spreads across his lips, sending chills down my spine. Before me, Van changes into some sort of frightening monster, clinging to me harder than before. A low, menacing chuckle explodes from his vibrating chest, and glee lights up the darkened shadows on his face, making him out to be the true villain he is.

Fear slithers through my veins at what he's capable of. Here I am in my own home, backed into a corner, forced to make out with the man who apparently has a hard time hearing no. Over and over again, I've asked him to fuck off, and repeatedly, he hasn't listened.

"You don't have to pretend you don't like it, Rivy. I know you do." With every word he speaks, his voice gets louder and louder, making my ears ring from the volume of his deep voice.

"I really don't," I grunt, attempting to push him away, but my hands become trapped between our bodies.

Every attempt to turn my head behind me is blocked by his massive hands gripping my hair with bruising force. Panic creeps up my spine, clawing at me to run the fuck away. From deep within, I find the strength to push Van off me and kick him straight in the dick. His brown eyes widen in terror, and he grunts, holding a hand to his balls, and sinks to his knees with a crazed expression. Betrayal flashes through his eyes when he groans, trying to ride out the discomfort of my kick on the ground.

It seems Van needs another—fuck around and find out—type of lesson because verbalizing my discomfort doesn't seem to register with him. So, without uttering a word, I grunt, pulling my fist back and heaving it straight into his face.

The burning, crunching pain hits my fist first as I shake it out in the air, wishing I could punch him again. Basking in the glory of his blood splattering against my fist, I heave a breath, trying to wash away the unwanted touch of Van as I make my getaway. How could someone so close to me force themselves on me like that? Again? How many times will it take for men to understand the word no?

My heart pounds in my chest at the phantom feel of him pushing against me, and I shake it off, running toward my bedroom. I slam the door shut, locking the damn knob, and turn toward my sliding glass door. Freedom is within my grasp until I stop dead, freezing in place.

My heart shatters when Callum stands outside the sliding glass door, shaking his head in disbelief. Tears run down his face in rapid succession, falling to the floor, agony twists his face when he wipes away the tears, and his jaw tightens as I've never seen before.

"You-you kissed him? So-so, it's true?" His face twists more, pain tearing through him and, in turn, splitting me open with his visual anguish.

"What? What's true? Callum," I say, reaching for him. "Listen..."

"Goodbye, River," he rasps through thick emotions in a low voice, sending shivers down my spine. The final nail in the coffin has sealed my fate.

"No, wait!" I shout with desperation cracking my voice when he walks as fast as he can down the sidewalk and fucking disappears into the night, not bothering to let me explain anything to him. I could chase him all night, and he'd still turn his back on me.

How could he walk away without letting me explain anything? How could he not see that Van had assaulted me in the kitchen? Pulling out my phone and texting the group, I don't waste a moment.

River: I know what you think you saw....

River: Please talk to me.

River: He KISSED me.... He did it against my will! I said no! I punched him for fuck's sake.

River: I didn't want it.

River: Please...can someone talk to me?

River: Why're you all ignoring me?

"River," Van murmurs through the door, lightly knocking against the wood.

"Go away!" I cry out, trying to hold the emotions clogging my throat. "You fucking psychopath! No means no, asshole!" I hiss, sucking in oxygen.

"Look, I'm sorry. I... I still love you, Rivey. I can't help it. I won't leave until I know you're okay," he says with concern, tapping on the door again.

"I'll be okay when you fucking leave!" I shout through shuddering breaths, feeling the warmth of my tears spreading down my cheeks as my heart breaks into a million pieces.

"Fine," he says softly, "but I'll be a phone call away when you need me. I'll always be there for you, Rivy. Whether you like it or not."

Crawling into my cold bed, I silence my sniffles with my comforter until the sound of my front door slams shut, leaving me with only the tumultuous thoughts wreaking havoc inside my brain. Here I am, once again alone like I always thought I'd be on the night before my mother's funeral.

I stare at my phone for hours, counting the minutes until the sun rises, and I heave myself out of bed. The same numbness sets in like before. This time, it wraps me in its arms like a hug that I embrace, carrying with me all day.

I expect to see the guys coming to pay their respects throughout the funeral, but they never show—not even a quick pop-in to say goodbye. Unlike them, Van dares to show his face, filled with massive amounts of sympathy. He even drops flowers at my front door with a note apologizing for his actions and asking me to call him. My heart sinks when the funeral wraps up, and I'm left with one last pitying look from a pastor I've never met before going home.

That night, I settle into my cold bed by myself. The loneliness presses in on me from all sides, squeezing my chest. Usually, Callum is here by now, kicking off his shoes and climbing into bed with me. Sometimes with Rad in tow. It's been three miserable nights without them. Longing sets in, making me reach for my phone again.

For the thousandth time, I check my messages and sigh. They've all been sent, but the boys have not seen or acknowledged them. What the fuck is going on? They can't seriously think I'd ever kiss Van voluntarily or enjoy it. They've seen how many times I've refused his advancements. There's something more going on than meets the eye, but I don't have the energy to inspect it.

My eyes refuse to shut as the painful memories of the last few days play through my head. The look Callum gave me when he shook his head full of disappointment and took off will haunt me for the rest of my life.

And, they got into the Battle of the Bands and didn't bother to tell the one person who rooted for them since the beginning—me.

RIVER

"And you haven't heard from them?" Ode asks, biting the edge of her nail with suspicion. Her eyes follow me through the entire disgusting bathroom of the bar I'm pacing through. Watching as I slowly spiral into the dark abyss of bullshit that my life keeps serving up to me on a pretty plate of fuckery. "Like, they just dropped off the edge of the earth?" Her shrill voice echoes throughout the bar bathroom, bouncing off the tiled walls.

I shrug, continuing my pacing in the small space of the bathroom.

"No. Not a fucking word," I seethe, anger brewing like a firestorm under my skin. If I get my damn hands on them again, I'll wring their necks and make them wish they had died a slow death. "I've fucking called and texted, and it always goes unanswered." Every goddamn day. Every hour. I'm desperate to get their attention or make them talk to me. Fucking cowards!

My fists curl at my sides, desperate to lash out and punch the damn wall, but I stop myself. Taking a breath, I waltz back over to Ode and shake my head.

"How the fuck does this happen, Ode?" Tears burn down my cheeks in a fury, glaring at the three innocent pregnancy tests lining the shitty countertop, all coming up positive.

Positive! How could my uterus betray me like this? I'm on birth control to prevent this kind of thing from happening! Millions of women pray for this tiny miracle every day, and I've been handed one without trying. How the hell is that fair? Especially when I'm not sure if I can handle this right now. A baby? Me? Not without a support system. And seeing as Odette and her family are the only people I have left, my options are limited. God. A hammer pounds in my skull, filling my ears with the sound of my beating heart. Panic swarms through my whole system, threatening to send me spiraling down the damn drain if I don't get ahold of myself and process what the fuck is going on.

Ode's eyes turn sympathetic when she pulls me into her arms. "Fuck them," she murmurs. "You don't need them. I'll be your baby daddy. I'll be a better daddy than them, anyway." I snort into her shoulder, cursing the fucking idiots who put me in this position. "But to answer your question. You usually get a little P in the V action, and then..bam! Baby batter makes tiny humans," she says with a sly grin, grunting when I smack her on the arm. "Ouch, bitch. I was just trying to make you laugh. No need for all that violence," she huffs, rubbing her arm with fake outrage.

If it weren't for Odette and her constant support, I would have curled up in a little ball on my bedroom floor, unmoving for days. Hot tears burn behind my eyes from the anger boiling deep under the surface, mixing with resentment. December 15th came and went without a word from the guys. The day we would have gone to the Battle of the Bands. My California dream sizzles into smoldering ashes right before my eyes. Not only did the guys stop texting and calling me weeks ago, but they also blocked me from every form of social media they had and changed their passwords and usernames so I couldn't access them like I had before.

So, my nosy ass looked it up, and wouldn't you know, they were as gorgeous as ever rocking out on the big stage at The KC Club. The crowd had roared with delight, throwing their hands in the air and waving them around at the sultry sound. Much like I had before, standing in awe before the Gods on stage. Then reality crashed, and I closed out the video, refusing to see if they won. And you know, I don't give a shit. Not at all. They can win or lose or walk off a cliff for all I care. Shit.

Where was I during their performance, you ask? Wallowing in my fucking grief all by my damn self. Stuck in my lonely apartment with no one at my side—my mom six feet deep, my boyfriends MIA, and my best friend on the fringes. My only reprieve has been coming to both jobs and making up my homework. I had a lot of shit to make up after getting beat up and then processing the fact my mom keeled over and left me with all this shit. But you know what? I've tried over and over to get into contact with these ghosting dickbags, and they've never responded. I could send an SOS, and they'd wave a hand and let me die.

One day, Odette drove me by Callum and Rad's place with little success. No answer. Dark house. It's like they never even existed. Maybe I made them up, and my boyfriends were figments of my imagination, and now I'm slowly going mad.

"Babe," Ode says, squeezing my shoulder. "You're going to have to go find them. Or something. I mean, they'll have to know, right? You can't just...have their kid and keep it a secret. Jesus. *Their* kid, Riv. Who is the father?" Her eyes widen as mine narrow into slits, and she grins. "Sorry, I'm just trying to lighten the dismal as fuck mood."

"Odette, you bitch," I say as a slight smile pulls at my lips. I might as well let a little humor crack through the bullshit of my life to keep me above water.

"I'm just saying! Four baby daddy possibilities!" she quips, shaking her head. "But seriously, you have to let them know."

I blow out a breath. "I know," I mumble, putting a hand on my flat stomach, trying to imagine the watermelon I will have in a few short months.

Images of my future with a baby flash through my mind as I pace in front of Odette. She sighs, leaning against the counter and watching me work everything out.

"You have options, you know. We'd never judge you for your decisions. Just saying, babe," Ode says with a sad grin.

"I know," I sigh, groaning when I put my forehead on the wet counter and groan more. "Fuck. This is bullshit! They fucking left me for weeks now! And they did this to me? Fucking Castle house on the lake..."

"Fucking sounds about right. Isn't that all you did on your little getaway? You were the main course, and they were the..."

"Please don't even finish that sentence, Ode," I mumble, trying to keep the pressure building in my brain at bay.

"Right. We're very pissed off at them," she mumbles with a defeated sigh. "Extremely pissed off at them." Ode's eyes fill with tears, and she sniffles. "I thought they were so good to you. And here they went and..."

"Acted like every other Lakeview guy on the planet. Who would have predicted that River West would get screwed the fuck over by four fuck boys? They succeeded, didn't they?" Tears fall freely from my eyes again, my fingers digging into my palm. "They fucking told me they got close to me for my name, and what did I do?

I got fucking knocked up by them. I let them in, Ode. I fucking..." My entire body trembles with rage, hurt, and disappointment. But mainly, my fucking heart shatters to the floor. "I fucking loved them," I whisper through my quivering lips and shake my head when Ode tries to wrap an arm around me.

"I know you did. And I swear the way they looked at you...I thought they loved you, too. I don't understand. How could they walk away without talking to you first?" she asks, running a hand over her forehead.

"Because they didn't want to," I say with resignation. "Maybe that was their plan all along." And I was too blind, once again, too fucking see what was going on in front of me.

And that's the gist of it all. Callum saw something, misunderstood it, and fucking walked away with a trampled heart before hearing what I had to say. It's like that shitty misunderstanding trope everyone loves to hate in movies and books. None of this would have happened if they had just talked it over like adults. The drama would cease to exist, and they'd come back with open arms and tell me they were sorry. But this isn't a book or a movie, this is real life, and somewhere along the way, it all got twisted into this entire situation. And it's entirely Van's fault. I'm going to castrate him beyond belief for kissing me. Then, I'm going to throw his body to the damn pigs and cackle as they eat through his bones and make him disappear entirely. Ah, that would be the dream. I'm no murderer—but I'll get my revenge if I ever see his face again. Lately, he's been in the damn wind, only texting me instead of showing his face, mentioning something about being in Europe for some damn internship I don't care about. I know I'll see him eventually. He's like a damn pest, always turning up.

"You need to go demand answers," Odette says, pursing her lips. "You need to knock on their doors, punch their faces, and force them to listen to you!" she harps on, raising her fist in the air. Next, she'll get the pitchforks and fire, and we'll storm their castle.

"Already tried that, remember? They weren't home. Hell, maybe they stayed in California," I say with a defeated shrug. Throwing my head back, I stare at the ceiling, letting more frustrated tears fall.

Odette doesn't say a word. Silence falls between us until I stare at her guilt-ridden face, and she huffs. "They won." Those two words punch me in the fucking gut, and all the air leaves my system.

The groupie part of me is fucking ecstatic they're living their dreams. But the baby momma part of me wants to yank their balls through their throats and dig their graves with my bare hands.

"Of course they did," I huff, throwing my hands in the air. "They fucking won. They're living their best life and shit...here I am. I'm knocked up and fucking fuming..."

"Direct that anger at them, babe. Take my car and go and confront someone. Maybe Kieran's mom? Ask her and see what she says. Oh shit, don't give me that look. I'm just saying," she says, placatingly holding her hands in the air.

"Every single person in that neighborhood hates my guts," I grumble, butterflies making my stomach swoop. "But fuck it. Someone has answers for me."

Ode hands her keys to me and pats my back. I shove all the pregnancy tests into my jeans pocket and quietly walk out of the bathroom and into my office, grabbing my coat.

"I'll hold down the fort here, okay? It's too early for a big crowd. So, we'll be good. Now, go get them bitch!" she shouts with encouragement, shooing my broken-hearted ass away.

I bet ten bucks she's tired of watching me pace and angrily cry out my frustrations. Ode won't admit it, but she wants me to handle this before I work myself up to stab someone. Again.

"So inspiring," I grumble, waltzing out the side door toward the parking lot, pulling my coat tighter around my body.

Cold air smacks me in the face as a few snowflakes float from the heavy clouds from above. Shaking off the shivers, I gasp for breath. If I thought Illinois summers were awful, meet Winter, her ugly, cold bitch of a sister, delivering several inches of snow today.

I shake my head, walking past my poor Bessy, and stop dead. Last time I checked, my poor Bes was covered in a thin layer of dust, yet she sits here, cleaned up, and... What the hell? My brows furrow at the small white note tucked beneath the windshield wiper, soaked from the weather. Picking it up, I carefully open it and nearly drop it on the ground.

"Stop fucking walking."

That's it. That's all it says. Clear and decisive, yet unclear about who it's from. Shivers roll down my spine when I dig my keys out and hop into my unlocked car. Every piece of trash is cleaned up—because I'm messy, so sue me—and the inside is wiped down. The smell of cleaning products wafts through the air. The hairs on the back of my neck stand on end when I put my key into the ignition. Holding my breath, I turn the key, and Bessy starts without a damn fight. Quickly, I press the buttons to heat instead of air conditioning, remembering the last time I drove Bessy was at the beginning of August. Now, here in December, I've finally gotten her going again. Well, someone did, at least. This time, I won't question this gift from God. Instead, I'll take Bessy out on her maiden voyage and hopefully find some answers.

The whole drive across town, my nerves flared to life again, slickening my cold palms. As I drive through the neighborhood entrance, I stare at the sign welcoming me to Lakeview Division. I raise my middle finger and salute the neighborhood the entire time I drive down the main road, turning off toward Callum's house.

To my surprise, two vehicles sit in his driveway and have been since the snow started twenty minutes ago. Thankfully, it's not coming down as hard when I stomp out of my car and walk onto the porch. Anger fuels my every move, and my heart pounds at the prospect of seeing them again. Maybe they're inside, or perhaps they're gone. Either way, I'm letting someone know I'm pregnant and moving on with my life—with or without them. I love them with my entire heart. More than I ever thought I could. They swooped in and stole every piece of me without even trying. I could repeatedly tell myself that I wouldn't give them my heart or love or hold tight to my reservations. But the reality is I'm a sucker for love, and they pulled me into their orbit. But I can move on and restart. I'll get over them...well, eventually.

As I raise my hand to knock on the door, it opens. An embarrassing yelp leaves my lips when I jump back, and a tall, blonde woman carrying folders against her chest stumbles out.

"Sorry," I say, shaking my head.

"Oh, that's all right," she says, wrinkling her nose like she has a bad taste in her mouth. Hell, maybe she swallowed a lemon the way her face morphs, and then she shakes it off. "Well, Gloria," she says, turning toward another woman I recognize standing in the doorway. "I had better get going. I'll get this listing up ASAP. Tell

Callum that it'll fetch a good price." She offers Gloria a tight smile, side-eyeing me when she walks back to her fancy car and gets in with a huff, slamming the door.

I swallow hard at the implications of her words and stare at the ground. Callum is selling his house after all this time, completely wiping away the memory of his family. I don't blame him for wanting to get rid of this place and start somewhere new. His family meant so much to him. But his place was a tomb filled with the ghosts of his past, constantly haunting him at every turn.

"Well, well, well," Gloria practically sings with glee, looking down at me with a smirk. "I was wondering when you'd show up. They don't have any money for you. So, you can go back to the slum you belong in," Gloria sneers, sticking her nose in the air and waving a hand.

I try as hard as I can to hold back the eye roll, but it slips through, making her scoff again.

"I was wondering if I could speak to them?" I ask with so much hope I'm practically puking it out of every orifice on my body. I shove my hands into my coat pocket when her assessing eyes stare me up and down.

"Why don't you come in," she says, sweeping a hand, gesturing for me to follow her through the front door.

Suddenly, I feel like I'm walking into a giant trap, and my face is about to be on the back of milk cartons everywhere. With words like 'Local Central City girl has gone missing after attempting to speak to her baby daddies and hasn't been heard from since December.' Shit. Ash may have plotted my demise from the moment he laid eyes on me, and now it's all coming to fruition. They planned to use me and then dump my body in the backwoods. I shake my head, tossing away the crazy thoughts going through my overactive mind.

I reluctantly follow Gloria through the front door, instantly relaxing in the heat pouring through the vents. Looking around, my heart sinks into my ass, and more tears burn the backs of my eyes. Where the couch and big screen TV once sat is empty, void of any furniture and life. Everything within the home is gone, except for the woman staring at me with a victorious smile.

"As you can see, they ran from you, Central girl. They don't want you anymore. They're onto bigger and better things," she says with glee, practically having an orgasm at the fact I'm here and they're...

"They're still in California?" I ask, raising a brow, knowing in my heart what the answer is.

Keep your shit together—no falling apart now.

Fuck. Every fear I had conjured over the past three weeks is coming true in vivid detail. They're gone. They left me here. And they don't fucking care about me like I thought they did. Was everything a fabrication for their benefit? Were all the things they said big, fat lies to capture my heart in their grasps and fucking crush it after they left? Who the hell does that? I don't give a shit if they thought they saw something that wasn't true. In my heart, I know Van kissed me against my will, and Callum saw it without waiting for an explanation. It's like they saw what they wanted to see and didn't hang around for an answer.

"Well, they did win the entire competition and got offered a record deal, not to mention the million dollars sitting pretty in their bank account, which you'll have no part of. I won't have you ruining their lives," she says, turning her nose up again.

What is with this lady and her prejudice about where I come from? Didn't she do the same thing and bag some rich guy who wasn't who she thought he was? She's really projecting herself onto me, and it's really beginning to piss me the fuck off.

"Well, I need to speak to them. It's pretty important," I grumble, hating to admit I need them right now. All I want to do is fall into their arms but also punch their noses into their faces. Is that too much to ask?

"No," she says, shrugging and giving me the stink eye. "There's no way..."

"I'm pregnant, lady," I say through clenched teeth. "And I'd appreciate speaking to the boys responsible. You know, all of them. So, can I please talk to them or what?" Okay, so that wasn't as polite as I had intended it to be. But my bullshit meter is flying through the damn red on dangerous levels, and I'm about to explode if I don't get any answers quickly.

Her face pales when her arms fall to her sides, and she shakes her head. "No... You can't be..."

"Yeah, I can be. Not that I did it on purpose. So, can I talk to them? They won't answer my calls," I say in a small voice, trying to reel back in all the rage brewing beneath my flesh. If Gloria isn't careful, I'll turn green, hulk out in Callum's empty living room, and destroy everything.

Gloria fumbles with the phone in her pocket, turning a sick shade of green. I take it back; maybe she'll be the one to turn green instead of me. Hers, of course, will be from sickness instead of burning rage. Or, perhaps I spoke too soon. Her blue eyes meet mine in a frenzy when she brings the phone up to her ear and holds up a finger.

"I'll contact them. They blocked your number for a reason," she snaps, turning her back to me, and waltzes into the kitchen.

Against my better judgment, I stand in the middle of the room, taking it all in. They blocked my number? That explains the lack of phone calls and texts. They must have done it the moment Callum returned with evidence of my infidelity—or lack thereof. At this point, I'd rather pounce on Gloria, drag the phone away from her ear, and give those assfaces a piece of my mind, but I refrain. I have manners—sometimes.

"Yes, she says she's pregnant and would like to speak to you," she murmurs into the phone, side-eyeing me as I stare daggers through her skull. "Of course," she says with a few head nods and then hangs up the phone, placing it in her pocket. Gloria sighs, reaches into her purse, sits on the empty countertop, and pulls out a little black book that I instantly recognize.

It's a fucking checkbook. Anyone could see that from a mile away. But why the fuck... Every part of me slumps when she grabs her pen and writes something quickly before tearing it out.

"Here," she says, waving it in the air until I snatch it from her hand. "The boys send their regards but want nothing to do with you or it. Kieran says to go ahead and get rid of it," she sniffs, putting her nose in the air again. "Something about Van being the real daddy?" she asks, raising a haughty brow. A victorious smile spreads across her face, and she nods. "That's probably right. They caught you red-handed slutting around, didn't they?"

"Slutting around?" I gape, rearing back. "Wow. For a grown woman, you sure speak like a catty teenager. Just wow, Gloria. Thanks for the check, but you can shove it up your tight ass and maybe knock something loose, like that haughty attitude you parade around with. Have a good life, bitch," I hiss, staring at the amount on the check and laughing. "Seriously? Nine hundred bucks for what? An abortion? Get fucked," I say, tearing it into pieces and throwing it like confetti around me. "Although, you probably don't care right now. Someday you'll see this child and want to be in their life, and I'll tell you the same thing. Get. Fucked."

Redness coats her cheeks when she vibrates with the same rage fueling my words. With stiff movements, she reaches into her purse again and slams down four separate envelopes with another grin.

"These are for you then," she says, tapping each envelope with her long nails. "They wanted to ensure you didn't follow them out there and ruin their lives again. So, here are your restraining orders forbidding you from ever contacting them again. No calls. No texts. No social media messages. The moment you do, they'll report you to the authorities. They will be famous, and they don't need the trash of their past slipping through the cracks. It also notes that you're not allowed to mention them on any form of social media and slander their name. Your hands are officially tied, Miss West." Her smug look makes my head rear back.

Anger builds more, and tears fall down my cheeks at her words. Restraining orders? Christ on a cracker, they've lost their fucking minds. But fine. Fine! If that's how they want to fucking play it, then so be it. I'll work my ass off for the rest of my life to forget about them and the fucked up games they played with my heart. My only hang-up is the constant reminder they left me with. The one they want nothing to do with. Whatever. Odette and I will give this baby as much love as they need without the help of the four idiots who helped create him or her. They can brainwash themselves for as long as they want with whatever lies they want to.

I know the truth.

And one day, they will too.

RIVER

SEVEN MONTHS LATER

The hot July sun beams down when I step out of Bessy, groaning when I can stretch my legs. Sweat sticks to every damn inch of my skin, slowly dripping down my back. I swear, it's only nine in the morning, and the sun is already trying to roast me like a Thanksgiving turkey. Shit. Turkey sounds delicious.

And now, not only am I starving for the thousandth time in the two hours I've been awake, but every bone in my body aches. Seriously, It was only a ten-minute drive to the local grocery store, but it was still Hell on earth for my hips and legs. My least favorite activity these days is walking or any form of exercise. Minus sex, now that'd be a pleasant activity. Except no one wants to bang a broken-hearted, pregnant girl. So, here I am, seven months along and hornier than I've ever been in my life and fucking lonely. Where's the good dick when you need it?

Normal women glow at this point in the pregnancy, raving about how their morning sickness has gone away and their acne has cleared. I call bullshit. I love this child with every fiber of my being, but I wish it were two months from now and she was here. Despite the circumstances and the lack of money, I'm over the moon to bring her into this world with me. It's just her and me against the entire world. As she ages, I plan to tell her about those assfaces who tucked tail to live their rock star dreams and left us here. All positive, of course. I don't want her to go a day without knowing who helped create her.

"If you could stop kicking my bladder, that'd be great," I mumble, rubbing a hand over my large stomach as she kicks me again. "Or not," I quip, reaching into my backseat with a grin. "Just you and me, Lyric," I say in a soothing voice, grabbing the grocery bags and hauling them into my hands. With a grunt, I shut the door and head up the back staircase of the record store to the apartment above it.

Seven months ago, my landlord informed me that I had to leave because my mom and I were in government-placed housing. We moved in there when I was a kid, and before my mom died, she had never added me to the lease. So, needless to say, I had to leave on a thirty-day notice, pregnant, grieving, and completely fucked up from the betrayal from the boys. Booker, bless his fucking heart, let me take over the abandoned apartment over the record store. I swear, when I'm a badass band manager, I'm buying him both businesses and a brand-new car for all the support he's given me over the years. The plus side? Van has no idea where I live and can't snoop around, knocking on my doors every hour of the day, begging me to let him in.

My new apartment is a small one-bedroom, maybe, eight hundred square feet of living space. But it's home now—a place to lay my head and a place for me to bring baby Lyric home when the time comes. It's mine for now until I get through school and work.

One day, I'll have more than an apartment above the record store. One day, I won't depend on the government to help me buy food and provide for my medical needs. But that's not today. Today, I'm still growing into the woman I'll be in a few years and taking what I can get to survive.

Checking my phone, I note the time and curse. Quickly, I put my groceries away and head down to the record store for opening with my laptop in tow.

For the past few months, I've been going through non-stop classes, getting closer and closer to my degree. Thankfully, the community college offers summer courses as a way to guarantee degrees at a faster pace. The faster I get this, the better off I'll be. And maybe, sometime in the future, I can get my bachelor's and expand my business degree in music.

Finally, I sit after hours of grocery shopping, walking, and moving around. Relief slams into my damn throbbing feet when I prop them up on the counter and pop in my one working earbud, groaning at the weight off my damn toes. God. Whoever said pregnancy was magical was a big, fat liar. Listen, I'll love this child until I die, but if I ever have to go through this again—I might pluck the child out too early and call it a day.

As I settle in and sign into school, the professor begins speaking in a monotone voice. One day someone will let this man know his class is boring and he should lighten up a little bit.

I internally groan when the bell above the door rings, announcing the arrival of... Fuckity, fuck...

"Van," I say through gritted teeth when he waltzes in with a grin, coming straight to the counter.

He cocks his head, taking me in when he leans on the counter, and his eyes widen. "I didn't believe the rumors, but here you are. And you're...."

"Very pregnant," I grit out, narrowing my eyes at his smug face when he whistles. "What the hell do you want, Van?" I say, pinching the bridge of my nose in exasperation.

I haven't seen this fool since the night he kissed me. So, to see him now up close and personal reminds me of the promise I made myself about castrating him and selling him as pig food.

"Just came by to see how you were doing," he says, grinning and looking me over. "How've you been? I've been away for a while." Genuine concern fills his eyes, but I don't fall into his manipulative trap like I used to.

"Oh, just peachy. Living the good life," I quip, dripping with so much sarcasm we're practically swimming in it.

"Rivey," he says in a low, pained voice. "I just... I just came by to see how you were coping with everything. And I wanted to tell you that I never took the money my dad offered me over you. I only broke up with you to go to college and get my degree. Not like them," he murmurs, shaking his head. "I would never take money over you. In fact, I've been away making a better future for us." I blink rapidly when he emphasizes the word *us*, and I wrinkle my nose.

"Like them? For us?" I indulge him just this once, hanging on to his words and ignoring my professor yapping in my ear.

Like I give a shit if Van took the money over being with me. That ship sailed a long time ago. Besides, that's all on him and his problem—not mine. He can do what he wants. And by the crease in his forehead, I'm not giving him the reaction he wanted.

"Yeah. I...listen, I wasn't supposed to say anything, but Kieran was bragging about the massive check his mom gave him to leave you," he says, watching my unmoving face. "And I would never do that. I went to Europe on my dad's dime for an internship, and now I have every arsenal in my pocket for us to have a better future. You, me, and the baby."

Even when it feels like a knife stabs through my fucking heart at the sound of his name. Kieran. The name I've refused to utter for months now. It feels like ash on my tongue the more my brain repeats it. Asher. Kieran. Callum. Rad. Shit. My stomach rolls, knotting around the memories we've shared.

Taking a deep breath, I shove that shit down as far as it'll go and lock them away. I'll remember them for Lyric and tell her every story I know, but I won't let Van barge into my place of employment and undo seven crucial months of mending my heart back together. Thanks to pregnancy hormones, it took many nights of crying myself to sleep and cursing their names for my heart to heal finally.

"He said that if they left you here, she'd pay for their trip to California and help their living situation and everything. I can't believe they took the money over you." Shaking his head, he runs a hand over the back of his neck, dropping his eyes to the floor with shame.

"Nice story," I say with a shrug, busting through my bullshit meter for the day. "They did what they did. That's fine. They can live their dreams in California without me, regardless if they took a paycheck over a human being or two." My nose wrinkles when I rub my grumbling stomach.

I see red when I roll my eyes, huffing at his mere existence. I'm holding back the angry tears welling in my eyes. Again, thanks to my pregnancy hormones throwing my body into some whacky ass emotions, I cry at every tiny inconvenience. Anger rises to the surface at the thought of those jackasses taking a big, fat check instead of hanging around. If I hazard a guess, I bet Gloria suggested the restraining orders, too. Among whatever else she thought of. Whatever. That's in the past, and this is the present.

Leaning forward with desperation, Van attempts to grab my hand. "I can take care of you, Rivey. I can...I have money. You'll have a good place to live, and we could be together. Half the town thinks it's my kid, anyway. I want... I want that," he murmurs, pleading with his eyes.

I blink a few times, letting his words register in my mind. For the first time, I'm seeing the true psycho he is. Like, really? He wants to take care of me after he stalked me and watched me for months when the guys were here. Even after the unwanted kiss and the groping. I knew he was a little unhinged in the head, but this takes the fucking cake. If I didn't know any better, I'd say he had something to do with this entire situation. Minus the pregnancy, of course. His tiny flesh flute didn't come anywhere near me. Thank God.

"Your kid?" I yelp, kicking my damn brain into gear.

"Yeah, I mean. They saw us at your house, babe. They know...." He waves a wrist, alluding to the horizontal tango we most definitely didn't do that night.

I grind my teeth and curl my fingers into fists. If I let my hands have free reign of the situation, I'll stab him in the throat. And there's no way I can go to prison now at seven months pregnant.

"You mean the kiss you forced on me. Or the way you cornered me in the kitchen? Or showing up uninvited? I could go on and on, but my answer would always be the same. Get fucked, Van. This isn't your kid. I'm not yours. And I'd really like to stab you right now." My eyes narrow when he swallows hard and takes a step back. Wise man, he's not underestimating me for once, probably because he's seen what my little knife can do and wants nothing to do with it.

"Jesus," he yelps, putting his hand in the air and staring at the knife in my hand.

Oh. Would you look at that? How'd that get there? I could really poke someone's eyes out with this, preferably Van's.

"I won't ask again. Please leave. I'm really, really not in the mood for people right now, and you're no exception." I shake my knife, making him lose all the color in his face.

"Fine. My offer still stands, even if you want to stab me. Shit," he says, bolting out the door like his ass is on fire.

Fuck. Finally, I can relax and pay attention to class. Maybe in five minutes, I'll head up to my apartment and grab the chocolate chip cookie cake I snagged at the grocery shop for cheap. It may expire tomorrow, but it sure as hell won't last that long in my home. Those things are my damn kryptonite right now. Take away the cookie cakes, and you might as well take away my life. Oh, and milkshakes. God. I can't shake this sweet tooth plaguing my every waking moment. It's no wonder I've already gained thirty pounds and am still growing. But fuck it, I'm building a tiny human one day at a time. I'll happily eat my weight in food.

Movement outside the store makes a grumble work up my throat. Great. Two guys linger outside, scrunching their stupid noses at the neighborhood. Narrowing my eyes, I watch the tattooed one secure his phone in front of his jeans, almost on instinct. I snort. That won't do anything around here, but I'm not breathing a word of that. They're already trembling in their designer shoes, giving their fancy schmancy lifestyle away. Looking them up and down, I furrow my brows. They may not be from around Central City, but they're not from Lakeview either. These identical guys stick out like a sore thumb. A hint of familiarity slaps me in the face the longer I stare at them standing outside the window.

The door overhead finally rings, indicating they've entered and are ready to browse or stare at me in awe. I feign ignorance like I wasn't watching their every move.

"Welcome to Dead Records. If you need anything, my name is River. Just let me know," I say through a heavy, tired sigh, suddenly feeling the exhaustion weighing me down.

Now that I'm seated and staring at the shocked faces of the guys in front of me, I need a damn nap, which won't come anytime soon. Not only do I have to deal with customers, orders, and pregnancy, but I have to get through my classes.

"You're River Blue West?" one guy asks overly seriously, making my eyes snap to his similar moss-green eyes.

Whoever gave me that name should be shot—AKA—my father. It's bad enough that the entirety of the West clan is named after our father's favorite bands. But to give me the middle name too? Sucks.

I frown, scrunching my nose with suspicion and taking out my earbud. I don't know who these fuckers are, but I'm too tired and pregnant to deal with bullshit.

"Whoever you are," I say, cocking my head to the side and examining them with a calculating eye. "I'm not interested. You assholes keep coming to me thinking I can get you whatever you think, but that's not how it works. I am a West. One of over a dozen, and I'm not the West that can get you fucking famous." I shake my head, trying to set my earbud back in my ear to listen to my professor's rambling, but I stall when the colder-looking twin opens his mouth.

"I'm Zeppelin, and this is Seger. We're—"

"My fucking brothers. Yup! I've heard that one before," I say with realization, narrowing my eyes and scoffing, waving a hand. "It's funny. Last I checked, my billionaire brothers were living it up in

California and signing douchebags like Whispered Words to their label and not coming to bumbfuck nowhere, Illinois. It's almost laughable. You scammers will do anything to get a buck. But newsflash, dickweeds—I'm as broke as an unfunny joke," I grumble, scrunching my nose again as the other idiot bends at the waist, barking out a sharp laugh.

"You're definitely a fucking West. Shit." He breaks out in a deep laugh, putting his hands on his knees, and wheezing.

I scowl. It really wasn't that damn funny.

"You done?" I ask, raising a brow at his antics. I swear he turns blue from all the laughter squeaking through his nose.

"Here, here, fuck," he wheezes again, digging into his wallet and throwing his license at me. On instinct, I catch it with ease from my seated position. My brows immediately furrow at the name, looking back at me.

"Jesus," I mutter inaudibly. My fingers tremble around his driver's license, and the realization of who they are smacks me in the chest like a runaway train, knocking the breath from my lungs.

"See? I'm Seger fucking West. The real fucking deal." Turning to his twin who can only be Zeppelin fucking West with a gigantic grin and murmur, he says, "I think she and Kace would get along fucking fine."

Zepp side-eyes Seger with a snort, steps up to the counter, and flips open his wallet. Everything inside me goes numb and haywire at the same damn time. My jaw drops open, and their shit falls to the counter with a loud thud.

"The fuck are you doing here? Listen, the shit I said about Dad, I..." I ramble through terror until Seger holds up a hand, stopping my words.

"Dad was the biggest fucking cock on the planet when he was alive..." he says with a cringe, running a hand across his neck.

"We're not here to discuss a dead man's shortcomings. We're here to discuss your inheritance," Zepp says, gaining my complete and utter attention.

I swallow the hard lump forming in my overly sensitive throat and shake my head. Rage once again boils in the pit of my stomach. How could a man who gave me life walk away without contributing anything and have his two favorite sons show up and tell me there's money? Nope. Even if I need it more than anything right now, I still have my morals.

"I don't want his fucking money. I don't want anything from the piece of shit. He kicked Ma and me out without anything but the clothes on our backs. Ma dragged us back here, and we've lived on food stamps and the medical card for fucking years. I don't need a damn dime from Corbin West," I hiss, jumping to my feet, which is a damn miracle these days. "I've done fucking fine without him."

My teeth grit when pity takes over Seger's eyes as they fall on my giant stomach protruding from my long band shirt. I frown when he doesn't take his eyes off it, staring like he's never seen something like it before

"What? You've never seen a pregnant woman before?" I chide, narrowing my eyes at him.

He snorts playfully, running a hand down his face. "Sure I have. It's just fucking uncanny. You're as far along as our wife. Twenty-eight weeks, right?" He looks at me as my hand flies to my stomach and my nose scrunches.

"Um, yeah," I say quieter before nibbling on my lip when he nods.

"Do you have time for lunch?" Zepp asks, gesturing toward a diner across the street.

I lick my lips, envisioning a delicious burger and strawberry milkshake, as a loud rumble erupts from my stomach. I could have denied lunch because of a lack of funds. My stomach, on the other hand, had other plans and outed me for the starving woman I am.

"Now that you know we're your brothers, we have some shit we'd like to discuss with you. And I think you may want to hear it," Seger says with a little too much enthusiasm, licking his lips.

When I finally meet his eyes, indecision weighs heavily on my mind. They showed me their licenses with their names on them. So, I shouldn't be afraid. But something holds me rooted to the spot. Every person I've ever trusted has left me dangling over the cliff with no way back up. Who is to say they're different? Are they lying to gain something from me? Is there an inheritance to receive? I blow out a breath, weighing my damn options. It isn't until Zeppelin speaks that I finally decide to say fuck it.

"Let's get some burgers, fries, and hell—a milkshake. We do have things to discuss with you—big things," Zepp tacks on with a convincing voice.

I lick my lips again and finally sigh. "Fine. Class was fucking boring today, anyway. Who cares about the history of business bullshit. Take me to lunch, but don't expect me to take a damn handout," I gripe, shutting my computer down and closing it. Quickly, I pick up a small backpack-style purse and fling it over my shoulder before grabbing a set of keys off the counter.

Whatever this lunch leads to, I'll listen. But I won't make any promises, especially regarding the people in my family.

"Hold the Weiner," I say, putting a finger in the air. My entire body trembles with my mouth hanging open. Did they say what I think they said? There's no way in hell. This can't be right. "Twenty million dollars? Shut the front door," I gasp, slumping on the bench as the waitress drops off my delicious strawberry milkshake and mounds of food. I've been starving all day, holding out for the food I got from the store. But when we came in, they said to order whatever I wanted. And who am I to deny that? "I just...I can't...he just..." I stutter, shoving a handful of fries into my mouth, and moan at the greasy, salty taste slithering across my desperate taste buds. God, this is even better than sex.

"Twenty million is just the tip of the iceberg, River. More will be deposited, according to our father's lawyer. He left money for each of you..."

"Each of us?" I ask, taking a swig of my milkshake. "You've met..."

"All fucking fourteen of the West children, yeah. We've been down that road, and you, dear sister, are the last damn one," Seger mumbles, shoving his cheeseburger into his mouth with the same zest as me. Maybe we're more alike than I thought. "Fuck. Nothing beats a quaint little diner's burger," he moans around his food, taking another bite.

"Animal," Zepp grumbles, taking a small bite of his burger.

Every muscle in my body locks up at the sultry sound blasting through the speakers. Looking around, every patron stops what they're doing to marvel at the song playing overhead with smiles. Seger bobs his head with a grin, closing his eyes and taking the tune in, seeming pleased with himself.

My milkshake turns to ash on my tongue, and heavy lead is in my twisting stomach. I've avoided everything Whispered Words from the moment they walked away without another word. I've avoided anything online mentioning their newly found success and articles interviewing them for various reasons. If I hazard a guess, I'd say they're taking over the world one song at a time.

"Is this?" Zepp asks, tilting his head.

"Fucking right it is. They're hella fucking talented, and I can't believe they came out of nowhere," Seger says with a grin, turning to look at me.

His face falls at the sight of what I'm sure is my pale face. Moisture beads above my lip as a heat of rage boils my blood, and my fists clench under the table.

Angry tears pool in my eyes, and my breath shudders in my chest. Of all the songs I could have heard today, why did it have to be theirs? And why did it have to be Roaring River? Like, do they seriously sing that still? Why couldn't they have lost and gotten what they deserved? To rot in the depths of hell. I swear to God, one day, I will enact my revenge on the boys who stole my heart, crushed it, and then abandoned me when I needed them most.

"Whispered Words," I mutter with my lips twisting into an angry scowl.

"Uh, yeah. That's them. They won the Battle of the Bands seven months ago and have taken the world by storm. They're absolutely..."

"Absolute fuck heads," I hiss, clenching my teeth and unleashing my anger.

Seger holds up a hand. "Um...I feel like I'm missing something," he mutters, side-eyeing his brother with confusion.

Licking my lips, an ingenious idea pops into my mind, easing some of the rage boiling over. I swear the moment my body decided to create a tiny human, my emotions ran rampant. So, with that thought, I'll use all my energy and become what I've always wanted to become—a band manager. And who better to give me a chance than the brothers I happened to meet?

"I'll sign the papers for the money," I say, taking a deep breath, but steely determination settles on my shoulders.

"Okay, cool," Zepp says, reaching down for the manilla envelope and placing it on the table.

"On one stipulation," I grind out, looking over the papers with so many zeros I nearly faint on the spot.

"What's that?" Seger asks.

"I want a job at West Records. I want to intern. I want to become a band manager," I say, nodding vigorously as I look over the papers again. "I have experience managing bands from the area. So, in return, I'll sign the papers if you give me a job. I'll move out to California and start as soon as possible."

Whatever it fucking takes. I'll start at the bottom again and work my way up. I'm not entitled enough to think they'd hand me a corner office and say, "have at it." No. I want to learn and dive deep into the music industry. So when my chance comes, and I come face to face with the dickless wonders who left me, I'll be in charge.

"I...Umm..." Seger looks at Zepp, who scratches his chin.

"To become a manager is a hefty undertaking. You'd have to intern at the bottom and get a feel for it. A bachelor's in Music Management is a necessity at West Records. We want the best of the best, but you're family. And if you want a job..."

"I'll start at the bottom. I'll sort fucking mail. I want this..." I say again with a snarl, taking another gulp of milkshake to calm myself down.

"But why? You could take your inheritance and never work another day in your life. Why would you want to?"

I rub my stomach, caressing the tiny human inside who depends on me and only me to provide for her. Looking out the window, heavy memories plague my mind. The laughs. The love. The fucking heartbreak. Everything I've endured over the past year sits on my shoulders daily. And I'm tired of it. I want a fresh start in the industry I've been dreaming about.

"I'm getting my business degree right now and working through summer programs to obtain it ASAP. I can change my major to music business. I'll put in the work. Anything to make those assholes pay for what they did to me." I frown slightly, shaking myself out of my haunting thoughts. I don't need to think of Callum's innocent smile or Rad's contagious laugh. I have to focus on what's suitable for Lyric and me.

"Who?" Zepp asks, furrowing his brows.

"They promised they'd take me with them. They promised...they loved me." A slight hiccup escapes from my trembling lips, but I look away, refusing to let them see me break. I've cried enough, and today, that stops. "They promised me everything, and I believed every lie they told." I swallow hard, vigorously wiping away the tears falling down my cheeks. "They left me, and they left her," I whisper, pointing to my belly.

Seger blows out a breath, filled with so much fucking confusion, and I have to bite my cheek to stop smiling. "Who?" he grumbles, shaking his head.

I stare out the window again, letting the emotions take hold. "Whispered Words promised me the world, and then they turned their back on me."

"They... They what?" Seger asks, curling his fists on the table.

"Not now," Zepp grumbles, putting a hand on his shoulder and squeezing. "We have watchers." With that, Zepp nods for us to follow him as he pays the bill.

The warm sun greets us when we step out of the diner, and I sigh, clutching the envelope tightly to my chest.

"They did this to you?" Seger immediately asks, pointing angrily to my stomach.

"Well, I was an active participant in the endeavor," I quip with a snort when he pales, looking away. "But yeah, this is one of theirs."

"I'll kill them," he murmurs, clenching his fists.

"No need," I say with a shrug, looking off into the distance. "I'll do it." Once I get my hands on them, I'll make them wish they never attempted to use me.

"Okay. You have a job, then," Zepp says, stroking his chin.

My heart soars with excitement, and I grin. "Thank you! Seriously, it's been my damn dream job to do this."

"Paid internship. We'll have you start in the office, delivering mail. Once you've had the baby and come back, we can start getting you more acclimated. And once you have your degree..."

"I'm working on it and have been for a year. I'm on track to get my associates in December through the quick pace program." Tears form in my eyes, and I sniffle. "Thank you for tracking me down and giving me this. I don't want his money, but..." I shake my head, rolling my lips together and gathering my emotions.

"By the looks of it, you need it. We had no idea that he saved it for you all these years. So, take the money and come start your new life in East Point Bluff with us," Zeppelin says, putting a hand on my shoulder and squeezing.

"I'll need maybe two weeks to get everything squared away here," I say, meeting Zepp's eyes, and he nods.

"Of course," he says with a slight grin. "I have a good feeling about you, River."

I snort, wiping away the stupid hormonal tears dripping out of my eyes. "Thanks for taking a chance on me."

"Eh, what's a long, lost, forgotten family for? We couldn't help you when we were kids, but we sure as fuck can help you now. Pack your bags, little sister. We're going to California."

California. All my dreams are coming true in the blink of an eye.

"To California," I mumble with an excited grin.

"But first, maybe sign the papers, and we can get all this wired into a secure bank account for you. That'll help with the move..."

And so much more than they even knew. That night, my brothers left on a private jet, needing to get back to their pregnant wife, leaving me to stew in my newly found fortune.

The next day, as soon as the money was within my grasp, I did what I always wanted to do. I paid off Booker's mortgage, the loan on the bar, and the record store. The man who took so many chances on me now lives a debt-free life and can focus on the greater things. Every cent of Korrine's, Odette's, and Leon's debt was erased with the money I paid for them to move into a beautiful new house with zero bills. From here on out, I'll pay their monthly expenses and let them live the life they deserve. They've been through everything with me and have been by my side for all of it, never turning their backs.

Over the next two weeks, I helped Booker rent the apartment above the record store to a new worker down on her luck. She was a great fit and took over my position. Leon managed to snag the manager title at the bar and quickly took over my duties easily.

Finally, the day came when I have to say my goodbyes. Odette cries the entire time we say our goodbyes in the empty airplane hangar, hugging for what seems like an eternity. My rock. My best fucking friend. And I was about to say goodbye to it all. Well, not goodbye, goodbye. But I hadn't lived more than ten feet away from her for the last ten years, and now, I was headed to a different coast by myself.

"I'll call every day," I murmur, hugging her tight.

"And my niece!" she wails, sprinkling her tears on my shoulder. "I'll miss her birth..."

"I'll fly you out. I want you there if you want to be," I say with emotions clogging my throat.

Odette chuckles, pulling back to cup my face. "You're a rich bitch now. I'll fly you out?" She snorts when I crack a smile.

"You're my sister," I murmur, patting her hand. "I'll miss the hell out of you," I grunt when she throws her arms around me again.

"You make them pay," she sniffles on my shoulder. "Make them regret ever fucking around with you, okay?"

"Believe me, Ode. By the time I'm done with Whispered Words, they won't know their ass from their elbows. Anyway, I know how. I'll fucking destroy them," I vow, formulating the long game I'll have to play to get at them.

By now, they're living their rock star dreams under the spotlight with their adoring fans at their feet. But my time will come, and they'll be under my heel, and I'll squish them like the little bugs they are.

"You ready?" Zepp asks, nodding toward the private fucking jet they brought to pick me up in.

"Yeah," I say, wiping my tears. "It's time for me to go," I whisper, squeezing Ode's hand one last time before getting on the jet. "Thanks for coming and getting me. The stupid airlines wouldn't let me travel," I grumble, putting my seatbelt over my belly.

"What's ours is yours now," Seger says, shrugging when he gets comfortable.

"So, are you ever going to tell us exactly what this band did to you?" Zepp asks, sitting back as the plane moves down the runway.

I shrug, staring out the window. "One day," I murmur, watching as the cornfields stretch in for miles and miles, and I settle back in my seat.

RIVER

FIVE YEARS LATER

"Hey! I'm on my way, I swear," I breathe into the phone, shoving my foot into my heel, instantly regretting the uncomfortable shoe.

But you know what? These heels make my legs and ass look amazing. And I'm all for feeling a little more confident in my skin these days. Ever since my baby girl graced me with her sassy appearance, my body has massively changed from the nineteen-year-old girl I was before. I'm a full woman now, blessed with wider hips, stretch marks, and a baby pooch that will never leave, no matter how many sit-ups I do. Whatever. I'm still me and damn proud of who I am.

"Uh-huh," Seger snorts into the phone. "Just, uh, meet us in the main office, okay? We have something we want to talk to you about." I raise a brow at his serious tone and peek out the window to the mansion across the street, biting my bottom lip.

"Is this about Break?" I ask, cocking my head. "They did it to themselves. They signed the pledge contract, and they blew it." I gave them many chances to clean themselves up from the booze, parties, drugs, and debauchery. They promised me in a contract that this was their last chance, and they blew it out of the water last night.

My eyes track the twenty movers across the street in fascination as they start tugging out Break's equipment, clothes, dishes, and whatever else they moved into the Band House with. The band shamefully watches with their heads hung low, berating Aiden, their lead singer, for his lack of self-control.

Shaking my head, I recall the surprise visit I paid the band last night at their first concert after moving into the Band House across from me. Call me their babysitter or the new manager, but most people call me The Fixer these days. Give me any band, and within six months, they're either making hits again or hitting the road with their tails tucked. Hence Break, hitting the damn road after breaking their contract with me and West Records.

I knew they were done when I walked into Aiden's backstage greenroom and witnessed him snorting drugs out of some groupie's asshole and then fucking her into oblivion. Nothing says tear up my contract more than breaking the rules within the first month of said contract being signed. So, after Aiden finished his little show with a shout, I let him know they were over by clapping my hands from the chair I sat in, watching as he fucked himself and his band over—literally.

Seger snorts again, bringing me back into the conversation. "Yes and no, you fucking ball buster. Shit. I can't believe that dumbass fucked his whole future up after signing a contract saying he'd give up the drugs, chicks, and improve his music," Seger growls, most likely ready to punch something or someone.

"Ballbuster? I resent that, asshole. I'm just doing my job, bro. You know, the fixer?" I roll my eyes, searching the kitchen for my missing tiny human. "Fuck, it's quiet in my house. Listen, we'll be there in about an..."

"An hour?" Seger quips at my lateness.

Shit. I never used to be late until I had my baby girl, Lyric. Now, I'm a perpetual hot mess, constantly late to everything–even work. Zepp says I'd be late for my funeral, and yeah, I think he's right.

"No! Not an hour. I have to find Ly, and then we'll be there! She's excited to see Maggie again and have a sleepover. So, she should stop hiding now!" I shout louder than necessary, greeted by crickets.

Great. She's probably slathering lipstick all over her face and giving herself a mustard face mask. Again.

"Yeah, see you at nine. Drive safe and all that fucking good stuff," Seger says as we say our goodbyes, leaving me with a suspicious feeling bubbling in my gut, feeling an awful lot like suspicion. My brothers don't call me into their office very often. Usually, it's to talk to me about a band or assign me another group.

"Lyric!" I shout for what seems like the millionth time this morning from the kitchen, tapping my heel with impatience.

I sigh, walking into the family room, and heading toward the little girl standing in front of the large screen TV with her head cocked to the side. Fuck. My heart sinks when one of the men who haunt my nightmares walks across the screen, bombarded by paparazzi.

Her long black locks hang past her shoulders, brushed straight, and her little nose scrunches in disappointment.

"Why is Daddy leaving another hotel with another lady?" she asks with a heavy sigh, turning to look at me with disappointment ringing in her beautiful mismatched eyes. Big, blue eyes stare up at me, making my heart sink into my ass. A dark brown streak takes up a portion of her right eye, similar to the man currently on the screen.

It's a kick in the gut to stare at this little human who baked in my belly for nine months and shot out of my vagina with no help from him—them—but turns into an exact replica of the man waltzing around on the celebrity gossip channel with another woman under his arm.

Huge sunglasses sit on Kieran's face, and a grim expression crosses his lips when he holds up a hand and tells the cameras to fuck off. He's been out of my life for five years and hasn't changed much in the looks department. He's still as delicious as he was years ago with those muscles and dark hair. But fuck. Loathing builds inside me as I stare at the same man who denied my child and walked out of my life without a second glance.

"Mommy. Why? This is..." She scrunches her brows, looking down at her fingers as she counts down the number of women he's been spotted within the past two weeks. "The fourth one. Daddy is a ho."

I choke on my spit, grabbing my throat, wheezing as she stares up at me, blinking like she didn't say the funniest thing on the planet.

"Ly, where the hell did you hear the word ho? You know what? Nevermind. Yeah, your daddy is a ho, but that's okay. That's the lifestyle he wanted, right?" I raise a brow when she shrugs, turning to look at him with sadness.

Every other kid in her kindergarten class has a daddy, everyone but Lyric. She has her four uncles who have managed to step up and wheedle their way into our hearts. But to Lyric, it's not the same. She wants him—them—in her life. And I can only hold out for so long before she gets some stupid idea about running away at midnight.

I've never lied to Lyric and never sugar-coated our situation. One day I knew she'd ask who her father was. So, I gave her the best possible solution—Whispered Words. They helped create her, but only one sperm won the frantic, impossible race. Sometimes though, when I watch her, I think their sperm merged into one massive bundle of cells and created my beautiful Lyric.

Sometimes my heart hurts when she laughs just like Rad or uses her brain just like Callum. The looks she gives me when she's upset were plucked straight from Asher's mean-ass scowl. And her attitude? Straight from the man who actually helped create her.

"We gotta get to mommy's work," I say, quickly shutting off the TV and grabbing her hand. Looking down at those gorgeous mismatched eyes, I sigh, tucking a strand behind her ear. "I know this is weird and hard to know who they are, but..."

Lyric bites her lip, seeming more grown up than any five year old I've ever known. "It's okay, Mommy," she mutters, looking to the ground with resignation.

"Are you ready to go to Aunt Kaycee's house?" I ask, accomplishing what I set out to do. Long forgotten is her sperm donor's face on TV. Instead, she beams, jumping on her toes with excitement, filling the house with her squeals.

"Yes!" she squeaks, grinning up at me. "Me and Maggie have lots of stuffs to do. I need to grab Barbie!" Lyric takes off through the living room, up the stairs, and into her bedroom on the second floor. "Got her!" she says, marching down the stairs with a bag, Barbie, and a smile.

"Let's go," I say, guiding her into my SUV, strapping her into her seat, and kissing her cheek. "It's you and me against the world, baby." Looking into her big, blue, mismatched eyes and running my fingers over her plump cheeks with a sigh. The love I've never felt slams into me every time I look into her little eyes.
She's mine. Always and forever.

"Okay, I'm here! And..." Slamming into Zepp and Seger's office, I hold a hand to my chest, begging for air.

"You're two minutes late," Zepp quips from the corner of the large room with a drink in his hand, swirling the ice cubes. "And did you run?" His brows raise when I flip him off.

Righting myself, I waltz into the office and heave myself into a leather chair across from Seger.

I scrunch my nose. "Sorry. Traffic sucks, and Ly was a little trouble this morning," I grumble, running a hand through my hair. "She flipped on that stupid celebrity gossip channel again and saw Kieran parading himself around with some new chick." Rolling my eyes, I huff out my frustrations.

"Fucking prick," Seger gripes from behind the large desk and blows out a nervous breath. "You fucking tell her. I'm not telling her." He waves a hand, fear washing over his expression.

Zepp's expression falls, and a slight paleness takes over his face when he nods, straightening his spine.

"What?" I ask, looking between the two of them. Fuck. My heart falls when they nod to each other, doing that weird twin talk without saying a word. "Whatever it is, tell me."

Zepp grumbles under his breath and sets his drink down. "You have a meeting right now. Follow me," he says, waving for me to follow and giving me his back.

I've gotten to know my brothers more than I would have thought possible over the past five years. We're best friends, something I never thought I'd have the chance to say. For years I resented them, unknowing what they were going through with their stepmom and our ailing father. Zepp and Seger are the best damn family I could ever ask for. Even when Ode comes to visit, which isn't as often as I'd like with her new baby and everything, they accept us with open arms. So, I can always tell when they're walking me into the lion's den and offering me up on a silver platter.

"If you fucking murder us, remember we have four innocent kids at home who would miss their daddies," Seger says, holding his hands up placatingly.

"I'm sure Chase and Carter could pick up the pieces after I dig your graves. Are you ever going to explain why I'm going to murder you?" I ask, raising a brow as we walk out of the office and head toward the conference room. "A new band?" I ask, tilting my head.

"You are the fixer, sis. And this fucking band needs your help. They're falling apart at the fucking seams. And you, dear, beautiful sister, are the only one who can help them," Seger says with a grin, buttering me up with his words.

Opening the back door, they lead me to the two-way mirror overlooking the conference room from a discreet position.

My heart drops, momentarily stopping inside my chest. I immediately shake my head, slowly backing away as my skin crawls in disgust. "No. No, Absolutely not. Fire me for all I care. I won't fucking do it," I rasp through the emotions bubbling in my throat after years of repressing them into the deep, dark abyss of my mind.

I can't. I can't fucking look through that piece of glass without tears burning the back of my eyes. I knew one day I'd run into them. I work for the company they signed with, but I've carefully avoided them for five years at every turn, until now. Here they are after all these years, ready for the damn taking. I promised myself five years ago I'd do everything in my power to bring them down piece by piece. But I've grown up since then, loving every aspect of my job and what it brings. I've met so many bands and helped them achieve their wildest dreams by picking them up by their bootstraps and forcing them to mend whatever is bringing their potential down. My heart pulls in every different direction. My stomach churns with heavy waves of bile climbing my throat. Lyric flashes through my mind with her curious, puppy dog eyes begging for scraps of knowledge on her fathers.

Fuck.

I can't face them.

"Wait!" Zepp pleads, grabbing me by the shoulders and halting my retreat. "I know that this is...not what you ever wanted..." Panic spears through his eyes, and he heaves a breath. "They're failing right now, Riv. They're going to implode within five months." He swallows hard when I narrow my assessing eyes. "They need you, the fixer of West Records."

"Or they're going to fucking dive off a cliff and never work in this industry ever again. It's either you fix them, or they're done," Seger pipes up, crossing his arms over his chest.

Swallowing hard, I turn on my heel, glaring through the two-way mirror. My heart pumps against my chest at the sight of them sitting around the conference table with their noses in their phones, barely paying attention to one another.

"You want me to fix them?" I rasp, looking between the boys, taking in their appearances.

"Take them under your wing. Have them sign the six-month contract and move them into the Band House. Repair whatever the hell is tearing them apart," Seger says, standing beside me with furrowed brows.

"But I..." Bringing my fist to my lips, I conceal the quiver taking over my bottom lip.

"You're their only hope, River," Zepp says, putting an arm around my shoulders and pulling me affectionately into his side. "They'll be done for after this."

"You can fucking do this. Think of Ly. Wouldn't she want to know her fathers are successful? Wouldn't she be happy to know the piece of shit is off the gossip station?" Seger raises a brow, crossing his arms over his chest, knowing he's right.

"That's low," I growl, flicking the tip of his nose.

"Ow," he gasps, rubbing the spot I hit. "Rude as fuck," he mutters, turning his attention back to the boys sitting silently around the table.

Their eyes avoid each other's, and their bodies stiffen when Rad shifts in his chair, giving a bored yawn.

"They hate each other," I mutter, intently watching their every move. "They..." Fuck. My brothers are right. "Give me their files," I groan with reluctance.

Seger grins, shoving every file on the band into my hands. "That's everything. Their numbers. Their profiles. Everything you need to light a fire under their fucking asses and get them back on track."

I sigh, flipping through the pages quickly and slamming them shut. A devious smile falls across my lips the more I watch them. At the lowest point in my life, they left me with nothing, depriving me of the partners I needed the most. They intentionally left without the knowledge that they could have cleared my name. If only they had understood. If only they had come back and talked it over like adults. A fire brews in my gut. My face hardens, and a new resolve festers in the depths of my mind. I hate them for what they did. But if this is my destiny, then so be it. Maybe they'll survive the boot camp I put them through. Or perhaps, I'll discard them within the first month of our contract. If they sign it, that is.

"Fine. I'll do it. But don't expect me to be nice or understanding. They may have been something to me at one point in my life. But not now. They'll have to work hard. No passes. And definitely no Lyric." I raise a brow when my brothers nod in agreement. "I'll have the movers on standby to collect their shit," I mumble, sending out an email to the company we always use in cases like this.

"Riv, they'll have to meet her at some point. You can't hide her forever. One look at her and him," Zepp says, gesturing to Kieran as he leans back in the chair, stretching his arms over his head. "They'll know."

"A problem for another day," I gripe, waving a hand. "Now, I'll go work my magic." Nerves eat away at me with every step I take in their direction.

Five years ago, Callum saw something he misinterpreted into something more. His tear-filled expression haunts every aspect of my life. For years, I wished I could go back in time and redo that entire thing, starting with not allowing Van into my apartment. Now, I'm faced with the four assholes who served me with multiple restraining orders in Illinois and told me they wanted nothing to do with our child. Thankfully, my beautifully brilliant sister-in-law looked into it a year ago and confirmed they expired within the first year.

"Get it, sis," Seger mutters, pumping a fist as I turn the knob on the back door and heave a breath.

"If this is a bloodbath, I'm claiming insanity and blaming you two," I quip, narrowing my eyes at my brothers.

"Fucking worth it," Seger says, barking out a laugh. "I'll get the fucking popcorn while you obliterate them into submission." Promptly, I flip him off, trying to shake the terror from my trembling fingers.

In two point five seconds, I'll be face to face with the assholes who broke my heart. And I'm supposed to guide them into a better future, eliminating any sort of distraction.

Fat chance.

As my heels click against the hardwood floors of the conference room, my heart beats double time. I'm breathing the same air as them again and standing before the four assholes still glaring down at their phones. They don't even have enough respect to look up and watch the person entering the room with a fire under her ass and revenge bleeding through her veins.

Once I step up to the long conference table, I set the files down lightly on the gleaming wood and take stock of the men around me. A smirk pulls at my lips as I gain their attention one by one, reveling in the paleness that takes over their faces.

"Hello, boys, my name is River West, and I'm your new band manager. Congratulations," I say, cocking my head when various emotions cross their pale faces.

Yeah. Revenge will be delightful, slow, and painful. Whispered Words will one-hundred percent get everything that's coming to them—all in due time.

"How about we get started?" I hum.

TO
BE
CONTINUED

THANK YOU
AND
GOODNIGHT

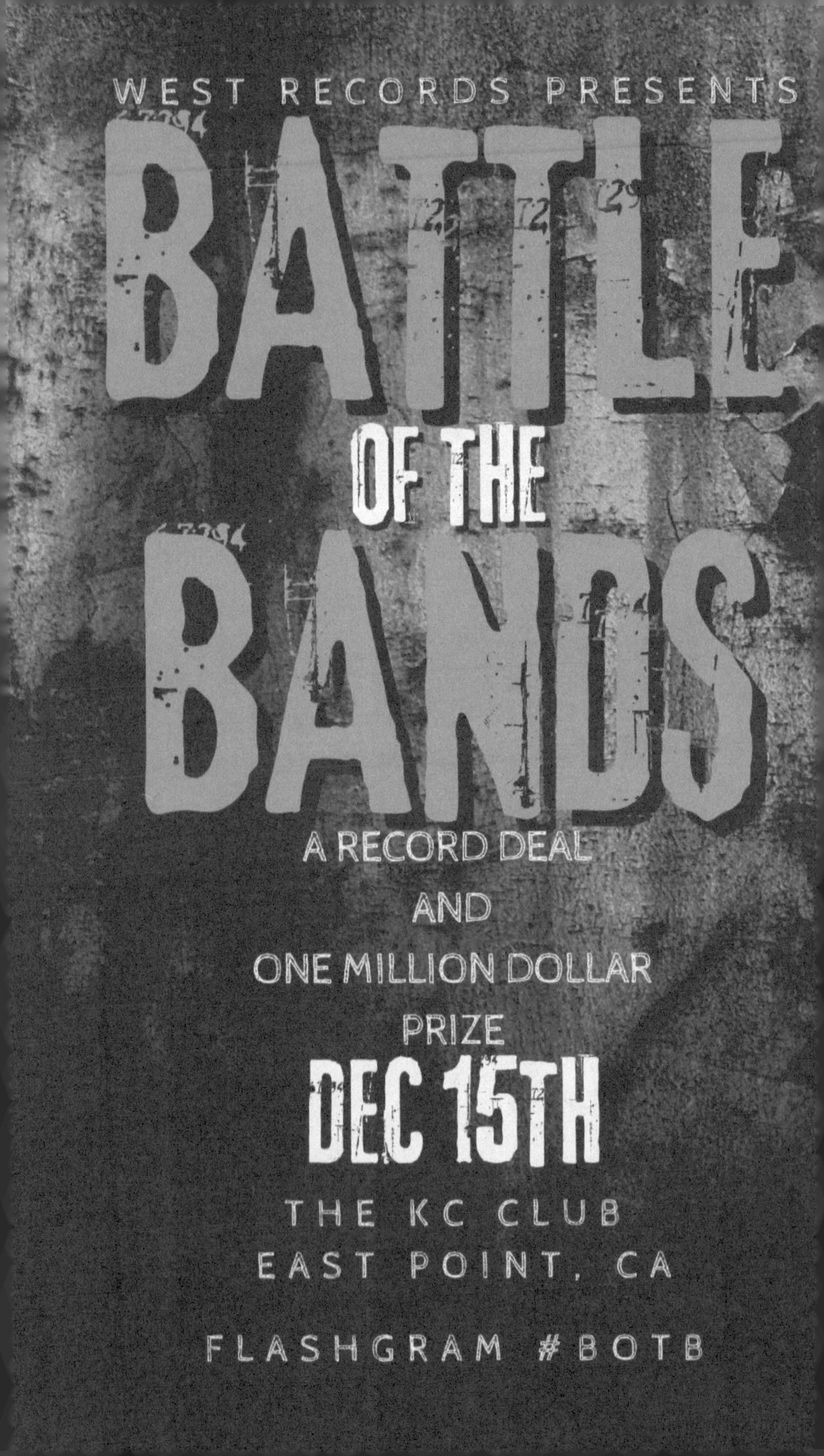

WEST RECORDS PRESENTS

BATTLE
OF THE
BANDS

A RECORD DEAL

AND

ONE MILLION DOLLAR

PRIZE

DEC 15TH

THE KC CLUB
EAST POINT, CA

FLASHGRAM #BOTB

The Roaring River
Whispered Words

OUR

Pretty Girl

Little Brat

River Blue

Little Star

FOREVER

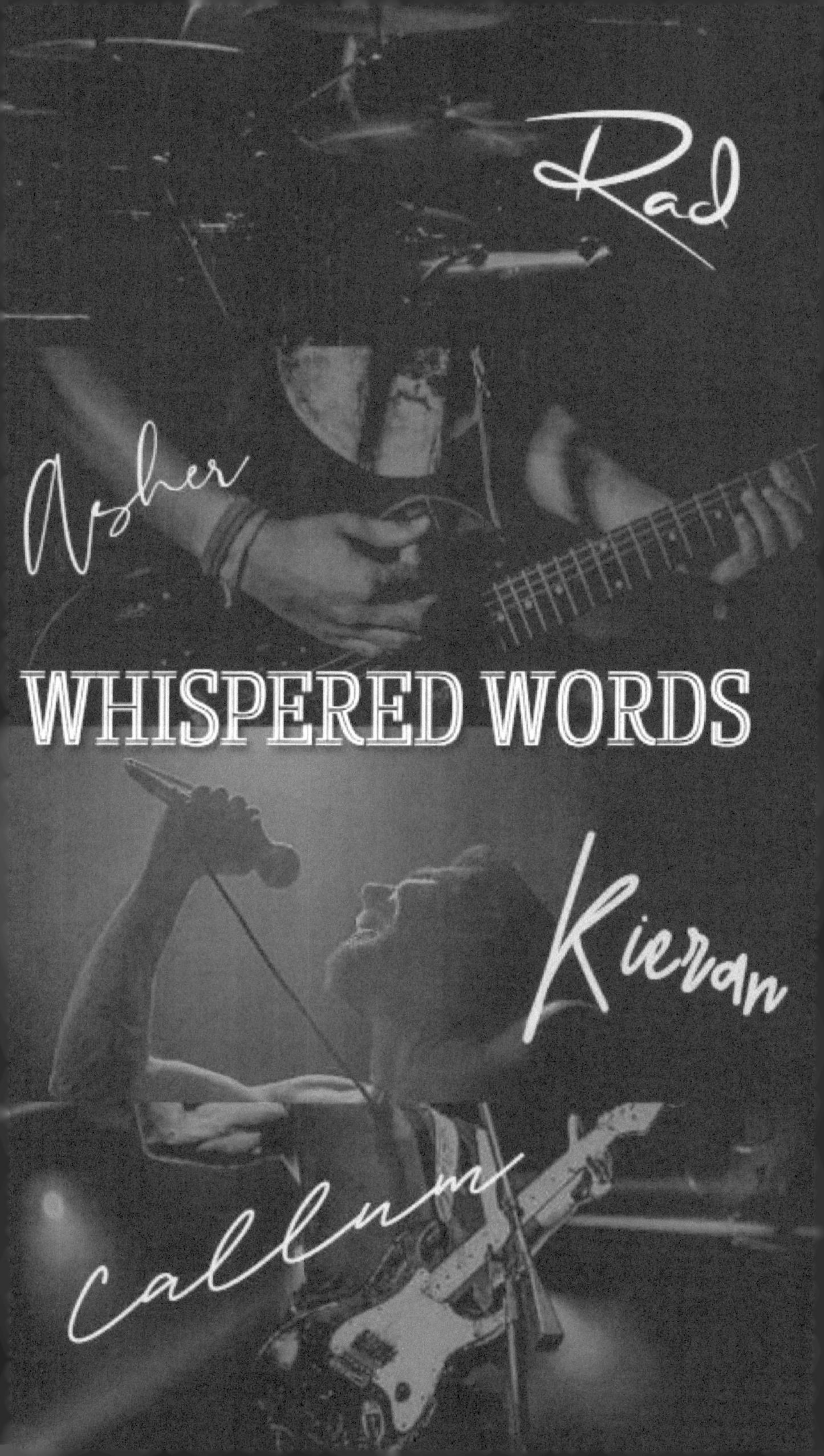
Rad
Asher
WHISPERED WORDS
Kieran
Callum

connect with

ALY BECK

Made in United States
Troutdale, OR
07/31/2024

21677990R00256